Island on Fire

A NOVEL

Sophie Schiller

ISLAND ON FIRE
Copyright © 2018 by Sophie Schiller
All rights reserved.

Summary: In the lush, tropical world of Martinique, an aristocratic French planter's daughter and an army officer enter a world of voodoo, intrigue, and deceit when a deadly volcano starts to erupt.

Model image Copyright 2017 by Mammuth
Used under license from iStock.com
Volcano image Copyright 2017 by jgroup
Used under license from iStock.com
Old map of Martinique image Copyright 2017 by Nicoolay
Used under license from iStock.com
Voodoo image Copyright 2017 by Atomazu
Used under license from Shutterstock.com
Cover Design: Tim Flanagan @ Novel Design Studio

Poem excerpt by Théophile Gautier
Translated by Sophie Schiller

ISBN: 978-1986210782

Printed in the United States of America

Part 1

Chapter 1

Monday, April 21, 1902
Saint-Pierre, Martinique

The city of Saint-Pierre was in a joyous mood. It was the end of the sugar harvest, a time for celebration and revelry. Music and laughter filled the air. The stars lit up the heavens, and the moon shone resplendent over the bay, where schooners and steamers lulled gently in the breeze. The strains of biguine music echoed from the cabarets, and the odor of piquant Creole cooking wafted from the cafés that lined the waterfront. No one noticed that on the summit of Mount Pelée, a thick plume of black smoke was rising steadily, growing larger by the minute.

In a villa nestled on the slopes of the mountain, Emilie Dujon felt the earth trembling. A picture rattled against the wall, and a lizard scampered away in fright. A rumbling noise that sounded like distant thunder drowned out the crickets and tree frogs. Startled out of her reverie, she dropped her copy of *The Mysterious Island* and grabbed her binoculars. Focusing them on the summit, her eyes widened in surprise. Smoke and steam were rising from the lower crater, the one they called the Étang Sec. It grew in size and curled outward, like an enormous gray mushroom, before blowing leeward over Saint-Pierre.

Emilie lowered the binoculars and scanned the mountain for several minutes, feeling a clenching pain in her gut. A young woman of nineteen with amber eyes, chestnut-colored hair, and a grave but lovely face, she had been watching these occurrences almost daily, and now they were becoming more frequent and, by the looks of things, more serious. For years the experts had claimed Mount Pelée was extinct, but if that was the case, why was there so much ash and smoke?

She made a note of her findings in a notebook, and sat down in front of her vanity mirror to brush her hair and reflect on the matter. Emilie was by nature very observant. She loved to study the world around her and uncover its mysteries. She spent long hours riding her stallion over the hills and valleys of Mount Pelée; exploring her tropical world was where she felt most at home. She had a good grasp of West Indian geography, having studied it at the convent school of Saint-Joseph de Cluny, and she knew that volcanoes were formed by subterranean fires deep below the earth's crust. But a piece of the puzzle was still missing. Dead volcanoes do not emit clouds of smoke and ash. She wondered if there was something more to Pelée that the experts were not saying.

Tonight was supposed to be a happy occasion, a chance to forget her worries and enjoy herself. Her fiancé, Lucien Monplaisir, was taking her to a gala performance of *La fille du régiment* at the theater in Saint-Pierre, and she was thrilled. Normally Lucien had no patience for cultural events, but tonight he was making the sacrifice just for her. Emilie smiled, thinking how strange and wonderful it was to be in love. In the span of a few months, it had changed Lucien from a world-weary sugar planter into a refined gentleman. And soon she would be his wife. Just thinking about it sent a surge of warmth throughout her body, and she felt a tingling in her knees.

At eight o'clock, spectators arrived in top hats and tails and long muslin gowns and turbans knotted in the distinct Martinique fashion. While the musicians were warming up their instruments, a murmur of anticipation rose up to the private box seat where Emilie sat with Lucien and his younger sister, Violette.

Emilie was brimming with excitement. She smoothed out her muslin gown and gazed at her surroundings. This was her first trip to the theater in years. It was considered an unnecessary luxury ever since her father's plantation, Domaine Solitude, started to lose money. The concert hall was even more splendid than she remembered. It shimmered like a golden Fabergé egg. The chandelier glowed, spreading warm light over the frescoes that adorned the ceiling. Gazing over at Lucien, her heart swelled with pride. She could scarcely believe how she, the daughter of a modest cocoa planter, had captured the heart of the richest sugar planter in Martinique.

The lights went down, and the play began. The audience watched with rapt attention, including Emilie, whose eyes scarcely left the stage. Even Lucien, who normally grew bored after only a few minutes, seemed to be enjoying himself.

In the middle of the third act, Emilie looked up and spied an old school friend, Suzette de Reynal, sitting in the opposite box. She seemed to be gazing over at Lucien. Emilie lifted her opera glass, and to her amazement, Suzette winked at him. Stunned, Emilie held up her program and saw out of the corner of her eye that Lucien met her gaze and winked back in return. For several minutes she watched the two of them engaged in silent communication. Clearly this was not the first time. Before long, Lucien got up and mumbled something about needing a drink. Panic spread throughout Emilie's limbs, and her heart pounded. Surely it had to be a mistake. She got up and followed him outside, but Lucien was nowhere to be found. She searched for him through the crowd, and when she reached a potted palm, she froze. Ensconced behind the plant were Lucien and Suzette, locked in a passionate embrace.

Emilie's face burned in anger. Time seemed to stand still. She took a few steps backward and fled to the safety of her seat. She willed herself to remain calm, but it took all the determination she could muster. Tears welled in her eyes. How could she have been so blind? How could she have been so naive? She blamed her own trusting nature. She was sure she had failed to see the clues that were there all along.

When Lucien returned to his seat, he put his hand on Emilie's shoulder, but she stiffened at his touch. All at once, she lost interest in the play. She lost all interest in Lucien. And then a great feeling of dread came over her when she realized that the wedding invitations had already been sent out. Perspiration beaded on her forehead. She tried fanning herself, but nothing could quell the anxiety and dread that had taken hold of her.

In the midst of her turmoil, a great rumbling noise filled the hall. The chandelier swayed, and the entire theater shook. Panic erupted in the audience. The rumbling noise grew louder, and the shaking intensified. The actors looked around in confusion. When a piece of scenery fell midstage, they shrieked and ran backstage in terror. And then, to everyone's horror, a marble statue fell into the audience, giving rise to mass panic.

Emilie gasped in fright. Someone yelled, "Earthquake!" and all at once everyone jumped out of their seats and raced toward the exits. The musicians fled the orchestra pit like wasps from a burning nest, and the once-cheerful hall turned into mass hysteria. People were shouting and jostling each other in their haste to escape. An old woman cried out, and an elderly man in a black suit and tails struggled to protect her as they were shoved aside in the melee.

Lucien grabbed Emilie's hand and said, "Come on, let's get out of here." He pulled her and Violette through the crowd, and they hurried down the marble staircase. They raced through the courtyard, down the stairs, and out to rue Victor Hugo, where the carriages were waiting. After they climbed inside, the driver proceeded north on rue Victor Hugo, dodging frightened residents and spooked horses. Emilie's heart raced and she felt as if she was having a nightmare. *Boom!* An explosion like cannon fire rocked the carriage. In the distance, the mountain appeared to be glowing. The blast was followed by a loud rumbling noise and tremors that shook the earth.

The horses whinnied and reared, and the elderly West Indian driver struggled to control them. "Ho! Ho!" he cried, pulling on the reins. Emilie feared the ground would split open beneath them, swallowing them up. Even Lucien looked terrified. The gas lamps swayed, and roof tiles smashed to the ground. A swarm of people hurried past their carriage on their way to the cathedral, crossing themselves and uttering prayers out loud.

Emilie's muslin dress was soaked with sweat. Heat and humidity hung in the air like a wet blanket. She glanced over at Lucien, but he was staring at the smoldering volcano with a mixture of fear and awe. *Dear God,* she prayed, *please don't let me die together with Lucien. Not here, not now.* Shutters flew open as fearful residents peered out into the darkness. A few horses broke free of their reins and were galloping down the street, chased by their furious owners. How quickly panic took over the frightened residents.

The carriage ground to a halt. Emilie pushed open the carriage door and scrambled outside. Lucien and Violette joined her, and they stood by the side of the road, watching the scene unfold before them like spectators to a disaster. Ash and volcanic dust rained down on their heads while the ground continued to shake.

"We really must get out of here," said Lucien as the party climbed back into the carriage.

The driver cracked his whip, and the horses trotted across the stone bridge that crossed the rivière Roxelane and then proceeded north for several miles along the coast before turning east onto a dirt road bounded by coconut palms and bamboo that led to the tiny hamlet of Saint-Philomène, where Emilie's father's plantation was located. As they climbed the western slopes of Mount Pelée, an ominous smell filled the air. It was not a burning kind of smell, like the occasional fumes that drifted down from the Guérin sugar factory across the savannah, but a different kind of smell, like rotten eggs. Emilie pressed her handkerchief to her nose and mouth. Lucien slipped his arm over her shoulders, but she again stiffened at his touch. As the carriage made its way down the dirt road, an uncomfortable silence followed, during which time Emilie pondered her dilemma. She had to find a way to break off her engagement without causing a scandal. But it would not be easy. No young woman of her social class had ever broken an engagement and survived the resulting gossip and slander. The scandal would crush her parents and brand her a social outcast. Her mind raced as she searched for a solution, but it seemed hopeless. She gazed up at the summit of Mount Pelée, but an ominous film of clouds blotted out the moon, reducing her world to utter darkness.

Chapter 2

Tuesday, April 22

The next morning Emilie awoke to the voices of the field workers reverberating through the jalousies. There was a clattering of dishes from the outside kitchen, and a rooster crowed in the henhouse. A memory of the previous night's fiasco flitted through her mind, and it all came flooding back. Pain gripped her, and a lump formed in her throat. In one fateful moment, her entire world had collapsed. She glanced over at the clock and groaned. Already seven o'clock. Her brother, Maurice, was waiting for her out in the fields.

Downstairs she found a copy of *Les Colonies* lying on the dining room table and leafed through the pages. Oddly, the newspaper seemed to be making light of the previous night's disturbance, as if it had been a burlesque performance gone wrong. The editor, Marius Hurard, wrote that "the trembling in the theater served to heighten the dramatic tension on the stage" and "the flashes of light on top of the mountain were more reminiscent of a Bastille Day celebration than an actual volcanic eruption" and "the only thing missing to make the evening more celebratory was the municipal band playing the Marsellaise." Emilie furrowed her brow. *Why no mention of the tremors? Why no mention of the ash clouds? Why no mention of the panic in the streets? What are they hiding?* She threw the newspaper down in disgust.

Behind her she heard a shuffling noise. Her old nurse, Da Rosette, came hobbling into the dining room bearing a breakfast tray and a pot of coffee. She was wearing her usual bright madras skirt over a white chemise, and on her head was a yellow turban. Rosette Desrivières, or Da Rosette, as she was called, had worked for the Dujon family for more than fifty years. She was the mainstay of the household. Rising in rank from cook to house servant to nanny, she had almost single-handedly raised two generations of Dujon children. Though she was getting on in years and needed a cane to walk, her hearing was still acute, and few details escaped her sharp eyes. It was almost impossible to keep a secret from Da Rosette. It pained Emilie that she would have to tell her nurse the truth about Lucien.

"What happened, doudou?" said Da Rosette, setting the tray down on the table. "You look like you have seen a zombie."

"Something terrible happened last night."

"You mean the tremors?"

"There was fire on the mountain. It was terrifying."

Da Rosette frowned. "All that drinking and carousing makes Father Pelée angry. But don't worry, cocotte, soon he will go back to sleep. Pelée is our protector, not our destroyer." She picked up a papaya and began to carve it with a pearl-handled knife. "The spirits dance a caleinda and play the tam-tam and drink too much rum, and the Bon Dieu gets angry."

"That's just superstition," said Emilie. "There has to be a scientific reason for what happened. It's not the spirits that are making fire on the mountain, but something much worse. But something else happened last night. Something awful . . ."

"Why the long face?" said Da Rosette. "Soon you will be the happiest bride in all Madinina. When the time comes, I'll take out the best linen and china, and you'll wear your grandmother's lace dress and pearls. Grandma Loulou would be so proud of you."

Emilie stared at her nurse. "Da, there's something I have to tell you. I found out Lucien has another doudou. He doesn't love me anymore."

The old woman looked shocked.

Emilie continued, "Da, do you remember the old saying: 'Even if you paid him all the money in the world, a monkey has enough sense not to climb a thorny tree'?"

The elderly woman put down the papaya. "M. Monplaisir is rich. He will make a wonderful husband for you. Don't talk such foolishness! Of course he loves you."

Emilie shook her head. "I know he loves someone else. I can't marry Lucien. It would be a terrible mistake . . ."

The old woman grabbed her wrist. "Shh! Don't talk like that! Of course Lucien loves you. No man is perfect, but a good wife always looks away from her husband's faults. Does the crab expect the mouse to soar like an eagle? The Bon Dieu has done you a great favor in giving you a rich husband. You should be thankful, or you will bring a terrible curse on your head. Do you want to end up marrying a zombie?"

Feeling vindicated, Da Rosette got up and began sweeping the floor, banging into furniture, clattering the dishes, and making a ruckus to show her displeasure. Her thin, bony hands clutched the broom like the claws of a raven. When she opened the door to sweep the dirt outside, she uttered a terrifying shriek.

Emilie rushed to her side. Outside, a huge crab with one leg missing was scampering down the path, trying to escape. Emilie felt instant pity for the creature. It had probably escaped from one of the workers' barrels. The field hands had a custom of fattening up their crabs by feeding them mangoes, green peppers, and maize before boiling them alive and stewing them in their favorite dish, *matoutou de crabe*, an island specialty.

Before Emilie could stop her, Da Rosette lifted up the broom and began to beat the crab without mercy until the poor creature scurried away into the bush.

"Go away, wretched beast!" cried Da Rosette, shaking her fist.

"Da, why did you treat the crab so cruelly?"

"That was no crab," said her nurse. "It was a little zombie. Tonight I will burn a candle to ward it away and to scare the others away."

Emilie grabbed the broom out of her hands. "Da, sometimes a crab is just a crab. Leave it alone!"

But the old woman would not listen. She waved Emilie off and began rearranging the dishes, singing one of her spirituals with renewed fervor. It was Da Rosette's way of shutting out all conversation. Emilie hated when she was like that; it was impossible to talk to her. Anyway, she would never see things Emilie's way, especially about Lucien. Although Da Rosette's heart was pure, she lived in a world of superstition, fear, and irrational beliefs tied to voodoo. It affected everything she did. When Emilie was little, Da Rosette would fill her head with all sorts of stories about voodoo and spirits. And whenever Emilie would stumble across strange voodoo ritualistic items such as a toad with its mouth chained shut, slaughtered chickens, or miniature black coffins filled with graveyard dirt, Da Rosette would jerk her away while crossing herself, warning her that she must never step over a *quimbois* (as a voodoo item was called in Martinique) or it would bring trouble. To

Da Rosette, canceling a wedding was tantamount to bringing a curse. It was simply not done. She was stuck in her ways and would never change. Emilie looked at her old nurse with pity, resigning herself to the fact that in the matter of Lucien Monplaisir, she was entirely alone.

Chapter 3

After breakfast Emilie grabbed her straw hat and gave Da Rosette an obligatory peck on the cheek, and then she ran outside to find Maurice, grateful for the chance to be out in the sunshine. She needed time to think—time to clear her head, time to plan her next course of action. She was determined to end their engagement, but it had to be handled delicately. Any rash action on her part could end in disaster.

As she made her way through the fields, the workers called out to her and waved. Most of them had known her since she was a baby. The Dujons were békés, white French Creoles who could trace their lineage back to the first French settlers of Martinique. Domaine Solitude, the Dujon family plantation, was sprawled across five hundred acres of the richest volcanic soil on the island. The plantation represented the only world Emilie knew and the only world she loved. Five generations of Dujons had grown up on the plantation, but it was her father, Georges, who had made the decision to switch from sugarcane to cocoa, believing that chocolate would one day become a prized commodity.

Although it was still morning, it was already hot and muggy. Soon it would be too hot even for the workers to labor outside. When the sun reached its zenith, they would clamber inside their thatched huts for their midday meal, which consisted of manioc, breadfruit, plantains, and black peas, after which they would lie down for their afternoon sieste. To sustain their bodies they drank copious amounts of tafia, white rum mixed with spring water, and to sustain their spirits they filled the church pews every Sunday. But Martinique was not, according to the strictest definition, a Catholic country. On an island steeped in voodoo, witch doctors, called *quimboiseurs*, wielded enormous power over the people and were not to be taken lightly.

Although life in Martinique was hard, it was punctuated by celebrations like Carnival, followed by a rousing Mardi Gras, when the people from the countryside would crowd into Saint-Pierre and engage in festive dances like the bamboula and caleinda and sing satirical songs while they paraded through the streets to the accompaniment of musicians on the ka drum, beating out African rhythms that stirred the crowd to a frenzy. Although Carnival drew many visitors from around the world, some aspects of it were morbid and frightening.

Every year as Carnival drew to a close, the Red Devil, whom they called Papa Djab, would make his appearance at night and always under cover of the darkness. From a dark alleyway, the Red Devil would emerge under the glow of the oil lamps, clad all in red, with a skull face and cow horns. Only his eyes were visible, and on his head he wore a wig made of horsehair, upon which he would place a shining lantern. Papa Djab was so terrifying and sinister, he could make even the bravest man climb a breadfruit tree.

As the crowd cheered, Papa Djab would parade down rue Victor Hugo, dancing in time to the music as he chanted incantations meant to raise the dead: "Bimbolo! Zimbolo!" Behind him, a devilish chorus all dressed in red would ring out, "Bimbolo! Zimbolo! The devil and the zombies sleep anywhere and everywhere!" After a while a hush would descend on the crowd while everyone waited to see what Papa Djab would do next. When she was little, Emilie would always hide behind Da Rosette's skirts, too fearful to face the Red Devil up close.

Over the years Emilie had heard rumors that Papa Djab was really the Grand Zamy, a quimboiseur who kept an herbal store in the mulatto quarter of Saint-Pierre. During the day, he wore a stylish European suit and waistcoat with a gold watch chain, and on his head he wore an authoritative pith helmet. Like all proper Frenchmen, he was baptized and given the name Gaston Faustin Jacquet, but to the people of Martinique, he was the Grand Zamy, a man to be feared, a man to be respected, a man whose voodoo spells often resulted in sudden and inexplicable deaths.

She found Maurice at the edge of the field. Tall, gentle, and easygoing to a fault, Maurice was a younger version of their father with his sandy-blond hair and blue eyes. He was loading baskets of cacao pods into a waiting donkey cart to be transported to the drying shack. All around, workers in their bakouas, wide-brimmed straw hats, were using their cutlasses to slash off the ripened pods from the barks of the trees. When the pods were too high, they would pull them down using poles fitted with a cutter at the end. Other field hands were weaving through the fields collecting fallen pods from the ground and putting them into burlap bags. Piles of yellow cacao pods began to collect under the trees to the constant chop-chop that reverberated across the fields.

Maurice was hard at work, but despite his youth, he looked tired and worn out. Clad in a white linen shirt and khaki trousers, his blond hair was streaked back from sweat, and his face was red from the heat. With each passing day, he grew thinner and more listless, his features more gaunt. Ever since Maurice had contracted consumption, he had fought a constant battle for his life. He refused to give in to the ravages of his disease and often pushed himself beyond his limits, even if it meant putting his own life at risk. Yet despite his constant pain, his blue eyes shone with mischief. He would never give up an opportunity to tease his sister. In this manner, he was relentless.

"Good morning, sleepyhead," he said, grinning. "Did you get enough beauty sleep? We must look ravishing for our wedding day."

Emilie frowned. "Not you too! That's all I hear from Da Rosette. It seems as if no one cares that last night the mountain was rumbling and spewing out fire and ash."

"I think I slept through it," said Maurice. "I don't remember a thing. And there was no mention of it in the newspaper this morning."

"It's almost as if they're hiding something." Emilie paused for a moment and added, "But something else happened last night. I found out Lucien is in love with another girl."

"That's impossible," said Maurice. "He's quite smitten with you."

She brushed a tear from her face. "I saw it with my own eyes. I saw him with Suzette de Reynal in a most compromising position. I've made a terrible mistake."

"I think you're actually serious," he said, staring at his sister.

"I've never been more serious in my life."

Maurice bent down to load another basket on the wagon. "It must be a mistake. Everyone gets cold feet before their wedding. Lucien's an odd bird, but he's a good man. There must be an explanation for it. I can't believe he would deceive you like that. Hey, grab me some of that water, will you?"

From a nearby bucket, Emilie spooned out a ladle of water and handed it to Maurice. He drank it in gulps and then poured the rest over his head, after which he wiped his face with the sleeve of his shirt.

"I know one thing for certain," said Maurice. "Lucien's as rich as Croesus, so you'll never lack for anything. I know he acts strange sometimes, but he's not a bad sort. I'm sure he would never intentionally hurt you. I'm sure it was all a misunderstanding . . ."

Before Emilie could respond, they heard a voice calling from across the field. Julien, their foreman, was heading toward them. Tall, handsome, and confident, Julien was her father's right hand. Like many others, he was the descendant of Hindu laborers who married mulatto women to create a unique West Indian blend of African, Indian, and European. Long-limbed, lean, and swarthy, he spoke the local Creole patois as if it was a musical sonata.

Julien doffed his straw hat.

"Bonjour, Mam'selle Emilie," he said, bowing slightly in her direction.

"How's everything going, Julien?" said Maurice, fanning himself with his hat.

"Very good, sah. The harvest is even better than last season. Come over here; there's something I want to show you."

The two siblings followed Julien across the field, past denuded cacao trees, luxurious banana trees, and various fruit trees, until they came to a clearing. Lying on the ground were two dead birds, a fine powdery ash covering their bodies.

"What happened?" said Maurice.

"They fell down from the mountain, sah."

"That's strange," said Maurice. "They appear to be covered in ash."

"Last night ash was rising from the top of Pelée," said Julien. "They must have suffocated and fallen from the sky. Take them to your father so he can see." He placed the dead birds in a burlap sack, which he handed to Maurice.

"Go now, sah. I take over for you." Julien gave a confident nod, but underneath his cool exterior, Emilie detected a hint of urgency.

Maurice grabbed his horse and mounted it. He pulled Emilie up behind him, and together they rode back to the house. After they left the horse with a stableboy, they went inside to look for their father. Aside from a few chattering servants polishing the silverware, the house was quiet. They passed the salon and the dining room and went straight to the office of Georges Dujon.

Their father was sitting at his desk, typing a letter deep in concentration. Bleary-eyed and sweaty, his hair clung to his forehead like a damp mop. Each time he tapped out a letter, a look of supreme discomfort would cross his face, as if he was in great pain. Though still handsome, Georges Dujon was beginning to show the effects of age. His sunburnt face bore the signs of worry and drink, his hair was all white, his reddish beard was flecked with grey, and his hands were calloused from years of hard work. The quintessential West Indian planter, Georges had a commanding presence, even while mired in paperwork. On his desk, a steaming mug of coffee sat beside an open flask of rum, while scattered about were a hodgepodge of invoices, telegrams, fountain pens, and paper clips. A palm frond peeked in through an open window, and Mount Pelée loomed behind him, its summit veiled in silvery-white clouds.

"What are you two up to?" said Georges, looking up from his typewriter.

Maurice opened the sack. "Papa, I have something to show you. Julien found these out in the field. Have a look."

He laid the dead birds out on his father's desk. Georges reached out and picked up a bird, turning over its ashen body several times as he inspected it. His brow furrowed into deep ridges.

"Strange," said Georges. "Their wings appear to be covered with ash, as if they flew into an oven. The poor wretches suffocated to death."

"Julien said the ash fumes from Pelée killed them," said Maurice.

Georges scoffed. "The old devil's air vent, eh? That's just superstitious nonsense tied up with voodoo and black magic. Everyone knows the volcano is extinct."

"Papa," said Emilie, "last night there were tremors, and ash was shooting out of the crater."

"The old volcano is just settling down," said Georges. "It's extinct. That's a scientific fact."

"According to whom?" she said.

"According to every geologist in the world," said Georges. "The West Indies is a known region of volcanic instability, so it's only natural there will be occasional tremors. Anyway, the volcano is quiet now, so there's no need to get all worked up. I'm sure there's a perfectly reasonable explanation for the dead birds . . . perhaps they were struck by lightning. I suggest you two get back to work. We have to make our sailing date."

"What about the rotten egg smell?" said Maurice.

"My boy, that is just sulfur, also known as sulfureted hydrogen, a harmless emission from deep within the earth," said Georges. "I hear in Guadeloupe they use it to warm their coffeepots. Now is there something else you'd like to discuss, or are you quite finished?"

Emilie glanced over at Maurice, but he looked tongue-tied. She decided to switch tack.

"Papa, this is not about the money," she said. "Our lives might be in danger. Didn't Pelée erupt only fifty years ago?"

"It was a partial eruption at best," said Georges. "As I recall, your grandfather said the ash did a remarkable job of fertilizing the crops, which brings us back to business." He pointed to a calendar on the wall. "The cocoa beans have to be packed and ready to sail three weeks from today. My customers send me urgent telegrams every day demanding to know the sailing date. If we miss the sailing, we'll be out of business."

"And if the volcano erupts, we'll be dead," said Emilie.

"Neither one of you is a geologist," said Georges. "All the experts say Pelée is nothing more than an oddity of nature. Now, are there any more questions or are we going to stand here all day chatting?" Emilie opened her mouth to speak, but no words came out. "Good; now get moving," he boomed.

Emilie looked at Maurice and frowned. There was no point in arguing with the old man.

Chapter 4

Tuesday, April 22
Telegraph Office
Fort-de-France

Jules Coppet pushed open the door to the telegraph office while it was still dark. He poured himself a cup of coffee and changed places with the overnight operator. When he eyed the basket full of messages, he let out a groan.

"Busy night, eh?"

"No, it's been slow," said the night operator, putting on his cap.

"Then why are there so many backed-up messages?"

"Don't get testy. I've been working on them for hours. Couldn't get a single message through to Guadeloupe. It's as if the whole island's been shut down. These messages are left over from yesterday. I think you'll have a busy day ahead of you."

Coppet's brow furrowed. "Stay a minute, will you? I want to show you how it's done."

He picked up the first message and tapped it out in Morse code. It was a routine commercial transaction involving two hundred hogsheads of sugar that were to be shipped on the steamer *Versailles* later that week. Simple enough. He sat back and took a satisfying sip of his coffee, waiting for a response. After a couple of minutes, he grew annoyed. After ten minutes, his annoyance turned to exasperation. Five minutes more, and his annoyance turned to anger. He tapped out the message again, this time with more vigor, but still there was no response.

Coppet shook his head. "Damn! I think the line is dead."

"What?" said the night operator with a bewildered expression.

"It's either that, or they shut down the whole island of Guadeloupe. The undersea cable must have snapped somewhere out on the seafloor. Send a message down to the cable office at once. Tell them to dispatch a cable repair ship to check on the damaged line right away. Until then, there will be no telegraph service to Guadeloupe."

Chapter 5

Wednesday, April 23

The next day Emilie was in the outside kitchen when Victorine, the cook, told her a rumor that Lucien was spotted recently with a woman from Le Carbet, and the woman was expecting his child. Hearing this, Emilie's face blanched. She dropped the knife she was holding and stared at the cook in disbelief. But the gravity in the woman's eyes told her it was true. Emilie's mouth went dry and she felt queasy. She took a few steps backward as the full weight of the cook's words came crashing down.

She fled the kitchen, tears stinging her eyes, and ran to the drying shack, where she knew she would find Maurice. Once there she joined in the work of turning over the cocoa beans with a wooden panel and then covering them up with banana leaves for the fermentation process. It was hot, sweaty work, but at least it took her mind off her problems. Maurice looked up and smiled when he saw her, but his appearance shocked her. He looked as if he was deteriorating by the day. His face was red and swollen, and he looked near collapse.

Maurice erupted in a violent coughing fit. Listless, he slumped to the ground. The workers next to him tried to lift him up, but Maurice was too weak. Dropping everything, Emilie ran to his side. She looked in horror as a streak of blood dripped from his mouth down to his shirt. Thinking quickly, she dipped her handkerchief in a bucket of water and smoothed it over his forehead.

"Maurice, you're very ill," she said, her voice tinged with fear. "You must go inside."

Maurice winced. "I'm fine. I just need a little rest."

She felt his forehead. Maurice was burning up with fever. *How long has he been hiding his illness?* He was so thin, she hardly recognized him. *When did he get so sick? How much longer will he be able to bear the heat and humidity before he completely collapses?* Emilie longed to spare Maurice the rigors of plantation work, yet she wanted to spare his masculine pride. But Maurice had to face the truth: If he was going to recover from consumption, he needed rest and proper medical care. Without it he would surely die.

Emilie unbuttoned his shirt and shuddered when she saw how thin he was. *My God, he's wasting away! How could I have been so consumed with my own problems that I neglected my own brother's health?* She swallowed hard and forced herself to put on a brave face. "Maurice, I think you've had enough for one day. Da Rosette made me promise to send you back if you got tired. Please don't force me to lie to her."

"I'm all right . . ." He winced. "Just give me a few minutes. . ."

Maurice was gasping for breath, and his face grimaced each time he spoke. He clutched his chest with each painful spasm, his face contorting in agony.

Alarmed, Emilie called out to one of the workers. "Césaire, come here! Help me get him up!"

Césaire came running, and together they lifted Maurice to his feet. They placed one of his arms over Césaire's shoulder, and the worker gently guided him back toward the great house.

Emilie stood in the drying shack watching Césaire lead Maurice back home with slow, uneven steps. It broke her heart to see how her brave, handsome brother was stumbling like an old man. How unfair life was! Maurice was the kindest, gentlest soul she had ever known. He was unsullied by the vice and immorality of the world around him. But Emilie knew the unspoken truth: that without proper care, Maurice would not be long for this world.

Several hours later, she trudged back home to eat dinner and check on Maurice. He was resting comfortably in bed. But he was perspiring, and Emilie knew that was a bad sign. Usually a broken fever was a sign of improvement, but she wasn't so sure in the case of consumption. She wished the doctor would come. She ran downstairs and brought Maurice some tea and crackers and suggested he see the doctor in the morning.

"I'll be fine," he said.

"But you haven't eaten a thing."

"I have no appetite." His face looked wan and tired.

Emilie frowned. "What did Da Rosette say?"

"She doesn't know. I came in through the back door."

Emilie sat down beside him. "Maurice, I think you have to go to the hospital."

"Don't be ridiculous. I'll be fine by morning."

Emilie locked eyes with him. "You were coughing up *blood* today. You need a hospital. You're wasting away. . ."

"It's not as bad as it looks," said Maurice. "I feel better already."

Emilie forced herself to smile; she didn't want to break his spirit. She left her brother to eat dinner and think the matter over. Life was becoming more complicated by the minute. She couldn't imagine losing Maurice. Without her brother, she was all alone in the world.

Later, as she sat at her vanity table brushing her hair, Da Rosette stuck her head in to announce that Lucien Monplaisir had come to pay an unexpected visit.

Emilie spun around. "Lucien is here? Tell him I'm busy."

Da Rosette's eyes sparkled with mischief. "He misses you very much. He say, 'Tell Mam'selle Emilie I wish to speak to her.' He say you are his only doudou and he loves you very much."

Emilie eyed her shrewdly. "He said no such thing."

"He said it with his eyes," said Da Rosette coyly.

"Tell him to go away. I have nothing more to say to him." Emilie began brushing her hair again, confident the old woman would do her bidding, but Da Rosette dug in her heels. She moved in closer and placed one of her shriveled claws on Emilie's shoulder. "Quick! Do not delay, cocotte. Do not keep your man waiting. He say he will make you the happiest bride in all Madinina."

"Stop lying to me!" said Emilie.

Da Rosette dug her claws in her shoulder. "Hush! Do you want to end up marrying a zombie? Lucien is your doudou!"

Emilie peeled off the woman's fingers. "That's enough of that voodoo nonsense. I don't believe any of it. You're just trying to scare me!"

"Don't be haughty or you will invite trouble. Now go and see your doudou. Do not be too proud, or the devil will tempt you. He will send a zombie to put a spell on you. I've seen it happen many times. Some women spend their whole lives married to a devil! You don't want to end up like them, do you?"

Something in the old woman's eyes spooked Emilie. She hated when the old woman used superstition and irrational fears to manipulate her and scare her. Stupid old woman! Emilie applied some rouge with furious strokes, but inside she was haunted by the old woman's words. Zombies, curses, voodoo. . .her mind raced. Somehow she had to find a way to get rid of Lucien for good.

Tramping downstairs, Emilie found Lucien in the salon with his boots on the coffee table. He was smoking a cigarette and flicking the ashes in her mother's favorite porcelain vase. She could smell the alcohol on his breath from several feet away.

She gave him an obligatory peck on the cheek and poured two glasses of rum punch. Then she settled on the sofa beside him and forced herself to chat, but her stomach was in knots. She had to find a way to get rid of Lucien for good, a way that wouldn't ruin her family's social standing and brand her an outcast. After a while Lucien brought out what he'd come to show her. In his arms he cradled a gleaming Browning M1900 pistol with a mother-of-pearl grip that he lovingly referred to as his "pistolet Browning." He turned it this way and that, explaining how it worked. She eyed it cautiously, wondering how he would react if she told him she was leaving him.

She cleared her throat. "Lucien, I have something to tell you."

"What is it?" he said, taking a deep draw of his cigarette.

"I've been doing a great deal of thinking lately, and I've come to realize that I'm not ready for marriage. I think we should cancel the wedding."

"Have you gone insane?" he said. "You don't expect me to take you seriously, do you?"

"I don't think we're suited to each other," she said. "We have nothing in common. I think you'd be happier with someone else."

"Who put these ridiculous notions in your head?" he said, scrutinizing her. "Was it that old nurse of yours?"

"No, I can think for myself," she said.

"Then stop talking such nonsense. You were made for me. You suit me just fine."

"It seems many women suit you."

Lucien's face reddened. "What are you talking about? Stop it right now! You don't know what you're talking about. I didn't come here to be attacked."

"I'm not attacking you," she said. "I just think we should call off our wedding."

"That's out of the question. Do you realize how crazy you sound? Stop it right now."

"I've heard rumors about you."

Lucien got up and started pacing the room. "Nonsense! I've heard enough of this. Every day you sound more and more irrational. There's no truth to anything you're saying. There are no other women."

Emilie was stunned. She stared at Lucien and felt her blood turn cold.

"My cook says you have a woman in Le Carbet."

"That's a filthy lie!" he said, his face turning colors. "If I see that cook of yours, I'll give her such a slap, she'll think twice next time. I forbid you to listen to such gossip!" He shook Emilie so hard she thought her neck would snap. She struggled to free herself, but Lucien held her with an iron grip.

"Lucien, stop!" she screamed. To her immense relief, he released her.

"Damned, filthy lies!" he said, his face a mask of rage. "You should fire that impudent woman at once. I won't tolerate such accusations. You're acting just as crazy as she is. Stop harassing me! I didn't come here to be attacked."

Emilie's mind raced. Lucien always managed to turn the tables and make himself the victim. It was maddening. No matter how rational she was, he always made her question her own sanity with his accusations and denials.

"Perhaps you'd like to have your ring back," she said as calmly as possible.

Lucien grabbed her by the shoulders. "Don't ever say that to me again. Don't listen to those vile rumormongers. You're the only woman for me."

Emilie's heart was pounding. This was not supposed to be happening. She was supposed to be the happiest bride in all Madinina. Isn't that what Da Rosette had said? Yet, all she felt was confusion and doubt. Why did she feel like killing herself to make the pain go away?

Lucien slipped his arm over her shoulders. "Enough with that nonsense talk. You're my fiancée. Don't you know how much I love you?"

He tried to force his lips on her, but Emilie squirmed out of his grip.

"Lucien, please stop! I'm confused right now. I have a lot on my mind. If we miss the sailing date, we may lose the farm. My father's very worried."

"Your father's a grown man and can take care of himself. If he loses the plantation, it will be because he's mismanaged it for years."

Emilie felt as if she'd been slapped. "What are you saying?"

"Face the facts, my darling. Your father made some serious errors along the way, the least of which is most of your equipment is outdated and malfunctioning. And he allowed a great number of trees to die from lack of proper care. For a planter, that's pure negligence. I run my plantation like a tight ship. Any worker caught shirking his duty is dismissed at once. And we invest in all the latest equipment. That's how we grew our plantation into the richest sugar empire in the West Indies. It takes hard work and know-how."

"I don't like what you're insinuating. My father is a respected planter. We're just having a hard time. I know this year we'll get out of debt."

Lucien frowned. "Emilie, when will you wake up? Your father is a terrible businessman. He's running the plantation into the ground. Everyone knows it. He could have cultivated twice as many acres and increased his output per acre. Now he's just running to catch up. At some point he'll have to sell or risk losing everything. It pains me to have to say this, but I think the situation is hopeless."

Emilie's neck was burning. "How dare you speak about my father like that! Please either change the subject or leave."

"Forgive my bluntness, but I speak like a businessman. If your father had handled things properly from the start, your plantation would be in better shape. Earlier in the day, I spied groups of workers lounging around when they should have been working. And there are piles of stray pods left on the ground, a surefire invitation for rats. And he let too many acres run fallow. Mark my words, sooner or later, he will be forced to sell the plantation, and when the time is right, I'm prepared to offer him a fair price, considering how much money I'll have to invest just to get it running properly."

"Sell you the plantation?" she said in a voice dripping with contempt. "Never! Domaine Solitude is not for sale."

"Listen to me," he said, his eyes blazing. "By combining our two plantations, I can corner the sugar and cocoa markets. It's the perfect marriage of convenience. But it's not just about the money. You present a unique *challenge* to me."

Emilie was taken aback. "How could you even suggest such a thing?"

Lucien laughed scornfully. "Emilie, don't you realize how naive you sound? When it comes to turning a profit, it takes more than good intentions. Your father is getting old. It's time he retired."

She stood up abruptly. "Lucien, it's late. I think you'd better go home now."

He stood up and grabbed his jacket. "As you wish, but I'll be back in a few days. I hope by then you'll be calm enough to have a civil conversation." He leaned over to kiss her, but she proffered only her cheek. In an instant, the smile vanished from his face. "I'm a patient man, but even I have my limits." He touched her cheek. "I understand if you're having last-minute jitters, but don't make this harder than it has to be."

After Lucien strode out the door, Emilie stood on the balcony watching his carriage roll out of sight. The only sound came from the chirping of the crickets and tree frogs. Down in the valley, lamps flickered in the workers' cottages like fireflies. She heaved a sigh. For the moment there was peace. But it was an ephemeral sort of peace, like a moth that flutters too near a flame and then disappears in a poof.

Chapter 6

Thursday, April 24

A rooster's crow broke the early-morning stillness. When Emilie entered the dining room, her parents looked up expectantly. She forced a smile, but she was in no mood for conversation. How could she tell them she had no intention of marrying Lucien? How could she tell them Lucien had deceived her? She poured herself a cup of coffee and kept her eyes averted. She knew that sooner or later, she would have to tell them the truth: that Lucien was a philanderer.

She stirred her coffee thoughtfully, taking great pains to avoid meeting her mother's gaze while her father pretended to be reading the newspaper.

"So how did things go last night?" said her mother with practiced nonchalance.

Emilie put the spoon down. "Unfortunately, Maman, things did not go very well. I've made some painful discoveries about Lucien that have forced me to reconsider whether I can spend the rest of my life with him."

Her mother's face drained of color. Her father threw the newspaper aside.

"What are you talking about?" said her father with incredulity.

"Lucien is not a good man," said Emilie. "I cannot go through with this wedding."

"That's preposterous!" said her father.

"You can't be serious," said her mother.

"Unfortunately, I'm very serious," said Emilie. "He's been unfaithful, and when I confronted him about it, he insinuated that I was crazy. He denied everything."

"Well, it does sound crazy," said her mother.

"That's exactly what I expected you to say, Maman," said Emilie. "All you care about is money and status. It doesn't bother you one bit that Lucien has no morals. I could never be happy with him. I want to love the man I marry."

The room went silent.

Her mother blinked a few times. "Where did you get these silly notions about marriage? You know nothing about men. Love is something that grows after marriage."

"You do realize the trouble this will cause us once word gets out," said her father, wagging his finger at her. "People will talk. That's how rumors get started. You'd better do an about-face and apologize immediately if you don't want this matter to escalate."

"How did he take it?" said her mother.

"He laughed in my face," said Emilie with derision. "Lucien never takes anything I say seriously. There's something unsettling about him."

"What's that supposed to mean?" said Georges.

"It means he's an insufferable boor. He orders his servants around like they're his personal slaves and refers to the striking workers as *scum* and all women as *flirts*. He's insufferable. I won't marry him!"

Her father looked as if he was going to explode. Her mother laid down her fork and looked at her with petulant eyes. Emilie heard a pattering of footsteps as the servants retreated to the outside kitchen.

"I've heard enough," said Georges, turning red. "We're under a great deal of financial pressure in case you didn't realize." He lowered his voice. "I don't even have enough money to pay the servants their wages this month. Do you realize we're in danger of losing the farm? I was counting on this marriage to ease our money problems."

"Emilie, darling," said her mother, "you must count your blessings. Lucien is a rich man. He can have any woman he wants, and he chose you. He comes from a good family, and he has a good name. You'll lack for nothing. Don't be foolish!"

Emilie felt her neck turning hot. "If you think Lucien is going to help us financially, you're dead wrong. He has a scheme to buy our plantation for a fraction of what it's worth so he can corner the cocoa and sugar markets. If you ask me, he's a ruthless scoundrel who wants to put all the smaller planters out of business. He puts ambition ahead of common decency. And this is the man you want for a son-in-law?"

Georges looked as if he'd been slapped. Her mother's jaw dropped.

"I don't believe it," said Mme Dujon, covering her mouth in shock. "Lucien is a decent, honorable man. He would never do such a thing."

"The Monplaisir family is fabulously rich. They can put out of business anyone they choose," said her father with a grimness that shocked Emilie. "But that's beside the point. The devil you know is better than the devil you don't. It's too late to cancel the wedding now. Do you want our names in the gossip columns?"

"Yes, think about the gossip," said her mother in a pleading tone. "You don't want to put us through that ordeal, do you?"

"Of course not," said Emilie. "But what choice do I have?"

"You have to compromise. You've always been so willful and headstrong, but now you have to think of others. Put away this silly notion and patch things up."

Emilie felt the bile rise up to her throat. What her mother was asking was impossible.

"Maman, I can't . . ." Suddenly her mouth went dry.

Her father stood up abruptly. "I've heard enough. As far as I'm concerned, nothing has changed. I want you to apologize to Lucien and act as if nothing happened."

"But, Papa. . ."

"Don't argue with me. Just do as I say. I have your best interests at heart. Look how upset you've made your mother. Don't make things harder on us."

All at once Emilie felt cold shackles pressing on her limbs.

"You haven't heard a thing I've said," said Emilie, her eyes blazing.

She jumped up from the table and ran out to the stable. Blinking back tears, she saddled up Balthazar, mounted, and galloped down the dirt road that led out of the plantation. She needed time to think. Time to clear her head. Time to make sense of her life. But most of all, she needed time to figure a way out of this mess. She knew they would never listen to her objections regarding Lucien. In their minds, the die was cast. As usual, she had to be smarter. She had to *think* her way out of this mess.

She headed up a nearby hill and gazed down at the sparkling blue ocean. In the distance she spied a tall sailing ship heading across the Dominica Channel, its white sails fluttering in the wind. Seagulls soared overhead, uttering lonely, piercing cries, and somewhere in the distance, a donkey brayed and a dog barked. Hummingbirds droned around a hibiscus bush, and a dragonfly sailed past her head. She patted Balthazar's neck. At least she still had her beloved horse.

She meandered through the tall guinea grass until her ire cooled and she began to feel strong again. Emilie was sure she would find a way out of this mess. Then, in the midst of her meditations, she began to smell something ominous. It was the same rotten egg scent as before, only stronger. It seemed to be drifting down from Le Prêcheur, the small fishing village to the north. She looked up at Mount Pelée and spotted a terrifying sight: an enormous black cloud was shooting out of the crater. It billowed outward like the ink of a squid, plunging the northern half of the island into darkness.

A thunderous roar filled the air. Balthazar whinnied and reared. Emilie grasped the animal's neck for dear life and tried to calm him down. In the midst of her ordeal, a great cry rose up that sent a shiver of fear through her. The field workers were shouting in terror.

Kicking Balthazar's side, Emilie galloped back to the plantation, dodging tall guinea grass and low-hanging branches. She arrived just as the ground started to tremble. The workers threw their staffs and cutlasses to the ground and ran to take shelter in the stone warehouse. Inside, they congregated with sweaty faces and worried expressions. From the drying shack, stables, and orchards, the workers scrambled to the building for safety. Emilie spied a small girl wandering in the field alone, crying pitifully. Her mother was nowhere to be found. Dismounting, Emilie picked up the child and ran with her to the shelter, pulling Balthazar behind her by his reins.

When she reached the warehouse, she placed the tearful child in her mother's arms and looked around. Maurice and her father were nowhere to be seen. She questioned some of the workers, but they told her they had ridden off with Julien to inspect the outer edges of the plantation and hadn't been seen since.

The sky was darkening. The rumbling noise grew stronger and more threatening. The air was tinged with the odor of sulfur, and there wasn't a bird in the sky. A powdery gray ash began to fall over the fields like a fall of snow. Occasional fragments of stones dropped from the sky as well. It was a shocking sight. The cattle and horses mooed and neighed incessantly. The donkeys brayed, stamping their hooves in protest. The workers crossed themselves and uttered prayers out loud. Some even dropped to their knees.

Leaving the shelter of the warehouse, Emilie brought Balthazar back to the stable, and then ran home to check on her mother and Da Rosette. The ash was falling faster and beginning to collect in small piles. The smell of sulfur became pervasive, giving her a sense of foreboding. After a few minutes, her father and Maurice rode back to the house looking slightly worse for wear. Their clothes were dusted with ash, and their faces had looks of dread. Her father described the scene at the edge of the plantation, which gave rise to much dismay. Piles of ash and cinders had begun to collect, and there were bodies of dead birds lying everywhere. The falling pumice stones had destroyed some of the crops and fouled the water in the streams. The horses and donkeys would soon lack for drinking water. Her father's face was pale, and Maurice was gasping for breath. The sulfurous air was irritating his lungs, making it difficult for him to breathe. Emilie brought him into the house and tried to make him comfortable, but her mind was racing at the disaster that seemed to be looming.

All at once, three distinct shocks like cannon fire rang out, causing the servants to cry out. Lizards scampered through the shutters, and Emilie felt her pulse racing. The blast caused glasses on the table to crash to the floor and dishes to fall from the cupboard. Panic spread throughout the house. Pictures rattled against the wall, and the chandelier began to sway. Outside, roof tiles crashed to the ground.

"Papa, it's an earthquake," said Emilie, looking around frantically.

"No, it's just a tremor," said Georges. "Nobody panic. It will soon pass."

"They're getting worse by the day," said Mme Dujon, visibly shaken. "How much longer can we hold out?"

Nobody answered her. Outside the servants were shrieking in fear. They had congregated on the porch, where Emilie could hear their nervous chatter through the shutters. Beside her, Da Rosette was crossing herself and praying silently. She looked smaller and more vulnerable than Emilie had ever seen her. Thinking quickly, she grabbed her father's binoculars and headed outside to observe the mountain up close. Looking up toward the summit, she saw a thick plume of black smoke billowing out of the crater and then spreading leeward toward Saint-Pierre, where it rained down ashes and cinders. Da Rosette hobbled toward her, her eyes full of terror. She gave Emilie a hug, but her arms never felt weaker and her eyes never looked more afraid.

"Doudou, you were right," said the old woman. "The sulfur mountain is boiling. The Bon Dieu is angry. We must repent before it is too late."

"Perhaps it's already too late," said Emilie.

The plantation was in a state of commotion. The field workers were deserting the fields in droves, calling out to each other to take cover, while in the house, the servants were running around trying to create order, picking up broken dishes and setting the furniture upright while her mother shrieked out orders. She was never good in a disaster. Many times she lost her head and had to be taken upstairs to bed. Emilie heard some coughing and hacking behind her and turned to see Maurice heading toward her. She had never seen his face so pallid or his shoulders so hunched. He looked near collapse. Da Rosette wrapped her shawl around him and set him down in a wicker chair.

"What happened to my boy?" said Da Rosette, patting his back.

Georges Dujon hurried toward Emilie and snatched the binoculars from her hand. "Blasted mountain!" he said. "It's wreaking havoc on the harvest. At this rate we'll lose half the crop."

"Papa, I think we should leave for Saint-Pierre until things quiet down," said Emilie.

Georges shook his head. "We can't leave until the harvest is finished."

"Look at Maurice," she said. "The fumes from the volcano are making his lungs sicker. He needs proper care."

Georges turned to look at Maurice and was repelled. Her brother was hunched over, coughing and spitting blood into a handkerchief. Blood streaked down his shirt, and a bloody mucous stained his handkerchief. Deathly pale, he was wheezing as if his lungs had collapsed.

Emilie rushed to his side and pushed his head back. She tried to stem the flow of blood, but Maurice was in obvious pain. He winced with each breath. Georges laid a hand on his son's forehead, and his eyes filled with worry.

"He's burning up with fever," said Georges. "How long has he been this ill?"

Emilie saw raw fear in her father's eyes, and it terrified her. Without waiting for a response, Georges called to some workers who were leading the horses back to the stable.

"Durancy! Césaire! Go and fetch Dr. Valentin—quick! Tell him Maurice is sick."

Mme Dujon rushed outside. When she saw her son's state, she cried out, "Da Rosette, help me get him upstairs to bed."

Supporting Maurice on either side, Mme Dujon and Da Rosette helped Maurice back into the house.

Emilie felt a lump in her throat. "Papa, I think Maurice needs a sanitarium. The fumes from the volcano are making him worse."

Georges shook his head. "Maurice is a strong boy. He'll be better in a day or two. I'm sure the doctor will say as much. I only sent for him as a precaution."

Emilie stared at her father in disbelief. Clearly he was fooling himself. Didn't he realize Maurice was dying? Didn't he realize that his consumption was getting worse? All at once it struck her that her father was no longer acting rationally. He was living under a grand delusion that everything would turn out fine, while in reality the world around them was falling apart. The volcano was erupting, and Maurice was slowly dying. The plantation lay in the direct path of the volcano, and it was waking up. She was sure it was going to erupt, but she had to be certain. Their lives could depend upon it. Tomorrow she would seek out the one person who could help her.

Chapter 7

Friday, April 25

When Emilie awoke the next morning, she was relieved to see only a thin wisp of smoke issuing from the crater of Mount Pelée. She hoped it was calming down, but by eight o'clock, an explosion larger than anything she had ever heard pierced the morning air. The shock caused her to drop a glass, and it shattered on the floor. The servants ran around in a frenzied state, and the workers fled the fields in droves. They headed back to their cottages in the valley, leaving their pruning sticks strewn on the ground. And then, to Emilie's amazement, huge projectiles shot out of the crater, rising to enormous heights and then falling back against the upper flanks of the mountain. The noise of the explosions was so shocking, she felt her heart racing. She fled to the stable, saddled up Balthazar, and without a word to anyone, rode down to Saint-Pierre, hoping and praying she would find her beloved cousin Abbé Morel. Surely he would know what to do.

Ever since she was little, Abbé Morel, or Tonton Abbé as she called him, had been a calming presence in her life. A distant cousin, he had been her tutor for as long as she could remember. She would listen for hours, wide-eyed with fascination, while he read from large volumes about natural history, botany, and geology. It was he who had taught her that volcanoes were formed from subterranean fires deep below the earth's crust. He was patient and kind, the wisest man she had ever known. With his flashing dark eyes, spectacles, black cassock, and round-brimmed hat, he resembled a scholarly medieval monk. The times she had spent with Abbé Morel were the happiest of her life. But their time together was cut short.

Several years ago, the Archbishop of Martinique had sent Abbé to Saint Vincent to minister to the flock there. Later he was shipped off to Port of Spain and then to Guadeloupe. Finally he was relegated to the tiny godforsaken island of Carriacou, where he served as parish priest to a congregation of plantation workers and fishermen. For many years, their only source of communication was letters and postcards. But after a while, his letters stopped coming.

When Emilie asked her father, he explained that Abbé Morel had grown sick and would soon be returning to Martinique. When she saw him alight from the ship, he was a changed man. He looked older and frailer. His eyes had lost their glow. The years of wandering had not been good for him. Emilie hugged him with all her might, but she could not erase the pain from his eyes. Abbé told Emilie that he had resigned his position so he could return to Saint-Pierre to tend to the convicts in the prison. Now, many months had passed since Emilie had spoken to her Tonton Abbé, and the hole he left in her heart felt like an open wound.

After crossing the stone bridge over rivière Roxelane, Emilie continued south on rue Victor Hugo until she reached rue de la Prison. She turned up the street and halted when she reached the prison. Dismounting, she tied Balthazar to a hitching post, unlatched the gate, and strode up to the entrance. The guard on duty told her that Abbé Morel was busy hearing confession, but she could wait in his office. She followed the guard down the passage past various cells containing sullen, hollow-eyed prisoners. The only sound she heard was a voice murmuring: *"Bless me, Father, for I have sinned. It's been six months since my last confession . . ."*

When they reached Abbé Morel's office, the guard told her to wait inside. Removing her straw hat, Emilie sat down and wiped the sweat from her brow. There was no breeze through the shutters. The air was stuffy and humid. Outside she could hear the trickling of the water in the gutters and a rooster crowing. Occasionally a carriage would trundle down the street, but otherwise all she heard was the clanging of the prison doors and the muted voices of the convicts.

She looked around. The office was bare. There were no mementos from home, no photographs, none of his personal belongings, just a wooden desk, a bookshelf, a washbasin, and a solitary crucifix hanging on the wall.

A few minutes later, she heard the clang of a metal door and a pair of heavy footsteps plodding down the passageway, the sound echoing off the stone walls. When she saw Abbé Morel's face in the doorway, Emilie flung herself into his arms. In an instant, time and distance melted away. In her beloved Tonton Abbé's arms, Emilie felt like a young girl again, innocent and free, without a care in the world.

Abbé Morel looked tired in his black cassock. His eyes were the same kind eyes and his arms were the same comforting arms, but something about him was different. He laid his hand against her cheek. "My dear Emilie, I've missed you so." He set his Bible down. "I can't tell you how happy I am to see you. What brings you here today?"

"I've missed you so much, Tonton Abbé. I just had to see you. So much has happened . . ."

He plopped down in his seat, removed his round-brimmed hat, and ran his hands through his hair.

"They never told us how hard it would be to hear confession. Sometimes it breaks my heart. These poor wretches seek only one thing, absolution, and all I can offer them is my ear. But somehow it gives them a glimmer of hope. I think I've finally found my true calling in life." He grinned. She thought she saw some color returning to his cheeks.

"Of course you did," she said. "You always had a generous and kind heart. I always believed it could cut through stone."

"I owe it all to prayer," he said. "Oh, I struggled with it for many years. But when I finally learned to allow the Holy Spirit to pray and struggle along with me, I broke through the barrier. It was the greatest accomplishment of my life. And now I share this gift with the men. They feel as if the world has forgotten them."

"Tonton Abbé, how can you be so peaceful when there are constant tremors and the ash clouds from the volcano? Sometimes I can barely sleep at night."

"It's an unfortunate side effect of living on a volcanic island," he said. "But all the scientists claim it will calm down. Perhaps I should go to the north of the island and pray with the people there."

"Prayer will certainly help, but I think there is something more serious at work here," she said. "I think the volcano is going to erupt."

Abbé Morel rubbed his chin for a minute and then went to his bookshelf. After perusing the shelf, he selected an ancient volume with yellow, mildewed pages, titled *The Natural History of the French West Indies*. He leafed through it, and when he found a relevant passage, he handed it to Emilie and asked her to read it:

Earthquakes belong to the phenomena of volcanic eruptions which take place in the West Indies . . .they have always preceded and accompanied the eruptions of volcanoes. Father Labat reported that there was an earthquake at the end of the 17th century when a prodigious quantity of sulfur ash and burnt stones was thrown out of a new opening in Mount Pelée . . .

"I think you're right, my dear," said Abbé Morel. "Perhaps M. Moreau de Jonnès is trying to warn us of an impending eruption."

"I want to find out for sure," she said.

Abbé Morel regarded her intently. "I see you are cooking up something. What's going through that mind of yours?"

"I want to climb up Mount Pelée and get a good look at the crater, and I want you to come with me."

The priest laughed. "I'm afraid my climbing days are over. But I can take you up to Morne-Rouge, where we can get a good view of the summit. With you on your horse and me on my donkey, we should be able to make it in two hours."

After filling up a canteen with fresh spring water, they headed up the winding road to Morne-Rouge, which traced the rivière Blanche through dense tropical foliage that grew wilder and denser the steeper they climbed. Gigantic ferns, clumps of bamboo, palm trees, and balisier flowers lined their path, providing much-needed shade from the blazing sun. It was a long and arduous climb, and by the time they reached the mountain village, they were exhausted.

When they arrived in Morne-Rouge, they stopped to rest in the shade of a breadfruit tree, eating the fresh fruit and coconut cake they had purchased from one of the marketwomen. After resting awhile, they left their animals to graze while they hiked up a nearby hill. It was a long, hot climb through brush and brambles, and when they reached the top, Abbé Morel collapsed on the ground.

"My dear, either you possess the strength of an ox to climb that hill, or the angels lifted you."

"No angels helped me, Tonton Abbé," she said. "At least none that I could see. I've climbed many hills, but I've never seen these angels of which you speak."

She took out her binoculars and scanned the summit of Mount Pelée, but there was no more smoke, not even a hint of a rumble.

During the climb to Morne-Rouge, the volcano had completely quieted down. Somehow this made Emilie more curious. She was certain it was only a temporary reprieve.

From his breast pocket, Abbé Morel pulled out a silver flask and took a long, satisfying sip. "Ah, much better," he said. "There's nothing like a bit of rum to restore one's soul." He gazed at the ocean in the distance. "The view from here is spectacular. You can almost see Dominica far off in the distance."

Emilie plucked some grass without responding.

Abbé Morel studied her. "Emilie, I suspect you didn't bring me up here just to study the volcano. Is there something troubling you?"

"Nothing. I'm perfectly fine," she said, avoiding his gaze.

Abbé lifted up her chin. "Emilie, I know something's bothering you. I've known you since you were a baby. I baptized you and taught you how to read, yet I see there's much more I have to learn about you."

She closed her eyes. "It's so hard to talk about these things."

"What things?" he said. "Oh, if only I could read your mind. Perhaps it's time we got to know each other a little better. Did I ever tell you why I decided to become a priest?"

"I thought you were always a priest."

"No, I was not born a priest," he said. "I guess it's time I told you the truth. What harm could come of it? Well, since this is to be my confessional, I suppose we should sit a little closer. That's better. You know, Emilie, I never told you this, but my parents, God rest their souls, waited many years for me to enter the world. After twenty years of marriage, their prayers were finally answered. Well, at least they were *partially* answered. I arrived in this world like most babies, but I was not a bundle of joy. I was difficult, colicky, headstrong, and decidedly nocturnal. As I grew up, I became conceited and smug. I'm ashamed to admit it, but I never had much respect for authority, so the priesthood didn't seem like a natural calling for me. At first I worked as a clerk, a bookkeeper, and a schoolteacher, but inside I had an unquenchable fire, a need to discover the truth. I read constantly from every book I could get my hands on. Most nights I stayed up late reading books with tiny print by the light of a kerosene lamp. One morning when I woke up, I made a startling discovery. During the night, I had gone blind! You can imagine my terror. The only way I knew it was day was by the rooster's crow, but everything was dark. My whole world collapsed. In one fell swoop, everything I loved was taken away from me. Without the ability to read and learn, life lost all meaning. I never felt more alone in my life. The thought that I would end my life as an invalid, unable to see, unable to read, unable to learn, was too much to bear. Right then and there, I promised God that if he restored my sight, I would take my vows and enter the priesthood. And so it happened. Several days later, after much prayer, my sight was restored. Soon thereafter, I took my holy orders and entered a monastery."

"That's fascinating," said Emilie. "I never knew that about you. What a terrible ordeal."

"So now you know the truth," said Abbé Morel. "That's how I became a priest."

"So in order for you to find your true calling, God had to first take away your sight."

"In a manner of speaking," said Abbé. "The Lord was testing me. He taught me a difficult lesson, that to reach a state of enlightenment, sometimes one has to go through a period of great hardship. We have to lose everything in order to realize what it is we truly want; what we truly need. Each one of us is tested in his own way."

"I think the Lord is testing me now," she said.

"My dear, what are you talking about?" said Abbé Morel.

Emilie stared at him. "I think I've made a terrible mistake. I can't marry Lucien."

Abbé's face turned serious. "Are you certain? What happened?"

"I've never been more certain in my life. I discovered that he's been unfaithful. He has other women."

Abbé's face blanched. "Good Lord, how could we have been so wrong about him?"

"When I tried to tell Maman and Papa, they wouldn't hear of it. They forbid me to call off the wedding and cause a scandal. I feel so alone."

Abbé brought his hand to his mouth, but he could not disguise his shock. "Oh dear, you can't marry that scoundrel. We have to call off the wedding, but it will cause terrible problems."

"Some days I wish I could just run away like you did so many years ago," she said.

"Running away won't solve this problem," said Abbé Morel. "Not with Lucien. He only respects strength, but I was convinced he was in love with you and would soften with time. Now I see now how wrong I was."

"Tell me the truth, Tonton Abbé, why did you leave Carriacou? Is it true what people are saying, that you threatened to leave the priesthood?"

"No, my dear," he laughed. "That's idle gossip. I'm afraid the real story isn't quite so dramatic. The simple truth is I got too old for the job. I entered the priesthood late in life. I grew tired of transferring from one parish to another, and I was desperately lonely on that godforsaken island. Sometimes the loneliness became so great, I would take to my bed for days. Before long, my old stomach ulcer started acting up, and I needed a doctor's proper care. They don't have a full-time doctor on Carriacou, just an English doctor who takes the ferry over from Saint Vincent twice a month. So, given my weakened condition, I asked for a position in Saint-Pierre."

Emilie touched Abbé's cheek. "If I had known how lonely you were, I would have come to visit you."

"Carriacou is no place for a young woman."

"But after you left, nothing was the same anymore. Life lost all meaning for me. Even Lucien couldn't fill the hole you caused when you left. And then when you came back, you were different. You had changed."

"So had you, Emilie," said Abbé, gazing at her. "You became a beautiful young woman. I don't want to see all that beauty and innocence go to waste. I don't want to see you turn cynical and bitter because life showed you her ugly side. I promise to do everything in my power to get you out of this predicament."

Emilie kissed the priest's hand. "Thank you, Tonton Abbé. I knew I could count on you."

Abbé Morel laid his hand on Emilie's cheek. He prayed that somehow he would be able to help her, even if he needed a miracle.

Chapter 8

Friday, April 25

Down in Fort-de-France, Gov. Louis Mouttet was facing a big dilemma. The election was days away, and for the first time, it looked as if the Radical Socialists were going to win. Their candidate, an influential mulatto named Louis Percin, was gaining in the polls and stood a good chance of being elected as the new delegate to the Chamber of Deputies. In Mouttet's mind, that would be a disaster. Percin's staunchest ally, Amédée Knight, was a wealthy mulatto industrialist who was pushing the Radical Socialist agenda to the consternation of the business community. Knight had power, money, and influence, and he represented the biggest thorn in the side of the bourgeoisie. Adding to the humiliation, Knight had befriended Mouttet's own boss, Albert Decrais, the Minister of Colonies, and was using every means at his disposal to usurp the powers of Mouttet's office in a bid to wrest total political control of the island. The situation was becoming intolerable. *Connard!* Mouttet crumpled up the latest issue of *L'Opinion* and threw it in the wastebasket.

For a small colony like Martinique, politics captured a large portion of the public's imagination. They treated it almost like a national sport. On the pages of *Les Colonies*, Marius Hurard mocked and demeaned Knight, calling him "The White Hater" or "The Little Machiavellian Sultan," and Knight retaliated on the pages of *L'Opinion* by calling Hurard a "Political Narcissist" or "The Man of Insatiable Ambition." Every day it was something else. The mudslinging was quickly reaching a boiling point. Instead of fighting duels in the old-fashioned manner, they launched offensives with pen and ink. And the posters they hung on the walls left little to the imagination. It took all the restraint Mouttet could muster to maintain an image of impartiality in the face of such smears. Some days he considered early retirement. As a representative of the French government, Mouttet was expected to stay neutral in political matters while maintaining order and control, jobs that seemed mutually exclusive. But now it looked as if power was finally going to swing in the opposite direction. To survive, Mouttet knew he would have to navigate safely through these muddy waters. It was a constant source of irritation.

Mouttet leaned back in his chair and sighed. At forty-five, he was in the prime of life and had reached what he believed was the pinnacle of his career. Not bad for a middle-class civil servant. A bulging middle hinted at his predilection for good food and wine, and occasional bouts of dysentery and malaria had coarsened his otherwise handsome features. His only claim to vanity was a walrus moustache that was still black, though there was a hint of gray at his temples, giving him the appearance of a wise sage. Yes, he had weathered many political storms in his career, but he was certain that with a little behind-the-scenes maneuvering, he could help the Progressives defeat the Radical Socialists at the polls. Although he personally liked Knight, the man had a way of getting under his skin. There was only one thing he knew for sure: on a small island it was nearly impossible to hide from one's political enemies, and therefore, it was better to remain friends.

Still, there were other matters to consider. There was the constant threat of riots, labor strikes, hurricanes, and rabble-rousers that sometimes curiously showed up in the homes of the wealthier békés, who comprised a small but powerful white minority on an island populated largely by the descendants of African slaves and mulattoes. The békés were an odd bunch. Strictly Bonapartists, they gave lip service to the ideals of the Third Republic, but they were no great lovers of republicanism. Ardently Catholic, they were even less fond of the new Socialist ideals, especially those espoused by Amédée Knight, which placed Mouttet in the uncomfortable position of being pitted between both sides. Personally, he was sympathetic to the Socialist cause, but he had learned over the years to keep his opinions to himself. The last thing he needed was to get on the bad side of either political party. He shuddered when he remembered how the previous governor, Merlin, was turned into a political football. When it was Mouttet's turn to leave, if that day ever came, he wanted it to be on his own terms. Even God couldn't deny him that.

He got up from his desk and peered out the window to the sun-drenched harbor of Fort-de-France. The bay was already starting to fill up with steamers and schooners for another day of brisk commerce. Statuesque coal women, *charbonniers*, were hard at work hauling countless baskets of coal into the coal chutes of the ships. Their skin glistened as they labored in the hot sun. Ranging in color from *café au lait* to bronze to deepest mahogany, the women displayed graceful features and long, curved necks that contrasted sharply with the harshness of their lives. Even in sooty rags, they displayed curves that would put Venus to shame. Without their labor, every port in the West Indies would be forced to shut down, including Martinique. Chaos would ensue. Money would be lost, and angry telegrams would pile up on his desk. A headache he could definitely live without. These women were a force to be reckoned with, and if he had learned anything from his years in colonial service, it was to never underestimate the power of a bribe.

Walking over to the mahogany cabinet, he poured himself a glass of rum, the island's best *rhum agricole*, distilled to perfection from the juice of fresh-cut sugarcane taken directly from the field. To this he added a twist of lime, a dash of spring water, and a spoonful of cane syrup. Sublime. The perfect elixir to calm his flagging spirits.

It wasn't his habit to drink so early in the day, but lately the pressures of the office had become burdensome. It was nothing to complain about. In fact, he thought he was lucky. If he played his cards right, Martinique would be his home for many years to come. Perhaps it would even be his *final* home, the tropical paradise of his dreams in which to spend his golden years. With such a casual style of living and abundant luxuries, he had no desire to uproot his family and move to another colonial outpost like the Ivory Coast or the Sudan. And moving back to France was out of the question. After spending half his life in the colonial service, he had no desire to ever return to the Métropole again.

And then there was the matter of the volcano. Another damned nuisance! There wasn't a single trained geologist on the entire island, yet every nitwit considered himself an expert. He lit a cigar, leaned back in his chair, and took a few satisfying puffs. He could almost smell Euphemie's *accras de morue* wafting down the hall. Those cod fritters seasoned with spices and fried to perfection were an island specialty, a delicacy. One that Euphemie had mastered with the skill of a great artist, like a Monet or Cézanne. In many ways these island women with their sumptuous cuisine, feminine wiles, coquettish behavior, and exotic clothing were like master artists. Artists who could . . . oh dear. He glanced at the clock. Time to get the meeting started.

Mouttet called for his assistant.

Didier stuck his head in. *"Oui, monsieur?"*

"Has Colonel Fournier arrived?"

"Yes, sir, he's waiting in the vestibule."

"Call him in please."

Mouttet rose when Colonel Fournier entered. After returning the colonel's salute, he shook his hand. This was a man to respect. Mouttet had admired him from their first meeting, but he wondered if the colonel wasn't getting too old for the job. He was still sprightly but was somewhat bent. Handsome, distinguished, and with a tolerable amount of gray, Fournier was sixty on his last birthday. As acting garrison commander at Saint-Pierre, he was perhaps the only man on the island whose opinion Mouttet truly respected, especially on matters of security.

"Care for a cigar? A glass of rum?" said Mouttet.

"What year?" said Fournier.

Mouttet grinned. "The cigar or the rum? For you, my friend, only the best: Rhum de Sa Majesté, 1892. Napoleon's choice for his troops. As pure as mother's milk and probably a lot better for you. As an inveterate drunkard once said after learning his cholera was incurable and he would soon be removed to a world of pure spirits: 'That's a comforting thought as it's impossible to get any in this world.'"

Fournier laughed. "That's a good one! What can I do for you today?"

"I'm developing a long-term strategy for the colonization of Martinique, which I'd like to share with you. I believe that once she's developed, Martinique will prove to be a magnificent asset to *la Mère Patrie*. Every day I receive correspondence from businessmen all around the globe expressing their interest in investing in our island. We desperately need to build up our infrastructure and secure our coastline. To do this, we'll need the best officers, men of good character whom we can trust. We have to make it clear to Decrais at the Colonial Office that we won't accept any officers with black marks on their record or who are deficient in character or lacking in moral stamina. And we certainly should not accept into our ranks any habitual criminals, lunatics, gamblers, or those considered constitutionally defective. As long as I'm in charge, Martinique will not be a place for shooting rubbish. Is that clear?"

"Absolutely. It has always been my policy. Is there any particular reason for your concern?"

"I heard we're expecting a new officer at the garrison, one who was shipped out of Africa quite abruptly under a cloud of suspicion. Are you aware of this case?"

Colonel Fournier looked thoughtful. "Yes, I'm aware of it, but let me assure you, Governor, that in all my years of service, there have only been a handful of cases that would fall into that category. I've learned not to question the Colonial Office in these matters. Telegrams have a way of getting misplaced; good men are sometimes caught in the bureaucratic shuffle. Plus, I feel it's only proper to give each man the benefit of the doubt. I assess each officer as he arrives and shuffle the derelicts down to Cayenne. I'm proud of my regiment, and you have no reason to worry about it."

"Very good," said Mouttet. "There's one more issue I'd like to discuss. It's concerning those infernal rumblings coming from Mount Pelée that's gotten the natives all jittery. To calm everyone's fears, I've decided to set up a scientific committee to climb up the mountain and write a report about it. I've put Prof. Gaston Landes in charge, but he needs a few good men with surveying experience. Is there someone you can recommend?"

Fournier perked up. "I've got just the man for you."

"Who is it?"

"That new officer you mentioned. The one that's due to arrive from Senegal any day."

"Does he have the necessary qualifications?"

"I've heard he has the best qualifications. He was responsible for conducting surveying missions in Senegal. He's the perfect man for the job."

"Splendid," said Mouttet. "Tell him to report to Gaston Landes as soon as he arrives. Perhaps we can make good use of the chap. Give it your top priority."

"Certainly, Governor."

Colonel Fournier saluted and left. As he walked out the door, Mouttet crossed off the word *volcano* from his list of pending issues, confident the problem would soon be forgotten.

Chapter 9

Friday, April 25

Standing on the deck of the French steamer *Versailles*, Lt. Denis Rémy watched as the island of Martinique sprang into view. What started as a blue cloud on the horizon transformed into a deep-green island of soaring peaks, lush valleys, and undulating fields of sugarcane and banana. Everywhere he looked, the island was teeming with life. Mango trees, sprawling bougainvillea, flaming flamboyant, majestic palm trees, and endless plantations dotting the hillsides like a patchwork quilt of sumptuous beauty. Every now and then, he caught sight of a wooden cottage or a chimney peeking through the foliage, adding to the mystery, while along the shore, native sloops sailed past silvery beaches lined with coconut palms. It was intoxicating and refreshing, like a tropical oasis that suddenly appeared out of the azure sea. As he was taking in the sights, the cry of a seabird broke his reverie.

Although it was late morning, it was already hot on deck. The tropical sun beat down on the passengers who had gathered near the railing while stewards passed around glasses of rum punch. With his blue tunic and kepi and his features bronzed from a lifetime in the tropics, Rémy stood apart from the others. At thirty-three, he was fast approaching middle age, with the scars of a lifetime to prove it. Lean and muscular, his most distinguishing characteristics were a jaunty moustache and pair of penetrating blue eyes that gave the mistaken impression he was a ruthless sort, which wasn't exactly a drawback for a career soldier. But in Rémy's case, it was far from the truth. His sense of duty and honor had cost him dearly.

But that was all behind him now. A great feeling of loneliness gripped his heart, a fear that his life had taken too many wrong turns. He wondered how long he would last out here in the West Indies. Between the cheap rum and the tropical diseases, he figured at most two years. He had gambled with his career and lost. Perhaps a younger man could overcome such a misstep, but not a man of his age. He remembered with a dull ache how the chief of the Bambara had warned him: "Ears that do not listen to advice accompany the head when it is chopped off." But Rémy did what he was compelled to do. He did what any man of honor would have done under similar circumstances, and he harbored no regrets. He accepted his fate, and now all he wanted was to make the most of whatever time he had left.

But maybe, just maybe, he would have a chance to redeem himself.

He inhaled the fresh sea air and felt invigorated. *So this is my new home,* he thought. *My place of exile, my Elba.* With Martinique's wild, untamed beauty, the island reminded him of Senegal. He gazed at the highest peak, a conical green mountain the deckhand had referred to as Mount Pelée in his lilting Creole. Even with his binoculars Rémy could scarcely catch a glimpse of the summit behind a veil of clouds. It looked well over four thousand feet high and reminded him of a poem his mother used to recite to him when he was a boy:

Du haut de la montagne,
Près de Guadarrama,
On découvre l'Espagne
Comme un panorama.
À l'horizon sans borne
Le grave Escorial
Lève son dôme morne,
Noir de l'ennui royal.

From the top of the mountain,
Near Guadarrama,
We discover Spain
Like a grand panorama.
On the horizon without bounds
The grave Escorial
Raises his somber dome,
Black from royal boredom.

The image of his mother's face brought a surge of pain. Memories like that popped up from time to time although he tried hard to bury them. His greatest regret was not being able to say goodbye when she lay dying. By the time he got word of it in

Senegal, it was too late. The pain crushed him. He was her only child, the only link she had to his father, who had died while Rémy was still a baby.

It was still early by the time the steamer glided into the harbor of Saint-Pierre. His first sight of the town brought him surprising contentment.

Stretched along the coast, the city of Saint-Pierre held its arms open in a welcoming embrace. Built at the foot of Mount Pelée, the town sloped down from the hills in a terrace fashion and spread out along the shore. Nestled between an abundance of foliage were stone villas with red roofs, walled-in gardens, a theater, hotels, a commercial district, and cathedrals with lofty steeples that peeked out through the mahogany and tamarind trees. Guarding the waterfront was a fort bearing the Tricolor, and beside it sat a contingent of stone warehouses. The marketplace was bustling with traffic, and horse carriages clip-clopped through the streets, creating a scene that was both charming and welcoming to the traveler.

When it was time to disembark, Rémy picked up his luggage and boarded one of the small skiffs sent to ferry the passengers to shore. Martinique was his new home now, for better or worse. As his commanding officer back in Senegal had stipulated, this was to be his final posting unless he committed another offense, in which case he would be shipped off to the penal colony in French Guyana, a veritable death sentence.

As he took his first steps on dry land, a feeling of relief washed over him. After weeks at sea, the hustle and bustle of place Bertin jarred his senses. The colors, the smells, and the cheerful sounds of bartering in the marketplace and the echoes of native music brought him a sense of calm. And the faces! Faces similar to those he had seen in Africa speaking in their own native patois. Charming native women in colorful madras skirts and headdresses sailed past with baskets laden with fruit and spices. Barefoot workers with glistening bodies were hard at work rolling hogsheads of sugar and rum down to the water. Fishermen in canvas trousers, schoolchildren, nuns, turbaned marketwomen with exotic, African faces, white-helmeted customs officers, and gendarmes in slate-blue tunics and pillbox hats—all created the bouillabaisse that was Saint-Pierre.

He walked over to a public fountain and took a refreshing drink. While he was taking in the sights, an old peasant woman carrying a basket of goods approached him. A wide-brimmed straw hat shielded her head from the sun, but it could not hide the poverty and misery that were etched into her face. She wore a faded muslin skirt and chemise stained yellow from dirt and sweat, but she wore no shoes. Her dirty, calloused feet displayed the direness of her predicament most wretchedly.

"Monsieur, would you buy something from pauvre petite Prospérine?" she said in a soft voice.

Rémy turned away. "No, thank you, madame."

She tugged at his sleeve. "Monsieur, buy something? Soap? Razor? Comb? Bay rum?" Staring into her eyes, Rémy was struck by the old woman's dignity. Her eyes had a purity that belied her wretched situation. His taut expression slackened.

"How much for a bottle of bay rum?" he said.

"Twenty centimes."

Reaching into his billfold, he pulled out a five franc coin and pressed it into her hand.

"Take this, madame."

Relief washed over the old woman's face. "Merci, monsieur. May the Bon Dieu protect you."

Something about the woman's words gripped him. Grasping the coin in her bony hand, the old woman disappeared into the crowd. As Rémy watched her meander through the marketplace, a stocky, redheaded soldier in his late thirties with a jovial face and a casual manner approached him.

"Welcome, Lieutenant," said the soldier, saluting.

Rémy returned the salute. "Thank you, Sergeant. My name is Lt. Denis Rémy, just arrived from Senegal."

The sergeant thought for a moment. "Ah yes, Lieutenant Rémy. I've heard your name mentioned. Colonel Fournier has been expecting you. Shall I take you to the commandant myself?"

"That would be splendid. And who are you?"

"I am Sgt. Jean-Alfred Aubert, attached to the Fourth Regiment at Fort Saint-Pierre, where I believe you are assigned. Allow me to show you the way. Follow me please, sir."

"My pleasure."

The sergeant motioned to a nearby soldier, who picked up Rémy's suitcase, and together they led him past the bustling place Bertin to the fort.

Heading north along rue Bouillé, they traced the curve of the harbor, past the customhouse, commission houses, cafés, and a long stretch of stone warehouses that Aubert explained was the Figuier Quarter, the commercial district. When they arrived at rivière Roxelane, they crossed a stone bridge over which passed most of the traffic through the city. They continued down rue des Bouchers straight to the entrance of the fort.

The guard on duty stiffened and saluted. Aubert led Rémy down a corridor lit by electric lights, and when they arrived at an anteroom, he instructed Rémy to wait outside while he went to inform the commandant of his arrival.

Sounds of metropolitan French filled the hallway as groups of young soldiers passed by on their way to the barracks. Aubert reappeared and motioned for Rémy to follow him into the commandant's office. When he crossed the threshold, he caught his first glimpse of the colonel, a broad-shouldered man in his sixties with a distinct Roman nose and a graying beard. He was sitting at his desk sorting through a pile of correspondence, at his side sat a gleaming revolver and a steaming mug of coffee. The office was a simple affair, containing only a simple wooden desk, chairs, a bookcase, and on the wall, a large map of the West Indies and a portrait of Waldeck-Rousseau.

Rémy saluted. "Lt. Denis Rémy reporting for duty, sir."

Colonel Fournier saluted and shook his hand. "Welcome to Martinique, Lieutenant. I trust you've had a pleasant journey."

"Yes, considering I was sick half the time."

"That's to be expected," said the colonel, chuckling. "I spent a few years in Senegal myself, but that was before your time. Most gorgeous sunsets I ever saw were in Dakar. Please take a seat."

"Thank you, sir."

"I've been reading up on you. Quite an impressive service record." Fournier put on his reading glasses and opened up a dossier marked *Lt. Denis Rémy*. "Hmm, five years with the Twentieth Battalion of the chasseurs à pied at Mézières, decent grades at the *École des sous-officiers*, a good service record at the penal battalion at Senegal, a transfer to the Camp des Madeleines near Dakar, an appointment to the general staff, advisor to the railroad project."

"Yes, sir," said Rémy. "I mapped much of the region between the Upper Niger and the Gold Coast. I acquired extensive knowledge about the region and the natives."

Fournier leafed through the papers. "And then it says you volunteered for a dangerous mission in Mali, but there's no report of the outcome."

"Yes, sir. You see, the mission was aborted."

Fournier removed his reading glasses. "Aborted?"

"We ran into some difficulties, sir. It was a personnel matter."

Fournier leaned back and observed him. "Care to elaborate?"

"Not really, sir. After that I was transferred here. I was not given a choice."

"Something is not quite adding up," said Fournier, furrowing his brow. "Is there something I should know?"

"It was a simple misunderstanding. The matter was officially sealed, and I'd rather not discuss it."

Fournier cleared his throat. "Well, so be it. I see you've accomplished much good work in Africa, but since we don't get many transfers from the general staff, you'll understand if the men are somewhat curious."

"I have no intention of becoming a carnival exhibit."

Fournier eyed him, then pushed aside the file. "Then I have no need to question you further at this time. Let's get on with it then, shall we? There's not much to say other than the life is hard here in the West Indies. We have occasional bouts of yellow fever, dengue fever, typhoid, and malaria, but I suppose you developed some immunity from your years in Africa. We have a pretty decent military hospital and an excellent surgeon. You'll find no lack of entertainment venues, although I would caution you to avoid certain establishments on rue Bouillé and rue Saint-Jean-de-Dieu, where there have been a number of knife fights. We also suffer from occasional hurricanes, earthquakes, and civil unrest." He stopped when Rémy gave him a quizzical look. "Regarding the civilians, two years ago there was an uprising on the island. Some workers went on strike and started fires on four plantations, using every means at their disposal to prevent the harvesting of the sugarcane. An infantry post sent to restore order was attacked and fired on its assailants, killing nine men and wounding fourteen. Since then the situation has quieted down, but there's still a great deal of tension. The lieutenant who commanded the troops that fired on the striking workers was removed from his post and transferred to Cayenne."

"What caused the workers' strike?" asked Rémy.

"As usual it was politics," said Fournier. "It was a classic political maneuver that backfired, resulting in those tragic deaths. Two of Martinique's delegates to the Chamber of Deputies won the election by promising the workers an increase in their wages, which the plantation owners refused to uphold. The situation grew heated, the delegates denied making such promises, and instead blamed the governor and the metropolitan government, whom they claimed were responsible for the uprising. The delegate from Guadeloupe denied their assertion, which resulted in two deputies coming to blows." When Rémy looked shocked, Fournier hastily added, "I should warn you that politics is a divisive issue in the West Indies. We have a new governor now, a man by the name of Mouttet, but there's a new election in a couple of days for two new delegates, so our main objective is to maintain law and order to ensure a peaceful election. As for you, however, I have a completely different assignment, one that promises to make use of your topographical skills."

Rémy perked up. "Oh? What is it?"

"We've been having some seismic activity coming from Mount Pelée. The governor formed a scientific committee to climb up the mountain and do some scouting around the crater to calm down the civilians, who've been understandably jittery lately. Given your extensive surveying experience in Africa, I went ahead and put you on the committee. Your orders are to report to Prof. Gaston Landes at the lycée. When you've completed your assignment, you're to report directly to the governor. Any questions?"

"Just one, sir," said Rémy. "I'm honored to serve la Mère Patrie in any manner that is required, but I have never surveyed a volcano before. My experience is limited to the jungles and rivers of Senegal and Mali."

"Take my copy of *Geography of Martinique*." Fournier handed a large volume to Rémy. "In it you'll find all the information you need. Anything else you need, you can find in the Schoelcher Library. And make sure to pick up your gear from the quartermaster. You'll need a good set of field glasses and a barometer. I hear the view from the summit of Mount Pelée is quite extraordinary. On a clear day you can see clear across the Dominica Channel."

Rémy hesitated for a minute. "Just one more question, sir: How likely is it the volcano will erupt?"

Fournier waved his hand. "Not likely at all in my opinion. There hasn't been a major eruption in hundreds of years. We expect it to die down shortly. Bear in mind the governor's main concern is to keep the civilians calm. The population tends to be highly superstitious. Their beliefs are tied up with voodoo and black magic. The government has had little success in uprooting these primitive beliefs from the people. One of their voodoo sorcerers thinks the extinct volcano is on the verge of erupting."

"Then would it be wise to climb up to the summit?"

"That's for the committee to decide," said Colonel Fournier. "I'm afraid it's out of my hands. Sergeant Aubert will show you to your quarters in the officers' barracks."

Rémy saluted. "Thank you, sir. I have one request related to this mission."

"What is it?"

"I would like to request that Sergeant Aubert be detailed as my aide-de-camp."

"That can be arranged."

"Thank you, Colonel," said Rémy, saluting.

Colonel Fournier returned the salute. "Good luck, Rémy, and welcome to Martinique."

Rémy strolled out, invigorated by his new assignment, hopeful that his stay in Martinique would be calm and placid. A fresh start to his life.

Chapter 10

Sunday, April 27

After settling into the officers' barracks and collecting his gear, Rémy strode over to the lycée to meet Professor Landes and learn about his new mission.

In Landes, Rémy found a sympathetic man with no pretenses other than an innate love of natural history. Landes was about the same age and sported a goatee and spectacles. In addition to a good sense of humor, he possessed an almost encyclopedic knowledge about the geography and botany of the West Indies. Landes gave Rémy a list of equipment to procure, and they agreed to head out the following Sunday.

When Sunday arrived, Rémy and Sergeant Jean-Alfred Aubert dressed in their khaki uniforms, helmets, and expedition boots. They saddled their horses and hired a porter with a donkey to carry all the gear they could not fit in their saddlebags, and then they headed over to the lycée. They found Professor Landes in his carriage, and beside him sat M. Paul Mirville, chief chemist at the military hospital. Trailing behind them was a porter on a donkey who looked less than thrilled with his mission.

After a brief introduction, Rémy sized up the newest member of the scientific committee. At sixty years of age and overweight, M. Mirville did not look capable of climbing the stairs of the theater, much less Mount Pelée. And to make matters worse, he walked with a pronounced limp, which he blamed on a nagging case of arthritis. With his fluffy white beard and shaggy eyebrows, Mirville resembled a mad scientist, and to their astonishment he even boasted that he had once climbed up Pelée in record time, prompting Rémy to wonder in which century, since the portly chemist seemed incapable of any form of physical exercise. After they had loaded all their gear, the men set out.

Landes explained that the first order of business was to hire some competent guides, which he would procure from a nearby plantation. Trotting up the coastal road, they began to smell the telltale scent of rotten eggs, an unmistakable sign of volcanic activity. Turning east, they headed up a road lined with leafy palms that led to the tiny hamlet of Saint-Philomène. After passing a small chapel and an outdoor market, they turned onto a dirt road bordered by dense vegetation, beyond which lay acres of cacao and coffee trees. Professor Landes announced that they had entered Domaine Solitude, the plantation of Georges Dujon, a respected landowner who hailed from a prominent old béké family.

Everywhere they looked there was a flurry of activity. Workers in straw hats were engaged in various activities related to the harvesting of cacao and coffee. Rémy had never observed a plantation up close. It seemed to be a small world within a world, a patchwork of fields, cottages, warehouses, wooden shacks, stables, a henhouse, and endless fields flanked by tropical forests that flanked the side of the mountain. The scene was picturesque and quaint, a glimpse into a world Rémy never knew existed.

They halted in front of a stately plantation house built in the Creole West Indian style. Luxurious and graceful, it sat atop a bluff overlooking the Caribbean Sea, and had a haunting beauty that harkened back to a distant age. The main entrance stood atop a grand staircase, which led to a wraparound balcony adorned with wicker furniture and potted plants. The air was fragrant, smelling of jasmine and ylang-ylang, and the trade winds provided a constant fresh breeze. Bougainvillea vines crept up the sides of the house, and lofty tamarind trees provided shade. But upon closer inspection, Rémy noticed signs of neglect. A few wooden shutters were damaged, and some roof tiles were missing. The lovely yellow paint looked faded and chipped in places. But the house was lovely. It reminded Rémy of those stories he had heard about the Empress Josephine's childhood in Martinique, a life of tranquility, innocence, and unspoiled beauty.

As he stood gazing at the house, Rémy had the oddest sensation they were being watched. Looking up, he spied a shadowy figure hovering behind a window. Whoever it was seemed to be staring at him intently, but no sooner did he look up than the figure vanished. He dismounted and handed his reins over to a groom, wondering what secrets the plantation house held.

An old native woman in a turban and colorful madras skirt was sweeping the porch. Upon their approach, she stopped to watch them with suspicious eyes. After Landes approached her and explained the nature of their visit, she hobbled inside and returned with the owner of the plantation, Georges Dujon, a ruddy-faced, white-haired older gentleman of aristocratic bearing. Rémy was immediately impressed with the man. Dujon was the epitome of a West Indian planter. Tall, barrel-chested, and with chiseled features, he had a commanding presence that drew attention. But it was his leathery skin and weathered hands that marked Dujon as a true man of the tropics. Rémy had heard these békés were a tough bunch, hardened by years of adversity and isolation from the Métropole. They were known to be generally suspicious of outsiders.

M. Dujon invited them in for refreshments. As they headed through the foyer, Rémy marveled at the exquisite mahogany furniture, Louis XIV gilded mirrors, pianoforte, planter's chairs, and porcelain vases filled with exotic flowers. He stopped to admire an old musket rifle hanging on a wall beside a portrait of a beautiful woman dressed in the style of the ancien régime. Standing off to the side, Rémy spotted a young woman observing him from a doorway. She bore more than a casual resemblance to the lady in the portrait. Their eyes met for an instant, and a blush crept across her cheeks. Before he knew it, she disappeared and later, as they moved into the dining room, she reappeared in a different location, her delicate figure hidden behind the leaves of a potted palm. It was only after she entered the dining room that he was able to observe her up close.

The young woman sauntered in like a cat that was used to the privilege of human company. She appeared to be no more than eighteen or nineteen and had the same lovely face and amber eyes as the woman in the portrait. Her hair was coiffed in an elegant chignon, with a few wisps left dangling over her eyes. She was slender and tall, and she wore a simple white cotton dress with a high bodice and lace collar, and in her hands she held a moth-eaten copy of *Around the World in Eighty Days*. By her appearance, Rémy assumed she was Dujon's daughter.

Mme Dujon appeared, and the men took turns kissing her hand. Rémy saw an older version of the young woman in the mother, but her eyes were creased from worry, and her hands were bony and somewhat shaky. Pale and stooped, she showed the men to their places while a servant poured glasses of punch from a glass pitcher. Before they knew it, other servants brought in platters of fruit, cake, fried fish, plantains, and loaves of cassava bread. While Professor

Landes explained the nature of their mission, the young woman listened with rapt attention, like a mongoose observing a henhouse.

"It was the most extraordinary thing I've ever seen," said Landes. "About a week ago, I was checking my seismoscope and saw wild scribbles that could only mean one thing, that sometime during the evening of April twenty-second, three small earthquakes were registered. It corroborated another sighting I had heard recently about whitish fumes rising from the upper valley of the rivière Blanche. When I reported this to the governor, he immediately created a scientific committee to investigate the matter and put me in charge. Lieutenant Rémy and Sergeant Aubert are with me to assist in surveying the area, and M. Mirville will take chemical samples to his laboratory."

Georges Dujon grunted his approval. "That's well and good. I'm glad the governor has decided to take decisive action. The tremors have gotten the workers all jittery lately. We've hardly gotten any work done."

Suddenly a delicate voice spoke from the end of the table.

"Papa, I would like to join Professor Landes on his expedition. That is, if it's all right with him."

All eyes turned to the young lady. Her cheeks colored, but her voice was persistent.

"My dear Emilie, our mission is purely scientific," said Landes. "It's not a pleasure excursion. I doubt you'll find it interesting at all."

"Oh, but I will," she said, growing ever more determined. "I want to get a good look at the crater. I have an interest in the volcano that's purely scientific."

"That's completely out of the question," said Mme Dujon. "Don't bring up the subject again."

"Please, Professor Landes," she persisted. "I've been watching the volcano for several weeks. I've even kept a journal about it. I promise I won't be any trouble. I can hike as well as any man. I've done it many times already."

Landes's eyebrows rose. "Emilie, you never cease to amaze me. Since your school days, you always had an inquisitive mind and a curious nature. I'd hate to dampen your enthusiasm."

Georges Dujon cleared his throat. "Gentlemen, that outspoken creature at the end of the table is my daughter, Emilie. She likes to think of herself as an amateur naturalist." He poured himself another rum punch. "But even if I wanted to, I can't spare Emilie right now. We're right in the middle of the harvest. I couldn't run the plantation without her."

"But, Papa, I want to go," she said with greater insistence.

"Absolutely not!" said her mother. "Can we please change the subject?"

As they were bantering and arguing, Rémy noticed that the old native woman from the porch was constantly hovering near Emilie. She never spoke but would pour drinks for the men or serve dishes from the outside kitchen, all the while keeping her eye on the young woman, like a protective shadow.

Interrupting them, Rémy said, "M. Dujon, is it true what you said, that your daughter helps you manage the plantation? That seems extraordinary for such a young lady."

"Don't let her youth fool you," said Georges. "She's as clever and capable as any manager I've ever had. She knows the plantation like the back of her hand. And the workers love her. Sometimes I think they respect her more than me."

"They respect me because I make sure they get paid on time," countered Emilie. "Even if it means we have to take a loan from the bank."

"See what I mean?" said Georges wryly. "She's as cunning as a fox. Well, I guess I can spare you for one day. But just one day. And I don't want you riding in those breeches of yours. You'll wear a proper skirt."

"How else do you expect me to climb a forty-four-hundred-foot mountain?" she said.

"Disgraceful!" said Mme Dujon, frowning.

Emilie assumed a look of indignation. "I find it much more modest to climb a mountain in breeches than in a skirt that billows up with each gust of wind."

"That's what they call a rational costume," said Professor Landes.

"Well, in her case it's highly *irrational*," said Georges.

While everyone laughed, Rémy noticed that the elderly black nurse would speak in the young lady's ears in hushed whispers. What few words he could catch were in the local Creole language, which was difficult to understand. She seemed to be a motherly figure to the girl, constantly giving her advice and admonishments, keeping her under her watchful gaze. Whatever the case, the old nurse and the béké girl seemed to exist in a world of their own; speaking a language only they could understand.

Professor Landes set down his fork. "Actually, Georges, I came to make an important request."

"Yes? What is it?" said Georges.

"I need a couple of experienced guides who can lead us up the mountain. Perhaps you could recommend some of your workers. Ideally we'll be heading out from Morne-Rouge on the trail they call the *Aileron*, which is the most practical and direct route up to the summit."

"Yes, I've used that route numerous times myself," said Dujon. "I have some men who I'm sure would be happy to take you for a fair price. It's a strenuous hike."

"That would be wonderful," said Landes.

"Has anyone here actually seen the summit of Mount Pelée?" said Rémy. "I'm new to the island and not so familiar with the geography."

"Yes, I've been there myself numerous times," said Georges Dujon. "Think of the crater as an enormous bowl that sits at an elevation of four thousand four hundred feet. It measures two hundred yards in diameter, and lying at the bottom is a clear lake of spring water, slightly sulfurous in taste but otherwise fresh. Around the rim are boulders and lava beds from previous eruptions. The lake is a favorite spot for swimming and picnics."

"How deep is the lake?" said Rémy.

"No one knows," said Georges.

"Come again?" said Rémy.

"They've taken soundings over the years, but no one ever found the bottom. They say it's bottomless."

The table went quiet while Rémy contemplated that revelation.

"Professor Landes, I still want to go," said Emilie. "I know the route up the Aileron as well as anyone else, and I can be a tremendous help to you. I promise I won't be any trouble." Rémy noticed that her eyes gleamed with excitement.

"I see no reason why not," said Professor Landes. "We'd love to have you come along."

"It's still out of the question," said Mme Dujon, glaring.

"Maman, I have every intention of joining this expedition," said Emilie. "I want to see the crater as much as anyone. I have a right to go."

Rémy cleared his throat. "Mademoiselle Emilie, perhaps you should listen to your mother. The trip could be dangerous, and I cannot guarantee your safety. We have no idea what we may find at the summit."

"I'm not afraid," she said with determination. "I've lived on the slopes of Mount Pelée all my life. I have a vested interest in the volcano."

After an awkward silence, Professor Landes said, "You give a convincing argument, Emilie. You're certainly welcome to join us. Rest assured, Mme Dujon, your daughter will be safe. I'm certain we'll be in no immediate danger. These small seismic shocks we've been experiencing are in no way indicative that the volcano is going to erupt. I still believe this is only a passing phase. Most geologists believe they indicate the mountain is just settling down. The governor is only sending us up as a precautionary measure. Does this reassure you?"

"Not in the least," said Mme Dujon. "But if she's that determined, I won't stand in her way. She's always had an adventurous streak. It comes from reading too many Jules Verne novels."

The table erupted in laughter. Rémy turned to watch the young lady, who was laughing in spite of herself. When they finished, Georges Dujon asked two of his best workers, Durancy and Césaire, to lead the expedition. As soon as they learned of their remuneration, they heartily agreed and went to saddle their horses. Before they set out, M. Dujon asked Prof. Landes if he would take Maurice up to Morne-Rouge and drop him off at the home of their cousin Luc Aubéry. Dujon thought the fresh air and mild climate of the mountain retreat would do wonders for his consumption. Professor Landes heartily agreed, and a short while later, the members of the scientific committee were saddled and ready to go. Emilie had already changed into a pair of khaki jodhpurs and riding boots, and she carried a knapsack with supplies and slung a canteen of water across her shoulder. When she reappeared, more than a few eyebrows were raised.

"Emilie, you look as if you're heading out on a trek in search of the mythical El Dorado or Shambhala," said Landes.

"My costume is strictly practical," she said. "A good pair of breeches is the best protection against mosquitoes and wasps, not to mention thorny plants."

Rémy mounted his horse, grinning. "All you need now is a Berthier carbine."

"Forgive me for saying so, but you look ravishing," said Sergeant Aubert, giving her an admiring glance. "And I'm glad you decided to join us."

"I don't recall anyone asking you your opinion," said Rémy. "Carry on, Sergeant."

The young lady blushed again, but Rémy pretended not to notice. He admired the young woman's pluck. She had a resolve that he found refreshing. She was nothing like he imagined the daughter of a West Indian planter to be. She was down-to-earth, spirited, and adventurous. But it was her outspoken nature and boldness that he found most charming. At the very least, Emilie Dujon would provide an amusing diversion for what promised to be a long and arduous climb.

After thanking their host, the party set off down the dirt road and then traveled the picturesque, winding road that followed the course of rivière Blanche up to Morne-Rouge. Once they reached the mountain village, they would leave the animals at a stable and pick up the walking trail that led up to the summit. And at that point, there would be no turning back.

Chapter 11

As she rode Balthazar at a steady trot, Emilie was acutely aware that Lieutenant Rémy was watching her out of the corner of his eye. She found herself growing curious about the lieutenant. He was quiet and unassuming, nothing like she imagined a seasoned army officer to be. He also had an elusive, mysterious quality about him. With his silent, watchful gaze, he seemed to be the polar opposite of Lucien's brash, arrogant nature. But what most attracted her to Lieutenant Rémy was his quiet demeanor and unspoken masculinity. He was so different from Lucien.

During the journey the climbers engaged in light conversation while they gazed at their magnificent surroundings. The scenery was changing constantly. At one moment they would be gazing down into valleys a thousand feet below them and later across a mosaic of banana and sugarcane fields. The horses trotted at a pleasant gait as they climbed higher and higher across vast chasms and cliffs and then through valleys that became ascending gorges. In the distance they spotted hills flanked by lush vegetation that ranged from pale green to emerald to sapphire. It was breathtaking. They climbed higher and higher, and as they climbed, the city of Saint-Pierre grew smaller and smaller until it was no larger than a chessboard. Flanking the road were leafy palms and gigantic ferns that resembled enormous ostrich feathers, clumps of bamboo, flamboyant trees with their canopy of orange-red flowers, breadfruit and mango trees, balata trees, and ceibas with their oddly buttressed trunks. Every now and then, they would spot a wooden shack in the distance or the spinning blades of a sugar mill. Sometimes a donkey cart would pass them by, its owner tipping his hat in greeting. Occasionally donkeys brayed from the bush. And looming ahead, bold and resolute against the brilliant blue sky was Mount Pelée, dominating the skyline as an ever-present reminder of their mission.

Professor Landes called out from his carriage, "Emilie, it's still not too late for you to turn around if you are so inclined."

"I have no intention of turning around," she said, patting her horse.

"Professor Landes, you don't know my sister very well," said Maurice. "She would rather climb a mountain or gallop through the fields than attend a fancy dress ball. Those were my breeches before she pilfered them."

Emilie feigned indignation. "Surely you don't expect me to climb a forty-four-hundred-foot mountain in a corset and a skirt, do you? And as to my outdoor excursions, I've found that one good gallop a day clears my mind of petty grievances and annoyances and opens my eyes to all the possibilities of life. Does that make me sound philosophical or adventurous? I can't decide which one I prefer. Anyway, breeches give me greater mobility despite the dictates of polite society."

Her brother grinned. "You never cared much for the dictates of polite society, did you? I believe Sister Marie said you were like a wild horse in desperate need of taming."

To Emilie's consternation, the lieutenant brought his horse next to hers.

"Mademoiselle, if you don't mind my saying so, while I was in Africa, I saw some Berber women riding horses just like you. Even with their veils, they had a true spirit of freedom. In fact, with your golden tan, you remind me of those mysterious ladies of the desert. Tell me something, is it true what your father said, that you help him manage the plantation?"

"Yes," she said. "I used to tag along behind my father and Julien, our manager, watching everything they did. From my youngest years, I learned all about the cultivation of cacao and coffee. I guess you could say managing the farm is in my blood."

"So you're one of those békés I've heard about?"

Emilie nodded. "We're a proud and independent bunch despite what you may have heard. Oh, I know what you metropolitans think of us, that we're provincial, that we're anti-Republican, that we're naive, that we were lucky to have escaped the guillotine. I've heard all those things and worse. But if you had lived here as long as we have, you'd see things differently. Martinique is our home. We're as much a part of the land as anyone else. It's the only life I've ever known. We have one foot planted in France and one in the West Indies. We have the best of both worlds."

"I noticed that right away," he said. "Your accent is a mixture of aristocratic French and the local Creole dialect. It's quite charming. How long has your family lived here in the Antilles?"

"More than a hundred years," she said. "My great-great-great grandfather came here as a militia officer and bought a parcel of land to fulfill his dream of becoming a rich planter. He started with sugarcane and gradually we switched to cacao and coffee. I could never see myself living anywhere else. I feel as if I'm a part of this land."

"That's plainly evident," he said. "Why did you come with us today?"

"Strictly out of scientific curiosity," she said.

"Coming from you, I would believe that," said Rémy. "You seem to have a very curious nature."

"And where are you from, Lieutenant?" she said.

"He thinks he's from the jungles of Senegal," said Sergeant Aubert, who had brought his horse alongside theirs. "And he thinks his father was the chief of the Bambara. He even speaks their language. Ask him; he'll tell you all about it."

"Is that true?" said Emilie with amusement.

"Don't listen to that buffoon," said Rémy. "He belongs in the stockade for gross insubordination. Actually, my dear, I was born in Strasbourg, but my heart will always be in Africa. My father died when I was a child, so I had to make my own place in the world. My grandparents helped raise me, but my mother had it rough. She never remarried, so I helped support her until she passed away a year ago. Being a proud Frenchman, all I ever wanted was to serve my country, so naturally I joined the army. As you can see, I am one of those dreadful metropolitans you békés disdain so much."

"Oh dear," she said, taken aback. "I harbor no such feelings. We're all French after all."

Aubert grinned. "Don't worry, mademoiselle, the lieutenant was just teasing you. Forgive me for interrupting, sir, but I think you've hurt the young lady's feelings."

"I'm aware of that, Sergeant," said Rémy. "But we were having a private conversation. Take no offense, mademoiselle. I'm a proud Republican, and I suspect that deep down inside, you are too. And please don't listen to those anti-Republicans who call us robbers, atheists, freemasons, Jacobins, and filthy Dreyfusards; I assure you I'm none of those. Carry on, Sergeant."

"Please continue," she said. "I find your story fascinating. And I didn't take the least bit of offense." Emilie loved the way the two soldiers seemed to be vying for her attention. She found the whole situation terribly amusing.

Aubert nudged his horse closer to Emilie's. "When he's finished telling you his story, I'll tell you mine, which is full of duels, glorious battles, and hair-raising adventures that will keep you up at night."

"Aubert, your stories are not for ladies," said Rémy. "Now, scat!"

Rémy continued, "As I was saying before, the day I enlisted in the army was the happiest day of my life. As a proud Frenchman, I was ready and willing to serve la Mère Patrie in any capacity she required. A short while later, I volunteered for service in a penal battalion in Senegal, a position that no other soldier in his right mind wanted, but I needed a chance to prove myself. During my career I explored over a thousand square miles of Senegal. Without a doubt the happiest days of my life."

"So why did you leave Senegal?" she asked.

"A soldier must go where he's sent," he said. "We learn not to question our commanding officers."

"Perhaps it was for the best," she said. "I've heard about the terrible conditions of our colonial soldiers in Africa, how ill-fed, ill-clad, and ill-lodged they are. And the cruel punishments they inflict on them."

He looked at her wryly. "I'm sure there are just as many bad stories out there as there are bad journalists, but if you would visit our camps, speak to our soldiers, join us on our marches, in the mess halls, and at our drills, you would get an entirely different picture, one of heroism and self-sacrifice. You would see a camaraderie and devotion to duty that would make your heart burst with pride. All we men speak of are battles, medals, and acts of heroism. That is what keeps us going."

"Will you ever go back to France?" she said.

"For many of us, there's no home to go back to," said Rémy. "For soldiers like me, fighting battles is our only hope, our only desire, and our greatest motivation. For some men it represents our only possibility for redemption since it is only in the heat of battle that we can meet a glorious death or a thrilling adventure."

"Tell me something, did you find your redemption in the heat of battle?" said Emilie.

Rémy shook his head. "No, mademoiselle, I'm still waiting for my redemption."

After rounding a bend they came to a clearing, where they got their first unobstructed view of Mount Pelée. Rémy whipped out his binoculars and focused on the summit.

"There's a column of smoke rising from the crater," he said.

Landes borrowed his binoculars. "They appear to be shooting out of a fumarole, a steam vent in the dry crater lake. I'm certain it didn't exist before."

"I've been watching it for quite some time," said Emilie. "The whole situation seems strange and bizarre. That's why I was so determined to join you on this expedition. I want to know the truth."

"Brave girl," said M. Mirville. "Something strange is going on up there, indeed, especially with regard to all the projectiles that have been wreaking havoc on the countryside."

"Have you read about the eruption of Mount Krakatoa?" said Rémy. "I've been studying the subject night and day trying to gain some insight into this volcano."

"There's no parallel between Krakatoa and Pelée at all," said M. Mirville. "One was a live volcano, and this one is most definitely extinct."

"I'm not so sure about that," said Rémy.

"I guarantee you this debonair old gentleman has just woken up from a deep slumber," said Mirville. "He'll soon go back to sleep."

"What can you tell us about Krakatoa?" said Emilie.

Rémy reflected for a moment. "Back in 1883, Mount Krakatoa in the Dutch East Indies erupted with an explosion so powerful it ruptured the eardrums of sailors forty miles away and caused a spike of more than two and a half inches of mercury in pressure gauges in the Batavia gasworks, sending them off the scale." He paused for a minute to let that sink in. "The pressure wave from the volcano was so great, it was recorded in barometers all around the world. The eruption was the greatest cataclysmic event of our lifetime."

M. Mirville harrumphed. "Our West Indian volcanoes have nothing in common with those in the Dutch East Indies. Pelée has been extinct for years, possibly centuries."

"If that's the case, then why are we heading up there now?" said Rémy.

"Purely as a precaution," said Mirville. "This is a scientific mission, after all."

"And if we find out Pelée is not extinct, then what?" said Rémy. "What if we find out it is more similar to Krakatoa than we ever imagined?"

"That's not likely to happen," said Mirville. "Our West Indian volcanoes have no historical record of lava flow. Any lava ejected is sure to run down the ravines into the ocean. I foresee no danger to the public whatever."

"That's just the point," said Rémy. "Krakatoa didn't emit any lava either. According to eyewitnesses, the volcano emitted clouds of hot gases that traveled at high speeds over land and sea, causing numerous deaths. But I don't wish to cause you any undue alarm. We have to investigate the matter first."

Emilie shuddered. She stared up at the volcano as it loomed overhead. The dense jungle vegetation that flanked the mountain could not hide its distinct corrugated shape, formed by dozens of ravines and gorges that raked down the mountainside, carrying fresh spring water down to the lower elevations. In many ways Pelée was like a living, breathing organism, a volatile creature of rock, soil, mineral, gas, steam, and fire that if angered could burst forth with a vengeance. For the rest of the journey up to Morne-Rouge, they noticed that instead of the air becoming cooler and fresher, the telltale smell of rotten eggs became more pervasive. The horses began to show signs of distress, balking and whinnying. The higher they climbed, the more the animals flattened their ears and whinnied. After a tiring journey, they reached Morne-Rouge slightly weary but eager to tackle the next stage of the journey.

Chapter 12

Sunday, April 27
Morne-Rouge

Sitting at an altitude of fifteen hundred feet, Morne-Rouge was the highest village in Martinique. It was nestled in a saddle-shaped valley between Mount Pelée to the north and the Pitons du Carbet to the south and consisted of a single street bordered by wooden cottages, shops, and a small church. Beyond the main square lay villas with orchards and fields containing bananas, limes, and papayas and bordered by hedges of hibiscus and Indian reeds. These were the country homes of the wealthy merchants from Saint-Pierre.

As they made their way down the street, the air was cooled by the trade winds that blew from the east, which diminished the smell of sulfur. But the scientific committee would not be staying long in Morne-Rouge. Before they set out on their climb, they took Maurice to his cousin's house and bade him farewell.

Standing in the doorway, Emilie tried to make the best of things. The worst part was the forlorn look in Maurice's eyes and the way he tried to disguise the lingering pain in his chest. But her brother could not hide the hacking cough that was plaguing him. Every time he coughed, she felt a lump in her throat and a stabbing pain in her heart.

She hugged her brother. "Goodbye, Maurice. I hope you feel better soon."

"I'd rather be going with you," he said with a tinge of sadness.

"Next time," she said, kissing his cheek. "And don't give Cousin Luc too much trouble. Try to be good."

"Yes, I'll try not to spill gravy on the tablecloth."

Emilie forced herself to smile. It pained her that Maurice was forced to give up his dream of becoming a doctor because of his chronic illness, and now he was denied even a simple pleasure like climbing a mountain. But his stoic nature would not allow him to complain. He kept it all bottled up inside, never letting on that he was suffering and slowly dying. It was this quality of self-sacrifice that hurt Emilie the most. Maurice was so different from their shallow, social-climbing parents, who had no capacity to appreciate their selfless, gallant son. She hugged Maurice and left him to rejoin the others, who were milling about by the horses, pretending to be searching through their equipment. By the time she mounted Balthazar, Maurice had already retreated inside the house.

"Emilie, there's no need to worry about your brother," said Professor Landes. "He'll be fine here. He's young and strong. By next year he'll be climbing Mount Pelée all by himself."

"I can't stop worrying about him," she said wistfully.

"Your brother has tremendous fortitude," said Rémy. "I'm sure he'll manage all right."

"Is it fortitude or stubbornness?" she said.

"I wasn't aware there was a difference," said Rémy.

They left their horses and donkeys in a barn and then set about organizing the supplies for the trip. To reach the summit of Mount Pelée, they would have to hike on foot, armed only with cutlasses and service revolvers in case they met up with the deadly fer-de-lance, the deadly pit viper that roamed the forests.

Once they were ready, the climbers hiked down the street until they came to a dirt road bounded by banana fields. Taking the lead, Durancy said, "I have to warn you, the hike will take us through dense tropical forests and steep slopes. It will be muddy and dangerous. Keep a watch out for the fer-de-lance. One bite has enough venom to kill a man. Above all, we must all stay together. Some people have been lost in the forests of Mount Pelée and barely made it out alive."

"With all due respect," said Sergeant Aubert, "the lieutenant and I are experienced surveyors. We're trained to operate on difficult terrain."

"Sergeant, with all due respect, you have not been to the summit of Mount Pelée," said Durancy. "It's my duty to warn you the journey will be replete with hazards. Are there any questions?"

Everyone shook their heads.

"Good, let's get started."

For the next hour they marched single file behind Durancy and Césaire up a sloped trail through dense vegetation consisting of bamboo trees, breadfruit and sandbox trees, cabbage palms, and enormous mango trees. The sun beat down mercilessly on their straw hats, and they welcomed the occasional foray into forested areas, where the lush foliage provided much-needed shade. There were nine climbers in all: Durancy and Césaire in the lead, followed by Lt. Rémy, Sergeant Aubert, Professor Landes, M. Mirville, Emilie, and finally the two porters who brought up the rear. They marched in a steady rhythm, stopping every now and then to take a drink of water or to gaze down at the town of Morne-Rouge, which was becoming smaller the higher they climbed. During the journey the path became steeper and more littered with rocks and tangled with vines, creepers, lianas, shrubs, and guinea grass. Swarms of mosquitoes buzzed around their heads, biting them, while birds called out to them from the branches above their heads. The higher they climbed, the more clearly they could observe the summit of Mount Pelée through wisps of clouds.

Rémy focused his binoculars on the summit. "Look there, Professor Landes, do you see those puffs of smoke coming from the crater?"

"Yes, they are coming from the Étang Sec, the dry crater on the lower summit," said Professor Landes. "By my recollection, that is where all the sulfur is being expelled, but it makes no sense since there have never been fumaroles spotted in that location before. I guess we'll discover more when we see it firsthand. But something odd is definitely going on here."

"I'm starting to believe Mount Pelée is an active volcano and not an extinct one as all the experts would have us believe," said Rémy.

Landes kept his eyes on the mountain. "Right now we're operating under the assumption that the volcano is just another curiosity in the natural history of Martinique. Our job is to ascertain that the earthquakes and fumarole activity are just a passing phase or if they pose an actual threat to the civilians."

"In other words, we could be heading into another Vesuvius," said Aubert, removing his pith helmet to wipe the sweat off his brow.

"Not likely," said Professor Landes. "In all recorded history, there's never been any lava ejected from any volcano in the West Indies. In other words, they're not half as volatile as our dear politicians, and they certainly blow out less hot air."

"Yes," added Rémy. "But even a debonair gentleman can have a short temper."

"Which reminds me of our previous governor, a debonair gentleman who resorted to fistfights to settle his political disagreements," said M. Mirville. "Not very reassuring."

Rémy lit a cigarette and took a few puffs. "For a small island, there's quite a lot of salacious gossip going around. Not to mention all those racy political posters that leave little to the imagination."

Emilie stopped drinking from her canteen. "Welcome to the West Indies, where political mudslinging is a national sport."

"I find it highly amusing," said Rémy. "I'm starting to get a picture of life here in the tropics: hot tempers, hot quarrels, and hot lava."

"Yes, but not necessarily in that order," added M. Mirville.

"There's something I still don't understand," said Emilie. "If the governor feels the volcano could pose a threat to the population, why not just evacuate everyone?"

"I suspect it's a lot cheaper to convince the people they're in no danger," said Aubert.

"Consider this scenario," said M. Mirville. "There are tens of thousands of people living within a five-mile radius of the cinder cone. It would be impossible to evacuate everyone. Where would they go? Who would pay for it? How long would they stay away?"

"You're talking about tens of thousands of people in harm's way," said Rémy. "I think I'm starting to get the picture. We could have mass panic on our hands."

"Think of it as one big carnival," said Aubert. "But instead of happy revelers, you have crowds of panicked residents stampeding over each other to escape the barrage of volcanic debris. Is that a comforting thought?"

"Personally, I try to keep a more positive attitude," said M. Mirville. "I'm of the opinion the volcano will settle down soon enough. Right now it's having a little attack of indigestion."

"Let's hope it stays little," said Aubert with a wink.

They continued on in silence behind Durancy and Césaire, who were using their cutlasses to slash the thick brush and vines that lay in their path. Insects swarmed around their heads, tormenting them, and thorns pierced their flesh and tore at their clothes. Relief came when they reached a rushing river that flowed over large boulders and debris. Landes decided that the guides should tie one end of a rope to a tree, then wade across the stream, then tie the end of the rope around another tree. Each climber, in turn, would wade across the river holding on to the rope, thereby reducing the risk of falling into the rushing waters.

One by one each member held on to the rope and gingerly made their way over the stream, balancing on the rocks that formed a sort of bridge across the water. When it was her turn, Emilie grabbed the rope and stepped onto the first rock. Cool water soaked her feet and ankles. She was surprised by the force of the current. Stepping onto the next rock, she slipped and almost lost her balance. Luckily, the rope saved her from the ignominy of falling in front of the others. Finally, after a few more near misses, she reached the other side. Behind her, Rémy stepped across with expert adroitness, followed by Professor Landes, the porters, and the portly M. Mirville, who likewise managed to reach the other side unscathed.

The last to cross was Sergeant Aubert. He grabbed hold of the rope and stepped onto the first rock. With the confidence of a frog on a lily pad, he hopped to the next rock but was knocked off-balance when a tree trunk floated past, striking him on the leg. Teetering on the edge, he fell headfirst into the raging waters.

When his head emerged, everyone uttered a collective sigh of relief. Aubert uttered a loud, colorful oath as he splashed around, trying to regain his footing. Finally he waded across the river and climbed up the riverbank looking only slightly worse for wear. Hoisting himself out of the water, he tore off his shirt and wrung it out good-naturedly as the men made sport of his predicament. One by one he removed his boots and emptied the water onto the muddy bank, but when he discovered that his cigarettes were soaked, he threw them down in disgust, saying, "I don't mind getting my boots soaked, I don't mind getting waterlogged, but this is where I draw the line in service to la Mère Patrie."

Rémy grinned. "Sergeant Aubert, your devotion to duty is admirable. I'll make a special mention of it when I write my report. Until then you can have some of mine." He tossed a pack of cigarettes to Aubert, who saluted and replied, "Thank you, Lieutenant, much obliged. And I believe it is my patriotic duty to inform you there's a huge black centipede wriggling in your boot."

Rémy looked down and froze.

An enormous black centipede was crawling down one of his boots with hideous movements of its legs. Emilie stared in horror. It was a *bête-à-mille-pattes*, a reviled monster capable of biting through shoe leather. They were sometimes found hidden in bedsheets, under pillows, in shoes, even in cribs. In a flash, Rémy grabbed his field knife, extracted the monster, and hurled it to the ground with a look of disgust, at which point Durancy stepped forward and slashed it with his cutlass, chopping the beast in two. The severed pieces writhed on the ground, filling them with disgust, until they finally lay still.

Still shaken from the incident, Rémy said, "Thank you, Durancy; that was a close call. And thank you for warning me, Sergeant Aubert. I owe the both of you a debt of gratitude."

"Be grateful at least that your trousers are dry," said Aubert.

"Believe me, Sergeant, I would much rather have wet *boules* than one of those monsters inside my boots," said Rémy.

Professor Landes bent down and examined the dissected beast. "That's the largest centipede I've ever seen. It must be at least sixteen inches long. These monsters are capable of devouring rodents and lizards with their steel-like jaws. As a professor of natural history, I find them fascinating, like holdovers from a previous age."

"I'll take your word for it, Professor," said Rémy. "I have no desire to meet up with one of these hideous monsters ever again. All right, men, let's get moving. We've got a lot of ground to cover."

They traveled half a mile across a savannah covered in a rich carpet of begonias and past a promontory called Calabash Hill, which was covered with guava trees bursting with ripe fruit. The air was redolent with the smell of fresh guavas, while the flowers lent a charming beauty to their surroundings.

After they had walked another mile, they entered a tropical forest teeming with every species imaginable, from primitive-looking ferns to wild orchids to mountain pineapples, lycopods, breadfruit and balata trees, cabbage palms, balisier flowers, birds of paradise, and endless varieties of palm trees. It looked as if they had entered a primitive jungle from the Pleistocene era. The air was fresh and moist, and the sound of trickling streams echoed down from the heights. Birds called out from branches sixty feet high, and they occasionally caught a glimpse of colorful, exotic feathers streaking past. The forest was shaded by a canopy of jungle vegetation that only permitted a few streaks of sunlight. As they tramped through the forest, lizards darted up the sides of trees, and *manicous* scurried through the underbrush. The closer they came to the upper reaches of Mount Pelée, the steeper and narrower the trail became, and the more exhausted they grew. Soon they were hiking at an angle of almost forty-five degrees and were almost completely cut off from sunlight. As the guides chopped through the brush, forging a path, Professor Landes pointed out evidence of seismic activity all around, including piles of ash, volcanic rocks, and occasional burnt trees.

At the base of the next hill, the party came to a halt. They had reached the buttress of the center mass of Mount Pelée, and it took the guides several minutes to locate the proper trail. Red-faced and sweating, M. Mirville stopped to catch his breath. He rested on a felled tree trunk and fanned his face with his straw hat.

"Mark my words, this is the last time I'll serve on one of these confounded scientific committees," said Mirville. "It's hotter and wetter than a Turkish sauna."

Emilie slumped down beside him. "I know what you mean. It's so humid you would hardly know we're over three thousand feet high."

"It's so humid you could grow mushrooms in your pockets," said Aubert.

"At least we'll get our names in the newspapers," said Emilie. "When news of Mount Pelée reaches the outside world, they will write stories about the brave team of explorers that climbed a rumbling, smoking volcano. We'll be famous!"

"If we're still alive by then," said Rémy.

"My dear, forgive me for saying this," said Mirville wryly, "but you have far too much courage for your own good."

"Even if the volcano erupts, I doubt the world would be interested in the problems of a tiny island like Martinique," said Sergeant Aubert. "Aside from the occasional riot, when has this island ever made the newspapers?"

"You may have a point," said Professor Landes. "If it weren't for the occasional fistfight in the National Assembly, I doubt anyone in France would know we exist."

"Oh, they'll know we exist all right if this damn thing blows its top," said Rémy. "Except by that time, it'll be too late, and we'll be blown to smithereens."

Emilie watched the men's faces and fell silent, contemplating that scenario.

For the next eight hundred feet, the ascent was slowed down by the heavy jungle foliage. Durancy and Césaire hacked at the undergrowth with their cutlasses, but the enormous trees and dense overgrowth blocked all sunlight, creating an eerie world where only lizards, snakes, and insects lived. The air reeked of sulfur, and the only sound they heard was the constant drip-drip of rainwater from the branches overhead. Their clothes were soaked, and the moisture was working its way into their boots. After another hour, the sun broke through the canopy, and the temperature soared, drenching their clothing with sweat. Emilie stayed close behind Durancy, while the rest of the group spread out single file behind them. Occasionally they would hear a fluttering of wings or the caw of a jungle bird in the branches above their heads. Their progress was maddeningly slow.

Spying a fallen tree trunk, Emilie jumped on top and balanced her way across. She froze suddenly when she spied a mottled brown coil of a snake dangling inches from her face, its eyes almost level with hers. She knew at once it was the fer-de-lance, the deadly pit viper. It was well over six feet long. She kept completely still, not even daring to breathe as her heartbeat pounded in her ears. Behind her she heard the men come to a full stop, their breathing coming in gasps when they spied the predator gaping at her from a low-hanging branch, its fangs poised and ready to strike.

Chapter 13

Emilie broke out in a cold sweat and she felt faint. She could not control her limbs from shaking as the snake hovered inches from her face, its fangs dripping with venom. Behind her Professor Landes whispered, "Don't move, Emilie. Keep absolutely still." Beads of sweat trickled down her forehead. She saw her whole life flashing before her eyes. Out of the corner of her eye she spied Durancy raising his cutlass above his head, but before he could let it swing, Rémy made a motion for him to stop. Then, in one swift motion, he extracted his revolver, cocked the hammer, and aimed for the snake's head.

"Nobody move," he whispered. "I've got him."

A blast rang out, sending the snake's head flying in one direction and the body in another. Birds squawked and scattered in all directions. Lizards scurried under the brush. The bushes rustled from unseen beasts, and Emilie's ears rang from the explosion as blood and tissue splattered everywhere. The snake's headless body continued writhing for several seconds before it finally went still. All that remained of the reptile was a mass of scales, tissue, and a pair of fangs attached to a lifeless head. The serpent's blood oozed onto the forest floor, creating an eerie red carpet. A wave of relief washed over Emilie.

"Are you all right?" said Rémy, giving Emilie an encouraging pat on the back. "I'm not sure I would have been as brave as you."

"You saved my life, Lieutenant Rémy," she said.

"Think nothing of it," he said, replacing his gun in his holster. Seeing her obvious distress, he handed her his bottle of water. "Here, drink this. It is tafia and spring water with a little rum mixed in. It will give you back your courage."

"Well done, Lieutenant," said Professor Landes. "Emilie, are you all right after that fright?"

"I'll be fine as soon as my heart stops pounding," she said.

"Let's just say if Mlle Dujon were a cat, she would only have eight lives left," said Rémy, grinning.

Durancy pushed the serpent's remains out of the way with his cutlass. "That's the biggest fer-de-lance I have ever seen. It's well over six feet long and as thick as a man's forearm."

"That's as close as I ever hope to get to one of those pit vipers," said Aubert.

"Rémy, you're damned lucky you got it with your first shot," said M. Mirville. "Those blasted things are like some mythological monster . . . like a Hydra or a Minotaur. They show no mercy and take no prisoners."

"Isn't that an exaggeration?" said Rémy.

Mirville shook his head. "Not in the least. If the Minotaur were alive today, he would be deathly afraid of that abominable reptile."

"Yes, but the ancient Greeks didn't have our modern firearms, which makes us stronger," said Sergeant Aubert.

"You mustn't let the Greek gods hear you say that," said M. Mirville. "We've already got one volcano furious at us. We don't need the gods fuming at us too!"

They continued hacking through the jungle vegetation until they reached a trail that was carved into the side of the mountain. Recent rains had made the surface slippery, causing them to lose their footing on several occasions. Soon their clothes were coated with mud and ash, giving them the appearance of survivors of a natural disaster. Unaccustomed to exerting himself, M. Mirville did his best to keep up with the others and was exceedingly grateful when Césaire presented him with a crude cane fashioned out of a branch. From time to time he would mutter, "Blasted creepers!" as he wielded his cane like a cutlass, slashing at the overgrowth of vines and shrubs with the zeal of a drunken horticulturalist. On these occasions, Emilie did her best to stifle a laugh, but occasionally she had to place a hand over her mouth to spare Mirville's masculine pride. With the danger of the pit viper behind her, Emilie was no longer afraid about what they might find at the summit, if anything, she was invigorated.

After another hour, they reached a steep rock face covered in moss. Balancing their knapsacks on their backs, they negotiated each step with great care, sweating through their khaki shirts as they climbed over boulders and steep ledges. When the terrain became too risky, the guides would scramble ahead, tie a rope around a tree, and use it to hoist the others up one by one. Complicating matters, a thick fog had descended over the mountain, making visibility beyond ten feet all but impossible.

Emilie proved to be a capable climber. By midafternoon she was exhausted but exhilarated. She noticed that Rémy had been keeping an eye on her ever since her near-fatal encounter with the snake, but that only made her more determined to carry her own weight. Behind her, the porters had the double burden of carrying the supplies on their backs, including the bulky photographic equipment. When she reached a steep ledge, she tried to scale it on her own, but it was more difficult than it looked. She redoubled her efforts, but nothing seemed to work. She wiped the sweat off her brow and rolled her sleeves as high as they would go. It mattered little to her that Rémy was watching from his perch above her, attempting to stifle a grin behind that jaunty moustache. When it began to look as if she wouldn't be able to scale it on her own, he threw down a rope, but she shook her head. "No, thank you, Lieutenant, I can do it myself." Grasping the rock with her bare hands, she hoisted herself up, but after she struggled and fell several times, Rémy dangled the rope in her face. "Take this, mademoiselle; what do you have to lose?"

Emilie looked at him with annoyance. "No, thank you, Lieutenant. I prefer to do it on my own."

"You won't get very far all by yourself. We're supposed to be a team."

"Do you think I'm not capable of climbing on my own?"

Rémy tried to hide his amusement. "Perish the thought. You climb better than most monkeys I've seen, but God had the good sense to give monkeys tails. That's why I threw you the rope. Even a monkey has enough sense to accept help when it's offered."

Emilie spat out some hair. "How do you expect me to concentrate when you keep interrupting me?"

After several more attempts, she lost her footing and fell over backward. Dirt and pebbles rolled down from the ledge, leaving a coating all over her clothes.

"Mademoiselle, why are you so stubborn?" said Rémy. "What are you trying to prove?"

"It's a personal matter."

"There should be no secrets between team members."

She stood up and dusted off her breeches. "If you don't mind, I have a problem I'm trying to solve, and the more we stand here talking, the more confused I get."

She climbed up between two rocks, but one of them gave way, causing her to tumble to the ground amid a shower of loose stones that rattled beside her. This time she was covered in dirt and pebbles, her hair streaming down her face. The porters hoisted her up as Rémy stifled a grin and once more threw her down a line of rope.

"I'm glad you find it amusing," she said, looking at Rémy with annoyance.

"Not at all, mademoiselle," he said. "You look lovely covered in mud. Actually, they say mud is good for the complexion. But enough of the heroics. Grab this, please. Tie it around your waist, and I'll pull you up."

Reluctantly, Emilie tied the rope around her waist and then braced herself against the rocks. When he hoisted her up, she gripped the rope and used her feet to guide her up the ledge step-by-step. Eventually she climbed the entire thirty feet in this manner. The men clapped and cheered her on until she reached the top. When she grabbed Rémy's hand, he lifted her over the ledge.

"There, that wasn't too difficult, was it?" said Rémy. "I think you handled that quite well, almost like an alpinist. What you lack in basic climbing skills, you make up for with sheer pluck."

"Thank you for the compliment, Lieutenant. I . . ." She stopped abruptly when she realized Rémy hadn't heard a word she had spoken because he had already climbed another fifteen feet and was well out of earshot.

Heaving a great sigh, Emilie stuffed her hair under her straw hat and followed him up the mountain. Something about the lieutenant's demeanor gave her pause. He was not as coarse or brutish as she might have expected, and he seemed almost gentle at times. She admired his strength, agility, and sense of humor. But she also admired his easygoing nature. More than anything, she liked the way Rémy kept an eye on everyone, always looking out for their safety. And it was downright comical the way he and Aubert always bickered and berated each other in colorful terms. There was no end to the indelicate phrases they used, such as oaf, blockhead, numskull, and the strangest one of all—badly groomed Merino sheep. Other times they communicated with barely a word passing between them.

Just a few grunts and gestures, and they seemed to understand each other, like well-mannered gorillas or chimpanzees, only clean-shaven and infinitely handsomer. She couldn't remember the last time she'd been so amused or felt so at ease. The men seemed to go out of their way to make her feel comfortable and not the least bit in the way. She almost wished the day would never end.

They stopped to rest in a forest of balisier flowers that were in full bloom. The scent was intoxicating; the fresh air invigorated them and provided a short diversion from the climb. A steady breeze blew in from the east, providing a much-needed respite from the heat, and the view of the surrounding countryside was breathtaking. They had reached the upper flanks of the mountain, where they were treated to a variety of exotic plant species that Professor Landes was only too eager to point out, including some that existed nowhere else on earth. There were great green ferns that resembled trees, ferns that were sensitive to the touch, and primitive ferns with wavy leaves like a sea anemone. Rémy sketched some of them in his notebook, and Emilie was impressed by his skillful hand. He would pluck an interesting flower and sketch it in great detail and then turn his attention to a green lizard that was quietly observing him from inside a balisier flower. She liked to watch him work; there was something comforting about his quiet presence.

Emilie opened up her canteen and took a swig. "That flower you are drawing is the *Heliconia bihai*, otherwise known as the balisier," she said. "There's an old legend that says the flower never dies, that it always springs up again."

"That's fascinating," said Rémy. "How do you know all that?"

"My tutor Abbé Morel taught me that. And he told me another legend that says Jesus was born in a balisier patch. He used to say, *'Jesu est né dans un balisier.'* And I always believed him. I used to believe everything he told me. Of course I was too young and naive to know better."

"It's not naive to trust the people who taught you and raised you," he said. "Old legends exist for a reason. There's always some truth in them no matter how outlandish."

She met his eyes for an instant and felt her face coloring. "Well, the summit is not far now. We should be reaching it in an hour."

"Too bad, I was just starting to enjoy myself," said Rémy. "In fact, I think I've found a friend in that lizard over there. Do you think I could train him to fetch my shoes?"

"I must admit, Mlle Dujon, your esprit de corps is admirable," said Sergeant Aubert. "In the army they would classify this as hazardous duty, yet you haven't complained once."

"I suppose that makes me a good little soldier," she said.

"You're certainly good for morale," said Aubert, easing closer. "In fact, I nominate you for the highest commendation, the Order of the Balisier Flower."

He snapped off a flower and stuck it in her hair. Emilie beamed, her cheeks glowing from the sunlight that filtered in through the foliage. The men laughed genially at this little joke except for Rémy, who looked up from his sketch pad and frowned.

"It's too early for celebrating," he said. "We still have some climbing to do."

"Anyway, Sergeant Aubert," said Emilie, "are you quite certain you wish to give me the honor, given I'm all covered in mud?"

"Definitely," he said, kissing her hand. "I gave you the award because of your extreme dedication to your regiment, your devotion to la Mère Patrie, and because even though your face, hair, and clothes are covered with mud, you are even more charming than the Empress Josephine."

Rémy pushed Aubert's hand away. "Carry on, Sergeant. We don't want her smelling like you."

The men burst out laughing. Emilie joined in, and when her eyes met Rémy's, she quickly looked down and pretended to search through her knapsack. Drawing out her binoculars, she peered through them but continued to watch him out of the corner of her eye. The men had launched into a discussion about the humorous aspects of Martinique society, which she found most amusing. Inevitably there was bickering, with Rémy observing that Aubert spoke French like a "Spanish cow" and Aubert countering that Rémy was a particularly annoying "nutcracker." M. Mirville burst out laughing, his portly body shaking with amusement as he described them as a sort of military Punch and Judy show. Even the scholarly Professor Landes had a good time laughing at the bickering soldiers. Emilie found herself enjoying the men's company as never before.

After a short break, they loaded up their knapsacks and ascended the last two hundred feet to the summit. When they reached the crater at an altitude of forty-four hundred feet, they were exhausted, muddy, and sweaty. Fighting heavy winds, they hiked across a rocky ridge to the Étang des Palmistes, the cool spring lake at the center of the caldera. What they found there shocked and terrified them to their core. The peaceful lake had turned into a pit of black lava that bubbled up with ferocious intensity. Emilie stared at the molten rock in shock. Her limbs trembled, and her heart pounded as she realized the volcano had entered a perilous new phase. It was spewing up all the magma from deep inside the chamber, and there was no telling how this would end. She looked over at Professor Landes, but the terror in his face told her all she needed to know: Mount Pelée was on the verge of eruption.

Part 2

Chapter 14

The climbers stood on the crater rim, staring at the horrifying scene. No one dared speak. The black lava frothed and hissed like a witch's cauldron, and it glinted with an eerie metallic sheen. It seemed to be coming from deep inside the earth. And there was no life anywhere. Ashes coated every surface. The climbers stared at it, shaken and disturbed. Emilie feared that if the black lava continued to bubble up, it would spill over the sides of the mountain, destroying everything in its path.

Adding to the gloom, sulfurous clouds floated over the lava pit like ghostly apparitions, leaving an overpowering stench of sulfur in their wake. Emilie realized that their very lives depended on the integrity of the crater rim, that if it were to suddenly give way from the pressure of the lava, they would all be engulfed in the boiling mud. That thought sent a shiver up her spine.

There was a slight rustling noise behind Emilie. When she turned, she saw that the porters had fled. Where they once stood was only a pile of baggage and a residual cloud of dust. Their footprints continued for several yards before disappearing down the side of the mountain. Crestfallen, she realized the expedition was now short two members. She pointed this out to Professor Landes, but he was too shaken to reply. She was suddenly gripped with a primal fear and a need to escape, but she remained steadfast, unwilling to desert her companions.

Rémy looked especially troubled. "Professor Landes, I think we've got a serious problem on our hands. This thing's going to blow."

"That's putting it mildly," said Aubert. "Who was it that said this blasted volcano is extinct? I'd like to have a serious chat with the bugger."

Durancy's face was noticeably grave. "Sah, I suggest we get out of here at once. It is not safe here. In a place where birds die, man cannot live for very long."

"Yes, yes, as soon as I take some photographs for the governor," said Landes.

"There's no need to panic," said M. Mirville. "I still think this volcano will die down and go back to sleep."

"Or maybe not," said Aubert. "We can't afford to take that chance."

The grim looks on everyone's faces told Emilie they agreed with Aubert.

Taking out her binoculars, Emilie scanned the lava field. She realized the situation was far worse than anyone could have predicted. The crater rim resembled the jagged edges of a gigantic vase that could at any point plummet off the side of the mountain, unleashing an avalanche of muddy lava on every plantation for miles, including hers.

"Professor Landes," she said, "it doesn't make any sense. If Mount Pelée is extinct, where did all the lava come from? Is this some kind of new geological phenomenon?"

Landes looked perplexed. "I wish I knew the answer to that. The lava you see here came from deep underground. It was forced up the chamber by high temperatures and high pressures, changing form and texture as it reached the surface. At this point it's impossible to predict when and if it will die down. Pelée has not had a major eruption for hundreds of years. We must hope for the best."

"I agree," added Mirville. "Most likely the lava signifies the worst is over, and the volcano will soon be on the wane."

"With all due respect," said Rémy, clearly agitated, "the volcano does not appear to be on the wane. I hope that's not what you plan on telling the governor."

"I haven't decided what I'm going to tell the governor," interrupted Mirville. "But nothing here changes my mind. I'm sure it's just a passing phase and the worst is over. Don't you agree, Landes?"

Professor Landes just stared at the black lava, lost in thought. His eyes looked haunted; his brow was furrowed and wet with perspiration. He coughed a little from the fumes and looked troubled by this new discovery, like finding out that an extinct species of dinosaur has been alive and well all along. As the team walked around the perimeter of the crater, the repercussions of their discovery struck Emilie as more disturbing than anything they could have predicted. The ramifications, she realized, could be enormous for everyone who lived in the vicinity of Mount Pelée. She stared at the men's faces—each one lost in his thoughts—and cried out when projectiles began bursting out of the crater. With a tremendous boom, rocks and boulders shot out of the crater like cannonballs, terrifying them. The expedition members stared in horror at the display of nature's power. Emilie clung to Durancy, watching as the missiles exploded like meteors; she was filled with a sense of impending doom. There was no end to the lava; it frothed up as if from a massive furnace. She watched with astonishment, her heart pounding so hard she could scarcely breathe.

"Professor Landes, this looks serious," said Emilie. "Our lives might be in grave danger. There's no telling what may happen."

Professor Landes scoffed at this notion. "We've got to remain calm. There has to be a reasonable explanation for all this magma. In all the years I've been studying Pelée, there was never any hint it was going to erupt."

Rémy looked frustrated. "As far as I'm concerned, all this lava points to only one conclusion: that the whole damn thing is about to erupt. We've got to take every precaution. We were sent up here to collect any data that confirm this, so the governor can take the necessary precautions to protect the public."

"Don't jump to conclusions," said Mirville, clearly agitated. "We've got to remain calm."

"I think we should leave at once," said Emilie. "Perhaps if we hurry, we can catch up with the porters. We must get back before nightfall."

Professor Landes shook his head. "I still have to take photographs for the governor and collect samples of the sulfur crystals. But I will try to be quick."

"The damn thing looks like the bloody pits of hell," said Aubert, his face reddening from the heat. "Gather all the evidence you want, but make it quick."

Rémy removed his pith helmet to wipe his forehead. "Yes, let's finish quickly and get out of here. The porters have already fled. Now we'll have to carry everything ourselves."

Professor Landes approached the crater to take some samples, his face turning red with each step.

"It's sweltering," said Landes, loosening his collar. "I can't begin to guess the temperature of the lava. I can't get close enough to take a reading."

"I don't advise you to get too close unless you want a permanent suntan," said Aubert, fanning his face with his pith helmet. His khaki tunic was soaked with sweat.

"Please keep a safe distance, sah," said Durancy, staring uneasily at the lava pit. "And Mam'selle Emilie, please stay next to me for your own safety. I promised your father I would protect you."

"Mlle Dujon, do as he says," said Rémy. "It's not safe for you to wander around by yourself, no matter how many times you've climbed the mountain. Now is no time for heroics."

Emilie backed away from the crater. By now the heat was almost unbearable. They were over thirty feet from the crater, yet the radiant heat was so intense they could feel it burning their clothes. As each projectile shot out, they cried out in astonishment, gaping at the fiery boulders as they soared through the air to dizzying heights.

After Landes had collected his samples, he set up the tripod for the camera. Rémy bent down to gather some pumice stones, which he stored in his knapsack. When he was done, he said, "Professor Landes, I think we've seen enough. When you're done taking photographs, let's head back and write our report."

"Yes, but before we go, I want to see the lower summit," he said, pointing westward. "It lies about fifty feet below us in that direction."

Rémy took out his binoculars and peered at the lower summit.

"I see sulfur clouds rising from there as well," said Rémy. "Seems odd."

They hiked around the perimeter of the crater, cognizant that the volcano could erupt at any moment. Professor Landes surveyed the ghastly scene with haunted eyes, sweat dripping down his temples. "Mon Dieu, for years we picnicked and swam here. I never imagined—"

"You never imagined that one day the volcano would start acting like a volcano?" interrupted Aubert.

"Well, I don't advise you to go swimming there now," said Rémy. "Not unless you want to turn into a petrified rock."

To demonstrate his point, he picked up a branch and threw it in the lava. All at once a reddish-orange flame shot out and consumed the branch, the fire crackling and dancing on the surface. The sight of it was terrifying. The noxious fumes that accompanied the explosion were so powerful they hacked and coughed despite covering their noses and mouths.

That's when they saw the dead birds.

Emilie was the first to see them. She hiked ahead of the others, and when she stumbled upon the bodies of hundreds of dead birds, she stopped short.

She pointed at their ghostly white bodies. "Look, they're all dead."

Landes's eyes went wide. "There are hundreds of them, asphyxiated. They must have died from carbon dioxide poisoning. The volcano is emitting huge quantities of it."

"What is carbon dioxide?" said Emilie.

"It is a gas that is denser than air and cannot sustain fire or animal life. It's all around us. If it wasn't for the constant flow of fresh air, we'd be as dead as these poor wretches."

Emilie felt the blood draining from her face. She saw the look of unease that overcame Rémy and Aubert, their muscles tensing, as if expecting a sudden attack.

"Come on, gentlemen, let's head down to the lower valley," said Professor Landes. "I want to see what the situation is like down there."

"That sounds reasonable," said M. Mirville, whose face did not exactly agree with his words. He pulled out his barometer, and Emilie watched his eyes widen with shock when he observed the wild fluctuations of the needle. She drew closer and watched with growing unease as the needle oscillated out of control.

"M. Mirville, what's going on?" she said. "Why is the barometer vibrating like that?"

"It means the atmospheric pressure is dropping rapidly," said Mirville. "I've never seen anything like it in my life. I've read that barometric depressions combined with microseismic movements indicate a high level of volcanic activity, but we shouldn't jump to any conclusions. There might be an approaching storm."

Rémy grabbed the barometer and studied it. "It's definitely picking up some magnetic matter in the atmosphere, some type of magnetic currents." He looked around with unease. Emilie stared in his eyes and tried to read his thoughts. But before he could say anything more, Mirville grabbed the instrument and stuffed it in his pocket.

"It could also mean nothing," he said. "We have to keep our wits about us. The last thing we need is a panic on our hands."

Rémy grew silent, his face a mask of worry.

They hiked around Morne La Croix and made their way down to the lower valley some fifty feet below. As they descended by means of a path cut into the side of the cliff, their progress was slowed by the overgrowth of vines and creepers. Durancy and Césaire took the lead, slashing at the overgrowth to make a path. One by one they descended to the lower crater, and when they reached the bottom, they were shocked once more by the sight that awaited them.

Chapter 15

Surrounded by clouds of steam, Emilie was shocked to see that the lower crater was an enormous field of black sludge. She willed her legs to carry her across the muddy surface when every instinct told her to flee. Yet something akin to fascination and curiosity pulled her forward. When they reached the edge of the pit, they looked on in horror. The dry crater had transformed into a frothing pit of black lava, from which noxious gases were rising. The men were noticeably troubled by the sight. They stared at it with palpable fear, sweat pouring down their temples. Their hands trembled as they surveyed the shocking sight through binoculars. To Emilie it looked as if the lava was bubbling up from subterranean fires, exactly as Jules Verne described them in *Journey to the Center of the Earth*. The only difference was they were atop a four-thousand-foot mountain five miles from a bustling town, not miles beneath the earth's crust. She shuddered, thinking there were now *two craters in active eruption.*

The party hiked across the muddy surface, enveloped in vaporous clouds that made them cough and gasp for breath. Everywhere they looked, pools of black lava were bubbling up from the depths, sending up wisps of smoke. Adding to the horror, the hissing steam became so loud it sounded like a deafening roar. Emilie looked at Rémy's eyes and saw raw fear. Even the normally jovial Césaire looked disturbed and Durancy clutched his cutlass so tightly his arm muscles bulged. They stared in shock at this new discovery. No one said anything. There was no explanation for this shocking phenomenon, but they all agreed that the dry crater looked even more fearsome than the first crater. It resembled a lake of boiling black lava. And even more disturbing, draped along the crater walls were the remnants of dead trees coated in a thick black slime. There was no sign of life anywhere. Every now and then, rocks and boulders would burst out of the crater with an explosion like cannon fire.

"Professor Landes," said Emilie. "The volcano is erupting. I think we had better get out of here as quickly as possible."

"Don't worry, I don't believe we're in any immediate danger," said Landes. "The volcano can experience seismic shocks like this for years before it dies down."

"Professor Landes is right," said M. Mirville. "It looks worse than it is. I think all this release of gas and steam signifies that the volcano will soon die down. Our job is to reassure the public they're in no immediate danger."

Emilie looked at him skeptically but said nothing.

Off to the side, they spotted an enormous cinder cone over thirty feet high that was spewing jets of boiling water and clouds of steam. Landes remarked that he had never observed a cinder cone before, and it appeared to be acting as a sort of plug for the magma below.

"God only knows what will happen if this cork blows its top," said Aubert.

"Gentlemen, I think we've seen enough," said Rémy. "The gas fumes here are quite toxic. Let's head back and write our report."

As they were getting ready to leave, Aubert called out to them.

"Look there!" He pointed to the middle of the lava lake. "Do you see those green leaves floating on the lava like tiny islands? It's amazing how they can survive at such high temperatures."

Landes strained to catch sight of the greenish leaves floating on the surface amid ashes and cinders. When he realized the source of the vegetation, his face paled noticeably.

"Gentlemen, those leaves are not small islands. I believe they are the tops of trees that once stood over sixty feet high."

Everyone stared in shock, the implications too frightening to imagine.

Stunned by their findings, the scientific committee hurried back across the black sludge, gathered up their equipment, and headed down the mountain as quickly as possible. Every now and then a boom would ring out, sending rocks raining down on the surrounding countryside. There was no sign of the porters anywhere.

During the descent there was no more laughter, no more joking. Everyone was exhausted and haunted by what they had seen. By the time they reached Morne-Rouge, they were covered in ash and soot, bruised, bleeding, and their boots were caked with muddy lava. Emilie stared in shock at her silver belt buckle, silver buttons, and coins. Each item had turned an eerie bluish-black color, instantly tarnished.

While they were retrieving their horses at the barn, Emilie said, "Professor Landes, what are you going to tell the governor?"

"I hardly know what to say," he said, looking perplexed. "I'm still stunned by what we found. I'm not sure I believe it myself. The volcano certainly looks as if it's on the verge of eruption, but it's hard to say . . ."

"We have to tell him the truth," said Rémy. "At the very least, we should warn him about the potential danger to the public so he can develop an evacuation plan. Thank goodness we took photographs."

"Our main job is to calm the public, not rile them up," said Landes. "But I'll give it some thought. Tomorrow we have to report to the governor at the Hôtel Intendance."

"I'll be there," said Rémy. "There are villages within a few miles of the crater. Those people have to be warned about the danger of projectiles. If the steam pressure builds, there's no way to predict where the debris will fall, not to mention the lava."

"Let's not get too hasty," said Mirville. "Any flow of lava will surely run down the ravines into the sea. And don't forget, Saint-Pierre is over five miles away. The civilians are in no immediate danger in my opinion. I'm sure the worst is over, and we should downplay the situation as much as possible so as not to cause a panic."

Emilie noticed that Rémy remained skeptical but said nothing.

After a light meal in a café, the travelers mounted their horses and set off for town. As they rode in silence, Emilie contemplated the worrisome scene they had witnessed. During the journey, she noticed Rémy never left her side. But he was in his own silent reverie. His eyes looked tired, and his dark hair was scattered over his sooty forehead. He looked like he had the weight of the world on his shoulders.

When they reached the fork in the road at rivière Blanche, they broke into two groups. Emilie, Durancy, and Césaire were heading north to Domaine Solitude, while Rémy, Aubert, Landes, and Mirville would head south to Saint-Pierre. Before they parted, Rémy pulled Emilie aside and said, "Mlle Dujon, may I speak to you for a minute?"

"Of course," she said.

"Regardless of what M. Mirville says, I feel it's my duty to inform you that if your family has a safe place to go, you should evacuate your plantation as soon as possible. No one can predict when the volcano will erupt, but it seems likely that it will."

"How can you be certain?" she said.

"It's a gut feeling I have."

She frowned. "That would be hard. We're right in the middle of the harvest."

"Then at least you should go, together with your mother and your nanny. I've been studying the trajectory through my binoculars, and if the volcano erupts, I'm almost certain your plantation lies directly in the path."

Emilie felt queasy. "It's just what I feared all along. Tell me something, Lieutenant, what do you think lies beneath that large cinder cone?"

"I'm no expert on volcanoes, but I think it's acting as an enormous plug for all the magma below it. If that cinder cone blows its top, some dangerous gases and huge amounts of lava could be released. If you stay in your house, I believe your lives could be in danger. Please take every precaution."

"Thank you, Lieutenant. Godspeed to you."

"Goodbye, mademoiselle." He doffed the brim of his helmet and went to join the others. She watched Rémy go with the sinking feeling that something terrible was about to happen.

Chapter 16

Monday, April 28
Saint-Pierre

While the scientific committee was climbing up Mount Pelée, a general election was being held in Saint-Pierre for a seat in the Chamber of Deputies. The favored candidate was Fernand Clerc, a rich béké planter who represented the Progressive Party. His adversaries, Louis Percin and Joseph Lagrosillière, represented the Radical Socialist and Socialist Workers parties, respectively. For Marius Hurard, editor of *Les Colonies*, the results were discouraging. Clerc was his favored candidate, and he had won only by a slim margin, thereby forcing a runoff on May 11.

Although Hurard was personally sympathetic to the Radical Socialist agenda, he was a pragmatist by nature. The son of a rich mulatto businessman, he was used to the privileges of his class and longed to keep the status quo. This meant doing everything possible to ensure a victory for Fernand Clerc. The idea of electing a Radical Socialist like Percin to the Chamber of Deputies was anathema to the business community; it meant an unholy alliance with Hurard's archenemy, Amédée Knight. For this reason, every vote counted in the runoff election. The only thing that stood in the way of a guaranteed victory was the rumbling on Mount Pelée, which was sending the people into paroxysms of fear. He decided that for the good of all, he would downplay the threat to the public. It was his civic duty to do everything possible to avoid a stampede out of the city. Naturally, this was a decision Mayor Fouché and Governor Mouttet supported wholeheartedly, also out of a sense of civic duty.

To everyone's surprise, Governor Mouttet had found a sympathetic ally in Marius Hurard. For a newcomer to the labyrinthine world of West Indian politics, Mouttet needed allies in every corner. While he would never be fully accepted among the rich and influential békés, he enjoyed the favors and attentions the bourgeois mulatto community showered on him. And he was only too happy to oblige by returning the favor whenever the situation called for it.

To rally his support for the candidates, Mouttet decided to spend the night in his suite at the Hôtel Intendance in Saint-Pierre. With its French elegance and Creole ambiance, the hotel's dining room was the perfect spot to hold court with the candidates and business community over a glass of Ti' Punch and a fine Cuban cigar. The hotel defined everything Mouttet loved about life in the French West Indies: tropical elegance, easy luxury, and a refined ambiance that transcended anything his civil servant's pay could afford back in France. But there were many irritating aspects about life in the tropics as well: malaria, yellow fever, cholera, Machiavellian politics, and all that volcanic activity. Since early February, he'd been hearing reports about a nauseating sulfur smell in Prêcheur that was sickening the residents. He had also heard that every silver object was mysteriously turning black. As the missives, telegrams, and reports began to pile up on his desk, he instructed his secretary, Didier, to file away the reports from Prêcheur so he could concentrate on more urgent matters. He promised to return to the situation as soon as his schedule cleared after the election.

Monday morning brought sunshine and a fresh breeze into Governor Mouttet's suite—all the proof he needed that the confounded volcano was on the wane. The only thing marring an otherwise perfect day was a slight rumbling that came from the mountain at varying intervals, but it was nothing to get alarmed over. He opened the French doors and strode out to the balcony. The streets were starting to come to life. Merchants, clerks, laborers, customs officials, schoolchildren, nuns, priests, and marketwomen paraded down the street. The harbor was already full with schooners and steamers. But nothing gave him greater pleasure than watching the workers loading huge hogsheads of rum and sugar onto the ships. A profitable colony was a guarantee of job security and a lifetime of carefree living. Perfect bliss.

Mouttet decided to have breakfast on the balcony, all the better to take advantage of the sunshine and cool breezes. After he finished reading the latest issue of *Les Colonies*, he kissed his wife and told her he was heading downstairs to meet with the scientific committee.

At precisely 10 a.m. Rémy entered the dining room to find the governor surrounded by prominent members of the business community. When Rémy strode up to the table, the governor greeted him and told him to take a seat beside Professor Landes and M. Mirville. Shortly thereafter, the businessmen began filing out, leaving the scientific committee with relative privacy.

"Gentlemen, let's get started," said Mouttet.

A servant brought a steaming pot of coffee and doled out cups for everyone. Landes gathered his expedition notes and prepared to speak. After taking a sip of coffee, Landes cleared his throat and said, "Excellency, yesterday we climbed up to the summit and made an extensive field survey of both craters. What we found was disturbing, to say the least. Both craters were full of black volcanic mud, and quite a few new steam vents had opened up, filling the air with sulfurous fumes. At times it was difficult to breathe. We took some photographs that will give you a better picture of the situation once they are developed. But what worried us most was the state of the lower crater, the Étang Sec. It was full of black volcanic mud that was bubbling up from deep inside the volcano. I won't mince words; it looks like Mount Pelée is experiencing some kind of eruption. How far this will go is impossible to predict. Hopefully it will die down as in past years, but there's no way to say for certain when or if this will occur."

Governor Mouttet's brow furrowed. "What about those loud detonations we've been hearing? How dangerous are they?"

Rémy leaned forward and said, "Governor, we believe they are caused by the ignition of combustible fumes in the volcano's chimney. While they sound dangerous, we don't believe they pose an imminent danger to the public. But our assessment may change. Right now they mostly do a good job of scaring the population."

"I agree," said the governor. "So what is the likelihood this episode will die down shortly?"

"We can't say for certain," said Professor Landes. "But right now we don't believe Saint-Pierre is in any direct danger. The city lies well outside the range of the volcanic projectiles. However, this may not be the case with regard to the small villages and plantations on the lower slopes of the volcano."

"I see," said Governor Mouttet. "What about the crater walls? Is it possible they could collapse from the buildup of steam and pressure?"

Landes paused for a minute. "If the sustaining walls collapse, then it's possible we could see some volcanic mud flowing down the mountain. If the quantity of lava is such that it overflows into the streams, then we could have a problem on our hands. And if lava invades populated areas, it could prove hazardous."

"How likely is that to occur?" said Mouttet.

"Doubtful," said M. Mirville. "I checked the rock formations pretty thoroughly, and they looked sound. Also, we can assume that since the steam and gases are venting regularly, they won't cause the lava to overflow the retaining walls. The lava may end up retreating back inside the volcano. The civilian population is safe for the time being. I would like to add that I believe the worst is over."

"That's encouraging," said Governor Mouttet. He turned to Rémy. "And you, Lieutenant? Is there anything else you'd like to add?"

"As a matter of fact, I would," said Rémy, sitting straighter. "While on the summit, I observed projectiles shooting out of the crater quite regularly. In most cases the rocks fell back to the upper slopes of the mountain. In the interest of public safety, we have to take every precaution in case the projectiles should change trajectory. You may wish to draw up an evacuation plan for the northern half of the island in case the volcanic bombs start heading toward populated areas."

Mouttet's face darkened. "Evacuate the northern half of the island? We're talking about five thousand souls. Where do you suppose I put them, in the barracks?"

There was a nervous laugh around the table.

"Lieutenant Rémy, with all due respect," said Didier, "the governor doesn't have the authority to quarter civilians. In most cases they would be safer in their own homes than venturing out on the roads during an eruption."

"Let's return to what we were talking about," said Mouttet. "So, Lieutenant, based on the situation with the projectiles, do you see any reason to evacuate Saint-Pierre at this time?"

"No, sir," said Rémy. "But the situation might change."

"We'll cross that bridge when we get to it," said the governor. "Right now, based on what you gentlemen have told me, the situation appears to be under control. I see no need to do anything further other than keep a watch on the volcano. Do you gentlemen agree?"

Rémy paused for a second and added, "Governor, there is one possibility that we haven't considered."

"Oh? What's that?" said the governor.

"I've been studying the situation with Mount Krakatoa, and I find it worrying. When Mount Krakatoa erupted in 1883, thirty-six thousand people were killed from hot gases that were traveling at high speeds from the volcano. If the same situation were to occur here in Martinique, we could have a similar catastrophic loss of life. In my opinion, we have to consider this possibility, which means a large-scale evacuation may be necessary."

"That's preposterous," said Mouttet, slightly flummoxed. "Think of the panic. And we simply don't have the resources to house everyone."

The governor dabbed his forehead with a napkin and drank a glass of water in one go. The men shot glances at each other and shifted uncomfortably in their seats.

"What Lieutenant Rémy mentioned is a worst-case scenario," said Professor Landes. "I don't foresee that happening at all. While I'm not overly optimistic about the situation with the volcano, I'm thankfully not quite as pessimistic. Other than that, I agree with Lieutenant Rémy about the projectiles. Some residents may have to move south temporarily."

Didier, the governor's aide-de-camp, added, "Gentlemen, let's consider the runoff election as well. The governor's job is to keep the public calm until then. If we emptied out whole villages, it could cause anarchy."

"There would be a lot more anarchy if we don't evacuate the civilians in the event of a major eruption," said Rémy.

The governor drew a deep breath. "Isn't it possible that all the ash and debris that have been ejected indicate that Pelée has exhausted itself and will die down shortly?"

"Yes, it's possible," said Landes.

"Which means we have every reason to believe the volcano is on the wane?"

"That is my opinion," said Mirville.

Landes nodded his consent, but his face told a different story.

"I believe the release of gas and steam is a prime indicator that the volcano will go back to its dormant state," said M. Mirville.

Rémy shook his head. "Forgive me for saying so, but there is no scientific basis for that position. It could also indicate the volcano will enter an even deadlier phase. We have to prepare for every possible scenario."

Governor Mouttet rubbed the space between his eyes. "Gentlemen, you do realize we're in the middle of an election cycle, don't you?"

"Indeed," said Professor Landes. "But unlike funerals, elections can be postponed."

"Hurard won't like this one bit," said Mouttet. "He's been pressuring me to keep the matter under wraps."

"I understand, Excellency," said Landes. "But even the esteemed editor of *Les Colonies* must serve the public interest first. I think the most prudent thing to do is keep watching the volcano and report back here in a week's time. Then we can decide if any further action is required."

Mouttet looked relieved. "That sounds reasonable. Do you gentlemen agree?"

The men nodded.

"Very well," said Governor Mouttet. "Let's adjourn for today and return on the fifth of May. Perhaps by then this strange episode will have died down, and we can drink to the future of Saint-Pierre."

Chapter 17

Monday, April 28

The next day Emilie awoke with a feeling of disquiet. When she had returned the previous night, she had found her parents in a state of great agitation. They were pacing back and forth, and her father's bleary eyes suggested he had been drinking. Her mother was nervous and agitated. She pounced on Emilie the minute she walked through the door, demanding to know why she came home so late and in such a bedraggled state.

Exhausted, Emilie had slumped in a chair and pulled off her muddied boots, trying to explain the terrifying sights they had seen on Mount Pelée. Her parents listened with concern when she described the bubbling black lava and the gas clouds, but neither of them believed her. They accused her of exaggerating the situation. They did not take the threat seriously at all. The final blow came when they told her that when Lucien Monplaisir found out she was hiking up the volcano with the scientific committee, he flew into a jealous rage. He ranted and raved, vowing to put an end to her independent streak. To placate Lucien, her mother had invited him to dine with them the following evening. When Emilie heard this, she felt as if the world was closing in on her. She could almost feel the cold shackles of a miserable marriage pressing against her ankles, binding her to Lucien forever. The thought made her nauseous. She had to find a way out of this disaster, even if it meant resorting to extreme measures. By the time she fell asleep that night, she decided she would do anything in her power to free herself from Lucien.

Early Monday morning Emilie took a small, two-seater carriage to Saint-Pierre on the pretext she had to do some shopping, but in her hand she clutched an address she had secured from the cook: 25, rue Longchamps. No doubt it was a desperate measure, but it was her last chance, perhaps her only chance. Under the circumstances, she believed God, the saints, and Sister Marie would forgive her.

She found the shop easily. The sign read, "GASTON FAUSTIN JACQUET, HERBALIST AND HEALER." After leaving the carriage, she collected her nerve, but all she could see was Sister Marie's stern but loving face flashing before her eyes. She felt a pang of guilt but pushed it aside and continued with her plan.

Pushing open the door, she entered the shop. Almost immediately she spotted a handsome, well-dressed older gentleman with stern eyes, tufts of white hair, and an imposing presence sitting behind a massive mahogany desk. He was writing in a ledger with neat, elegant script, but as soon as she entered, he fixed his eyes on her, as if sizing her up. She felt uneasy but browsed around the shop for a few minutes, pretending to peruse various objects. But when the pounding of her heart became too great, she turned and was halfway to the door when a deep voice called behind her: "Bonjour, mam'selle, may I help you?"

Emilie stopped short, her heart pounding. Slowly she turned and said, "Thank you, monsieur; I was. . . uh. . . just looking."

The gentleman invited her to continue browsing with a gracious smile that disarmed her. He was smooth in his manner and handsome enough to beguile her. She walked around the store with as much casualness as she could muster, as if browsing through the shop of a notorious voodoo witch doctor was the most natural thing in the world to do. From time to time she would catch him studying her while he pretended to be perusing his ledger books. He had an almost paternalistic quality about him, but he was suave and elegant to a fault. Although she couldn't say for certain, she was sure the man behind the desk with the penetrating eyes and wizened face was the Grand Zamy. She had a strong intuition about it. Was this handsome, older gentleman the infamous quimboiseur who held the people of Martinique in his grip?

Emilie turned to meet his gaze. He smiled, showing a row of gleaming white teeth, yet there was nothing particularly friendly about his smile. As she continued browsing through the store, M. Jacquet's eyes followed her every move. But Emilie sensed another quality lurking beneath the surface. Whether it was cunning or deviousness, she couldn't say for certain. There was something haughty and domineering about him, as if he could see right through a person to his core and then use his cunning to control him.

The store was unlike any other Emilie had ever seen. There were rows of bottles filled with various contents, such as scented oils, herbs, powders, bone fragments, dried insects, flowers, holy water, eau de cologne, roots, snakeskins, berries, nuts, and desiccated chicken feet. Each bottle was labeled with a yellowed parchment on which mysterious symbols were written that could have been Latin, Greek, or Kabbalistic. There was also a large assortment of candles in various colors and sizes, talismans, crucifixes, charms, rosaries, and statues of saints and African deities. On one wall there were pictures of saints with eyes that looked curiously alive. It was enough to make her skin crawl, but she had come too far to back down.

The Grand Zamy laid down his fountain pen. "Is there something I can do for you, mam'selle?"

"I, uh—" Emilie froze.

He leaned forward and urged her to continue with a kindly, paternalistic voice.

"I. . . uh. . . need some help," she said, feeling strangely awkward.

The Grand Zamy motioned toward a chair. "Please sit down, mam'selle. What is your name? Don't be afraid. I'm here to help you."

Emilie slithered into the chair and met his gaze. His face looked so normal, so paternalistic, almost like a kindly grandfather. She could hardly believe this debonair gentleman was responsible for so much death and turmoil, most of which was only spoken about in hushed tones. She had heard a rumor from Victorine that his first wife went insane and was shut up in the lunatic asylum on rue Levassor, although no one knew for certain. She simply disappeared one day, and the sisters of Saint-Paul de Chartres who cared for the patients were notoriously tight-lipped about them. But Victorine's face went grim when she told Emilie that no one had ever seen or heard from his wife again. But that was many years ago. Most people had forgotten about her. No one knew precisely what went on inside the stone walls of the asylum, although some people claimed they heard screams in the night. Others told stories about restraining chairs and other forms of torture. Victorine said she had heard of people who were poisoned by him. And some who were turned into zombies. It was all terrifying to Emilie. Adding to the mystery, everywhere he went he was trailed by an alluring servant girl, even when he went to mass each morning. The exact nature of their relationship was always the subject of gossip and innuendo. Still,

Emilie reasoned that this sinister character was her best chance for breaking free of Lucien.

"Bonjour, my name is Emilie Dujon, and I have a problem." As she spoke, the Grand Zamy fixed his eyes on her, as if he was hypnotizing her. She shifted in her seat and continued, "You see, I'm engaged to a man who is unfaithful. . ." She paused for a moment to let that sink in. The Grand Zamy nodded, sphinxlike, and urged her to continue. "Since I no longer love him or wish to marry him, I must find a way to end our engagement without causing a scandal."

The Grand Zamy leaned back in his chair and put his hands behind his head. "So if I understand you correctly, you're engaged to a man you do not wish to marry."

"That is correct."

The Grand Zamy regarded her through narrow slits. "Does this man love you?"

"Yes, I believe he does, in his own way."

"But you don't love him."

Emilie shook her head. "No."

"Then, mam'selle, you have a serious problem indeed." The Grand Zamy closed his eyes and rubbed his forehead, as if deep in concentration. "Let me think for a moment. Love, you see, is a powerful emotion. Once it takes hold, it is very hard to uproot. But there are certain herbs that can help mitigate the situation, provided of course you use the correct mixture and in the correct dosage. Luckily for you I have great experience in these matters. As you can see, I have a well-stocked laboratory." He motioned toward the shelves with the assortment of bottles. "In addition, there are powerful incantations that can increase the effectiveness of the potion. I recently assisted a young man from the village of Pointe-Noir who fell in love with a young lady whose family objected to their engagement. They whisked her away to the other side of the island, which enraged him. He came to me in a state of great agitation, vowing revenge against anyone who would take away the love of his life."

"What happened?" said Emilie.

The Grand Zamy gave a mysterious smile, like the Mona Lisa. "I don't think you want to know the exact details of that case. Thankfully I solved the young man's problem to his satisfaction, and in the end, that's all that counts, correct?" Emilie nodded. "The medicine I prescribe is tailor-made to suit each patient's needs. It takes years of experience to know the correct formula and spells. That is the art of the herbalist. But it's a mistake to think I alone hold full control over the outcome. At most I am only an intermediary. I ask the spirits to intervene on behalf of my clients. Some herbalists—my competitors, some of whom are quite unscrupulous—think the best approach is to simply eliminate the obstacle. But that is an extreme measure I rarely employ. First, let us consult the cards and see what they have to say."

Standing up to his full height, the Grand Zamy lit the black candles on the chandelier and said, "Spirits, I invoke you, tell me how to solve this young woman's problem."

The black candles flickered for a moment and then mysteriously snuffed out. Taking out a deck of tarot cards, he shuffled them and asked her to cut them. He spread the cards out on his desk in the shape of a cross, then he turned them over one by one, studying them with great concentration. Finally he looked up and said, "You have recently discovered a painful truth, or perhaps you have been betrayed. You feel lost, isolated, and alone. Perhaps you have seen your man in the arms of another woman. That is the Three of Swords. I see much anguish and despair. You feel as though you have been pushed to your limits, and you're going through a dark night of the soul. You are filled with worry and sadness. You lie awake all night, worrying and fretting. That is the Nine of Swords." He pointed to a card and gazed at her through narrowed eyes. "I sense you are experiencing an upheaval, a sudden change, or perhaps you have realized the truth about something. Something that was once hidden but has now been exposed. You are in a crisis. This is evidenced by the Tower card over here." He pointed to a card that showed a tower that was struck by lightning and was in flames. Emilie shuddered at the sight of it.

"And look here." He pointed to another card. "This is the Nine of Pentacles. It represents a lady of refinement and grace. She does not seek the easy way out but learns to take matters into her own hands. She relies on herself to solve her own problems. This, mam'selle, is you. You must learn to trust your own abilities. And do you see the Ace of Cups over here? This represents a new love or a fork in the road, a new path or a struggle between two choices. Beware of overconfidence and the danger of rushing in too soon. I see difficult times ahead of you. Great strife. I see a maiden, bound and blindfolded, surrounded by danger and unable to see her way out. She is overwhelmed. She feels trapped by her circumstances, lost and confused. This is the Eight of Swords. Don't look worried, mam'selle; I am sure you will find your way out. Look here, there is a powerful, broad-shouldered man carrying a great burden. That is the Knight of Wands. He is confident and courageous. He carries the duty of responsibility on his shoulders. He will risk anything without fear. That card is a good sign. Finally, I see an awakening to a new and even greater challenge. I see a large goal ahead of you." The Grand Zamy looked up from the cards. "Unfortunately, that is all I see. I believe your problem is not too severe and can be solved by a simple ritual and potion."

"Are you sure?" said Emilie.

"I've dealt with much worse cases."

"Are these potions dangerous? I mean, can they cause great harm?"

"My dear, anything can be harmful if applied in the incorrect dosage. That is why you must always consult with an expert. For ten francs I will prepare a powder that will calm your fiancé's ardor and cause him to break off your engagement. Perhaps it will set your destiny in motion. Have no fear that harm will come to him. I assure you the effects are not permanent." He erupted in house-shaking laughter that sent a shiver up her spine.

With quivering hands, Emilie extracted ten francs from her purse and handed it over to the Grand Zamy. He placed the money in a strongbox and locked it. He explained to her that she must take three strands of her hair and three strands of Lucien's hair and wrap them up in a sheet of silk paper. Then she must go to the cemetery and stand at the edge of an open grave and recite the following incantation: *Sator arepo, tenet opera, Rohas, Enam, Binah Jhedulah, Teburah, Jiphereth, Netzah, Hod, Jesode, Malrouth, Meschache, Obdenego! Come all to help me destroy the love that oppresses my heart!* Emilie wrote down all the instructions, including the spell. The Grand Zamy continued, "Then, while still standing at the edge of the grave, you must light a candle and say, *Good souls of purgatory, I entrust my love to you in order to let it fall asleep in the same way that you were plunged into your eternal sleep. So be it.* As you recite the words, throw the silk paper with the hair into the grave."

The Grand Zamy stood up and strode over to the wall. He selected an assortment of bottles containing various powders and herbs. After mixing them in a wooden bowl, he added some crushed beetles, a drop of lavender oil, and a bit of tafia. He poured the mixture into a vial, which he sealed with a cork and handed to Emilie.

"Here you are, mam'selle," he said. "This is the potion that will change your life. Now give me the young man's name and date of birth." She gave him the information. "Now listen very carefully. When he comes to visit, light a white candle in front of a mirror. Place the powder into a glass of punch and serve it to him. In a short while his behavior will start to change. He may seem a little intoxicated at first, perhaps even a little erratic, but he will soon ask for his ring back, and your problem will be solved."

"Is it that simple?" she asked.

Eyeing her, the Grand Zamy said, "For you, my dear, it is simple. For me it is a bit more complicated. I will recite the appropriate spells, perform sacrifices, and petition the spirits—that is the special task of the herbalist. I do not expect a fine lady to sacrifice a chicken."

The Grand Zamy roared with laughter, causing Emilie to almost jump out of her seat. Clutching the vial, she raced out of the store.

Chapter 18

When Lucien arrived that evening, Emilie was ready. Just before dinner she had stolen away to the cemetery with a candle and a sheet of silk paper containing three strands of her hair intertwined with three strands of Lucien's hair, which she had procured from a locket he had given her. She located an empty grave, lit the candle, and recited the mysterious incantation. Then she tossed the paper in the grave and rushed home. She rehearsed in her mind what she would do when Lucien arrived until she knew it like the back of her hand. By the time the clock struck seven o'clock, she was as nervous as a lobster before a pot of boiling water. Her mind conjured up all sorts of terrifying scenarios, which she tried to shrug off but found it impossible. She sighed and rubbed her forehead. She had invested ten francs to rid herself of Lucien. If it failed, she would be in a terrible predicament.

As Emilie got dressed for dinner, she took great pains to hide her inner turmoil. All the lessons she had learned from Sister Marie in the convent school of Saint-Joseph de Cluny came back to haunt her—all her old fears and worries, her anxieties about voodoo and black magic. She had always striven to be an example of virtue and piety, but circumstances had caused her to fall to a level she could never have foreseen. She was dabbling in voodoo! She could almost see Sister Marie's admonishing eyes upon discovering the truth. It filled her with intense shame and remorse. Outwardly she looked exquisite in a pale-blue tea gown and her grandmother's pearl necklace, but inside she felt anxious and afraid. As Da Rosette brushed her hair, Emilie looked at her reflection in the mirror and felt like a hypocrite. She had never lied to her nanny before, and now she was reduced to sneaking around behind everyone's back hiring a quimboiseur to sacrifice chickens on her behalf! She felt lower than a chicken thief. If word got out that she had resorted to voodoo, it would create a terrible scandal. She could never face her friends or even her relatives. And poor Maurice! He would be so disappointed in her. Black magic and sorcery were taboo, reserved for primitive and superstitious people. As Emilie stared at her reflection, she saw the Grand Zamy's face laughing at her, mocking her with his yellow eyes and his white teeth gleaming like a skull. She shivered and rubbed her shoulders. She wished the night would end quickly.

Later, as Emilie marched down the stairs, she was utterly focused on her mission. She was determined to succeed. By the end of the night, she wanted to be rid of Lucien forever.

For the first time in ages, even her mother looked pleased with her.

"Well, look what we have here," said Mme Dujon, beaming from ear to ear. "I'm glad you've finally come to your senses. Lucien will be overjoyed when he sees you." Then she flitted about the house putting fresh balisier flowers in the vases. Like Emilie's mother, even Da Rosette was exuberant. She had changed into her best muslin dress and matching turban and draped her silk foulard over her shoulders like a royal mantle. She hobbled through the house with her cane, but her back was straighter than Emilie had seen in years. Da Rosette laid out the crystal wineglasses and a plate of cake on the table, remarking how much she wished that Grandma Loulou could be there to share such a special occasion.

A knock on the door caused everyone to jump. To Emilie's relief, standing on the doorstep was none other than Abbé Morel in his black cassock and round-brimmed hat. As soon as he saw Emilie, his face lit up, and he rushed into the house. Pulling her aside, he whispered that he would speak to Lucien about calling the wedding off. He thought that if he applied the right pressure, he might persuade the young man that she was not yet ready for marriage.

"That's not necessary, Tonton Abbé," said Emilie. "I have it all figured out."

He looked at her quizzically. "Have what figured out?"

"How to end my engagement," she whispered. "But I can't talk about it now. You'll see soon enough."

Soon they were joined by her father, and by the time Lucien arrived, Emilie's heart was pounding.

When Lucien's carriage arrived, Georges was the first to greet his future son-in-law. He shook Lucien's hand and patted him on the back while the latter beamed from ear to ear, especially when he spied Emilie standing resplendent in the glow of the chandelier.

"You look ravishing," said Lucien, giving her a peck on the cheek. "I'm glad you've finally come around. If anything, when you played hard to get, you made me crazier about you. But I hope there will be no more of that foolish talk. You're the only woman for me."

Emilie offered a wan smile but was too nervous to speak.

Georges led his guests to the dining room, and after Abbé Morel said grace, servants brought out platters of food, and everyone dined. After a while the conversation drifted to the subject of politics, giving Emilie the perfect chance to put her potion to work.

Jumping up, she realized she had forgotten to light the white candle. She hurried to the salon, grabbed the candle, placed it in front of a mirror, and then lit it with a match, almost burning herself in the process. From her pocket she extracted the bottle with the voodoo potion and emptied the contents into a glass, which she filled with rum punch. With shaky hands she filled the remaining glasses with punch and carried the tray back to the dining room. One by one she handed out the glasses, careful to reserve the tainted one for Lucien. She was so nervous she could scarcely breathe.

And then disaster struck. Just as she sat down, Abbé Morel knocked over his glass of punched. She jumped up, but before she could pour him another, Lucien handed the priest his own glass, saying he had already drunk too much. Horrified, Emilie tried to snatch the glass away from Abbé Morel, but before she could grab it, he had already brought it to his lips and begun to drink.

Emilie sank into her seat, feeling her face draining of color. She watched Abbé Morel finish his drink and set the glass back on the table. When the conversation resumed, no one noticed that Emilie failed to touch her drink. No one saw the look of horror in her eyes when Abbé Morel drank from Lucien's cup. What happened next almost made her heart stop.

Abbé Morel's face flushed, and his eyes took on a glassy appearance. He broke out in a sweat and started mumbling. Soon it was visible to all that he was in great distress. Emilie lifted her glass to take a drink, but her hand was so shaky she dropped it on the floor, where it shattered in a thousand pieces.

"Emilie, what's got into you?" said her mother with a scornful expression.

"Nothing, Maman," said Emilie. "I'm so sorry. Please forgive me."

A servant rushed over to clean up the mess. Emilie bent down to help her, but the servant shooed her away. Left with no choice,

Emilie squirmed in her seat, feeling a growing unease at the distressing situation.

Abbé Morel's head began to sway, and his face turned colors. Emilie's stomach churned. Time stood still. As the priest suffered the effects of the potion, she saw her life flashing before her eyes.

Hovering near her, Da Rosette gave Emilie a quizzical look, but the panicked expression on her face told her to remain silent. When the broken glass was cleaned up, the conversation resumed, but Emilie was filled with dread. Her beloved Tonton Abbé's face took on a pallid color. His eyelids fluttered, and he looked queasy. She tried to revive him by patting his cheeks and offering him some fresh water, but nothing worked. Abbé was slipping into a drugged state, and sooner or later, her crime would be exposed. The idea left her nauseated.

"Tonton Abbé, talk to me. Are you all right?" she said, shaking the intoxicated priest. His eyes were dazed, and he looked delirious. He began to mumble something incoherent in Latin. Was it the Hail Mary? The Apostle's Creed? The Lord's Prayer?

Her mother affixed her lorgnettes and observed Tonton Abbé with a quizzical look. "Good God," she said, wrinkling her brow, "what's the matter with Pierre? I hope he hasn't been hitting the bottle again."

"It sounds like he's saying mass," said Georges, raising an eyebrow.

Emilie shook his shoulders. "Wake up, Tonton Abbé!" When she realized the priest was in a catatonic state, she was filled with an overwhelming feeling of dread.

"I think Monsieur l'Abbé has had a bit too much to drink," said Lucien.

Emilie ignored his comment as she attempted to resuscitate her cousin with some bitters, but nothing worked. Abbé Morel was slipping away before her eyes.

"I've never seen Pierre so sick before," said Mme Dujon, looking worried. "It looks like he caught something serious, like malaria or yellow fever."

"I heard he fell back on the bottle while he was in Carriacou," said Georges. "The archbishop wrote to me about it. That's why they sent him back here."

"That's not true!" said Emilie with indignation. "Abbé Morel doesn't drink. I don't believe a word you're saying. It's a terrible lie!"

"Don't worry; he'll be fine," said Georges, leaning over to give Abbé Morel a light tap on the shoulder. "He just needs to sleep it off. Let the servants put him to bed. By morning he'll be back to his old self."

Abbé Morel opened his eyes and gazed at Emilie as if for the first time. The color returned to his cheeks, and he had a gleam in his eye. He loosened his priestly collar and inched closer to Emilie. Slipping an arm over her shoulder, he tried to kiss her, but she squirmed out of his grip. But that just served to increase Abbé Morel's ardor. He clung to her with unchecked affection. And then, to Emilie's horror, he put his lips on hers, and it took all her strength to wriggle out of his grip. Across the table, she saw Lucien's expression change to one of shock. Emilie's discomfort grew as Abbé Morel kissed and caressed her with unchecked affection.

"Tonton Abbé, stop!" she cried.

"What the devil is going on?" said Lucien with outrage. Apparently he had never seen a priest kissing a young lady before.

"I've never seen him like this before," said Mme Dujon, bewildered. "I almost can't believe it."

"What the devil was in that drink?" said Georges.

Emilie tried to get away from Abbé Morel, but that only made him cling to her tighter.

"Papa, please do something," said Emilie. By now she was squirming in the priest's grip. "Something's wrong with Tonton Abbé. He needs a doctor!"

"There's nothing the matter with me," said Abbé Morel. "I'm perfectly fine. Never felt better in my life. Come closer, my dear. I want you near me."

Abbé Morel pressed his lips to Emilie's, causing her to cry out and wriggle out of his grasp again. Mme Dujon peered at her cousin through her lorgnettes, her face turning white with shock.

"Good Lord," said her mother. "What happened to him?"

"Papa, please make him stop," said Emilie. She glanced over at Lucien, but he was watching the spectacle like a bettor at a cockfight. His ire dimmed somewhat when he realized his rival had completely lost his senses. He laughed at the absurdity of the situation, but Emilie didn't find the matter the least bit funny.

"Emilie, my darling, I think your whole family has gone insane," said Lucien. "But I'm starting to feel at home. In fact, I find your family most amusing."

Two servants came and managed to drag Abbé Morel upstairs to the spare bedroom. Emilie attempted to fix her ruined coiffure, but her mood was utterly spoiled. She was furious at the disastrous outcome.

"Please forgive Abbé Morel," said Georges. "He can't be held responsible for his behavior. I think his new job at the prison is proving too much for him. He must be suffering from overexertion and found his only comfort in the bottle."

"I think he just got a little overexcited," said Emilie.

"A little overexcited is an understatement," said Lucien. "He almost makes me want to become a priest." Everyone laughed, and the matter was soon forgotten. By the time Lucien left that evening, Emilie was so overwrought, her stomach was in knots. She had failed in her mission and had been on the receiving end of all sorts of strange looks from Lucien and the servants. The evening had been a complete disaster. She was running out of time, running out of money, and running out of patience. Her wedding date was drawing near, and there seemed to be no way out.

Chapter 19

Tuesday, April 29

Emilie tossed and turned the entire night. She was riddled with guilt over the terrible fiasco she had caused and dreaded the idea that her marriage to Lucien was almost a certainty. She felt as if she had fallen into a black hole from which she would never escape. His arrogant, conceited personality was anathema to her. The thought of spending a lifetime with him caused her to double over with pain. Even sleep was not an escape; her dreams were full of torment. Tears coursed down her cheeks. Even the droning of the insects outside didn't bring her peace. She racked her brains for hours trying to understand why Abbé Morel had acted so strangely. It was almost as if the potion had done the *opposite* of what the Grand Zamy had promised. It looked to her as if the potion had made the priest *fall in love with her*. It seemed too illogical to be impossible. Yet the more she thought about it, the more logical it seemed. Yes, that's what happened! The potion caused Tonton Abbé to fall in love with her. It was a far-fetched notion, but it seemed like the only logical explanation. And if this was true, how could she explain this to her parents? Or worse, how could she explain it to Abbé Morel? Would he be forced to leave the priesthood? Had she inadvertently ruined his career? The fear and worry kept her in a state of unremitting anxiety the entire night.

The next morning she went to Abbé Morel's room and was relieved to see that he was alert and awake. He lay in bed in a peaceful state, although by the bags under his eyes, it looked as though he hadn't slept much. His face was pallid, but he looked renewed at the sight of her. As soon as she stuck her head in, he perked up and asked her to sit down beside him. It pained her to see him in a love that would remain forever unrequited.

Abbé Morel grasped her hand. "Emilie, it's not easy for me to say this, but it's time I did. I want you to know how much I love you. You have always been the light of my life. I feel as though we are kindred spirits." He pulled her head down on his chest, where she heard the thumping of his heart. "And now I see that with the passing of time, my love for you has only grown. It's much deeper now than anything I could have imagined. I feel almost reborn inside. Tell me, Emilie, do you feel the same way?"

Emilie lifted her head and stared into his eyes. It was all too obvious that Abbé Morel was hopelessly in love with her. She was sure the drug was responsible. The stunning revelation filled her with new purpose. She had to find a cure for his malady, but until then, she had to tread carefully with his tender feelings. It was the least she owed her beloved cousin.

"Of course I love you, Tonton Abbé. But what did you mean when you said you felt reborn?"

"It's hard to explain. I feel. . . different."

"Can you be more specific?"

"It's just an odd feeling."

"And you love me?" she said.

"More than I ever thought possible," he said with childlike eyes. "Tell me, do you perhaps love me too?"

"Tonton Abbé, it's not easy for me to say this, but I believe you've been drugged. That's why you feel feverish and out of sorts. I'm going to ride down to Saint-Pierre to fetch you some medicine to cure you. Please stay here and await my return. I'll be back as soon as possible."

She tried to leave, but the priest grabbed her hand and pulled her down on the bed.

"Don't leave me, Emilie," he said. "Not just yet. I can't bear the thought of parting from you. I need you near me at all times. I feel as if I've reached the end of my life, and I want you close in case something happens. I no longer fear death. My love for you will continue long after I'm gone . . ."

Squirming out of his clutches, Emilie dipped a washcloth into some water and rubbed it on his forehead.

"You're not going to die, Tonton Abbé. You only have a mild fever. I promise you it will soon go away. Perhaps it's a touch of dengue fever. I have to go now, but I'll be back soon. By this time tomorrow, you'll be cured. I promise you."

Emilie kissed Abbé Morel's forehead and hurried out to the stable. As much as she hated to do it, she had to solicit a cure from the Grand Zamy. There was no other way around it. Since voodoo had caused the malady, the only cure would be through voodoo. She instructed the groom to hitch Balthazar to a carriage, and without another word, she headed down to Saint-Pierre. When she reached rue Longchamps, she dismounted and tied the horse to a hitching post, and then she hurried to number 25 for what she hoped was the last time.

As usual there were no customers in the herbal shop. She had the oddest feeling M. Jacquet was waiting just for her. When she opened the door, he was sitting at his ledger deep in concentration, but as soon as she stepped over the threshold, he rose to his feet.

"Bonjour, mam'selle, it is so nice to see you. Can I help you today?"

Emilie rushed to his side. "M. Jacquet, there's been an accident. Something terrible happened. I need your help."

"An accident?" He looked puzzled.

"Due to an unfortunate mishap, I fed the herbal potion to the wrong patient. But the strange thing is the powder had the *opposite* effect."

"I'm not sure I'm following you," said the Grand Zamy.

"Instead of giving the potion to my fiancé, I gave it to my cousin, but the strangest thing is the medicine seems to have had the opposite effect. I'm afraid my cousin has fallen madly in love with me. I need an antidote urgently."

The Grand Zamy scratched his chin. "Let's start at the beginning. If I understand you correctly, you say the medicine I gave you was inadvertently administered to the wrong patient? Not the young man whose name you gave me?"

"That is correct," she said.

He narrowed his eyes. "And it had the *opposite* effect, you say?"

"Yes, that is correct."

"That is indeed unfortunate but not unheard of." The Grand Zamy rubbed his chin. "And where is the unfortunate patient now?"

"He's resting in bed. But there's something else. The patient, you see, is a priest."

The Grand Zamy's eyebrows shot up. *"A priest?"* He looked incredulous for a moment and then erupted in house-shaking laughter. He laughed so hard his whole body convulsed. Emilie's knees quivered, and she felt queasy. She was terrified someone would catch her in the voodoo shop. She broke out in a sweat as her mind raced.

The Grand Zamy sat down and began leafing through an ancient volume. When he came to a certain page, he marked the passage with a long, yellow fingernail and said, "I see what happened. It's an unusual occurrence, but I think I've found a solution. When an herbal remedy is misapplied, it sometimes has the unfortunate side effect of producing the opposite result. When this happens, we give the recipient an appropriate antidote."

Emilie's heart skipped a beat. "Are you certain?"

"Yes, it's written right here in Latin. I'm afraid the language is too esoteric for those untrained in the art of the herbalist."

"Can you prepare an antidote?" she said, breathless.

A huge grin broke out on his face. "Of course I can! For you, mam'selle, it would be a pleasure, but I'm afraid it will cost you a considerable sum."

Emilie froze. "How much?"

"Fifty francs."

Emilie gasped. "Fifty francs?"

The Grand Zamy tented his hands. "To increase the effectiveness of the potion, we add certain rare and costly ingredients to appease the spirits, such as dried orchids, wasp stingers, ground lizard bones, and rum that has been buried in a graveyard for thirty years."

Emilie felt faint. The price he was asking was exorbitant. How could she possibly afford it? That was almost all the money she had. Her gaze shifted to a makeshift altar in the corner, where a white candle was burning beside a crucifix, a vial of oil, a statue of a saint, and a carved African deity, while a human skull grinned at her, as if mocking her. How had she sunk so low? What would Sister Marie think of her now? She thought of poor Abbé Morel, and it sickened her that the quimboiseur was using her predicament to extort money out of her, but what choice did she have?

She gazed at him in dull horror. "But, monsieur, fifty francs . . ."

The Grand Zamy gave her a piercing stare. "This potion is twice as powerful as the last one, mam'selle. You should expect to see immediate results. It comes with a money-back guarantee in case the patient experiences a sudden . . . relapse. But I don't foresee any complications. However, if you don't pay me, the priest will suffer the full consequences, and that would certainly bring, shall we say, divine retribution . . .?"

Emilie's mouth went dry, and her stomach lurched. Fifty francs was an exorbitant sum, but since she had no other choice, she opened up her purse, extracted the money, and placed it in his hand.

After locking the money in a safe, the Grand Zamy went to the shelf and took down a handful of bottles. He took them to his worktable and proceeded to mix them in a bowl and then emptied the concoction into a vial, which he handed to her.

"Here you are, mam'selle."

"Are you certain it will work?" she asked.

"No need to worry. After I recite the special incantations, your problem will be solved. Go and may the spirits guide you."

Emilie stepped out of the shop, feeling the weight of the world on her shoulders. She hurried through the crowd and in her haste, bumped into a man, the force of the jolt knocking her off-balance. When she regained her footing she shielded her eyes against the sun and was shocked to see it was none other than Lieutenant Rémy.

"Pardon me . . . oh, Lieutenant Rémy, what a surprise," she said. "How nice to see you again."

"Good day, mademoiselle," he said, doffing his pith helmet. "This is certainly an unexpected pleasure."

"I wanted to thank you again for saving my life," she said, slightly flustered.

"Think nothing of it," he said. "It was good target practice. What brings you to Saint-Pierre today?"

"Oh, nothing, I was just . . ."

"I saw you exiting that shop over there." Rémy motioned to the herbal shop. "What is that place? I've noticed it before."

She felt her cheeks turning crimson. "It's an herbal shop owned by a native healer. They say he's quite good."

"A native healer? Not a doctor of medicine?"

She stuttered. "Oh, everyone uses him. They say he can cure almost anything."

"I hope you're all right," he said. "But are you sure his cures are safe? Sometimes these native healers are charlatans. Something about that place gives me an odd feeling." He walked over to the store and peered in through the window. "Who is that dapper looking gentleman with the waistcoat and gold watch chain?"

"That's the owner, M. Jacquet. He's the best herbalist in Martinique. He has quite a reputation."

Rémy furrowed his brow. "Forgive me for saying this, but I hope you're not in some kind of trouble."

"I'm perfectly fine. Why do you ask?"

"I've heard that only the most desperate people go to these native healers."

"Ah, yes . . . actually the medicine isn't for me. It's for a friend of mine."

A worried look crossed Rémy's face. "A friend of yours? I guess I'll have to take you at your word. Are you certain that man is reputable?"

"Oh yes," she said. "At least I believe he is." She watched as Rémy assumed a serious countenance, and his voice became somber.

"I've heard stories about these healers who take advantage of people's naiveté to extort huge sums of money from them. Perhaps you should go to a regular doctor, one who doesn't deal in native quackery."

Emilie tried to appear calm, but she felt a sudden tightness in her chest.

Rémy continued, "Please don't think me nosy, mademoiselle, but I have some experience in these matters. My only concern is for your safety. You're young and innocent, and some of these charlatans can be quite sinister."

Deciding to drop her guard, Emilie moved in closer and said, "Lieutenant, I believe your instincts are correct. I think I may have made a terrible mistake, but it's too late to back out now. Can I tell you something in strictest confidence?"

"I give you my word as a gentleman."

Emilie sighed. "The truth is, I'm in a bit of a fix. Can we talk someplace private? I wouldn't want anyone to overhear our conversation."

Just across the street was a café called *Aux Enfants de la Patrie*.

"Come with me, mademoiselle," said Rémy. "Perhaps I can be of some assistance."

Taking her hand in his, Rémy led Emilie across the street.

Chapter 20

When they entered the restaurant, Emilie was relieved there was no one there she knew. Luckily there were only a few merchants, sailors, and laborers seated around wooden tables laden with bottles of rum and steaming plates of fried seafood and cassava bread. Other customers were seated around rickety tables playing dominoes or cards. Emilie felt vaguely uncomfortable but decided to go along since Lieutenant Rémy was doing everything possible to make her feel comfortable.

They found a quiet corner table on the second floor, where Rémy ordered a bottle of wine and two plates of seafood, *dorade grillée* and Creole rice. A breeze blew in from the window. Looking outside, they had an unobstructed view of the harbor, where a dozen schooners rocked gently in the breeze. Laughter and chatter from the marketplace filtered into the restaurant; no doubt the people were oblivious to the fact that five miles away, Mount Pelée was belching out a cloud of black smoke that was blowing toward the city, sprinkling ashes and cinders along the way.

Rémy poured two glasses of wine. "Salut."

They clinked glasses.

After drinking his wine, Rémy said, "You smell wonderful. What is that scent?"

"*Bouquet Nouveau,*" she said. "A mixture of orange flowers, hyacinth, jasmine, musk, and sandalwood."

He breathed in deeply. "I shall never forget that scent. It will always remind me of you."

Emilie beamed. She was not immune to the lieutenant's charms. She took another sip of wine, and they ate their meal in silence. Occasionally one of the men would cry out when he had won a game of dominoes, and laughter would erupt amid the swirling cigarette smoke. Bottles of rum clanged on the tables, and the cooks yelled at each other in the kitchen, adding to the rustic ambiance. Emilie felt her inhibitions start to evaporate. When they had finished, Rémy lit a cigarette and sat back. "All right, mademoiselle, you've kept me in suspense long enough. Tell me about this trouble you're in."

She blushed in spite of herself. "Actually, I am a bit ashamed. I hardly know where to begin."

"It's always best to start at the beginning."

She took a deep breath. "Very well. Not long ago I found myself in a difficult situation. There was no way out, so out of desperation, I went to that native healer, but instead of fixing the problem, he only made it worse. You see, the medicine the herbalist gave me was really a voodoo potion."

Rémy's eyebrows shot up. "A voodoo potion? Do you mind explaining that?"

Emilie looked sheepish. "This is where it starts to get complicated."

Rémy took a puff of his cigarette. "Then go back and start from the real beginning. I have a feeling you're leaving out some important details. Don't worry about the time; I'm not needed back at the garrison today."

"They'll be expecting me back home," she said.

Rémy laid a hand on her arm. "You'll be home soon enough. I want to make sure you're not in some kind of trouble."

Emilie nodded. "Very well, the reason why I went to see M. Jacquet is because I had to find a way to break off my engagement. You see, I was desperate."

"That sounds serious," said Rémy. "Why would you. . .?"

"Allow me to explain. You see, I'm engaged to a wealthy planter named Lucien Monplaisir, but I discovered that he's been unfaithful to me. I told my parents about it, but they insist I go through with the wedding. They want to avoid a scandal. So out of desperation, I started searching for another way out . . ."

"A way out that involved voodoo?" he said, raising one eyebrow.

Emilie clutched her shawl tighter. "Perhaps you think I'm superstitious or provincial, but I felt trapped. You see, Lucien is a shrewd devil. The only reason why he wants to marry me is so he can take over my father's plantation. He's an unscrupulous, ruthless cad, but my parents refuse to see his faults because they think our marriage will improve their social standing. Our farm is almost bankrupt. Now do you see my dilemma?"

Rémy sat back and examined her. "I understand it perfectly. You're in quite a fix, mademoiselle, but how can the herbalist fix your problem? It would be easier to send Lucien a goodbye letter or put a bullet through his head. Finish him off with one clean shot."

She laughed ironically. "Very funny, but here in the West Indies, people use voodoo to rid themselves of their enemies. It's much safer and infinitely cheaper. The natives swear by these voodoo practitioners."

"Ah, so the herbalist is really a voodoo witch doctor."

"Oh, he'll never come out and say it. But I've heard he's one of the best, a notorious quimboiseur, as we call them here. His name is the Grand Zamy, a quimboiseur with a legendary reputation. I know it sounds primitive and superstitious, but people swear by them. They claim they can solve all sorts of problems with just a little potion and magic spells."

"Potion . . . magic spells?" said Rémy, taking another deep draw of his cigarette. "Don't tell me you go in for that sort of thing. Are you telling me that elegant-looking gentleman with the waistcoat and the gold watch chain is really a quimboiseur? I find it too absurd to believe."

Emilie leaned in closer. "It gets even stranger. They say on Carnival he wears a red devil's mask and parades through the streets dressed as the devil."

"This is starting to sound bizarre," said Rémy. "Would you please explain why a respected herbalist would parade in public dressed as the devil?"

Emilie lowered her voice. "He has two distinct personalities. By day he's a respectable herbalist, but under cover of darkness, he operates as a quimboiseur, the Grand Zamy, a man who makes pacts with the devil. It's all tied in with voodoo. Almost everybody here believes in it, although few will admit to it. Even some respected members of society."

Rémy eyed her. "Tell me, Mlle Dujon, do you believe in voodoo?"

Emilie paused for a moment. "I'm not superstitious, but I've seen things that cannot be explained. One night while my old nurse Da Rosette was sewing, a beetle flew into her room and started circling the candle and buzzing in her ear. Quick as a flash, she caught the beetle and singed its head in the flame. I was horrified, but I knew better than to question her. Sure enough, the next day one of the cooks came running into the house with her head all bandaged. When Da Rosette asked her what happened, the cook looked furious and said, 'You have some nerve asking me what's wrong when it was you who burned my head in the candle last night!' Da Rosette threw her out of the house, and we never saw her again. I stood there watching the whole thing shaking with fear. I was only ten years old at the time. Later Da Rosette confided that the cook was a gagé, a person who had sold her soul to the devil."

Rémy laughed. "What superstitious nonsense. No sane, rational person would believe such tripe. Surely you don't believe it. You're an intelligent, educated young woman."

Emilie assumed a grave face. "Lieutenant, I consider myself a sane, rational person, but if you had grown up here and seen the things that I've seen, perhaps you would believe it too. Isn't it easier to believe that a potion or a magic spell can change your destiny? If you had the chance to change your fate, wouldn't you take it?"

Rémy reflected for a moment. "That's a good question. While I was in Africa, I heard all sorts of strange stories, but I'm a realist. Voodoo can't solve my problems or anyone else's. When fate happens, you have to accept it and move on. We all pay a price. Voodoo isn't going to change anything as far as I'm concerned. As for you, you're far too young and innocent to be mixed up with a charlatan like that. I'm almost certain that suave old herbalist with the waistcoat is nothing but a common criminal."

"It's too late; I'm already involved," she said.

Rémy stubbed out his cigarette. "Then you must uninvolve yourself, mademoiselle. I would feel better if you stayed away from that quimboiseur, or you could become his next victim."

"Do you think I was foolish?" she said sheepishly.

"Foolish is too strong a word. I would say naive, gullible perhaps."

"I had no other choice. He promised to solve my problem, but a mishap occurred, and now my problems have multiplied."

"This is getting more interesting by the minute," he said, pouring another glass of wine. "Would you care to elaborate?"

"When I served the voodoo potion to Lucien, I thought my problem would soon be over, but unfortunately my cousin, Abbé Morel, spilled his drank and Lucien gave him his. Before I could stop him, poor Abbé drank the whole thing."

Rémy almost spat out his wine. "A priest? That's sacrilegious!"

"I feel awful," she said. "I watched my poor Tonton Abbé changing right before my eyes, and I was powerless to stop it. He trembled a bit, became delirious, and then looked at me with lovelorn eyes. Before I knew it, he had his hands all over me and was trying to kiss me! I realized he was in love with me. Of course everyone was shocked by his behavior, but only I knew the cause. They assumed he was drunk, but I knew it was because of the voodoo potion. If this remedy doesn't cure him, he may be like this forever. And then there's still the matter of Lucien . . ."

Rémy appeared shocked. "I've never heard anything so bizarre in my life. It sounds as if you're in quite a fix. Your cousin, the priest, is in love with you, and you are mixed up with a criminal voodoo witch doctor who has made you his unwilling pawn. I suspect soon he'll be extorting large sums of money out of you to 'fix' all these problems. The man should be jailed."

Emilie blanched. "I feel terrible."

Rémy poured her another drink. "Don't make too much of it. I'm sure we'll sort it all out. The law is on our side. Here, drink this and calm yourself. I'm sure we'll find a way out of this mess."

"Thank you for listening to me," she said. "I feel as though a great weight has been lifted off my shoulders."

Rémy gave her a stern look. "Mademoiselle, I won't mince words. I think you're in a bit of hot water, but with some careful strategizing, I believe we can free you from both that menacing quimboiseur and your scheming fiancé. They have a saying back in Africa: 'Smooth seas do not make skillful sailors.' I think you're about to become a first-class sailor."

Emilie laughed. With the ice now broken, they resumed their conversation, but this time they talked about lighter topics, such as their childhoods, their school memories, places they had traveled, their dreams, goals, aspirations. Emilie told Rémy all about life in the West Indies—the balls, the horse races, the picnics in the botanical garden, the quarrels, the duels, swimming in fresh pools of spring water, and spending hot summer days lounging on hammocks. During that time Rémy watched her with fascination, his eyes twinkling as he occasionally laughed at her little jokes, while she found herself enthralled by his pleasant demeanor. She had never met someone so unlike herself, yet who made her feel so comfortable, so natural. And despite the scars and creases in his weather-beaten face, Rémy was almost *handsome.*

"Tell me something, why did you go to Africa?" she said.

Rémy looked pensive for a moment. "It was the only way to advance in my career. I knew my obscure family background and my reputation for being a loner would hold me back from getting promoted, so I decided to take a big risk. I volunteered for service in the penal battalion in Senegal. From there I ended up in the yellow-fever-ridden Camp des Madeleines. A short while later I volunteered for an expedition to Casamance. That was when my journey in Africa really began. In Casamance I found all sorts of people speaking many different languages. There were the Wolof, the Jola, the Felup, and the Mandinka, some of whom lived in the great forests, while others lived along the banks of the Casamance River. For me it was a journey into the unknown, an escape from rigid society. I learned to speak Bambara, and through hard work, I earned their trust. My regiment formed strategic alliances with the tribes, and we attended their celebrations and their funerals. The chief of the Bambara became my close friend, and in the end, he was almost like a father to me . . ." Rémy's voice trailed off, and he stared into the distance, as if seeing the past. "I advanced up the ranks to full lieutenant, and two years later, I was promoted to captain. That was when I decided to become an explorer. I signed up for my most challenging assignment yet, to map the area between Senegal and the Niger Rivers and to study the route for a proposed railway from Kayes to Bamako. I knew the dangers I was facing, but I didn't think twice. I had found my life's calling, and that's all that mattered. The only problem was there were some dangers I could never have foreseen . . ."

"Such as?"

"There's no point in continuing," he said.

"Please do. I find it fascinating."

Rémy assumed a downcast appearance. "My plan was to explore the Mossie country before heading to Grand Bassam. Together with a fellow captain, an *ordonnance,* a type of soldier-servant, and a team of thirty natives, we set out on the greatest expedition of our lives. I didn't realize the trials that lay ahead of me."

"It sounds dangerous," she said.

"It was in more ways than one," he admitted. "I risked my reputation to save an innocent man's life, and in the end, it destroyed my career. That's why I'm here talking to you today." Rémy swirled his glass. "But I have no regrets. If I had to do it all over again, I would do the same thing, and I would still suffer the same punishment. Honor has no price. It's all that a man has."

"Please tell me what happened."

"There's no point in talking about it now," he said. "What's done is done. It's all in the past now. I was demoted in rank and suffered the consequences. The rest, they say, is history."

"I'm sorry," she said. "Perhaps someday you'll tell me all about it."

"Be careful what you wish for," he said. "Perhaps you'd be better off with that Lucien fellow. At least he can afford to keep you in grand style, with a lovely villa, an army of servants, and annual shopping trips to Paris. Everything a girl like you could want."

"It's not what I want," she said. "I don't love Lucien, and I would never sell my soul for money."

"Yet you'd do business with a voodoo witch doctor."

Emilie stiffened. "I'm not proud of it."

"Don't worry, my dear," he said. "I would have done the same thing had I been in your shoes."

She looked at the clock. "Oh dear, it's getting late. I must be getting home."

She got up to leave, but Rémy held her arm. "Don't leave so soon, mademoiselle. Stay for another drink. We may never have another moment like this."

His touch sent shock waves through her body.

"I really can't. I must be going . . ."

He clutched her arm. "Mademoiselle, take my advice: don't marry that man. I can promise you you'll regret it. You would fall into a trap from which you would never recover. But you probably know that already."

Emilie stared in Rémy's eyes and felt weak in the knees. Before she could respond, there was a commotion outside. Screams and shouts reverberated from the street, and everyone ran to the window to see what had happened. Rémy tossed a few coins on the table, grabbed Emilie by the hand, and headed outside.

People were racing through the streets shouting and pointing at Mount Pelée. A huge black cloud was billowing out from the crater and drifting over the city, where it rained ashes and cinders on everyone's head. Women screamed and searched frantically for their children. Everyone ran for cover. A man yelled that rivière Blanche had swollen and was turning black. Someone else shouted that a flash flood at rivière Roxelane was so powerful it had swept several washerwomen out to sea, where they vanished in an instant.

Chapter 21

The streets erupted in chaos. People scattered in all directions, screaming and shouting. Straw hats flew, and women with their shawls and turbans askew fled in terror. The crowd at place Bertin dispersed as horrified shouts erupted from rivière Roxelane. In the distance a loud roaring noise rang out, adding to the terror.

Rémy and Emilie raced down rue Victor Hugo, through the throng of terrified residents fleeing place Bertin and the marketplace. Dodging donkey carts and carriages, they turned left down rue Impératice, where the situation became even more confused, with people rushing around in a panic. When they arrived at rivière Roxelane, the reason became clear. The river had turned into a raging torrent, with water so high it threatened to flood the surrounding streets. Only the embankments on each side kept the water from inundating the north side of town. Caught in the raging tide were tree trunks, boulders, and debris, sweeping everything in their path to the sea. Along the shore people were shouting and screaming, trying in vain to rescue the remaining washerwomen who were caught in the flood. They held on to the rocks for dear life. Fishermen in canoes had paddled seaward in search of the unfortunate washerwomen who were swept out to sea, but it appeared to be hopeless. Down in the river, they heard desperate cries. A woman's turbaned head was all they could see struggling to stay above the white foam. A washerwoman was fighting for her life, clinging to rocks. Her screams were muffled by the water as it pounded against her, pushing her out with the tide.

"Oh no," cried Emilie, pointing. "That poor woman is drowning!"

Rémy watched the struggling woman with a grim countenance. He hesitated for only a moment and then raced to the water's edge and attempted to grab the woman's hand through the floodwaters, but she was too far away. And then, before their eyes, the current tore her away and carried her downstream. Emilie was frantic. In a flash, Rémy tore off his jacket and helmet and dove into the river.

Emilie held her breath until his head broke the surface. When he finally gasped for breath, he looked helpless amid the torrent.

Kicking with all his might, Rémy fought valiantly to reach the woman. When he finally grabbed her, he turned her on her back and struggled to reach shore. Several times their heads disappeared beneath the churning white foam, and each time when they resurfaced, Emilie felt a surge of hope. The crowd along the shore called out encouraging words. Some held branches for Rémy to grab hold of. But it seemed as if the odds were against them.

After fighting against the tide, Rémy managed to drag the poor woman to the shore, where the crowd pulled her to safety. He was exhausted and looked half-drowned himself, but he'd managed to save the woman's life. Emilie was overcome with pride. She rushed to his side, where he had collapsed to the ground, trying to catch his breath. Removing her shawl, she wrapped it around his shoulders. He looked like the victim of a shipwreck disaster, but his sinewy muscles were taut under his wet khaki shirt, and his eyes were shining. He leaned back, took a few satisfying breaths, and then glanced back at the recovering woman as the rescuers attempted to pump the water out of her lungs.

"That was very brave of you," said Emilie, slumping down beside him. "You saved that woman's life."

"It was close for a minute there," he said. "I wasn't sure if we would make it."

They turned to look at the stricken woman. Some gendarmes were pounding on her back, trying to resuscitate her. She coughed out water, which was a good sign.

"She's damned lucky," said Rémy. "The poor soul came close to being swept out to sea. It's odd. For the life of me, I can't figure out why the river flooded when it hasn't rained in days." He rose to his feet to survey the raging river. "I suppose it'll be flooding for quite some time." He turned to Emilie. "Well, mademoiselle, I think you've had enough excitement for one day. Tell me something: Is life here always so dramatic?"

The stone bridge over rivière Roxelane was inundated with the floodwaters, making it impossible to cross. Traffic was at a standstill, and the carriages were beginning to back up down rue Victor Hugo. The situation was worse than Emilie had ever seen it before.

"I don't advise you return home tonight," said Rémy. "It's far too dangerous. I'm afraid the priest will have to wait for his herbal remedy."

"But my family will be worried about me," she said.

"Your safety is much more important. I think it would be more prudent if you spent the night here in town. Do you have a place you can stay?"

"My aunt has a small villa on rue de Cathédral, but it's on the other side of the river. It's useless to me now."

"Come with me. I'll put you up in a small inn. You'll be much safer here in Saint-Pierre than attempting to cross the river. I can't imagine rivière Blanche is any better. I'm sure by tomorrow you'll be able to return home."

"I wish I shared your confidence," said Emilie.

Rémy gathered his tunic and pith helmet, and together they headed down rue Victor Hugo, past frightened Pierrotins running in all directions and frantic mothers looking for their children. Many were heading down to the shore, where some fishermen were launching their boats in a last-ditch attempt to find the missing washerwomen.

They located Emilie's carriage and brought it to a barn for safekeeping, and then they located an inn on rue Petit Versailles that still had a vacant room. After the innkeeper handed Emilie her key, Rémy told her he would return at dinnertime, but first he had to report back to his regiment. Just to be safe, he paid for her lodging ahead of time.

As the appointed hour approached, Emilie waited in the foyer and tried to calm her nerves with a Ti' Punch the innkeeper had given her. It slid down her throat and sent a warm feeling to all her limbs. She was grateful for the elixir's ability to make one forget one's problems, something she needed now more than ever.

At seven o'clock, Lieutenant Rémy marched into the inn sporting a fresh uniform and a wide grin. As soon as he spied Emilie, he beamed, and she felt her heart fluttering in her chest. As soon as she saw him, all her fears melted. She no longer cared that she was meeting him without a chaperone. Tonight she would learn to rely on luck alone.

Rémy stepped forward to greet her.

He kissed her hand. "Good evening, Mlle Dujon. You look charming. Much better than when you were all covered in ash and soot, although you didn't look too bad then either."

Emilie laughed. "Please call me Emilie. And you look splendid as well, Lieutenant, much better than when you were trying to impersonate a fish out of water. Actually, as I watched you dancing on the riverbank, I couldn't help but notice how much you resembled a plucked chicken."

"You're too clever for your own good," he said.

Together they strolled down rue Petit Versailles under the glow of electric streetlamps. The ash had settled on the rooftops and streets, giving the town a wintry look. A few cats could be seen licking their haunches, and a few birds lay dead in the piles of ash. But the mountain had settled down for the night, and it was quiet. With any luck, they would have a peaceful night in Saint-Pierre. The pungent smell of Creole cooking wafted from behind closed shutters, and the sounds of crying babies and clattering dishes broke the otherwise tranquil atmosphere. They stopped at a café along the water's edge and dined on *accras de morue* and Ti' Punch. Later they went for a twilight stroll along the beach. Sitting together under a pavilion, they watched the fishermen singing while they folded their nets, their yoles bearing names like *Dieu Merci, Ange Gabriel*, and *Protection de Marie*. Gazing out to sea, they caught the last rays of sunlight dancing on the water's surface. Emilie was filled with an enormous sense of calm. And while her proximity to a strange man should have made her feel awkward, strangely enough it didn't. Rémy put his arm around her, and she lay against his chest, smelling his musky odor mingled with the scent of bay rum. She felt so natural beside him. His presence filled her with a tremendous sense of belonging.

Snuggling closer to Rémy, she said, "While you were saving that woman's life, what was going through your mind?"

He looked reflective for a moment. "Nothing. I pushed aside all extraneous thoughts and concentrated solely on my mission. That's what soldiers are trained to do in life-and-death situations."

"Where do you find the courage?"

"My commanding officer once told me that a strong will and a sense of duty often lead to greater results than enthusiasm. Once your resolution is fixed, whether good or bad, never lose sight of it until you've carried it out. Soldiers are trained to turn aside all obstacles and never flinch. Dogged perseverance often compensates for a lack of genius."

"Tell me something," she said.

"Shoot."

"I noticed that you hesitated briefly before agreeing to meet me tonight. Why?"

"Personal reasons," he said.

"Can you share them with me?"

He paused for a moment. "I try not to get involved with the locals if I can help it. It tends to complicate matters. In my field one must always keep one's wits about him."

"Yet you agreed to meet me. Tell me why."

"That information is classified, but I tend to enjoy your company."

Emilie blushed. "And here I was thinking it was my voodoo stories."

"A good storyteller and a bottle of rum make for the best company on any mission."

Following the pulsating rhythms of music, they arrived at a cabaret, where a band of native musicians in top hats, waistcoats, and cravats were playing biguines while couples danced. The beat was lively and infectious. The women in their colorful madras skirts and turbans and the men in their straw boater hats and duck suits twirled on the dance floor, filling the room with laughter and song.

Rémy stood watching the dancers, transfixed by the cheerful scene. Before she realized it, he held out his hand. "May I have the pleasure of this dance?"

Emilie flushed with excitement. As she placed her hand in his, they began to dance, absorbing the rhythm with their feet, legs, and hips. Colors blended into one, and song and laughter rang in their ears, the music almost lifting them off their feet. Rémy did his best to follow the steps, which were faster and more free-flowing than what he was used to, while Emilie sang along in the local patois. As they twirled across the dance floor, the rum coursed through their veins, making their steps lighter, their laughter merrier, their closeness more apparent. All of a sudden, a mischievous thought made Emilie burst out laughing.

"What's so funny?" he said, gazing into her eyes.

"I can't tell you," she said.

"You better tell me, or I'll never let you go."

"You'll never get it out of me." She smiled coquettishly.

"I have my ways," he said.

"Be careful what you wish for, lest it come true," she said with a boldness that astonished her.

He held her firmly in his grip. "Now you'll have to tell me, or I'll never let you go."

Emilie relented. "I was just thinking that when I went to see the quimboiseur, I was looking for a solution to a problem that seemed insurmountable. It's ironic that the voodoo potion helped me in ways no one could have predicted."

"But I thought you said the potion was a disaster; that it made the priest fall madly in love with you."

"But it's only on account of the voodoo potion that we met today. It's the only reason why we're here tonight."

"Yes, but let's not forget the volcano had something to do with it as well," said Rémy. "Anyway, if we hadn't bumped into each other, you'd be home in bed and infinitely much safer."

"Who says I want to be safe?" she said with womanly guile.

Rémy's eyebrows shot up. "I should have known by the way you tackled that mountain that you were no ordinary young lady. You have the pluck of a Legionnaire, but don't let it get to your head. First you insist on climbing an erupting volcano, then you stare down a pit viper, and then you take on an infamous voodoo witch doctor. It seems as if you have no intention of living a safe life."

"What about you?" she said. "Didn't you risk your life today by saving a drowning woman? That took no small dose of courage."

"I was in desperate need of a good bath," he said.

"Have you always had such a dry sense of humor?" she said, staring into his eyes.

"No. In my younger years, they say I was quite funny."

"I would have thought the life of a career soldier would have turned you into a hardened, callous individual. But you're not like that at all."

"I'm a realist, Emilie. I learned that bravery gets you nothing but hurt. But when I looked into that woman's eyes, I knew I had to do everything possible to save her life. I figured she needed a second chance."

"Maybe you need one as well," she said.

All at once they stopped dancing. Rémy pulled her close and kissed her. Emilie melted into his embrace, caressing his head and neck, forgetting all her problems and worries. It was only until this moment that she realized how much she longed for him.

"You are lovely," he said, caressing her face. "But I suppose many men have told you that."

"You are the first," she said. "The first man I've ever loved."

He stared in her eyes and said nothing. She laid her head against his chest, and they continued dancing until the early-morning hours. Then, when all was quiet, they headed out into the night, the laughter and music still ringing in their ears.

Later, while Emilie lay in her room, she listened to the drumming of the raindrops on the tin roof. The wind howled and beat against the shutters. She worried that the river would still be raging in the morning. Memories of the day flashed in her mind. Rémy's voice, his eyes, and his strong embrace had utterly captivated her.

Later, after the music died away, he had brought her back to the inn and kissed her in a hidden alcove. He spoke words of love that filled her with desire. The feelings he awakened in her came as suddenly as a West Indian hurricane, raging and powerful yet surprisingly peaceful. Rémy was so different from Lucien. He was a soldier, a leader of men, but above all, a gentleman. As she lay in bed, all she saw was Rémy's face until sleep eventually took her.

Chapter 22

Wednesday, April 30

The next morning Emilie rode her carriage down rue Bouchers toward rivière Roxelane. When she arrived at the river, she was surprised to see that the floodwaters had actually receded. There was no hint of the raging flood from the previous day, and no reminder of the innocent lives lost aside from the tolling of the church bells. The only evidence that something was amiss was a light sprinkling of ash that had fallen over Saint-Pierre early in the morning, which gave the town a wintry look. A few brave souls were out on the water in skiffs searching for the missing women, but most people had given up hope of finding them. As Emilie crossed the river, a procession of mourners dressed in black was heading to church for the funeral mass, but there was no carriage and no bodies. From what she heard from the innkeeper, they had not recovered a single body.

When Emilie returned to Domaine Solitude, Abbé Morel was waiting for her on the front porch. As soon as she approached, he jumped to his feet and began waving his arms. She waved back, relieved to see that he was improving. But when she looked around, she was shocked to see the entire plantation was coated in a layer of ash. There were mounds of it on the roofs, the paths, and the fields. Some of the workers were brushing it off their shoulders and shaking it off their bakouas, but most of them continued harvesting nevertheless. Emilie felt a crushing guilt that during her brief interlude in Saint-Pierre, she had neglected her beloved cousin.

As soon as she got close enough, her spirits lifted. Abbé Morel seemed to come alive at the sight of her. He didn't look sick as much as he looked *lovesick*. By all appearances, the voodoo potion had not physically harmed Abbé Morel, but he was still deeply in love with her. Her only hope now was that the antidote in her pocket would free him of this tragic love. It was her last chance to make things right again.

She ran up to the porch and flung herself in Abbé Morel's arms.

"Tonton Abbé, I've missed you so much," she said.

"Emilie, where have you been? I've been worried sick about you."

"Please forgive me," she said. "But I was forced to spend the night in town because of the floods. Rivière Roxelane turned into a raging torrent, sweeping several washerwomen out to sea. Men in canoes went out looking for them, but they disappeared beneath the waves. The river didn't recede until this morning."

"Good Lord! What's to become of us?" he said. "Thank goodness you're safe. The forces of nature seem to be rising up against us. Those poor, poor women!"

"Did you read what Léon Sully wrote in *Les Antilles* this morning?" She handed him the newspaper.

> *If April has not been comic, it has been doubly tragic. We have seen two volcanic eruptions, one in people's minds and the other at Mount Pelée; one electoral, the other physical; one of speeches, propaganda, rum, money and voting papers, and the other of smoke and ashes. One of them is still not finished, because the electoral volcano is still smoking and will not be extinguished for another 12 days. The other is still going on, for our Pelée is still active, and will put its fires out we know not when. We don't know what the result will be in either case. Let us hope that it will be nothing bad.*

"Rubbish!" said Abbé Morel, throwing the paper down in disgust. "He seems to think the ash and tremors are some comical April fool's joke. How many people have to die before they take it seriously?" He took a small Bible from his pocket, opened it up to a certain passage, and read, "Hear my prayer, oh Lord, and let my cry come unto thee. Do not hide your face from me in my hour of distress. Turn your ear to me and when I call, answer me quickly. For my days vanish like smoke. My bones burn like glowing embers."

Emilie shivered. "What is that?"

"Psalm 102, the one we say in times of grave misfortune."

She rubbed her shoulders. "It sounds like a chilling prophecy. I feel that something terrible is in store for us."

Abbé Morel tousled her hair. "Emilie, we must have faith. We must pray for deliverance."

She took his hands and kissed them with great tenderness. "You'll be happy to know I brought you some medicine from Saint-Pierre. The chemist said it should make you feel better. Take it, and I guarantee you'll be like a new man." She laid a hand on his forehead and was relieved to see he was not burning up with fever, but she spied a faint blush creeping across his cheeks. She jerked her hand away and attempted to pull him inside, but Abbé Morel grabbed her hand and wheeled her around. "My dear, I just want you to know that no matter what happens, I love you dearly. I have a strange feeling the end is near, but I have no regrets. Whatever happens, I don't want you to worry about me. I'm prepared to accept whatever fate has in store. Perhaps it's good that I retired from my post in Carriacou. I believe it was Providence that brought me back here to you."

"Of course it was," said Emilie, hugging him. "Not because you're going to die, but so that you can be near to your family. When you were gone, my life was so empty. I missed you so much."

Abbé Morel assumed a wistful look. "And to think I wasted all those years chasing my vanity and pride while I was overlooking the one thing that truly meant the most to me." He sighed. "I was blind to not realize that what I most needed was right here all along."

"Don't speak like that, Tonton Abbé," she said in an admonishing tone. "You were serving your flock on an impoverished island. That is the noblest endeavor. And now you're needed here in Saint-Pierre. I've heard the prisoners cry out for you. You've brought many of them back to the faith."

"My only wish is to serve them fully. But right now my mind is in a state of turmoil."

"You'll feel better after you take the medicine. Go upstairs and lie down. I'll bring it to you shortly."

"Thank you, but I'm not sure I want to be cured."

She led Abbé Morel inside and asked a servant to take him upstairs to his room. She had just removed her shawl and hung up her straw hat when the room began to shake. The bottles in the liquor cabinet rattled, and the chandelier swayed ominously. A glass fell off the table and shattered on the floor. The servants rushed outside in a panic and began crossing themselves. Just then Mme Dujon and Da Rosette came rushing downstairs with panicked looks on their faces.

"Emilie, where have you been?" said her mother in an admonishing tone. "We were worried sick about you. Your father was frantic."

"I'm sorry, Maman; I was trapped in Saint-Pierre on account of the flood. This horrible volcano! When will it ever end?"

"Doudou, you must stay home," said Da Rosette.

"Where's Papa?" said Emilie, looking around.

"Out in the fields," said her mother. "A whole slew of workers ran away on account of the tremors. We're falling farther and farther behind schedule. I fear this will not end well . . ."

As soon as they started cleaning up, the tremors stopped. The only remnants were the shards of broken glass on the floor and the worried looks on everyone's faces. Da Rosette picked up a broom and started sweeping up the glass, while Emilie ran outside to the kitchen to fetch a glass of tea for Abbé Morel. Clutching the tea and the vial, she hurried upstairs to the priest's room. She poured the contents of the vial into the tea and then bade Abbé Morel to drink it.

"Here, take this," she said. "It will make you feel better. I promise."

He sat up in bed and took the glass. "Thank you, Emilie. You know, I fear all this trembling is a warning from heaven that the people of Saint-Pierre should repent."

"Why do you say that?"

"Last Carnival something unusual happened," he said, sipping the tea. "Late one night I left the rectory and followed the sound of drumbeats to rue Victor Hugo. The crowd was thick. I stood among them for quite some time as bottles of rum were passed around and people laughed and sang and clapped their hands in merriment. There was much carousing. And then the usual group of devils began parading down the street, all dressed in red with shiny horns and demonic faces. They were dancing and twisting and turning their bodies in an unholy fashion. My heart started pounding. One of them in particular stood out from the crowd—it was Papa Djab himself. His eyes were like yellow orbs, his mouth like a grinning skeleton. He thrashed his arms and twisted his body in an ungodly manner, like a demon straight from hell."

"What happened next?" she said.

"Papa Djab called out to his followers and led them up the stairs to the cathedral. I suspected something devilish was up, so I followed them, making sure to keep to the shadows. Then, before my eyes, he committed a sacrilege by throwing ashes into the holy water basin! I cried out in shock, but my voice was drowned out by the revelers. Another group had lifted up the Virgin Mary's skirt. I was beside myself. They shrieked and howled at this blasphemous display, and then they fled the church and ran outside to rejoin the parade as it continued marching down the street. Frightened out of my life, I tried to clean out the basin, but I felt that a great sin had been committed, a sin for which the whole city would suffer, a sin that even I could not prevent. Later, when the bishop found out what had happened, he raised an outcry, promising the scoundrels that they would all roast in hell for what they had done. A chill went through the cathedral, as if the entire assembly was struck dumb. In his booming voice he ordered the sinners to repent immediately. He said, 'He who throws cold stones will receive hot stones.' A hush went through the crowd, me included."

"How terrible!" said Emilie. "It seems like a shocking premonition. I wonder how this all will end. Sometimes I have bad dreams about it."

"I only pray that no harm comes to you," said Abbé Morel. "Your soul is pure and unblemished."

But Emilie felt weak in the knees. She was overcome with nausea for having visited the voodoo witch doctor. If Abbé Morel ever found out, she would be mortified. She could not face losing his respect. How much longer could she keep this terrible secret?

Abbé Morel finished drinking the tea in one shot. Lying back against the pillow, a beatific glow came over his face, and he said, "Thank you, Emilie. If that medicine was my punishment for all my worldly sins, then I'm guaranteed a place in the heavenly kingdom."

With trembling hands, Emilie took the cup and saucer and placed them on a side table.

"Just try to rest now," she said. "When you wake up, I hope you'll be better."

Later, as they played a game of whist, Abbé Morel seemed like a changed man. The color returned to his cheeks and he had renewed vigor, but a closer look showed dullness in his eyes. His eyes became dazed and unfocused, and he barely responded when spoken to. He looked like a man who was present in body but not in spirit. Soon he fell into a deep sleep. Emilie caressed his hand and then left his room, heartbroken.

As she lay in bed that night, Emilie's body was soaked with sweat. She tossed and turned in the hot, humid air, listening to the croaking and chirping of the insects. They seemed to be mocking her, admonishing her. She was filled with a growing fear that her life was about to spin out of control.

Chapter 23

Thursday, May 1

The next morning brought a slight improvement in Abbé Morel's appearance. He sat up in bed reading his Bible, sipping a little tea, but he ate almost nothing and spoke very little. Emilie checked on him from time to time, and he would look at her longingly in return, but his eyes had lost their spark, as if his soul was slowly dying. Her heart ached for her Tonton Abbé, but there was little more she could do.

There was also a slight improvement in the countryside. The rain had washed away most of the volcanic dust, and the workers were reporting that Saint-Pierre gleamed in the sunshine. The workers floated in between the cocoa trees, their bakouas visible above the dark green leaves, their chatter more cheerful and hopeful. Even Georges Dujon seemed to be in better spirits. He helped load sacks of cocoa beans into the warehouse, where they would wait until they were transported to the dock the following week. It looked as if their money problems would soon be over.

Later, after Emilie returned from the drying shack, two letters had arrived for her. One was from Maurice, who reported that he was concerned about the constant rumbling from the volcano. He told them he felt better and wanted to return home as soon as possible.

The other letter bore unfamiliar handwriting.

She tore it open and was surprised to see that it was from Lieutenant Rémy. She cradled the letter in her hands and drank in every word. He told of how much he had enjoyed their evening together in Saint-Pierre, and he wanted to invite her to dine with him that evening in the Hôtel Intendance if the idea was not displeasing to her. Emilie's heart raced at the prospect. Ever since their impromptu meeting in Saint-Pierre, she couldn't stop thinking about him. But to meet him again in public entailed enormous risk. The hotel's dining room was frequented by many people from high society who would recognize her. How could she find a way to keep the matter from reaching Lucien's ears?

While she read the letter, something in her demeanor drew the curiosity of her mother and Da Rosette, who was hovering near the piano, pretending to be dusting it.

"Who's the letter from?" said her mother.

"It's from Maurice," said Emilie with nonchalance. "He says he wants to come home."

"Not that letter; the other one," said her mother, inching closer.

"Oh . . . that's from Lucien," said Emilie, forcing a smile. "He's inviting me to dine with him this evening at the Hôtel Intendance."

Her mother beamed. "Wonderful! I'm so happy he's willing to overlook your behavior and patch things up. He's such a gentleman. You'd better hurry and get ready."

Emilie felt her stomach churning. She placed the letter in her pocket and retreated to the safety of her room, overcome with guilt for having lied again.

Later, as she was seated at her mahogany vanity table brushing her hair, Da Rosette knocked on the door and entered. The elderly woman hobbled into the room wearing a look reserved for petty thieves and public drunkards, her muslin dress brushing against Emilie in silent admonition.

"Doudou, where are you going tonight?" said Da Rosette, eyeing her suspiciously.

"I'm having dinner with Lucien."

"Tell me the truth."

Emilie gave her a sly half look but continued brushing her hair. "That is the truth. Why are you being so mistrustful lately?"

"Don't give me that cock-and-bull story," said Da Rosette. "I know you're not going to meet Lucien tonight."

Emilie eyed her sharply. "Why do you say that?"

"Because I know when you're lying."

Emilie feigned indignation. "I'm not lying!"

"I know you better than anyone else," said the old woman with a reproving look. "I saw the look on your face when you read the letter. I saw the way your eyes lit up. I saw how you bounded up the stairs as if you were the Empress Josephine waiting for her Napoleon." She crossed her arms and raised an admonishing eyebrow. "You were never like that for Lucien. The last time he came to visit, you looked as if you were facing a firing squad. So don't tell me that nonsense that you are going to meet Lucien tonight. Tell me the truth."

Emilie put the brush down. *"Zaffè cabritt, pas zaffè mouton.* What the goat does is not the sheep's business."

Da Rosette grabbed her arm. "Doudou, in this house what the goat does *is* the sheep's business. *You* are my business. Now tell me the truth."

Emilie's cheeks flamed. "Why are you always so suspicious? Everywhere I go, you spy on me; you watch everything I do. You probably even read my letters. Very well, if you must know the truth, I'll tell you, but you must promise not to tell Maman and Papa. I'm meeting someone tonight."

Da Rosette's eyes narrowed. "I know that but *who?*"

"An officer from the garrison." Da Rosette sucked in her breath. "Do you remember those two soldiers who came here with Professor Landes? It's the dark-haired officer with the moustache."

Da Rosette looked horrified. "Bon Dieu, when Lucien finds out, he'll kill that innocent man, and he may turn his pistol on you as well. He's more jealous than an old Spaniard with a wife of eighteen. You'd better not let him catch you with him."

"The officer carries a revolver and can defend his own life. As for me, I'm not afraid of Lucien. I'm not his slave. I don't love him, and I have no intention of marrying him."

"Cocotte, do not talk like that!" said Da Rosette, eyes blazing. "It brings bad luck. *Crabe pas mâché, li pas gras;—li mâche touop, et li tombé dans la chôdiér.* The crab that walks around too much falls into the pot!"

"Doudou-Da, stop talking like that. It's old superstitious nonsense. I want to be happy. I want to be free to marry the man I love."

Da Rosette clutched her necklace of gold beads. "Doudou, I think you do not love me anymore. Aye! You give me so much pain . . . so much grief!"

Emilie grasped the old woman's arms. "Don't say that. You know it's not true! You know I love you, but I don't want superstitions and voodoo curses to haunt me all my life. And I don't want Lucien to haunt me all my life either. I must be free of him, or I will surely die."

Da Rosette shook her head. "No, cocotte, you do not love me one bit! If you loved me, you would not say these things. You would marry the sugar planter and be his adoring wife. To spurn him is to make a pact with the devil."

Emilie shook her head. "I can't marry Lucien. I'm sorry, I just can't . . ."

"Doudou, you must stop seeing that soldier, or you will both wind up dead."

"If I marry Lucien, I will surely die. Oh, it will be a slow death for sure, but the end is the same: misery and despair. A slow death that will suck all the life out of me—all my hopes and dreams. Do you want to see me end up like that? A soulless, lifeless zombie trapped in a loveless marriage? Haven't you seen women who end up with men like that? They are miserable and pray for death. Perhaps they are better off dead."

"Don't talk like that," said Da Rosette. "You'll bring an evil eye! And don't think you can cross the Monplaisir family and get away with it. Nobody makes a fool out of them. Lucien is a dangerous man. I know he loves you, but if you cross him, he will turn his gun on you."

Emilie stared at her nanny, but her throat was too dry to speak.

A few hours later, after Emilie had left for Saint-Pierre and her parents had settled down for the evening, there was a sharp knock on the door. A servant ran to answer it and announced that M. Lucien Monplaisir had come to pay an unexpected visit.

After giving each other a quizzical look, her parents went to greet their future son-in-law in the foyer. Slightly breathless, they found him with a look of great expectation on his face.

"Lucien, to what do we owe this pleasure?" said Georges. "I thought you were having dinner in town tonight."

"I apologize for the inconvenience, but I had to see Emilie. May I speak to her for a minute? It's urgent."

Mme Dujon looked perplexed. "But I thought . . ."

Lucien produced a jewelry box. "I bought this for Emilie. Do you think she'll like it?"

Georges and his wife exchanged a worried glance.

"Oh dear, it's beautiful," said Mme Dujon, gaping at the glittering gold bracelet.

"There must be some mistake . . ." said Georges, hemming and hawing. "I thought you had gone to meet her in town."

Lucien looked surprised. "In town? What are you talking about?"

Mme Dujon cleared her throat. "We were under the impression you had invited her to dine with you at the Hôtel Intendance at seven o'clock tonight."

Lucien's brow furrowed. "Dinner at the Hôtel Intendance?"

"I saw the letter myself," said Mme Dujon. "Perhaps you meant some other night? She seemed very excited. She left about an hour ago."

A shadow fell across Lucien's face.

"Ah yes . . . how forgetful of me," he said, his face turning pale. "Please excuse the intrusion. I must make haste. Don't want to keep her waiting."

Lucien thrust the jewelry box into his jacket pocket and stormed out of the house.

As he slammed the door shut, Mme and M. Dujon looked at each other with eyes full of panic.

Chapter 24

The ride to Saint-Pierre was exhilarating. Emilie's heart raced as the horse trotted down the coastal road past fields of sugarcane and bananas, towering coconut palms, and barefooted laborers with baskets piled high on their heads. She gazed out to sea. The sun was dipping low on the horizon, casting shimmering rays that danced like sparks of fire on the water. The air was cooler, smelling faintly of the sea. Overhead, a bird cried out and disappeared in a splash of foam. Many times she thought about turning back, but each time she resigned herself to press onward. She would not shy away from her destiny, whatever it was.

She crossed the bridge over rivière Roxelane and arrived at the Hôtel Intendance. After leaving the carriage at the stable, she hurried through the courtyard and up the main steps, breathless and trembling with excitement.

The lobby was bright and cheerful. Tropical flowers peeked out of colorful vases. Soft piano music was playing, and the voices of the guests added to the exciting atmosphere. She wended her way through the lobby and stopped short when she spotted Rémy. He was pacing back and forth with an air of great seriousness. He looked freshly scrubbed and was wearing his navy tunic and pith helmet, and his boots were polished to a brilliant shine, while slung across his shoulder was his service revolver. She watched him for several minutes, aware of the beating of her heart. When he looked up suddenly, their eyes met. Before either one could speak, Rémy stepped forward to greet her.

"Bonsoir, Mademoiselle Emilie, you look charming. Just like the day we first met." He bowed slightly and kissed her hand. "I was worried you wouldn't come. I hope my invitation did not offend you."

"Not in the least," she said, smiling. "I was delighted to receive your letter. And quite the contrary, I feel honored by your invitation."

Rémy's face brightened. "I wanted very much to speak to you again. I enjoyed your company so much the other day that I felt I had to see you again. I enjoyed our time on Mount Pelée immensely. I have very pleasant memories of that day."

Emilie laughed. "I think your memory is playing tricks on you, Lieutenant Rémy. If I remember correctly, I fell in the mud more times than I care to remember. I think there was even mud inside my boots."

"You speak like a true soldier," he said, "for whom no sacrifice is too great. Always willing to sacrifice his life for la Mère Patrie, like Napoleon, whose only wish was to serve in the army with éclat and, if necessary, die the glorious death of a citizen soldier."

"You're quite amusing, Lieutenant," she said.

"Please call me by my given name of Denis. After completing such a dangerous mission together, I feel as though we are comrades in arms."

Emilie laughed in spite of herself. All her fears and worries were melting away. She felt so comfortable and natural with Rémy that Lucien was becoming just a distant memory.

Rémy took her arm. "Come; let's sit and get more acquainted, shall we?"

He led her to the dining room with its tiled floor, potted palms, and crystal chandeliers. Emilie scanned the room. There was an assortment of prominent members of society, including merchants and politicians she knew from the newspapers. She tried to keep her face averted, although she noticed several of them eyeing her. The maître d' showed them to a corner table with a white linen tablecloth and a flickering candle. Rémy ordered a bottle of champagne, and after the waiter popped the cork, he lifted his glass in a toast.

"To your health," he said, studying her with his blue eyes.

"Cheers," she said.

They clinked glasses and drank.

Emilie took a sip and put her glass down. "Denis, I have something to confess. I hope you'll forgive me, but I told my parents I was meeting Lucien tonight. I didn't want to arouse any suspicion about where I was going. I hope you don't mind the secrecy."

"I understand completely," he said. "This shall be our little secret, but how long do you think you can keep it up? Eventually you will have to tell your father the truth. And Lucien is bound to find out. Anyone here who may recognize you could inform him within a matter of hours. There could be trouble. I just thought I'd warn you."

Emilie nodded, grim-faced. "I'm aware of that. I took a tremendous risk in coming tonight. But I'm glad I did. You see, I've tried every way possible to end my engagement and convince my parents that I can't marry Lucien, but they refuse to listen. They see this marriage as a last chance to save the plantation and their falling social status. You see, we're practically penniless. Nothing in the world will change their minds."

"What do you propose to do about it?" he asked, studying her face over the flickering candle.

"I don't have a clue," she said. "Everything I tried has failed, including voodoo, which I'm ashamed to admit."

Rémy took her hand in his. "No need to be ashamed. I understand why you did it. If I was in your situation, I probably would have done the same. Back in Africa they have a saying: 'If you marry a monkey for his wealth, the money goes, and the monkey remains as is.'"

"So you understand my situation perfectly," she said, gazing into his eyes. "You're quite charming, Denis. Tell me something about yourself. You're a mystery to me."

"What would you like to know?" he said.

"Like you say, it's always best to start at the beginning."

Rémy poured himself another drink. "I think I'll need a dose of liquid courage to answer that one. Not much escapes your scrutiny. You're a very inquisitive young lady."

"It's because I observe everything. For instance, I noticed how you slipped the maître d' money for this choice corner seat."

Rémy lowered his voice. "I had a very good reason for that. I wanted to sit as far away as possible from that captain over there. Do you see the officer with the deep-set eyes, pockmarked skin, and rigid bearing? That's Captain Renoult. In my opinion he's no credit to his regiment. He's angry, violent, and given to drunkenness. I've seen him making threats against junior officers. There's no place in the army for a guy like that. He's bad for camaraderie."

"Has he threatened you?"

"I mostly stay out of his way," said Rémy.

"He looks like an alligator," said Emilie.

"An alligator is more predictable," said Rémy.

"Denis, please don't think me too forward, but there's something I wish to know. Have you ever been in love before?"

He took another sip of champagne and said, "I'm deeply in love with the army, although I can't say she loves me back."

"I meant with a woman."

"Don't knock the army; she can be a jealous lover. She hates it when other women try to steal her men away. She's vengeful, spiteful, and entirely without mercy. She'll throw a starry-eyed soldier into jail if he should dare switch allegiance. She demands complete fidelity. So I hope you'll understand if I try to avoid getting on her bad side. I honor her as required by saluting my commanding officers and pledging eternal devotion, but when I lie down at night, I never tell her what's in my heart. Some things must remain secret."

"You're teasing me."

"Actually, I'm quite serious," he said with gravity. "You see, I'm married to the army. I've sworn allegiance to la Mère Patrie, and I'm prepared to lay down my life for her. Beyond that there's not much more to tell."

"Have you never been in love with a real woman?"

"There may have been one or two in the past, but that's all over now. All I want is to serve my country to the best of my ability with whatever time I have left. That is the highest form of love in my opinion. Is that a fair answer to your question?"

She cocked her head to the side and regarded him boldly. "Don't you want more out of life?"

"Now you're wading into treacherous waters," he said, assuming a philosophical look. "My dear girl, I've learned to live moment by moment and ask as little from life as possible. It's impossible to predict the future. Who knows what tomorrow will bring? So let's make the most of the present, shall we? My only regret is that I was exiled from my regiment in Africa. At that moment I knew what it was like when a woman slaps your face in a fit of jealousy. The army can be a cold and vicious lover. And to me she was merciless. I had grown quite fond of Africa and her people. To the chief of the Bambara, I was almost like a son . . ." His voice broke, and he gazed off in the distance.

"Why did you leave Africa?"

"Perhaps it's best we don't talk about it," he said.

"Please, I want to know everything about you—the good, the bad, and the in-between. I'm not afraid of the truth."

Rémy reached out and touched her cheek. "Emilie, you are unlike any person I have ever known. I hold you very dear to my heart for many reasons. Your love, trust, and support are unsurpassed." He finished his drink in one gulp. "Well, since we've come this far, I suppose there's no turning back. During my last mission, the one I told you about before, I discovered that a fellow officer was mistreating his soldier-servant, an *ordonnance*. I reported it to our commanding officer, and when he interrogated the *ordonnance*, he refused to implicate the officer. I suppose he was frightened for his life. The officer in question was a vicious brute. The next thing I know, I was accused of filing false charges. After a court-martial, I was demoted in rank and sent into exile. My superiors warned me that any further misconduct on my part would get me shipped off to the penal colony in French Guiana, which is tantamount to a death sentence."

"Why didn't they believe you?"

"It was my word against his, and the *ordonnance* refused to testify, and that, my dear, is the whole sordid affair."

"But you did an honorable thing. You tried to save a man's life."

"Yes, but I disgraced myself in the process and ruined my career." Rémy's voice tapered off, drowned out by the voices in the restaurant. "I try not to think about it too much. It doesn't matter anyway. At least here the rum is cheap and plentiful. The only thing I don't care for is the politics."

Emilie laughed. "You'll have to get used to it. Mudslinging is almost a national sport in the West Indies. I suppose you've seen all those scandalous posters covering the walls."

"They leave little to the imagination." He grinned.

"Anyway, you have more important matters to attend to, even more important than drinking yourself into oblivion. You have to convince the governor to evacuate the people before the volcano erupts."

"That will be an uphill battle."

"Why?"

Rémy's face turned serious. "Because the governor is dead set against it. I was in a meeting with him last Monday right here in this hotel with Professor Landes and several other officials. Based on my observations, I believe he thinks the runoff election has top priority over the volcano. He fears creating a panic, so he prefers to sweep the whole business under the carpet. Apparently the election has serious ramifications for the business community and the landowners. The men in charge want the Progressives to win at all costs. I suspect the governor only sent us as a matter of formality. I don't think he ever had any intention of evacuating Saint-Pierre."

"You can't be serious."

"I'm dead serious," he said. "But don't let it get out. I'm telling you in strictest confidence. If the people find out the governor is deliberately withholding information about the volcano, it could create a panic."

"What are you going to do about it?"

"Right now I don't have a plan. As a soldier, I'm just following orders."

"So they intend to do nothing—just sweep everything under the carpet. But surely if you told them your suspicions, they would listen—"

Rémy shook his head. "It's not that simple. There are powerful political headwinds. During our meeting, the only subject that seemed to concern the governor was the issue of separation of church and state. When confronted with the danger from the volcano, he cried out, 'Gentlemen, we must get our priorities straight! The economy is far more important than the rumbling volcano.' I looked at Professor Landes, and we both fell silent, thinking it better that we keep our concerns to ourselves rather than risk repercussions from interfering in their precious election."

"It's clear he doesn't understand how serious the matter is," said Emilie.

"He understands what he wants to understand. I'm no politician, but he seemed more interested in appeasing M. Decrais at the Colonial Office than protecting the civilians. I'm a simple artillery officer, so I can't say for certain when and if the volcano will erupt; only that it seems likely. What am I basing it on—fear? That's hardly scientific now, is it?"

Emilie fell silent for a moment. "Perhaps M. Mirville was right when he said the worst was over. Perhaps we are exaggerating the danger."

Rémy looked at her wryly. "And if he's wrong? Can we afford to take that chance? But let's not talk about that now. We have a few precious minutes together, so let's not spoil it. Do you know how often I think about that trip up the mountain? Do you know, that's the first truly enjoyable day I've had in months, years even."

"And I suppose it was fun seeing me covered in all that ash and mud."

Rémy held her hand tight. "I was moved in ways I cannot explain. I see you as a product of this unspoiled tropical world, as beautiful and natural as the balisier flowers and the hummingbirds. Sometimes I feel like Degas in Tahiti. To me you're more fascinating than those Tahitian girls he painted."

Emilie's cheeks flushed. "Look, you've got me blushing."

"Forgive me for my candor," he said. "I realize you belong to another man. I can't offer you the life he can, not on my salary. Perhaps you should marry M. Monplaisir. He'll keep you in grand style with a villa and servants and annual shopping trips to Paris. You'll lack for nothing. Maybe he'll even land a seat in the National Assembly or the governor's mansion. You would like that, wouldn't you?"

"I'm not in love with Lucien."

"Then, Emilie, you indeed have a serious problem. Here, let's have more champagne. It will help us to drink away our sorrows. I'm not needed at the garrison tonight."

Emilie was taken aback. "Pardon me?"

"Forgive me; I didn't mean that," he said hastily. "I'm a gentleman, after all. I was referring to champagne's reputed medicinal qualities. It's been known to heal many broken hearts. If you feel half of what I feel, you'll need a few bottles to forget your worries."

Emilie sipped her champagne and watched as he drank. She was so moved by Rémy's heartfelt words that she sat motionless for a few minutes, feeling an intense longing that enveloped her in warmth. He took her hand in his, pulled her close, and whispered words in her ear that she'd never expected to hear. She felt her resolve slipping away. Her heart pounded with desire. As they laughed and chatted, a sullen figure entered the dining room, a tall man with a scowling face, dark hair, broad shoulders, and a heavy gait that Emilie knew too well. He made his way through the dining room, shoving his brooding form past the waiters until he reached the table where Emilie and Rémy sat, and then he came to an abrupt halt.

Lucien stood before them, his face a mask of rage.

"What the devil's going on here?" he said.

Emilie paled. "Lucien, what are you doing here?"

"I should ask you the same thing," he said, visibly trembling. "Who is this man?"

Rémy stood up. "My name is Lt. Denis Rémy of the Fourth Regiment at Fort Saint-Pierre. How do you do?"

Rémy held out his hand, but Lucien refused to shake it.

"I don't care who you are," said Lucien with derision. "What are you doing with my fiancée?"

"As you can see, we are having dinner."

"Not anymore." Lucien grabbed Emilie's hand. "She's coming with me."

Emilie struggled to free herself, but Lucien held her with an iron grip.

"Lucien, stop!" she said, glancing around nervously. "People are watching!"

Lucien pulled her out of her seat. "I said we're going. We'll discuss this later."

Rémy laid a hand on Lucien's shoulder. "The lady said she doesn't want to go with you."

Lucien shoved Rémy away. "Don't touch me. She's coming with me. You have no business with her."

"M. Monplaisir, let her go, or I shall have to use force."

Struggling, Emilie said, "Lucien, you're embarrassing me in front of all these people. We were only having a simple dinner."

"You should have thought of that before you agreed to meet this scoundrel. I know his type—a useless piece of rubbish, the kind the Colonial Office is always trying to pawn off on us. I see them congregating on rue Bouillé, starting fights and causing trouble."

Rémy stepped forward and held on to Emilie. "Leave the lady alone, or I shall have to—"

Before Rémy could finish, Lucien punched him in the jaw. Rémy staggered backward and then returned the punch, knocking Lucien sideways, where he landed on a table. The dishes crashed to the floor, causing the other patrons to shriek with fright. The waiters moved in, circling the combatants. Furious, Lucien lunged at Rémy's throat with murderous intent, but the older man was too quick and blocked his arm. He struck Lucien across the face, hurling him to the floor, covered with spilled cutlery and broken plates. By now pandemonium broke out, as the two men were locked in combat. The maître d' raced toward them, calling for the gendarmes as silverware and plates crashed to the floor. And then, to Emilie's horror, Lucien sprang at Rémy, and they ended up in a heap on the floor, fists flying as they pounded each other. Suddenly Lucien grabbed a bottle and smashed it on Rémy's head, causing the officer to collapse in a heap, blood dripping from a cut on his head. Staggering to his feet, Lucien grabbed Emilie by the arm and dragged her out of the hotel.

As they fled past the startled onlookers, Emilie struggled to free herself.

"Let me go!" she screamed. "You're an animal. You have no right to spy on me!"

"I have every right to spy on you," said Lucien, seething with anger. "You lied to me; you lied to your parents, and you acted like a tart, sneaking off with another man. I caught you red-handed. How could you do this to me? I'll be the laughingstock of tomorrow's newspapers. I saw Marius Hurard in the cafe."

He led her to his carriage and opened the door in a huff. "This will teach you not to humiliate me in public!" Seething with anger, Lucien slapped her across the face and shoved her into the carriage. Emilie screamed, and the carriage driver tried to intervene, but Lucien ordered him to leave her alone. She clawed at Lucien's face, but he was too quick, and he blocked her.

"How dare you?" she said. "And you call yourself a gentleman?"

"And you call yourself a lady?" he said with derision. "I can only guess as to what else you've been lying about. I'll soon get to the bottom of it. You're lucky I caught on to the affair early enough before you got yourself into real trouble."

"What I do is none of your business. You don't own me."

"It's every bit my business," he said, seizing her with his iron grip. "You're my fiancée, and I intend to make that scoundrel pay for what he's done. If I catch him near you again, I'll shoot him, and you'll pay for it as well."

Emilie's face turned white. "You wouldn't dare."

"It would be my pleasure to blow that bastard's brains out. Of course, under the circumstances, the court would show me every leniency. Dozens of people saw you with him tonight. The trial would be a mere formality."

"You would resort to murder?" said Emilie. "Like a savage?"

"No court in the civilized world would convict a man of murder if he could prove he was defending his honor. The law is on my side."

"Not entirely," said Emilie in an icy tone. "First a defendant has to prove he has any honor worth defending, which you obviously don't."

"And what about you, my darling?" said Lucien with a sneer. "Did you behave like an honorable lady tonight?"

Emilie recoiled at Lucien's insult. She had never seen him so filled with rage. She was suddenly petrified.

As the carriage trundled through the darkened cobblestoned streets, Lucien lit a cigarette and drummed his fingers on the windowsill. He continued to rant and rave, flicking his ashes in a show of fury. Emilie turned her face away and tried to stifle the tears, but it was impossible. She endured his curses, his raging, and his threats, wishing the ground would open up and swallow her whole to end her nightmare. She closed her eyes, but she could not squeeze back the tears of frustration at the idea of spending her life with this intolerably abusive man. Life with Lucien was a long, slow, torturous agony. The brief interlude she had spent with Rémy had shown her there was happiness to be found in this world, and maybe, just maybe, one day it could be hers. Or maybe I'm deluding myself, she thought. Maybe my fate is to spend the rest of my life with Lucien in sorrow and misery. The thought sent a shiver up her spine. A sob escaped her throat. When she glanced over at Lucien and saw him fingering his revolver, terror seized her.

Chapter 25

Friday, May 2

The next morning began with a violent, driving thunderstorm. Rain pelted the island with a vengeance, coating every surface with wet volcanic ash that muddied the streets, the buildings, and all the fields with an ugly gray film. In the northern district of Saint-Pierre, several inches of wet, cementlike paste accumulated over every surface. In the distance, a distinct rumbling noise could be heard that was deeper and louder than before.

Cattle and horses began to keel over from hunger and thirst from the contaminated water. Ash and cinders coated everything. Rats scurried through the gutters looking like white mice, their fur covered in a fine, powdery ash. Every now and then, shutters would fling open as worried citizens peered out, troubled by the sight of volcanic debris that had begun to collect on the ground. In their eyes was a deep sense of foreboding.

Emilie awoke with a pounding headache and a sense of impending doom. Memories of the previous night flashed through her mind, followed by pangs of mortification and guilt. The shock on the diners' faces, the look of betrayal on her parents' faces, the horrible end to the evening was a crushing blow. When Lucien had dragged her into the house screaming like a madman that she had betrayed him with another man, her parents looked stricken. Her mother's face turned white, and her father looked as if he'd been slapped in public. Their shock and horror were palpable. Emilie was so heartbroken and humiliated, she was filled with a blind rage toward Lucien. And when she saw the pain he caused Da Rosette by dashing all her hopes while all Emilie could do was stand by helplessly, her soul was crushed. When the old woman crossed herself and whispered a prayer, Emilie's heart broke. She ran upstairs to her room, where she passed the night tossing and turning, hating herself for causing everyone so much pain. She was overcome with worry, fearing that Lucien would turn his vengeance on Rémy. That fear sent paralyzing waves throughout her body, leaving her frantic and numb.

The next morning when she woke, the first thought that popped into her mind was that she had lost the respect and love of her beloved nanny. The next thought was that she would never see Rémy again. Both notions gave her tremendous pain. And there was the additional likelihood that Lucien would use her betrayal as an excuse to abuse her for the rest of her life. She had seen the way he abused his servants with a callous eye and a cruel mouth. He ordered them around like slaves, tormenting them with his sarcasm and arrogance. He used his position to torment anyone he considered beneath him. And now he would certainly consider Emilie beneath him—indeed, beneath contempt. She shuddered. The queasiness in her stomach would not go away. In fact, it was getting worse. When she could no longer stand it, she dashed for the porcelain washbasin and vomited into it. And then she sobbed.

Out came all the fear, anguish, pain, and agony that had been festering inside of her like a cancer. She collapsed on the floor and sobbed. *Dear Lord, please save me from Lucien's wrath! Please don't let him harm Denis.* She closed her eyes and felt the anguish flooding her body. She sobbed as she had never sobbed before. Lucien was insanely jealous. He was cruel enough to kill the both of them to salvage his dubious honor. She didn't doubt for a minute he would try. She knew from personal experience that Lucien was incapable of feeling any remorse for his victims. He was cold and ruthless, lacking any human empathy. And now she was his enemy, deserving of all his rage and hatred.

Emilie slumped on the bed with hunched shoulders and swollen eyes. She forced herself to drink the cup of coffee that Da Rosette had brought for her. The sight of her beloved nurse left Emilie reeling. She had never seen Da Rosette looking so hurt and tormented. Putting on a brave face, the old woman sat down and rubbed Emilie's back.

"Doudou, what happened to you? Why did you run away like that?" Da Rosette's arms were so thin and bony. She had aged terribly these past few months. For the first time, Emilie realized how old and feeble her nurse was. She was little more than skin and bone, her once-beautiful face a picture of sadness, her eyes mirrors of her wretchedness.

Emilie clung to the old woman's shawl and sobbed. She never meant to cause everyone so much pain, but she had to face the truth:

she was in love with Lieutenant Rémy. Hopelessly and utterly in love. She could never go back to Lucien now. And for the first time in her life, she was happy. Meeting Lieutenant Rémy was the best thing that ever happened to her. It changed her life. He showed her what true love and affection could feel like. The feeling was overwhelming, like the cross between a gushing waterfall and a quiet stream. It was like nothing she ever felt before. And for the first time in her life, she had experienced true happiness. She tried to squeeze back the tears, but they gushed like a hurricane. Why did it have to come to this? Why did her love for Denis Rémy have to bring ruin to her family? And worst of all, why did it have to cause her beloved nanny so much pain?

Later, when Emilie went searching for her father, she found him in his office with his nose buried deep in his ledger book, his brow furrowed with worry.

"Papa, about last night—" she said.

Georges Dujon looked up suddenly. His face was red and bloated from rum and lack of sleep; his eyes were full of rage. Emilie winced at the sight of him.

"What about it?" he said. He got up from his chair and stalked over to the window to gaze out. "You caused us a great deal of trouble, young lady. Your mother is taking it very hard. Her melancholy came back. She won't leave the bedroom . . ." His voice broke as he turned to face her with scorn-filled eyes. Emilie took a step backward. "How could you do it? What were you thinking? Do you hate us so much?"

"Papa, I can explain . . ."

"Save your words. You've made a mess of things, but that's the least of my problems." He rubbed his forehead. "We're not going to make the sailing date. This was our last chance, and we lost it. We're going to lose everything—the house, the farm . . ." His voice broke as he watched the rain drenching the fields through the open shutters. "Half the workers didn't show up today on account of the ash and the rumbling. The rest are complaining about their salary. They're demanding a raise to come back to work. I've already taken out bank loans to pay them what I owe them from last month, but I can't manage . . . It's hopeless . . . utterly hopeless."

He buried his face in his hands. To Emilie's horror, she thought she detected tears gliding down his cheeks. She drew back, aghast.

"Papa, I'm so sorry . . .please . . ."

"Save your words," he said. "What's broken can't be mended. Your marriage to Lucien was our last hope of saving our sorry situation, and now that's gone. We're finished." His face was a mask of wretchedness.

Emilie felt the blood draining from her head. She reeled from shock and remorse. Her father's ire now unleashed, he pounded the desk with his fist and uttered a curse that sent a chill up her spine. Emilie let out a cry like a wounded animal, then turned and fled.

Thinking quickly, she grabbed her purse and headed out to the stable. She instructed the stableboy to prepare a carriage, and without another word, she headed down to Saint-Pierre and went straight to 25, rue Longchamps, the herbal shop of M. Gaston Faustin Jacquet. As much as she hated the idea of returning to the quimboiseur for advice, she felt she had no other choice. Her situation was now intolerable, and she needed the power of *quimbois* to regain control. Everything was falling apart like a house of cards. What irony! The primitive superstitions she had grown up fearing and detesting were starting to take control of her life.

Saint-Pierre was unusually quiet. The streets were empty of passersby, and the marketplace was shut down. The sidewalks were muddy from the wet ash and cinders. The rain was running down from the corrugated roofs and flooding the gutters. Ships in the harbor bobbed like dark, empty hulks, and the Figuier Quarter, with its tiered rows of warehouses, was all but deserted. Even the normally ebullient fishermen were gone. The rumbling volcano probably scared the fish away, she thought. It certainly wasn't a day to brave the seas; the skies were dark and ominous from the ash clouds that were rising from the lower crater of Mount Pelée, blocking out the sun. There was a whiff of death in the air.

A sudden loud explosion detonated on the summit of Mount Pelée, shattering the quiet. Gasping in fright, Emilie sought shelter in a doorway and watched with fearful eyes as huge projectiles shot out of the crater. The sight was terrifying. Turbaned women stopped and stared at the spectacle, their voices shrill and their eyes as wide as saucers. Emilie took flight, and when she reached the shop of M. Jacquet, she tied the horse to a hitching post, then pressed her nose to the glass and looked inside. The shop was dark and quiet. The front door was locked. Seeing no alternative, she banged on the door and called out, "Hello! Is anybody there? Please open up!"

A light went on, and a pair of feline eyes belonging to an attractive mulâtresse peered out through the glass window.

"What do you want?" said the woman, eyeing her suspiciously.

"I have to see M. Jacquet."

"What is your business with him?" said the woman.

"I have to see him right now. It's urgent."

Reluctantly, the woman retreated to the back of the store and then reappeared a few minutes later and opened the door. With an air of suspicion, she ushered Emilie inside and locked the door behind them. The woman was young, perhaps no more than thirty, and she wore an expensive blue madras dress over a cotton chemise that was trimmed at the neck and wrists in expensive lace. It must have cost a small fortune in addition to the necklaces of gold beads that glittered around her neck. The woman was charmingly seductive and had a coquettish air about her. She moved in sinewy waves, with her hips swaying side to side rhythmically. Emilie assumed the woman was the servant girl everyone talked about since his wife had disappeared. With slender fingers the woman lit a match and used it to illuminate the chandelier with the six black candles that hung over M. Jacquet's desk. The light cast eerie shadows on the makeshift voodoo altar in the corner, giving a flicker of life to the grinning skull and statues of saints that stood in a semicircle around it. The cloying scent of incense mixed with traces of rum, chicken feathers, and burnt candles wafted through the room, causing Emilie to gag. How ironic it was that now she was utterly at the Grand Zamy's mercy!

"Sit here, mam'selle; I will fetch the proprietor," said the woman through sensuous lips. Emilie did as she was told and sat alone in the voodoo shop, feeling vulnerable and afraid, tortured by the fear of being found out, and riddled with shame and guilt at betraying her religious upbringing. She imagined Da Rosette's horror at finding out what she was doing. She fixed her gaze on the makeshift altar and was repulsed by the sight of a necklace made of snake vertebra lying beside a goat skull that still had flesh clinging to it. Behind the ritual objects was a fresco containing bizarre images, such as interlocking serpents, monsters with blazing eyes, bizarre humanoid plants, and ships in the middle of a raging storm pursued by ravenous sharks. The message was clear: where man and nature intersect, there is a brutal struggle for survival, and only voodoo has the power to overcome disaster. Emilie was struck with the notion that she was like one of those helpless fishermen alone in a raging sea of confusion and doubt. This helped alleviate her guilt, but only a little.

She heard a door open and a pair of heavy footsteps plodding down the hall. Despite his age, the Grand Zamy walked with swift, forceful steps, as if he was twenty years younger. As usual he was dressed in an elegant suit and waistcoat, and his gold watch chain glinted in the light of the chandelier. With calculated precision, he sat down behind his desk and fixed his eyes on Emilie. A hint of a smile formed at the corner of his lips that sent a chill up her spine. She was suddenly at a loss for words.

"Bonjour, mam'selle," he said. "My assistant tells me you have urgent business."

Emilie squirmed in her chair. "Oui, monsieur, I'm afraid I need your help again. I'm in a dire predicament."

"Fixing problems is my specialty," he said, grinning. "Can you explain the matter to me?"

"Yes. You see, my fiancé, the gentleman I was trying to get rid of, caught me with another man, and now he wants to kill us both. I'm in great fear for my life."

The Grand Zamy's eyebrows rose in surprise. "That sounds serious, indeed, mam'selle. But perhaps it's not beyond hope. Let's see what the cards have to say."

He pulled out a deck of tarot cards and chanted, "Spirits, I invoke you, tell me how I can solve this young woman's problem."

Once again a black candle on the chandelier snuffed out, leaving a thin wisp of smoke rising to the ceiling. The Grand Zamy shuffled the cards with great concentration and then handed the deck to Emilie and asked her to cut them. He spread them on his desk in the shape of a cross and meditated over the results.

"I see mental anguish and despair, fear, sleepless nights, great worry." His face took on a look of paternal concern. "This is shown by the nine of wands." He pulled up the card and showed it to her. "I also see combativeness, hot tempers, a great struggle or a great competition between two potential suitors. This is shown in the five of wands." He pointed to the card with utmost gravity. "Over here I see a young woman in shackles who is tied up against her will. She's in bondage, despairing and hopeless. This is the devil card." He lifted up an ominous-looking card that showed a winged devil with goat horns seated on a throne to which a young man and woman were shackled. The figures were naked, helpless, and the devil had an insidious control over them with eyes like empty sockets of fire. Emilie's eyes went wide with terror.

The Grand Zamy locked eyes with her. "Focus on the young woman. Do you see yourself here?" Emilie stared at the card and nodded. "The card represents Lucifer, Mephistopheles, Satan, the Prince of Darkness, or whatever you choose to call him, but they all symbolize evil. We try to vanquish the evil in our lives so good can prevail, but in fact, good and evil cannot be separated, just as one cannot separate a shadow from its source. Darkness is merely the absence of light and is caused when truth is obscured. From this card I see that forces outside of your control are forcing you into a perilous situation. You feel tied down against your will, controlled. To escape your shackles, you must untie the bonds that are keeping you in this bad situation. Only you hold the key to your own freedom. And only you can find the key." He put the card down and studied the remaining cards. "I also see a religious figure, one who has a great love or a deep passion for you and with whom you share a deep bond or a joining of the spirits; that is the hierophant." He paused for a moment, scrutinizing the final card with unblinking eyes. "I also see a duel and a raging fire . . ."

"A fire? What kind of fire?"

"A fire that will consume everything in its path," he said with great solemnity. "Like a fiery furnace. There will be utter and complete destruction, a natural disaster of some sort, an upheaval. This is the Tower card." He held up a card that showed a blazing tower with people dying all around. "I also see death, tremendous death—a massacre." At the last word, the Grand Zamy looked up abruptly, sweat beading on his forehead.

"Mam'selle, I think you are in a great deal of trouble," he said. "I have never seen such a bleak reading, but I do not believe your situation is beyond hope. With the right incantations and potions, I'm certain I can fix your problem. I will make your fiancé disappear for a price, and no one will be the wiser. No one will be implicated in the crime, and you will be free. He will simply vanish without a trace."

A cold fright came over Emilie, the implication of his words too chilling to contemplate, like a noose around her neck. "Isn't that rather extreme?"

"It depends on how badly you want to solve your problem," he said, regarding her with his cool, unblinking orbs. "Based on the reading, I would say you are facing a severe crisis. A vision of death. But in your case, perhaps we can solve your problem without having to resort to such violence. The price, however, will be steep for such a job."

She could feel her stomach clenching. "How much exactly?"

"Ten thousand francs," said the quimboiseur.

Emilie's heart stopped. "Ten thous—"

That was impossible! The amount he was asking was extortionary, completely out of the question. Even if she had the money, she could never hand it to him in good conscience. It was like paying off the devil. There was something unholy about it. She dropped her purse on the floor. The quimboiseur stared at her with cold, malicious eyes, his expression never wavering, never displaying an ounce of emotion. Emilie felt as if she was suffocating. Her blood ran cold in her veins, and her palms broke out in a sweat. It was simply not possible. He was demanding a fortune! He was using her distressing situation to extort vast sums of money out of her—exactly as Rémy had predicted. She felt the blood rushing from her head, leaving her dizzy and light-headed. The Grand Zamy pulled out a ledger book and began to leaf through the pages. When he came to a particular column, he marked it with a long, yellow fingernail and fixed his eyes on her.

"Yes, that is correct. It will cost you ten thousand francs," he repeated. "For this amount I can solve any problem, no matter how complicated, no matter how dangerous, no matter the risk. And I give you my word, the gendarmes won't come snooping around your house asking difficult questions. I have ways of making them—shall we say, blind?" He roared with laughter, causing Emilie to almost fall off her seat. "And rest assured, your hands will be as white as snow. You'll have no fear of going to jail."

"You don't understand," she said, shaking with fear. "I don't have that kind of money."

The Grand Zamy rested his elbows on the desk and scrutinized her face. "That is no problem, mam'selle. I can put you on a payment plan. My clients come from all walks of life. We aim to please every customer no matter what his financial situation by offering a wide variety of options." He grinned like a jackal, exposing a full set of white teeth, while his eyes took on an almost seductive quality. "And when a customer such as you cannot make his payments, we put him on a special program. But that is used only in rare cases. I hope it will not be necessary in your case. Mam'selle, do you know what a gagé is?"

Emilie's throat went dry. "No," she croaked. "I mean, not exactly. I've heard of them, but I don't really know . . ."

"Then allow me to explain. A gagé is a person who has made a special pact with the devil," he said, smiling maliciously. "When a person cannot pay his debts, he sells his soul to the devil until he can collect the full amount, at which point he can buy his soul back. It's all very simple and quite legitimate. I've handled quite a few cases myself. However, I'm sure that in your case, we won't have to resort to such extreme measures. You're in good hands. I have hundreds of satisfied customers all over Martinique and as far away as Trinidad, Dominica, Guadeloupe, and Saint Lucia. People come to see me for every sort of problem. I'm the doctor that makes their problems go away . . .forever." Again he erupted in a house-shaking laughter that caused Emilie to almost jump out of her chair. Trembling like a leaf, Emilie watched the Grand Zamy pull out a huge file containing hundreds of yellowing contracts written in elegant longhand and sealed in blood, which he waved under the glowing candles.

"Each contract represents a satisfied customer and a soul that has found greater purpose."

Emilie's eyes went wide. "I don't want to be a gagé." She could feel her toes curling inside her shoes.

"That is no problem. As I stated, that is only used in extreme cases. In your case I am sure you will have no trouble making your payments."

"And if I can't?"

"No need to discuss that now," he said soothingly. "Empty your mind of all fear and worry. Trust me, and together we will make your problems go *poof* and disappear."

Emilie struggled to catch her breath. Her chest was so tight she felt like she was suffocating and her temples were throbbing. What the quimboiseur was asking was impossible. She could never raise that kind of money.

"Ten thousand francs is an enormous sum—"

"Mam'selle, do you want your problem solved or not?" By now his face turned to stone. His black eyes stared at her in a threatening manner, as if willing her to act.

With trembling hands, Emilie opened up her purse. She handed him her pearl necklace, the one her Grandmother Loulou had given her.

"I can give you this as a down payment," she said, swallowing hard. She had no idea how much the necklace was worth, but it was all she had to offer.

"Very nice," said the Grand Zamy, admiring it. "I will put you down for two thousand francs. You have one month to pay me the remaining eight thousand francs, agreed?"

Emilie was stunned. "One month? How can I . . .?"

He eyed her sharply. "Mam'selle, it is your responsibility to fulfill your side of the contract. I will do my part to make your fiancé disappear, and you must rely on the spirits to help you find a way to pay. Don't worry, though. We can always amend the contract at a later date to more favorable terms." From his desk he took out a prewritten contract and began filling in the blank spaces. "Very well; sign here, please." He handed it across the desk to Emilie, who barely had time to scan the fine print before she signed it and handed it back to the quimboiseur.

"You see, that wasn't so hard," said the Grand Zamy, flashing his charming smile. He reached behind him to a shelf that contained a colorful assortment of bottles. After selecting a few, he placed them on the desk and called out each name as he set it down. "This is strength powder, this is moon powder, this is star powder, this is subterfuge powder, this is shark powder, this is proficiency powder, this is hexing oil, and this is devil oil . . ."

He mixed the ingredients in a bowl and poured the contents into two vials, both of which he handed to Emilie. He instructed her to drink the first bottle immediately and the second bottle in a week's time. She downed the mixture in one gulp. It tasted surprisingly of mint. Then he recited a long phrase in Latin, inserting Lucien's name at the end and telling her to repeat after him: *"Acceso alius sententia ut mihi, phasmatis of interregnum ego dico, solvo meus mens mei, ego dico phasmatis audite meus placitum meus mens quod iacio Lucien Monplaisir."*

Emilie recited the phrase, feeling as if somehow she had crossed an invisible line.

"Very well; we are done," said the Grand Zamy. "I expect the final payment of eight thousand francs in a month's time. I am confident that by then, your problem will be solved, and you will be satisfied."

Shaking like a leaf, Emilie got up to leave.

"Oh, and another thing," said the Grand Zamy. "You must be punctual in paying your debt. If you miss the payment, the amount you owe will be double."

"Double?" she said, feeling faint.

"It's in the contract, mam'selle," he said, snapping the file shut.

Chapter 26

Friday, May 2

By the time Emilie returned to Domaine Solitude, the clouds of volcanic dust were so thick, the sky had darkened, as if there was a solar eclipse. Flashes of lightning lit up the summit of Mount Pelée, adding to the eerie atmosphere.

Most of the workers had refused to show up for work, citing the danger, but there was a small group standing in a nearby field, chatting nervously. After leaving her horse in the stable, Emilie looked around frantically, but her father was nowhere to be found. Neither was Julien. She felt a gnawing pain in the pit of her stomach. Something was wrong. She could feel it. When she ran in the house, the chandelier started tinkling, and the dishes rattled in the cupboard. A roof tile crashed to the ground, and voices in the outside kitchen shrieked. Before long the servants ran back to the house, shouting in fear. Some were crossing themselves and praying out loud. The walls were shaking so hard it sounded like horses were galloping on the roof. Thinking quickly, she rescued a glass that tipped over and almost crashed to the floor. Then she froze. Outside she heard a distinct loud roar that sounded like a landslide.

Her mother and Da Rosette raced down the stairs and cried out when they saw Emilie standing there. She asked about Abbé Morel, and they told her he was upstairs in bed, calmer and more relaxed. But the rumbling and ashfall had set her mother's nerves on edge, and Da Rosette was frantic with worry. It seemed as if their world was coming apart at the seams. No one could deny the volcano was in active eruption, but it was impossible to predict when or if it would settle down. Emilie knew she had to get them to safety, but where? Thinking quickly, she asked a servant to bring everyone, including Abbé Morel, to the storm shelter. Certainly they would be safe there.

"Where's Papa?" she asked.

Nobody knew. Her mother looked fearful, saying he had left the house an hour ago and hadn't been seen since. Da Rosette erupted in tears. Racing outside, Emilie called over to a group of workers that was in the courtyard. They were huddled under the tamarind trees with sweaty brows, fearful eyes, and heaving chests, waving their cutlasses to and fro and shouting all at once. One of the men was pointing toward the slopes of Mount Pelée and shouting in a voice full of distress that the volcano was erupting. Emilie felt the crushing weight of the world on her shoulders. With her father gone, they were looking to her for answers. But she had no answers.

"Have you seen my father?" she asked Durancy.

Immediately his shoulders slumped. He removed his straw hat and looked at her with eyes filled with terror and uncertainty.

"Mam'selle, your father and Julien and four other men rode out to inspect the fields, but they have not come back yet."

Her brow furrowed. "In which direction did they go?"

"About two miles east of here." He pointed to the far edge of the estate, the valley that flanked the lower slopes of Mount Pelée. "They said they were heading to inspect the stream that feeds the orchards. Someone reported seeing water rising and flooding the nearby crops."

"Oh dear, we have to find them," she said.

Before Durancy could respond, a burst of orange flames shot out of the crater, flickering and crackling in the sky, then disappearing with a boom that almost burst their eardrums. Emilie gasped. For several seconds, reddish-orange sparks continued to glow on the summit before vanishing into the cone. The rumbling of the volcano increased, and a great black cloud billowed outward, raining ash and cinders for miles around. As they coughed and gagged, Emilie saw terror in the men's eyes. Workers in the fields began shouting in alarm and then abandoning the field in droves, shrieking with fright as they ran to the warehouse for cover. Some others ran down to the cottages in the valley, screaming in terror.

Mustering up all her courage, Emilie said, "Durancy, are you coming with me?"

He nodded bravely. "*Yes, mam'selle.*" Emilie breathed a sigh of relief, knowing his loyalty extended to such a strange and frightful occurrence.

"I'll get Balthazar. Tell the others where we're going and tell them to send help if we don't return in an hour."

"*Yes, mam'selle,*" said Durancy as he ran to mount his horse.

After fetching Balthazar, Emilie climbed into the saddle, and together with Durancy, they took off at a canter through the fields. Ash and cinders rained down on their heads, almost blinding them. Emilie used her shawl to shield her nose and mouth from the barrage, but it did little to help. As they rode, branches whipped their faces and cut their skin. When Balthazar began to snort and whinny from the ashes, Emilie kicked his sides, urging him to keep moving forward. After a while they heard a suspicious roar reverberating from the direction of the stream. As they drew closer, the noise grew louder until it resembled a rushing waterfall. The sound was powerful and frightening. It sounded almost unnatural. And then, through the noise, they heard faint voices. Emilie was sure it was the missing workers. They hurried toward the voices, which began to sound like men in distress. Alarmed, they kicked their horses into a gallop and raced to a clearing. There, in the distance, they saw a sight that turned their blood cold.

The stream had turned into a raging torrent of black mud. It gushed down from the heights, spreading thickly across the valley floor, scorching and uprooting everything in its path. Caught in the flow were branches, tree trunks, dead cattle—even men. Emilie screamed in terror. Hopelessly trapped in the lava were six men on horseback: her father, Julien, and four workers. They were surrounded by the mud and sinking fast, on their faces a mask of fear.

Jumping off Balthazar, Emilie raced toward the sinking men, but she could not get close enough to reach them. The lava was rising quickly, swamping the horses and threatening to submerge them and carry them away with the debris. She felt weak and dizzy when she realized there was nothing she could do. The men were doomed.

The horses neighed pitifully. They lifted their haunches and struggled against the mudflow with their powerful bodies, but it was no use. Frantic, the men kicked their horses, shouting and urging them on, but by now the lava had completely engulfed them and was threatening to pull them under. The men screamed in terror, but their voices were drowned out by the deafening roar. Soon they would disappear under the torrential flow.

Emilie's heart raced. Valuable minutes were ticking by. Beside her, Durancy tried to reach the men, but the mud was spreading so quickly, it was threatening to overpower them as well, sucking them into its deadly current.

"Help us! Help us!" cried her father. He thrashed his horse with all his might, but the poor animal was hopelessly trapped. The mud was climbing higher, burning and searing its flesh, sucking the life out of it. The rest of the horses were in a similar predicament. The horrifying smell merged with the odor of sulfur and hot lava, sickening them. The men cried out in agony, their horrifying shrieks echoing across the valley, but there was nothing Emilie or Durancy could do. Tears stung her eyes when she realized that soon it would be all over.

Suddenly she had an idea. Untying a length of rope from her saddlebag, she threw it across to Julien, but the rope snapped back, unable to bear the weight of his horse. She threw it again, this time to her father, but he could not reach it. The situation was past critical. The horses were weaker, and some had started to give up. Seeing their doom, the men were in a state of panic. They thrashed at their horses and tugged at their reins as they screamed and shouted, but the animals were hopelessly burnt and had lost the will to fight. Whipping his horse's flank, Georges tried in vain to get the animal to move, but they were helpless to escape the death trap. The more his horse struggled, the farther they sank into the mud. Emilie stared in horror at the terrifying sight, her body convulsing with sobs.

By now the horses were almost buried up to their chests. The men were screaming for dear life, but the horses were dying. As the mud pulled them under, all struggling stopped. The men uttered their last prayers, crossed themselves, and prepared for the end. Soon they would be buried alive.

"Jump, Papa, it's your only chance," she shouted.

But her father shook his head. "It's no use, Emilie. Tell Maman I love her."

The mud rose up to his horse's neck, searing its flesh. Only its head and tortured eyes could be seen above the black lava. By now her father had given up all hope. His limbs too were scorched by the volcanic mud. A cry slipped out of Emilie's throat when she saw the look of resignation in his eyes.

Without a word, Georges pulled out his pistol, unlatched the safety, and shot himself through the head. His lifeless body sank in the mud and slowly disappeared. "Papa!" she screamed and collapsed on the ground.

The workers' cries reached a crescendo. The sight of Georges Dujon's suicide left them frantic. Julien called out to her, "Emilie, go now! Save yourself before it's too late!" The sight of her father's body in the lava and the heart-wrenching cries of the men had left Emilie in a state of shock, paralyzed with grief. The mud continued its vicious assault, swallowing up the men and horses as it spread across the valley floor, cutting down trees, shrubs, crops, everything in its path. Slowly the men's bodies disappeared under the mud. Emilie cried and screamed, the tears almost blinding her. A few minutes later, it was all over. The men and their horses sank beneath the scorching lava until there was no trace of them, as if they had never existed.

When Durancy brought Lucien to Emilie a half hour later, she was collapsed on the ground, perilously close to the river of volcanic mud. Lucien called out her name, but she was unresponsive. Jumping off his horse, he grabbed her, but she refused to budge. When he shook her, she screamed as if she had gone mad. He looked at Durancy in a panic, but the latter shook his head with pity. Lucien stared at Emilie and saw his life crumbling to pieces. The woman he loved had lost her senses.

By the time they reached the house, she was still screaming.

Part 3

Chapter 27

Saturday, May 3
Governor's Residence
Fort-de-France

In the early morning hours of Saturday, the volcano was spewing out massive clouds of black smoke, which coated Saint-Pierre in a thick layer of ash. The column of smoke rose three miles in the air, sending ash particles and cinders high up in the atmosphere, blowing southward as far as Fort-de-France. Explosions like cannonades rattled the people of Saint-Pierre and the smaller villages to the north. It sounded like a war, yet there were no invading ships, just a natural enemy that was more terrifying, more powerful, and more merciless. The Pierrotins closed their shutters and prayed by the light of candles and kerosene lamps. Some brought their children through showers of ash to the cathedral for a hasty baptism, while others packed their belongings into donkey carts or horse carriages and headed south to Fort-de-France.

Governor Mouttet awoke to an alarming sight. The town of Fort-de-France was covered in a layer of ash. The problem was getting worse, not better as the committee members had assured him. His instincts told him that something had to be done. He wondered if he should declare a state of emergency, but he needed guidance and permission from Decrais of the Colonial Office. It would be impossible to reach him on a Saturday, even if the telegraph cables were open at all. In all his years of colonial service, he had never been in such a predicament. He hesitated to take such drastic action without the Ministry's seal of approval. The last thing he needed was a bureaucratic inquisition if it all turned out to be nothing. And then there was the matter of keeping the public calm. He had to avoid a panic at all costs. Perhaps if they sent a cruiser to help evacuate the citizens up north and bring food and supplies, a state of emergency could be avoided. That would certainly go a long way in keeping the citizenry calm and placated. And then there was still the matter of vaccines. Had Mirville solved that problem yet? Why hadn't he received the report? He threw on a shirt and trousers and headed downstairs for a hasty breakfast. As he sipped his coffee, his valet threw down the latest issue of *Les Colonies*. When Mouttet saw the headline, his jaw dropped.

SPECIAL EDITION
Mount Pelée and Saint-Pierre: Yesterday the people of Saint-Pierre were treated to a grandiose spectacle in the majesty of the smoking volcano. While at Saint-Pierre, admirers of the beautiful could not take their eyes from the smoke of the volcano and the ensuing falls of cinder; timid people were committing their souls to God . . .

Grandiose spectacle? Admirers of the beautiful?

It would seem that many signs ought really to have warned us that Mount Pelée was in a state of serious eruption. There have been earthquake shocks. The rivers are in overflow. The town of Prêcheur has been inundated with large stones and torrents of dust. People are abandoning their homes in droves. The need now is for the people outside Saint-Pierre to seek the shelter of the town. Citizens of Saint-Pierre! It is your duty to give these people succor and comfort. Meanwhile, the excursion of the Gymnastics Club to the crater of Mount Pelée has been cancelled due to the harsh conditions. All those planning to attend will be notified when the event is rescheduled.

What the devil is he talking about? Has everyone on the island gone mad? Mouttet threw down the newspaper in disgust.

He got up from the table and headed out to the balcony, where the barometer was nailed to a pillar. He studied the needle for a few seconds. It was trembling. *Good Lord, is this normal?* He had heard about those infamous West Indian hurricanes, but the needle was not quivering because of an approaching storm. The pressure was dropping for another reason altogether. His mind raced . . . when the atmosphere is full of vapor, the barometer usually falls. The mountain was expelling a great deal of smoke and steam. He was sure that was the reason for the precipitous drop in atmospheric pressure. So in point of fact, the eruption of Mount Pelée was causing a decrease in atmospheric pressure. Could that be a good thing? Didn't that imply that once all the steam was expelled, the volcano would soon die down?

He gazed northward in the direction of Mount Pelée, but the mountain was enveloped in a thick gray cloud. There was an ominous low rumbling that resembled underground thunder and the air smelled foul again. Didn't all the experts say the volcano was extinct? What a ludicrous assessment! Nobody in his right mind would believe that. Then again, there could be some truth to the claim that the volcano was settling down again. But what if they were all wrong? He sat down and jotted out two telegrams, and then he went upstairs to pack an overnight bag, and he told his wife he was heading up to Saint-Pierre for a meeting with the scientific committee. He looked at the clock. It was seven a.m.

On his way to the ferry, Mouttet stepped into the telegraph office. When the operators saw him, they bolted upright.

"Good morning, Governor," said one of the wireless operators. "Nice seeing you today."

"Which one of you is Coppet?" said Mouttet.

"That would be me, sir," said the young man standing up straighter.

"I need you to send this urgent telegram to the Colonial Office, and I must have their response today. I've written it down for you. And here's another one for Mayor Fouché. Give them top priority. I'm heading up to Prêcheur to inspect the damage in the town, but I should be back to Saint-Pierre by noon."

"Yes, sir. Right away."

Coppet put on his headphones and began tapping his Morse key as fast as he could.

> *Fort-de-France 3 May.*
>
> *To Decrais, Minister of Colonies: The volcano known as Mount Pelée is in eruption. Large quantities of ash and cinders are covering the surrounding countryside where the inhabitants were forced to flee and find refuge in Prêcheur, Saint-Philomène, and Saint-Pierre. Explosions have been heard and at 2:00 am the crater spat forth flames and ejected large projectiles, some of which fell on the district of Prêcheur, more than 2 km from the summit. Please advise if*

*large-scale evacuation is in order. We are in desperate need
of food, supplies, and vaccines. Large loss of cattle and
agricultural produce. Heading up to Prêcheur to deliver first
round of aid and to inspect the damage.*
L. Mouttet

"There, sir, it's been sent," said Coppet. "Here's your copy."

"Thank you," said Mouttet, pocketing the slip of paper. "I'll be
staying at the Hôtel Intendance. Please send the reply there as soon
as you receive it."

"Certainly, sir."

After Coppet had sent the second telegram, Mouttet left the
telegraph office and headed to the wharf. Crowds of people were
pointing at Mount Pelée in alarm, their fearful voices rising above
the noise of traffic. When he arrived, he was relieved to see they
were already loading boxes of supplies onto the *Rubis* for transport
to Prêcheur. Waiting for him was his aide-de-camp, Didier, who was
organizing the transport. *Good, plenty of food and supplies. That
should keep the people happy and settled for the time being.* For
once Mouttet was starting to feel as if the situation was under
control. As the steamer pushed off from the dock, he felt the weight
coming off his shoulders.

Chapter 28

Saturday, May 3

Emilie woke to find a nurse opening the shutters. The sky was dark outside, as if a black cloud had blotted out the sun. When the wind blew particles of ash inside, the nurse quickly closed the shutters and covered them with a white sheet. Then she turned on a kerosene lamp for light. Emilie blinked a few times, but her vision was still fuzzy. It looked as if she was lying in a hospital bed in a room that smelled of urine and disinfectant. Everything was white—the walls, the sheets, the porcelain receptacle, the nurse's uniform, even the hospital gown she was wearing, but the bed was made of cast iron, and she could feel the steel slats beneath the thin mattress. Beside her bed was a table containing a metal tray with a syringe and a bottle labeled morphia, and on the wall facing her was a crucifix and a basin with free-flowing spring water, the only adornments in the otherwise bare room.

The nurse noticed her fluttering eyelids and came over to check her pulse. She was a beautiful mulâtresse who wore the white habit and veil belonging to the order of Saint-Paul de Chartres, the nuns responsible for caring for society's most vulnerable: the orphans, the poor, and the wounded soldiers in the military hospital. They also cared for the lunatics in the asylum on rue Levassor. Emilie's eyes widened and she felt a surge of panic. She tried to sit up, but she couldn't move her feet. Something cold and hard was restraining her.

"Where am I?" said Emilie, struggling against the restraints.

"No, no, no," said the nurse, pushing her back down. "You're not ready yet. Doctor said you must rest. You've had a terrible trauma."

Emilie groaned as the painful memory came flooding back. She could remember only traces of it: shouting men, struggling horses, an avalanche of black mud, her father's terrified face, a gunshot, and bodies sinking in the mud. Then came darkness. After that, her memory went blank.

"I must go and find my mother," said Emilie with renewed vigor. She tried to sit up again, but this time she realized her feet were shackled to the bed. *Shackled?* "What's this? Why am I being held like this?"

"It's for your own good," said the nurse, pushing her back down. "The doctor was afraid you would hurt yourself if you got up too soon. He ordered strict bed rest. Anyway, now is not the time to be out on the road. The entire town is covered in ash and soot. There's almost no fresh water to drink. Animals are dying of suffocation. People are panicking, and rivière Roxelane is flooding again."

The entire town is covered in ash?

"Sister, how long have I been here?"

"Since yesterday," said the nurse. "Last night at midnight, loud explosions were coming from Mount Pelée. I was afraid you would wake up. When I looked out, I saw lightning and a huge column of black smoke shooting out of the crater, sending ashes and cinders raining all over the city. About two hours later, flames were shooting out, and large pumice stones began to fall on the roofs. We could hear them bouncing on the rooftops. Everyone ran to the chapel to pray, and this morning when we awoke, the entire city was covered in ash. The patients were howling in fear, but you managed to sleep through it. We kept you heavily sedated."

"I don't remember a thing."

The nurse looked at her with pity. "Given what you've been through, you're lucky. Some people have recurring memories of tragedies, and they never fully recover. I think you'll be fine once you've rested. The doctor has high hopes for your full recovery. Anyway, you're much safer here than out there. Everyone is anxious and afraid. Fights have broken out. Some people are packing up all their belongings into donkey carts and heading south. I heard from Sister Marie-Denise that people are crowding into the churches and fighting for places at the confessional."

"Why?" said Emilie.

"They want absolution. They want peace in their hearts. People think the end is near. Thank goodness the governor arrived this morning to calm everyone down. Hundreds of people from Prêcheur are flooding into the city, but most are stuck along the coast with nowhere to go. There's almost no food left, so they're getting panicky. People are so frightened they are fleeing their homes and are paying exorbitant amounts to leave on steamships and ferries.

The roads are almost all blocked. But no matter where you go, there's no escaping the constant ashfall and the horrible smell of rotten eggs. There are so many extra mouths to feed, I don't know how we'll cope."

From outside her room, Emilie could hear the agonizing moans of the other patients. They were demanding to be set free. She also heard the sound of metal clanging, as if the patients were banging their chains. She felt a shiver up her spine.

"Nurse, where am I?" she said.

"The Colonial Health Institute," said the nurse, avoiding her gaze.

Emilie froze. *The lunatic asylum?*

"Why am I here?" she said. "Who brought me here?"

"Your fiancé found you in a catatonic state after an avalanche buried part of your plantation. He brought you here yesterday. He said you had witnessed a terrible tragedy and needed help. But perhaps you're not ready to talk about it yet."

Lucien brought me here? "What day is it today?"

"Saturday."

"I meant *what date?*"

The nurse eyed her. "The third of May. Why do you ask?" She poured a cup of water from a pitcher. "Here; drink this."

Emilie brought the cup to her lips and drank. She could take only a few sips before the trauma returned, a haunting vision of death that caused her stomach to clench, her heart to race, and perspiration to ooze from her pores. The blood drained from her face as the memory came flooding back. *The horses, the mud, the terrified faces, the screams, the shouts, her father's anguish . . . the gunshot . . . the final gunshot . . .* She handed the cup back to the nurse, laid her head against the pillow, and sobbed, her cries mingling with the anguished shrieks that reverberated from down the hall until it was a ghastly chorus. Tears streamed down Emilie's face. She felt a cold compress against her forehead and the pinch of a needle in her arm, and soon everything went black again.

The next time she opened her eyes, it was night. It was quiet. The only light came from a kerosene lamp beside her bed. Her legs were still shackled to the bed, and cold beads of perspiration ran down her temples. She had no idea how long she had slept, but she felt as if she would burst. Left with no choice, she called for the nurse, and when there was no answer, she grabbed the cup and banged it on the metal tray as she screamed for help. Soon a nurse appeared in the room with a jangle of keys in one hand and a porcelain bedpan in the other. After Emilie had relieved herself, she said, "Nurse, please take these shackles off. I want to get up and stretch my legs."

The nurse shook her head. "I will ask the doctor tomorrow, but tonight that's impossible. I'm sorry."

The nurse ran a cold compress against her forehead.

Emilie turned to face her. "I have to see my mother and nurse. Are they all right?"

"Your mother is being cared for at home. Your nurse is with her. Your fiancé has assumed all responsibility for your care."

The implications of that were terrifying. Emilie felt a tightening in her throat.

The nurse picked up the syringe and gave her another shot of morphia. Emilie closed her eyes again, tormented by the feeling of utter helplessness. The cold shackles pressing against her legs reminded her of her imprisoned state.

The next time she awoke, it was morning. Suddenly her mind was clear. She lay in bed for several minutes, remembering the events that had led to her being brought to the hospital. She recalled Da Rosette's anguished cries when Lucien had carried her back to the house. "Doudou, what happened to you?" the old woman had said through tear-streaked eyes. Emilie was paralyzed with grief and shock, but she remembered Abbé Morel's worried face as Lucien carried her inside. The house was in complete disorder, and when Lucien and Durancy told her mother and Da Rosette about the tragedy, her mother had collapsed on the floor. The servants swarmed around her and lifted her to the sofa, while Da Rosette crossed herself and prayed feverishly. Everything was in chaos. Several workers had grabbed horses and tools and raced to the avalanche in the hopes of rescuing the trapped men, but it was too late. The men's anguished cries echoed across the fields, sending the remaining workers into a frenzy. The plantation had suffered a devastating death blow.

Da Rosette tried to revive Emilie with smelling salts, but she was too much in shock. Left with no choice, Lucien decided to take her to the hospital on rue Levassor, where she would be better cared for. Hearing this, Abbé Morel became noticeably agitated. He tried to reason with Lucien that no one would take better care of Emilie than her nurse, but Lucien refused to listen to him. Abbé Morel tried to prevent him from taking Emilie, but it was no use. When Lucien picked up Emilie and carried her outside, Abbé rushed after him, begging Lucien to allow him to accompany them, at which point Lucien pushed the priest away. "No, Abbé! Go back to the house and keep watch over her mother." Through tearstained eyes, Emilie saw Abbé Morel's face fall. His countenance clouded over, but he said nothing. And then the carriage rolled away, and Abbé Morel's figure grew smaller and smaller while she sat there feeling helpless. It was all hazy now, but bits and pieces were starting to come back.

When the nurse came in to check on her, Emilie said, "Nurse, what day is it?"

"Sunday, the Lord's day."

"I mean, what day of the month is it?"

The nurse looked at her. "The fourth of May."

Emilie tried to appear strong. "May I leave now?"

The nurse shook her head. "No, my dear. Now is not the time. The whole city is covered in ash. The air is foul, and everyone is afraid to leave their homes. Horses are collapsing from asphyxiation. Even dogs and cats are dropping dead. Everywhere you look, hummingbirds lie dead by the hundreds, covered with ash. It's too dangerous to leave the hospital grounds. Many of the wealthier families are fleeing to Fort-de-France, which leaves the poor people in greater anguish. They have nowhere to go. Last night in the cathedral, some desperate people ran to the altar yelling that they were going to die. A young woman fainted. They had to carry her to the hospital. The priests tried to calm the people down with prayers and blessings, but it did little to quell the fear. Here, I brought you a copy of *Les Colonies* to read with your breakfast. Later I will come and pray with you." She placed a newspaper in Emilie's hands and a tray of food in her lap.

Emilie picked it up and read the headlined article.

The rain of ashes never ceases. At about half-past nine the sun shone forth timidly. The passing of carriages is no longer heard in the streets. The wheels are muffled. The ancient trucks creak languidly on their worn tires. Puffs of wind sweep the ashes from the roofs and awnings and blow them into the rooms whose windows have been imprudently left open. Shops which had their doors half-closed are now barred up entirely . . .

My God, is the world coming to an end? Emilie set the newspaper aside. She tried to calm the beating of her heart, but it was impossible. An intense feeling of claustrophobia came over her, which she tried to conceal in her attempt to appear strong. But truth be told, the room was small and growing smaller by the minute. Her fear and anxiety were threatening to overcome her powers of reason. She had to fight at all costs.

"Nurse! I have to get out of here. My mother needs me. My father is dead, and someone has to take care of her. I'm sure Da Rosette is frantic with worry. Our house lies in the direct path of the volcano . . ."

The nurse shook her head. "I'm sorry; I can't let you go. Not even to the courtyard. The air outside is not fit to breathe. Doctor's orders."

Emilie felt the sweat trickling down her forehead and her heart racing. With the shutters closed, there was no fresh air; the acrid odor of rotten eggs was nauseating, suffocating. Her mouth was dry, and her feeling of claustrophobia was increasing. She saw the walls of the hospital crashing down over her head, crushing her.

"Please, Nurse. Please take these shackles off. I have to get home."

"No, dear, you must eat. You're getting weaker by the day."

Suddenly Emilie saw a vision. She recalled what the Grand Zamy had told her when he lifted up the tarot card that depicted a tower and a vision of impending death: *A fire that will consume everything in its path, like a fiery furnace . . . a great destruction . . . and death, tremendous death: a massacre!*

By now Emilie was gasping for breath. "Please let me go! I'm in grave danger. I must get out of here!"

The nurse shook her head. "Nonsense; you are perfectly safe here."

"You don't understand. The volcano . . . we're all in grave danger. Please let me go."

But the nurse only shook her head again and took Emilie's pulse. She frowned as she made a note on her chart. Desperate, Emilie tugged at the nurse's habit. "Please listen to me. The volcano . . . please let me out of here!"

But the nurse pretended not to hear her. She turned her back and poured a fresh cup of water from a pitcher. She left it on the table next to Emilie and then set about tidying the room, sweeping the floor, and emptying the bedpan in the gutter. Then, without another word, she left. Emilie watched her go with sad resignation. She felt invisible, powerless, and helpless. It was all too apparent the nurse was used to dealing with the insane, those written off as a lost cause. She took a bite of food but spat it out. Then she collapsed on the pillow, groaning as tears coursed down her cheeks. Her mind was numb from the tragedy, and her heart ached from the trauma. The pain was still raw. Now she had to contend with her own inevitable grim fate. She was locked up in a lunatic asylum with an erupting volcano only five miles away, and there was nothing she could do about it. Her fate was sealed in the cards. Suddenly the room felt more like a prison than a hospital. Maybe it really was a prison. A prison for the insane. Listening to the moaning and shrieking of the patients down the hall, Emilie realized her only chance of survival was escape.

Chapter 29

Saturday, May 3

In the infantry barracks, Rémy was starting to get uneasy about the situation. He barely slept the whole night. Since midnight, the volcano was belching out enormous black clouds, while lightning illuminated the purple-gray sky. It was like being in the middle of a maelstrom. He could not understand how the people of Martinique could take the volcano's pyrotechnics in their stride. He had never seen such a display of nature's power. It was like a message from heaven. When he finally awoke on Saturday morning, the entire town of Saint-Pierre was coated in a thick layer of ash. There was a pervasive sulfurous smell, and rivière Roxelane had turned into a raging torrent. The usual gaggle of washerwomen was gone. Even the usually cheerful fishermen looked gloomy.

As he read the morning newspaper, he laughed in derision. The editor of *Les Colonies* stated that an unnamed "leading authority" on volcanoes had told the newspaper that the ash fallout was nothing more than a passing phase and the crater would soon become dormant. Rémy wondered who the leading authority was since no one on the scientific committee had any more specialized knowledge about volcanoes than the boy who polished his boots.

Setting aside the newspaper, he picked up a book on Pompeii that he had borrowed from the Schoelcher Library. Leafing through the pages, he stared at the pictures of toppled columns, ruined villas, writhing humans, skeletons embedded in ash, a once-beautiful town in utter ruin. He found some striking similarities between Pompeii and Saint-Pierre. It was almost uncanny. Both Pompeii and Saint-Pierre were resort towns built in the shadow of a volcano, both had a reputation for loose morals and a careless, pleasure-seeking approach to life, and both suffered from endless political backstabbing and bickering. Saint-Pierre even boasted Roman columns in the fort cathedral and a plethora of public fountains and baths, just like in Pompeii. Some of the expensive villas on the hillsides even resembled the villas of ancient Roman officials. And like the citizens of Pompeii, the Pierrotins seemed to be oblivious that they were living in the shadow of a smoldering volcano, as if they were living under a grand illusion about their own mortality.

He meditated on a certain passage:

> *The eruption begins after the lavas have risen within the crater up to what may be called high-lava mark. When the pressure from the vapors generated and confined below and from the hydrostatic pressure of the lava column is too great to be withstood by the containing mountain, the mountain consequently breaks; the conduit is rent open on one side or the other, and the lavas run out . . .*

A cold sweat broke out on his forehead. Perhaps it was the suffocating humidity or a touch of malaria. Or maybe he was suffering from an unnamed tropical malady that was clouding his better judgment. Perhaps the situation wasn't so bad after all. *Maybe by tomorrow the volcano will settle down, and life will go on as normal. The air will be fresh, the streets will be clean, birds will stop falling from the sky, cattle will stop dying, and the tremors will stop.* Or maybe he was losing his mind.

Rémy's eyes wandered across the desk to the photograph of his mother. He picked it up and stared at her sad features, a lump forming in his throat. Had it really been a year since she died? Was a person's life really so fleeting? With the earthquakes and ashfall, he had begun to think about his own mortality. Life in Martinique seemed very fragile, like a voodoo apparition that vanished in the night. His meager possessions gave little clue about his life: a fountain pen, a silver pocket watch, a few scattered books, and an African mask, a gift from the chief of the Bambara. Slung from a hatstand was his leather holster containing his service revolver, and on a shelf was his shaving kit. Aside from a bed and a chair, the rest of the room was bare. As bare and empty as the life he had lived up to now.

And then he remembered Emilie.

A cool breeze blew in from the bay, rustling the papers on his desk. Rémy sat in his shirtsleeves, wondering what happened to her since that horrible night when Lucien stormed into the Hôtel Intendance and took her away. She had started to invade his thoughts like a recurring dream. He was imagining all sorts of frightening scenarios when his thoughts were interrupted by a knock from Sergeant Aubert. He entered the room and stood at attention.

"You wished to see me, Lieutenant?"

Rémy looked up. "At ease, Sergeant. I have a few questions for you about a matter that I was hoping you could clarify."

Aubert smirked. "If it's about that tripe in the newspaper, I can assure you I wasn't the leading authority they quoted. It's a pile of rubbish."

"My thoughts exactly. I'm glad I'm not the only person who found it comically absurd. It's almost as if the editor, Marius Hurard, wrote it himself."

"Knowing his skill with a pen, it's a safe bet he did."

Rémy looked at him with bewilderment. "Why would he do that?"

Aubert put his hands in his khaki trouser pockets and assumed a philosophical look. "Politics, pure and simple. He has a valid reason for calming everyone's nerves. He's a staunch supporter of the rich béké landowners, and he'll do anything possible to make sure the election goes for Fernand Clerc. So in order to ensure the maximum number of votes, he has to keep the public calm, no matter what."

"I suppose Hurard thinks Pelée will comply with his demand and behave like an obedient voter," said Rémy with a wry face.

"I think you're starting to get the picture," said Aubert. "By the way, that's a nice bump you've got there." He motioned toward his head.

Rémy smiled wanly. "A mosquito bit me."

"Must have been a very *large* mosquito. Did you lose at cards again?"

"No, I—"

"Don't tell me, let me guess . . ." Aubert fell silent for a moment. "Does this concern that spirited béké girl with a penchant for wearing breeches? If so, Lieutenant, take my advice and stay away from those békés. They're a closed society and rarely admit outsiders. Most of them are bourgeois royalists, Legitimists, anti-Republican, and downright snobbish."

Rémy raised an eyebrow. "And they think we're atheists, Republicans, Freemasons, thieves, mischiefs, and Jacobins who suffer from poor table manners."

"Who would have thought the brave explorer of West Africa is nothing more than a mischievous Jacobin with poor table manners?" said Aubert with a smirk.

Rémy twitched his moustache. "I appreciate your dry sense of humor, but that's not why I called you here today. I need some information about local customs. What can you tell me about these quimboiseurs?"

"That's a strange question. I'm not an expert on voodoo."

Rémy looked thoughtful for a moment. "My question is more of a general nature. It's my understanding that these quimboiseurs exert a lot of influence over the local population. The young lady mentioned something about meeting one of these characters. I found her exiting a shop on rue Longchamps that she claims belongs to an herbalist by the name of M. Gaston Faustin Jacquet, who is some kind of notorious voodoo witch doctor known as the Grand Zamy. Later she confessed she had gone to see him to find a way to break off her engagement to a sugar planter with an aggressive left hook. I have to admit, there was something disturbing about the guy. I went back and surveilled him for a few days. I didn't like him one bit."

"The sugar planter or the herbalist?"

"Both, actually," said Rémy, rubbing the bump on his head. "But there was something especially sinister about that quimboiseur."

Aubert rubbed his chin pensively. "I find it odd that someone of her class would dabble in voodoo. Although I've heard that on rare occasions these obeah men are employed by whites, this is the first time I've had firsthand knowledge of such a case. Usually these quimboiseurs are people of considerable cunning and craftiness. They hold the bulk of the native population in fear on account of their mysterious powers, which are rooted in knowledge of plants and herbs more than black magic. By dabbling in herbal medicine, they commit all sorts of crimes, including murder. Very few people would be willing to testify against one of these charlatans lest they become their next victim."

"Why do the quimboiseurs thrive if everyone is so afraid of them?"

"Everyone has enemies," said Aubert. "People use voodoo to rid themselves of a bad neighbor, a business competitor, or even a romantic rival. Oftentimes their enemies end up dead or missing, and since the authorities rarely perform autopsies or exhume dead bodies for inquests in the West Indies, they get away with it scot-free. It's almost too easy for these obeah men to furnish a customer with poison if he wants to rid himself of a rival. In some cases, the quimboiseur doesn't even have to actually poison the victim. All he has to do is deliver some kind of sign, like a tiny black coffin filled with graveyard dirt or a note bearing occult phrases and symbols, or even just give his victim a strange look and that's enough to give the poor fellow a heart attack."

"So they're in the business of scaring people to death," said Rémy, narrowing his eyes.

"So to speak," said Aubert. "But their most effective weapon is poison. You've heard about zombies, haven't you?"

"I always assumed they were fairy tales," said Rémy.

Aubert shook his head. "It's rooted in scientific fact. If a quimboiseur chooses to turn a person into a zombie, he feeds him a concoction that renders the poor soul comatose, after which he is pronounced dead and buried. Hours later, the quimboiseur goes to the cemetery, digs him up, and revives him with a revitalizing cocktail, and then uses the poor bloke to commit all sorts of crimes. By that point the victim has lost all will and all memory; they become almost like slaves to the quimboiseurs. I've even heard these quimboiseurs carry vials of snake venom, which they administer to their victims by placing it under a sharpened fingernail and then puncturing their victim's flesh. These men are dangerous criminals, and they mostly get away with their crimes because no one in his right mind will testify against them. It's a hopeless case."

"We shouldn't allow them to run loose," said Rémy, feeling a surge of anxiety. "They can be dragged into court on trumped-up charges of disorderly conduct or practicing medicine without a license."

"If that were the case, then we'd have to arrest every traditional healer on the island, and there could be hundreds of them. It's a complicated, messy situation. These sorcerers are powerful criminals who hold the people in their grip. And they always tell their victims the same thing: 'Tonight the devil is coming to get you,' which is usually enough to scare the poor devils half to death. The government has had little success in uprooting these primitive beliefs from the people."

Rémy let out a sigh. He knew Aubert was right. He knew he shouldn't get involved in the béké girl's life and her problems. It went against his better judgment. It went against his instincts for self-preservation and survival. But it was already too late. He was in love with her. It bothered him to no end that she would soon be trapped in marriage to that vile, philandering sugar planter. He didn't think she would survive long in a marriage like that. Cynicism or the bottle would eventually get to her. All that innocence and virtue would be used up and discarded like a crab shell. Lucien could never love her; he was too arrogant and narcissistic to love anyone but himself. The thought of it crushed Rémy inside. Thinking about Emilie made it difficult to concentrate on his work. Everywhere he went, he saw her face, heard her voice, smelled her perfume. Yes, it was already too late. He was in love with her. Somehow he had to help her.

"There's one thing I can't believe," said Rémy at last. "And that is that Emilie Dujon would try to kill her fiancé. She's too good for that. She has no malice inside of her. She's a pure soul, absolutely innocent in every way. I'm sure she only did it as a last resort. I believe the quimboiseur exploited her vulnerability. He looked like a shrewd operator. Someone has to protect that girl."

Aubert locked eyes with him. "With all due respect, Lieutenant, I think you should stay out of it. Keep away from that béké girl and the quimboiseur. They'll bring you nothing but trouble. Mark my words."

Rémy got up and went to stare out the window. "Life has a way of pushing you to the edge of reason. People get desperate; they attempt to change their fate by using anything at their disposal, even if it involves black magic and voodoo. Perhaps it becomes a self-fulfilling prophecy . . . a voodoo of the mind. I heard of stranger things while I was in Africa. They have their own version of voodoo and witch doctors. People believe in black magic because they want to believe in the impossible. They want a feeling of control . . ." He turned around abruptly. "But their black magic is not powerful enough to overturn our French system of justice. If I have to, I'll charge that maniac with extortion and assault and bring him in for trial."

"I wouldn't do that if I were you," said Aubert, shaking his head. "You'll never get a living soul to testify against him. These devils are cunning, devious, and able to exert a powerful influence on their ignorant countrymen. Your best bet is to forget the young lady and carry on as if nothing happened."

"I can't do that," said Rémy. "Sometimes in life you have to do what's right, regardless of the consequences. You have to listen to your gut, and right now my gut is telling me that if she ends up with that sugar planter, she'll die a slow, miserable death. I can't let that happen . . ."

He was interrupted by a young corporal who rapped on the door.

"Yes?" said Rémy, looking up.

"Lieutenant, the colonel is requesting your presence, sir."

"Where?"

"At the Hôtel Intendance. The governor arrived this morning from Fort-de-France and called another meeting about Pelée."

"Thank you, Corporal," said Rémy, grabbing his jacket and pith helmet. "Carry on, Aubert. I think it's time I gave the governor a piece of my mind about the volcano."

Chapter 30

Saturday, May 3

As Rémy strode up to the Hôtel Intendance, a crowd had gathered in the courtyard, eager to hear the latest news of the scientific committee's findings. Pushing his way to the entrance, he hurried through the lobby to the dining room, where he found the meeting in progress.

The governor was in a state of nervous agitation. He was surrounded by various officials whom Rémy recognized, including the mayor of Saint-Pierre, Rodolphe Fouché; Colonel Fournier of the garrison; Fernand Clerc; Marius Hurard of *Les Colonies*; Capt. Matthieu Alexandre of the gendarmerie; Joseph Ferdinand, chief engineer in charge of roads and bridges; and finally, Prof. Gaston Landes and M. Mirville, the latter looking none too happy.

Removing his helmet, Rémy took his place beside Landes while the men were in the midst of a heated discussion. Cigarette smoke swirled. The men shouted over each other, waving their arms and pounding the table. Rémy shifted in his seat. It looked as if they had reached another roadblock. It was the usual case of clashing wills. No one on this island could reach a decision about anything. It was always one political party against the other, and now there was a worrisome new announcement. In addition to the fright caused by the tremors, a new disaster appeared on the horizon: an outbreak of smallpox.

Mouttet rubbed the space between his eyes, looking like he would rather be anywhere but at the center of this conflict. "Gentlemen, why wasn't this brought to my attention sooner? How many cases do we have right now?"

"Three," said M. Mirville. "For the time being, they are being kept under strict quarantine in the military hospital and are being given the standard treatment, namely, wound care and infection control. But the only way to stop an outbreak in its tracks is to immunize every man, woman, and child on the island, and of course, every traveler who steps foot on our shores. This means we'll need to post health officers at every landing site. And we must do it urgently. We can't sit on something like this."

"Won't that create a panic?" said the governor, his brow furrowing. Rémy could see tension etched into his forehead by the laxity of the health officials.

"We have no other alternative," said Mirville. "Our standard protocol is to go from village to village according to the census data. But to do this, we have to order a fresh supply of vaccines from France, which could take weeks. We have to stop the smallpox from spreading. And believe me, it can spread quickly."

Mouttet rubbed the back of his neck in frustration. "But going from village to village is sure to alarm the civilians, which is precisely what I'm trying to avoid at this time. I just came from Prêcheur, where the people are desperate to get out. It was all I could do to calm them down. The church is filled with people crowding around the altar praying for salvation. If they hear of an outbreak, we'll have a mass panic on our hands. We have to keep this quiet until after the election."

"I'm afraid we can't afford to do that," said Professor Landes. "During the last outbreak, whole areas of the native population were decimated by the virus. If we don't take prompt action, we could have a potential disaster on our hands. At the very least, we should evacuate the schoolchildren down to Fort-de-France."

Mouttet shook his head. "Gentlemen, you're not listening to me. The election is only a week away. With the added pressure of the volcano, it won't help matters by riling up the public. There has to be a better way of handling the situation. I shall refer the matter to Decrais at the Colonial Office."

A grim-faced Mayor Fouché was the next to speak. "Governor, the situation is quite desperate. We need medical assistance urgently. At the very least, we should summon help from Dominica or Saint Lucia, both of which have extensive medical facilities. On our own, we won't be able to handle the situation. And if law and order starts to break down, we'll need reinforcements from the garrison to patrol the town."

"Certainly," said Mouttet, writing in his notebook. "But in my experience, the best way to ensure public safety is to keep everyone calm and in their homes. The last thing we need is rioting, looting, or mass panic. With the influx of refugees from the north, we're running out of food and lodging, and hospital beds will be in short supply as well. I've received reports that a third of all fruit and vegetable shops have shut down because they have nothing to sell. And there's only one bakery still functioning. Can anyone give me some suggestions on how to quell the shortage?"

"We can ship food in from Fort-de-France," said Mayor Fouché. "That is the quickest method."

"I second that motion," said Joseph Ferdinand, the chief engineer. "Right now the roads are blocked with all the refugees heading in and out of the city. We can't handle large transports over the roads and bridges. There is too much pressure on them with the tremors as it is. I agree that we should try to bring everything in by steamer. I also recommend that you barricade some of the roads to keep traffic at a minimum."

"Good idea, I'll make that a priority," said Mouttet. "Anything else to add?"

"Yes, Governor," said Ferdinand, consulting his notes. "From an engineering standpoint, we have been studying the ability of the structures to withstand the shock from the tremors as well as the accumulation of ash, pumice, and other projectiles. Then there's always the risk of fire. At the present rate, the buildings will hold out, but if the debris increases in size and intensity, we could have a serious problem on our hands."

"Point noted," said Governor Mouttet. "M. Fouché, put your firemen on high alert. We must avoid the risk of fire at all costs."

M. Ferdinand continued, "And one final point I wish to make is this: Are the roads capable of supporting a full evacuation?"

"Why wouldn't they be?" said Mouttet.

"Well, for one thing, there is only one coastal road that leads directly to Le Carbet and Fort-de-France. Right now the conditions are poor. If it rains and floods, we can expect massive delays and further problems."

"Such as?"

"In their present condition, the roads will never withstand the heavy wagon traffic that a massive evacuation would entail," said Ferdinand. "Within a few hours, it would become a quagmire, vehicles would get stuck, and most of the civilians would only be able to get out on foot, which means only the young and strong would make it. The sick and elderly wouldn't have a chance."

"He's right about that," agreed Mirville.

Ferdinand continued, "With regard to the ongoing earthquakes, our office feels the multistory masonry buildings are in no direct danger of collapsing, so rest assured that on that issue alone, there is no reason to evacuate Saint-Pierre."

"Excellent; thank you very much," said Governor Mouttet. "Now, Professor Landes, with regard to the sulfurous fumes, do they pose a health hazard to the public?"

Landes tented his hands. "I have thought about this matter a great deal. While we have all seen birds plummeting to the ground after being asphyxiated and we've heard rumors about horses dropping dead in the same manner, I've concluded this is mostly exaggeration. While it's true the birds can fly directly into clouds of fumes and grow disoriented and die, this is not a problem for horses and certainly not for humans. With regard to asphyxiation, so far we have seen only the severely ill coughing and wheezing. I have no reason to suspect it will become a health hazard for the general population."

"I agree with Professor Landes," said Mirville. "If the atmosphere were truly poisonous, wouldn't dozens of people be dying already? So far not a single person has died of asphyxiation, and it seems highly unlikely."

"Very well," said Governor Mouttet. "Now moving forward, based on your findings at the summit, gentlemen, can you give us an approximate date as to when the volcano will quiet down? I seem to recall you mentioning at a previous meeting that the volcano was on the wane."

Landes shook his head. "Governor, I'm afraid we can't do that. It's impossible."

"I don't need a scientifically accurate date. Just give me a reasonable date, something we can print in the newspaper—perhaps Ascension Day?"

There was a stir around the table.

"That's absurd," said Landes. "No one can predict when the volcano will settle down. It may take weeks, months, or even years. Mount Vesuvius was rumbling for several months before it erupted." He fell silent before adding, "Given the severe nature of the ashfall and tremors, I think we have to consider the possibility that we may soon have a major eruption on our hands."

The room fell silent. Rémy and Landes exchanged a quick glance but said nothing.

Mouttet twitched his moustache. "Professor, I was under the impression that this was just a passing phase. That's what you and M. Mirville have been telling me all along. That's what the newspapers have been printing. Are you telling me this has all been a farce?"

"No, but—" began Landes.

Rémy interrupted Landes. "Governor, allow me to shed some light on the matter. Last night while I was observing Mount Pelée, I heard several explosions coming from the crater, followed by flashes of lightning. The rivers are inundated with mud and debris. The carcasses of cattle are floating out to sea, and the ash is beginning to pile up on every surface for miles. As we speak, the water supply is becoming tainted by sulfur and volcanic mud. Animals are dying. Frankly, I'm not sure how much longer the city can hold out. I think we have to start taking the volcano more seriously. We may have a life-threatening situation on our hands."

"He's right," added Capt. Matthieu Alexandre of the gendarmerie. "Saint-Pierre is being besieged constantly by refugees. If law and order break down, my men will be outnumbered. The situation is reaching a critical point."

There was a loud murmur around the table and a great shuffling of feet.

Mouttet motioned for them to be quiet. "Gentlemen, you're making it sound as if we have a genuine crisis on our hands. I need assurance this is not the case."

"And there's something else," added Rémy, looking around the table. "I hesitated to voice my opinion before, but I've been doing a great deal of reading on the matter, and I believe I've found some striking similarities between Saint-Pierre and Pompeii."

"Do you care to elaborate?" said Mouttet.

"Both Saint-Pierre and Pompeii are ports. Both cities were built in the shadow of a live volcano and experienced similar earth tremors and a pervasive sulfur smell. In addition, both towns experienced lengthy fallout of ashes and cinders prior to eruption . . ."

"Isn't that just a coincidence?" interrupted Mouttet. "By all accounts, Mount Pelée is extinct. Isn't that what you gentlemen have been telling me since last February, that the volcano is just going through a passing phase?"

"Well, yes and no," said Landes, leaning forward. "No one can say for certain Pelée is extinct, nor can we say for certain when it will erupt, but I'm of the opinion that anything can happen. I believe we must prepare for a worst-case scenario. That is the only responsible way to handle the matter."

The room burst into anxious chatter. Some of the men burst out laughing. Rémy gazed at their faces, feeling utter disgust. *Don't they realize they could all be dead in twenty-four hours?*

Rémy added, "Actually, Governor, there's something else I neglected to mention. There's one very important distinction between Saint-Pierre and Pompeii."

"What's that?"

"Most of the residents of Pompeii fled before the eruption, while here in Saint-Pierre, our population swells every day with refugees. And we have an administration that refuses to face the fact that we may have a potential catastrophe on our hands."

Mouttet's face darkened. "Thank you, Lieutenant Rémy, but now is not the time for hysterics. We must be sober and deal with the situation one crisis at a time."

"My point is that the people of Saint-Pierre are reacting with too much indifference," said Rémy. "Everyone seems to have a blind faith that the government will protect them. Look around: everything is covered with ash. It blows in your eyes, gets inside your clothes, and contaminates your food. Every home has layers of ash and cinders inside, and they penetrate into the cupboards and the closets. Every piece of silver is tarnished. When you walk outside, your clothes, your hat, your shoes, everything is covered with ash. And I hear in the botanical garden the birds are asphyxiating. We have actual cases of horses dropping dead in the streets—not rumors. The countryside is covered in so much ash and cinders, it looks like a winter scene. We ignore these signs at our own peril."

Marius Hurard, who had been sitting in the corner watching with interest, spoke up: "Gentlemen, up to now I've held my tongue, but on this issue I feel compelled to voice my opinion. I'm of the belief that spreading alarm is part of the Radical Socialist policy, the policy of our dear friend, M. Knight. If we cave in to fear, we clear a path for their victory in the upcoming election. I propose we remain composed until the whole thing blows over. The only volcanic eruption I'm seeing is in everyone's minds."

Rémy and Landes exchanged an almost imperceptible glance.

"Hear, hear," said Governor Mouttet. "I'm prepared to post troops outside of town with orders to stop any citizens from leaving who might spread panic or false rumors."

Colonel Fournier, who had been silent up to now, spoke out. "Governor, I see no reason why we can't evacuate at least the women and children. The safest and most effective route is by sea. There are a dozen ships in the harbor as we speak, any one of which could take several hundred people at a time. The refugees could camp as far south as Trois-Islets, safe from any potential lava flow. In my opinion, this is the only sensible course of action."

"That's preposterous," said Marius Hurard. "There's no history of lava flow in any West Indian volcano. An evacuation of any sort is likely to cause panic and will most certainly cost the Progressives the election."

"M. Hurard, that is unconscionable," said Colonel Fournier. "And I won't stand for it. We're talking about human lives, but all you seem to care about is politics. At this point, the election is of secondary importance."

"The fact is," said Professor Landes, "based on the position of the craters and the ravines that run down the slopes, we cannot guarantee the security of Saint-Pierre. I believe an evacuation, even a partial evacuation, is warranted."

The men erupted in more squabbling and shouting. As Mouttet tried to quiet them down, Didier, the governor's secretary, stormed into the dining room.

"Governor, I've just received word that the undersea cable linking Saint-Pierre and Dominica has been ruptured," he said. "We've ordered the cable repair ship *Grappler* out to fix the cable to Guadeloupe, but they still haven't solved the problem. We have loads of backed-up messages, so I took the liberty of requesting immediate assistance from Saint Lucia. I've just received word that Admiral Pierre Goudon has ordered the cable steamer *Pouyer-Quertier* to leave Castries at once and attend to the repairs. Meanwhile, our telegraphers are rerouting all messages over the remaining six cables."

"Have we heard back from the Colonial Office?" said Mouttet.

"Not yet, sir."

Mouttet looked noticeably agitated. "Resend the telegram at once, informing Decrais the situation is urgent, that Pelée appears to be in eruption. Tell him large quantities of ash are falling on the north side of the island, and the explosions are becoming more frequent and more volatile. Tell him to send aid at once, including medical aid for the smallpox victims. Meanwhile, Captain Alexandre, send some of the gendarmes down to Le Carbet with a wagon instructing the grocers to fill it up with supplies for the civilians flooding into Saint-Pierre. We must reassure them that they are safe and food is on the way. Otherwise, I fear we may have a breakdown in law and order."

Captain Alexandre stiffened. "I assure you the gendarmes are well trained to ensure that law and order are maintained. And we will distribute the food as soon as it arrives."

"And there's one more thing, sir," said Didier. "I've just received word of some civilian deaths on a plantation due north of here. They are asking for immediate assistance from the gendarmerie."

"A plantation?" said Rémy, suddenly alarmed. "Which one?"

"Domaine Solitude, just north of here," said Didier. "It's owned by a man named Georges Dujon."

Chapter 31

By the time Rémy reached Domaine Solitude, the plantation was in a state of chaos. The field workers were deserting the fields in droves. Cutlasses and pruning sticks lay strewn about like the remnants of a deserting army. The henhouse had been raided; not a single chicken remained. The few horses remaining in the stable were being guarded by a vigilant young stableboy, but the animals were in such a state of distress, they were neighing and stamping their hooves. There was no sign of Georges Dujon. When Rémy asked a passing worker what had happened, the man made the sign of the cross and fled to the cottages down in the valley.

Rémy ran up the stairs to the front door of the villa and entered. Inside, the sounds of crying and wailing reverberated down the hall. He spied a young servant girl heading for the door who told him that most of the household help had already fled, leaving only a few remaining servants to take care of Mme Dujon, who was in an agitated state. He asked about Emilie, but the woman only shook her head and departed. Alarmed, Rémy headed to the salon, where he found Mme Dujon in hysterics, flanked by the elderly nurse, a young servant girl, and a priest. Mme Dujon was sobbing violently, clutching her rosary beads while the priest prayed over her in Latin. As soon as he saw Rémy, he nodded toward the officer, and after blessing the woman, ushered him out to the hall, where they could speak in confidence.

"Pardon me for intruding, Abbé," said Rémy, removing his helmet. "My name is Lt. Denis Rémy of the Fourth Regiment, sent by the garrison commander to assist you. Can you tell me exactly what happened?"

"There was an avalanche and a large loss of life," said the priest, ashen-faced. "It came down from Mount Pelée in torrents, burying several acres and half a dozen men, including Georges Dujon himself. They have yet to recover the bodies."

Rémy was horrified. "And you are quite certain M. Dujon is dead?"

The priest nodded. "Two people witnessed it, including his daughter Emilie, but there was nothing anyone could do. It happened so quickly. And now the poor girl is distraught. I don't know what will become of her."

"Where is she?"

"A gentleman came and took her away."

Rémy grabbed his arm. "Please tell me the name of this man. I must know!"

"It was her fiancé, Lucien Monplaisir."

A wave of alarm swept over Rémy. "Did he say where he was taking her? I must find her before something terrible happens."

"He said he was taking her to the hospital on rue Levassor."

Rémy's eyes widened. "The lunatic asylum?"

"The poor girl was in shock," said Abbé Morel. "She was screaming and crying. The situation was chaotic. Madame was beside herself with grief . . ."

"I should have known, the scoundrel!" said Rémy, his voice tinged with disgust. "Abbé, why did you let him take her?"

"She was in hysterics," said the priest. "There was nothing we could do. I figured the sisters would take good care of her."

"God help her!" said Rémy; he made a fist and banged the wall. *Why, oh why did I let her come back?* In his mind's eye, he could see the expression of blind terror on her face as she witnessed her father sinking in the mud. He blamed himself for not keeping her in Saint-Pierre, where at least he could have protected her. Damn that scoundrel, Lucien!

Abbé Morel's eyes clouded over. "I tried to calm her, Lieutenant, honestly I did, but she was so overcome with fright, I couldn't reason with her. And when I tried to stop M. Monplaisir from taking her away, he pushed me with such a violent force I feared the worst. By that time, it was too late. Emilie tried to warn me about Lucien's character, but I didn't act quickly enough. I failed her. I fear she will never forgive me."

The priest buried his face in his hands.

Rémy put a hand on his shoulder. "Don't blame yourself, Abbé. Now is not the time for regret. I have to find her and get her out of there. I should have known Lucien would be capable of doing something like this. I only wish I had gotten here sooner."

"Do you know the man?" said the priest, still ashen-faced.

"Unfortunately, I do," said Rémy. "He's a ruthless scoundrel. He gave me a nasty crack on the head with a broken bottle. I'm not surprised he would lock Emilie up in the lunatic asylum. The man has no scruples. I have to get her out of there. She must be terrified."

"Oh dear, this is all my fault . . ." said Abbé Morel, his voice breaking. "I should have done more to protect her. If only she knew how much I love her, how much it pains me that I failed her."

"I'm sure she knows," said Rémy. "But right now we're in the middle of an emergency. There will be time for explanations later. I have to find her and get her out of there."

Abbé Morel's face turned grave. "Lieutenant, if something were to happen to me . . . and by this I mean if I should not survive this disaster, please take good care of Emilie. You seem like an honorable man. Her father's dead, her brother is dying, and her mother had a nervous breakdown. She has no one else. Please promise me that."

Rémy assured him that he would.

"Lieutenant, there's something I don't understand," said Abbé Morel. "How do you know Emilie?"

"We met while I was on the scientific committee. She asked to join our party, and I didn't have the heart to say no. The truth is, I grew quite fond of her during the expedition. When I heard about the mudslide, I feared for her safety. I knew the Dujon plantation lay in the direct path of the volcano, and I blame myself for letting her return home while the danger was so evident. I only wish I'd gotten here sooner."

Abbé Morel's face radiated with understanding. "Then I fear not for your safety for it is written, 'Blessed are the merciful, for they shall obtain mercy.' Please find her and take good care of her. I'm sure she's terribly distressed."

The priest poured Rémy a glass of rum. "Here, drink some of this. It will calm your nerves."

Rémy downed it in one gulp and then studied Abbé Morel's face as a realization dawned on him.

"Abbé, are you Emilie's cousin, the priest?"

"Indeed, I am," said Abbé Morel.

"She told me about you. You can rest assured she loves you dearly."

"I just hope there's some way I can make this up to her," said the priest. "I must return to Saint-Pierre now, but please do everything you can to get Emilie out of that place. You can send her to her cousin's house in Morne-Rouge. She'll be safe there. As for me, I'm needed back at the prison."

"What about Mme Dujon?" said Rémy, motioning to the stricken woman who lay on the couch.

Abbé Morel reflected for a moment. "We should send her up to Morne-Rouge as well. She'll be safe there. As for me, I will ride back to Saint-Pierre with you. I'll tell Da Rosette to prepare Madame for the trip."

He bent down and whispered something to Da Rosette, who looked at the stranger with immediate understanding. She whispered something back in Creole, of which Rémy could only pick up a few passing words.

"The nurse says Madame is still in shock from losing her husband. Perhaps they should stay here until she improves."

Rémy shook his head. "No, I have reason to suspect the plantation is still in danger from the volcano. We have to evacuate everyone for their safety."

After making plans to send Mme Dujon and Da Rosette up to Morne-Rouge with the remaining house servants, Rémy ordered all the workers to evacuate their cottages and head south until the volcano calmed down. Then he mounted his horse while Abbé Morel mounted his donkey, and together they headed back to Saint-Pierre. During the ride Rémy found Abbé Morel to be a warm and affable companion. The Jesuit shared with him many stories about his travels to far-flung islands to minister to the poor. Rémy was deeply moved by Abbé Morel's accounts of self-sacrifice; he could easily understand why Emilie was so fond of him.

Just as Saint-Pierre was coming into view, they heard cries and wails echoing from the town. A crowd of people had gathered near the Mouillage. Everything seemed to be in disarray. A few ships hoisted sail and were heading back out to sea, which threw the remaining ships in panic. Sailors were rushing about on the decks trying to put order as the small skiffs paddled back toward shore. Rémy raised himself in the saddle so he could see better and was shocked to see waves of people running through the streets, causing pandemonium as ashes rained down over their heads. It was just as he feared.

A soldier galloped furiously toward them. When he approached, Rémy could see it was Sergeant Aubert. He halted just in front of them, saluted, and explained that Captain Renoult had ordered Rémy back to the garrison for urgent new orders.

"Thank you, Sergeant," said Rémy. Turning to Abbé Morel he said, "It seems I'm needed back at the garrison after all, but I will search for Mlle Emilie the first chance I get. Please don't worry. She'll be safe with me."

"Thank you, Lieutenant," said Abbé Morel. "Go and may God protect you."

Riding back toward town, Rémy watched the priest heading down rue Victor Hugo on his faithful donkey, a lonely figure with the weight of the world on his shoulders.

Chapter 32

When Rémy reached Saint-Pierre, the city was in a state of panic. Ash was falling, creating confusion. The streets were clogged with refugees who were camped outside, milling about aimlessly or seeking shelter and sustenance. Aubert and Rémy rode over the ash-covered cobblestones, wondering how much more the refugees would have to endure. The crowd was so thick, especially near the cathedral on rue Victor Hugo, that it was almost impossible to wend through the disorder. Desperation showed on everyone's faces. People were fighting to get through the doors to baptize their children or to confess their sins. Babies were crying. Mothers looked frantic. Troops from the garrison were attempting to clear the area, but there was no place for the people to go. The city was swiftly running out of accommodations. A few nuns were distributing food and water since the public fountains were clogged with ash, but there was little to go around. Everywhere he looked, there were piles of ashes with the crumpled bodies of dead birds. He wondered how much longer it would be before the people started asphyxiating as well.

The air was cloudy from swirling ash, causing the people to cough and wheeze. Almost everyone had a damp handkerchief tied around their nose and mouth. A young barefoot mother in tattered clothing and a forlorn turban sat nursing her infant in an alleyway. An old man with a cane stood outside place Bertin praying the rosary, while two gendarmes led a shackled man who'd been accused of looting to jail. Clearly the people were starving. They were desperate. A young corporal told Rémy the people were so hungry, they were looting the shops and warehouses in the Figuier Quarter. To Rémy the situation looked bleak, yet all he could think about was Emilie. He wondered if she was safe. He felt a tightening of his chest at her dire predicament. He loathed Lucien Monplaisir as he had never loathed a man before for locking her up in a lunatic asylum. That he could tear the young woman away from her loved ones and lock her up against her will made him seethe with anger. He was certain Emilie was alone and frightened, forgotten on an island gone stark raving mad.

When he arrived at the fort, he left his horse at the stable and marched into the captain's office, feeling a knot in his stomach.

"Lieutenant Rémy reporting for duty, sir," he said, saluting.

Captain Renoult stubbed out his cigarette and returned the salute. "Ah, Rémy, just the man I wished to see. The governor has asked for additional troops to keep the peace and supervise the distribution of food. I'm putting you in charge of a detachment of thirty infantrymen to stop the looting and to evict people from hotels and bars, where they have been demanding free food and shelter. After that I want you to guard the southern road that leads out of town."

Rémy furrowed his brow. "Guard the southern road? Wouldn't it be more effective to evacuate the people to relieve the overcrowding?"

Renoult shook his head. "The mayor refuses to evacuate the town. He wants law and order restored. Fights have been breaking out between the local residents and the refugees over food and shelter."

"How can we calm the people down when there is no food or shelter?" said Rémy.

"That's not my problem," said Renoult. "The main issue right now is restoring law and order. See that something is done about it."

"Yes, sir," said Rémy. "But there is something important I must attend to first."

"What's that?" said Renoult, fixing his hooded eyes on him.

"There's a young woman in the hospital who—"

"There's no time for that now," said Renoult with a dismissive wave. "We have much bigger problems to handle. I'm sure the woman, whoever she is, is in good hands. Carry on now."

"Yes, Captain." Left with no choice, Rémy saluted, did an about-face, and marched out.

Rémy spent the day patrolling the streets of Saint-Pierre with his soldiers, breaking up fights and removing squatters from inns and public areas and then relocating them to the barracks, the hospital, and other areas that had been set aside for the refugees. Some of the people showed signs of smallpox, in which case they were hauled off to the isolation ward in the military hospital. By midafternoon Rémy was worn out, wondering what would happen if a massive outbreak of smallpox occurred in the middle of the volcanic eruption. Thousands could be stricken. Did the island have enough resources to deal with a large-scale disaster?

In the midst of his turmoil, he arrived at a bar called *Le Vieux Cocotier*, where a disturbance was in process. Some drunken patrons were demanding free food and rum, but the owner was ordering them to leave. People were leaning in through the windows, shouting and yelling, adding to the disorder. Marching in through the crowd, Rémy ordered the men to disperse. The leader, a strapping young field hand who was clearly drunk, threw a punch at Rémy. He blocked the man's fist and heaved him aside, where he crashed into some tables, tumbling to the ground. Furious, the man recovered and lunged at Rémy, but luckily he retrieved a bottle and broke it over his assailant's head, knocking him unconscious. Seeing that no other rioters dared raise their fists at him, Rémy ordered the soldiers to carry the recalcitrant field hand to prison for the night. Then he ordered everyone else to clear out of the saloon and told the owner to lock up and send everyone home.

In this manner Rémy and his soldiers went from saloon to saloon and from inn to inn, clearing out the ruckus. But it did little to improve the situation, as there was almost nowhere for the people to go. Many were reduced to sleeping in alleyways or camping out on the beach in makeshift tents. Some were cooking on the side of the road with pots and skillets set up over small fires. Fear and uncertainty showed in everyone's faces. Children were sleeping in the arms of their weary mothers. Fish bones, crab shells, and empty rum bottles lay strewn about on the roads and sidewalks, adding to the disorder. *Will this madness ever end?* Rémy tried putting as many homeless people as possible in the barracks, but conditions were becoming increasingly unsanitary. They had run out of beds, and people were reduced to sleeping in the hallways. He began to feel as though the situation was hopeless, that the city was somehow doomed.

Chapter 33

Sunday, May 4

When Emilie awoke, it was night. At least by the darkness, it appeared to be night. The hospital was quiet. The rumbling had abated. The shrieking of the patients had died down, if only temporarily. The only light came from a small kerosene lamp that glowed in the corner. She was thankful for the light, as without it the room would have the warmth of a stone crypt. She shuddered, thinking how terrifying it would be to wake up in the dark not knowing what was going on around her, whether she was alive or dead, whether she had been forgotten in the chaos. That alone could drive a person mad, she thought. The lack of fresh air and the nauseating smell of rotten eggs caused her to cough and gag. The fumes were relentless and only served to increase her feelings of claustrophobia and helplessness. Outside, she could hear rivière Roxelane flowing furiously toward the sea. It sounded like an overflow. She tried to guess what time it was, but it was impossible. Ash blew in through the sheet-covered shutters and was collecting on the floor in small mounds; it was beginning to spread all over the floor. The sight of it unnerved her. She wondered how long it would be before the situation became intolerable and everyone began asphyxiating from the fumes. *I have to get out of this dungeon*, she thought as a sweating terror came over her. *I have to save myself.*

She called out for help, but this time no one came to check on her. Even the water at her bedside tasted funny. Was it sulfur? She spit it out in disgust. Her thoughts drifted once again to escape. She had to break her shackles and make her way back to the plantation, back to her mother and Da Rosette. She had to find them and bring them to safety. Perhaps they could head down to Fort-de-France, where they had relatives. She feared they were frantically out looking for her, not knowing what had become of her. She was sure they must be searching for her. They couldn't have forgotten about her. The feeling of isolation plagued her. She didn't want to die alone in these two-foot-thick walls with not a soul knowing what had become of her. She didn't want to end her life like a madwoman in a cell.

And then her mind drifted off to Rémy.

She saw his face in the glow of the kerosene lamp. She longed to reach out and touch him, to hear his soft voice, to feel his body close. She wondered if he was thinking about her, if he was worried about her. Why had it come to this? Why had fate come between them like an insurmountable ocean? Deep down inside, she feared she would never see him again.

The shackles around her legs were beginning to feel like slave irons. She tugged at them, but there was no chance of escape without a key. *A key!* Something about the word stirred her memory. What was it? Oh yes, *only you hold the key to your own freedom.* Isn't that what the Grand Zamy had said? *I must get the key*, she thought. And then she remembered the tarot card that depicted a young maiden shackled to the throne of the devil. Her heart beat furiously when she realized the prophecy had come true. The Grand Zamy had predicted her future. She was shackled to the devil, and she was trapped inside the burning tower. If she didn't break out, she would die in the flames. Somehow she had to escape before it was too late.

Mustering all her strength, Emilie pounded on the metal tray and screamed for help. Luckily, this time the door opened. In the darkness she could make out two shadowy forms slithering in through the door. A man and a woman. Emilie lay paralyzed with fear as the nurse came closer and peered in her eyes. In the glow of the lamp, Emilie could make out the nurse's features. There was something unusual about her eyes. They had an almost feline quality about them. She was not the same nurse as before. Of this, Emilie was certain. For one thing she wore perfume and had sensuous features that vaguely resembled the beautiful mulâtresse she had seen in the Grand Zamy's shop. The more Emilie scrutinized her face, the more certain she was that the woman was the mysterious shop assistant.

The nurse laid a damp cloth on Emilie's forehead. Standing behind her was the doctor. He was a suave, older gentleman with tufts of white hair and an expensive suit and waistcoat, but around his nose and mouth, he had affixed a wet handkerchief to protect him from the sulfur fumes. It was hard to make out his features, but there was something oddly familiar about him as well. Emilie was certain she had seen him before.

"Is this the patient you told me about?" said the doctor in clipped tones.

"Yes, Doctor," said the nurse solemnly.

The doctor leaned forward, peering into Emilie's eyes. "You're certain this is the young woman who asked to be discharged from the hospital?"

"Yes, Doctor, this is the one," said the nurse.

Suddenly Emilie sensed something was wrong. The doctor was the same approximate height and had the same deep, resonating voice as the Grand Zamy. The resemblance was uncanny. The realization caused Emilie to break out in goose bumps, as if she had awoken in the middle of a nightmare.

"Very well; let's get started," said the doctor. "I must ask you a few questions first. Are you indeed Mam'selle Emilie Dujon?"

"Yes," said Emilie in a faint whisper. She tried to inch her body away from the doctor, but it was impossible since the shackles kept her immobile. He moved in closer until he was only inches from her face, scrutinizing her. She could smell the acrid odor of rum, incense, and cigars emanating from him.

"Ah, that's better," said the doctor, smiling. "I'm glad you're still with us. We were worried about you for a while. We haven't met before, but I'm your doctor. You can call me Dr. Faust." He roared with laughter. Emilie's eyes widened in shock. "According to official hospital policy, I cannot release you unless you sign these discharge papers. Are you prepared to cooperate?"

"Yes! I'll do anything to get out of here," she said.

"In time, in time," said the doctor. "First we must take care of a little business." From his breast pocket, he produced a folded sheet of paper, which he opened and scrutinized in the candlelight.

"Everything appears to be in order," he said. "There is, however, the matter of payment. How much are you willing to pay to leave the hospital?"

Emilie was taken aback. "Pay?"

"Of course you must pay," he said. "Did you think the hospital was free? The only question is how much are you willing to pay to get out of here?"

Emilie was stunned. She looked at the doctor and the nurse, but their eyes betrayed nothing. Her body began to tremble. Her teeth rattled, and she felt strangely cold and clammy, though the air was hot and humid. With no money, how could she pay? As far as she knew, there was only a hundred francs in her father's strongbox, money he kept for dire emergencies. But he was dead. The plantation was in ruins. The volcano was on the verge of eruption. Somehow the hospital did not seem that important.

"I'm sorry, but I don't understand," said Emilie at last, feeling dizzy.

"Then allow me to explain," said the doctor with mounting impatience. "You wish to be released from this hospital; I hold the key, but how much are you willing to pay to regain your freedom? How much is your life worth?"

"I want my freedom, but I have no money with me," she said.

"That's most unfortunate, because if you don't pay me, you'll never leave this hospital alive. The cards have foretold it. You will be consumed in a great fire. Your body will be incinerated. We have spoken of this before. You were warned about the danger. Now you must decide your fate."

Emilie's eyes widened. "Who are you? What is your name?"

"We are old friends," said the doctor. "Now, mam'selle, if you want to leave this hospital, it will cost you a small fortune—or your soul. It depends on how much you value your life. The only question is, how much are you willing to pay?"

Emilie's heart began to pound. What he was saying was impossible. The Grand Zamy was using her predicament to extort money out of her. He was trying to crush her with fear and threats. She felt the bile rising from her stomach to her throat.

"I truly don't understand," she said, looking at the doctor and nurse in disbelief.

The doctor dangled a key in front of her. "I hold the power to save your life. How much are you willing to pay to save yourself? Do you remember we spoke before about a gagé?"

A sudden realization dawned on Emilie. She was overcome with horror.

"Are you asking me to make a pact with the devil?" she said. "That's impossible! I'll never sell my soul to the devil. Give me the key now! If you don't, you're guilty of murder."

The Grand Zamy roared with laughter. The sound of it filled Emilie with terror. Even the nurse laughed too, showing pearly white teeth, fine features, and glowing, catlike eyes.

"Mam'selle," he continued, "I am holding a contract for which you already owe me eight thousand francs. If you sign a new one, I will gladly rip it up."

He dangled a sheet of paper in front of her.

"What does the contract say?"

"Here, you may read it." He handed the new contract toward Emilie, but she could not make out the writing in the dim light. It was written in some foreign script, possibly Arabic or Greek, although she couldn't say for certain. "Don't worry, mam'selle. I assure you the terms are quite favorable. By signing on the dotted line, your debt will be erased forever. You will be like a new person. On this you have my word." The nurse nodded. The woman's eyes displayed no emotion, but they looked so trustworthy, almost beckoning. Still, Emilie hesitated. She knew these contracts always had clauses that were impossible to fulfill, clauses that could ruin her financially and damn her soul for all eternity. She refused to take the contract from his hands. "Go ahead, mam'selle." He beckoned. "Don't be afraid. Take the contract. You'll be out of here in no time. You have my word."

Emilie's eyes blazed. "I refuse."

The Grand Zamy leaned in so close she could smell the rum and cigars on his breath.

"Let me repeat, if you don't sign, it's as if you have sealed your own death warrant."

"And if I do sign, then I will also be signing my own death warrant," she said. "I will be selling my very soul to the devil."

"Why are you so mistrustful?" he said. "I came here to offer you salvation. Sign the contract now, and I will set you free. It's your only hope. It's the only way out of here. There's no time to lose. Hurry now before it's too late."

He handed her a gold fountain pen and the contract. With shaky hands, she took them and signed where he indicated. She tried to read the contract but couldn't. The words were as foreign to her as hieroglyphics. When she finished, she handed the contract back to him, so terrified that her whole body was shaking.

"There, that wasn't so hard, was it?" he said, stuffing it in his jacket pocket.

"What does it say?" she asked.

"You have just signed over the deed to your plantation. But don't worry; your debt of eight thousand francs is hereby forgiven."

Emilie gasped. "What did you say?"

"It's a small price to pay for freedom, isn't it? And I promise to keep up my end of the bargain. Sister Alphonsine, please hand me the key."

The nurse pulled out a jangle of keys and handed them to the Grand Zamy. He located one and used it to open the lock that held her feet in the shackles.

"Here, put on this shawl and come with us," said the nurse.

"Let me go," said Emilie. "I'm not going with you! I'm going home to find my mother and Da Rosette. I've bought my freedom."

The Grand Zamy slapped Emilie across the face. She cried out and felt a trickle of blood oozing from her mouth onto the shawl. She looked at the red stain in horror and threw the wrap on the floor.

"You'll come with me until the debt is paid," said the Grand Zamy. The woman shoved Emilie's dress over her head and buttoned it in the back. Then, grabbing her by the arm, the Grand Zamy pulled her out of the room and down a stone corridor lit only by glowing oil lamps. As they passed each cell, the inhabitants shrieked in voices that made her skin crawl. Sometimes she would catch sight of a ragged patient with sunken eyes and matted hair covered in volcanic dust, and she would recoil. Their haunted expressions gave her chills. They were prisoners in a jail from which they would never escape. But at least death would free their souls.

They descended a flight of stairs and proceeded down another stone corridor and then through a back door. The Grand Zamy flung open the door and pulled Emilie toward a waiting carriage. He opened the carriage door.

"Get in," said the Grand Zamy. "This is your carriage to freedom."

Left with no other choice, Emilie climbed in. The Grand Zamy and the nurse climbed in after her and slammed the door shut, and the carriage took off down rue Levassor and out into the dark, moonless night.

Chapter 34

Monday, May 5

The next morning when Emilie awoke, she was in a strange bed. She was famished, and her face still stung where the Grand Zamy had slapped her. A streak of dried blood stained her dress. She looked around. The room was small and bare; sunlight filtered in through the wooden shutters. A broken-down chest of drawers sat opposite her, and beside it was a wooden chair and a shelf that contained statues of saints. A chicken was walking around, clucking and pecking at insects on the wooden floor. All she could remember from the previous night was a strange doctor and nurse, a long carriage ride, and a struggle before everything went black. She couldn't remember how she had gotten into the bed or even who had brought her here, as if her memory had been wiped clean.

The smell of fried food wafted in through the wooden shutters, mingling with the cloying scent of burnt incense and chicken feathers. Her head throbbed. She tried to sit up but realized her legs were tied to the bed frame, this time with rope. She was wearing her cotton shift, and her dress was draped across the wooden chair, out of reach. All her muscles ached, and she felt despondent. Her strength was ebbing, and her mind was fuzzy.

Presently a woman peeked in. Emilie looked at her and froze. All at once she realized she wasn't alone. She was in a house and was being watched. They were holding her prisoner. And there was something familiar about the woman. Emilie was sure she had seen her face before.

"Where am I?" said Emilie, breaking the stillness.

The woman set down a tray of cassava bread and tea on the night table. "Bonjour, you are safe here; do not worry," she said.

Although the woman was wearing a plain madras skirt and turban, Emilie was certain she had seen the woman's face before. She was lovely. She had the same feline eyes and sensuous lips as the nurse, the same coffee-colored skin, but in the daylight she looked somewhat tired and drawn. She wore no jewelry, and she gave Emilie almost no eye contact. A sickening feeling came over her.

"Madame, how did I get here?" said Emilie.

"You were brought here last night at your request."

"At my request?" said Emilie.

"Yes, it is in the contract," said the woman with deadened eyes. "According to the contract, you will stay here until you have completed your end of the bargain."

"My end of the bargain?" Emilie felt a chill down her spine. It was all starting to come back: the mysterious doctor in the dead of night, the contract, the gold fountain pen, the strange writing, the impossible terms, the veiled threats, the slap, and the taste of blood in her mouth. The horrible, excruciating pain.

"I know you," said Emilie, feeling her neck grow hot. "Your name is Alphonsine. Tell me what was in the contract."

"You made a bargain with M. Jacquet," said the woman with nonchalance. "And now he expects you to fulfill it. Until then, you are his guest. All your needs will be met, but you must remain here. Don't worry; you have nothing to fear."

"I have to go home," said Emilie. "Please untie me."

"That's impossible," said Alphonsine. "You are a guest of M. Jacquet. Drink this tea. It will make you feel better."

Emilie picked up the tea and sipped it. She didn't realize how parched and famished she was until she had finished the cup. After a few minutes, she felt a slight burning sensation in her stomach. Soon she was drowsy and fell asleep.

She had no idea what time it was when she awoke again. She was alone in the room. It was dark outside, and there was no smell of food. The air was stale and humid. She was hungry and frightened. The only sound came from a dog barking in the distance and a deep male voice coming from down the hall, but she saw no one. As she lay in the darkness, the pain of the previous day came flooding back. Fear and loneliness gripped her. She tried to stop the tears, but it was impossible. She cried into her blanket, releasing all the pain and frustration she had been harboring. She was quickly losing hope.

Presently, the woman reappeared with another tray of food and tea. She urged Emilie to eat and drink, and after she had downed the liquid, she once again felt the same burning sensation in her stomach. Several hours later, after a few more glasses of tea, she felt as if her body was on fire. She cried out in pain. The burning sensation started in her stomach and spread to all her limbs, causing indescribable pain. It paralyzed her. She felt as if she was burning on the inside. Soon she was writhing in bed. She was in utter agony. She tried to scream, but the words would not escape her throat. Even her throat was scorching.

Then Emilie developed a vertigo that caused the room to spin all around. She became dizzy, incoherent, and delirious as the fiery sensation coursed throughout her body until her insides were red-hot and scorching. She felt as if her insides were burning with fire. The terror and fear caused her to cry out, but only a muffled sob escaped her raspy throat. She couldn't focus on anything, and the burning sensation kept rising to her throat, threatening to burn a hole through her neck. Even her heart was burning. The pain was paralyzing, and she was seized with fear. Then she realized the horrible truth: the quimboiseur was poisoning her to death. Her body was slowly dying, burning to death. The poison was eating her alive from the inside. They had no intention of letting her leave, and soon she would be dead and no one would ever know the truth. They would bury her in an unmarked grave, and no one would be the wiser. Escape was impossible. Thinking quickly, Emilie realized her only chance for survival was to expel the poison from her body.

She felt her body convulsing, and she prayed for salvation. She had the sudden strange sensation that she was in an endless dark tunnel, trying to reach a glimmer of light, but it was too far out of reach. No matter how hard she tried, she could not reach it. She was collapsing, dying. Her muscles and organs were shutting down. She was burning to death. Soon the light would be out, and she would never reach it. She would slowly, methodically burn to death, like a moth in a flame. Poof! She mouthed a silent prayer, stuck a finger down her throat, and vomited the contents of her stomach.

Chapter 35

Monday, May 5

At noon, a deafening roar shook the town of Saint-Pierre.

From his makeshift post guarding the southern road, Rémy looked up toward Mount Pelée and saw an enormous avalanche of black mud plunging down the slopes at a terrifying speed, heading toward the plantations lower down. He felt a chill go up his spine. *Good God, the volcano is erupting!* He fumbled for his binoculars and focused them on the mountain. Through the clouds he could make out an enormous dark mass a quarter of a mile wide. It swept everything out of its path. People were pointing and shouting as the mudslide hurtled down the mountain, kicking up enormous clouds of dust and causing a thunderous boom that set off a wave of alarm. People clung to each other and cried out for mercy. Rémy stared in horror, feeling utterly powerless.

Later, men began shouting that the Guérin sugar factory had been completely inundated in the avalanche. Dozens of people were buried alive. Workshops and warehouses were overrun. Some of M. Guérin's own family members had perished. Of the entire estate, only a solitary chimney remained visible above the volcanic mud. By a stroke of luck, M. Guérin was rescued and reportedly stated the only reason he survived was because he ran back to the house to retrieve his hat. The enormity of the damage was impossible to comprehend. All of Saint-Pierre was in a state of mourning and nervous agitation on account of the Guérin sugar factory disaster. And just as frightening, rivière Blanche was flowing at five times its usual volume. No one knew what to make of it, only that it seemed as if the laws of nature had been repealed.

Rémy braced himself for mass panic. Alone he felt helpless, but something had to be done to quell the anxiety and fear of the people. Leaving Sergeant Aubert in charge, he hurried back to the fort to see Colonel Fournier. When he reached his office, he found the older man anxiously writing out a telegram. By his side was a half-empty bottle of rum.

"Request permission to speak, mon colonel," said Rémy, saluting.

Fournier looked up. "Permission granted." His face brightened somewhat as Rémy approached, but the junior officer could see the deepened lines on his forehead, the haunted look in his eyes, and his drooping shoulders. The colonel he admired and respected looked like a shell of his former self.

"Sir, about the orders to keep the citizens contained in the city, I fear we will soon have a breakout of civil disorder on our hands. I think we should change tactics."

Fournier shook his head. "I'm sorry, Lieutenant, but that's not possible. Our orders are to keep soldiers posted on all routes in and out of the city to seal it off. The only people who are authorized to leave the city are military personnel, gendarmes, and clergymen. Mouttet threatened several high-ranking civilians, including judges and customs officers, with dismissal if they leave their posts. He's using them as exam—"

"Examples? Of what, foolishness?" interrupted Rémy.

Fournier's face reddened. "He's acting on orders from Minister Decrais of the Colonial Office."

"That's ridiculous," said Rémy. "The Colonial Office has no idea of the situation down here. The governor should use every power of his office to save lives."

"I know Governor Mouttet very well," said Fournier. "He's a disciplined, thoughtful civil servant, a credit to the Republic, but he's under extreme pressure. I know of one judge who tendered his resignation and is heading down to Fort-de-France as we speak. He was a good man, that judge. His career is finished."

Fournier poured himself a glass of rum and downed it in one gulp.

"Good Lord, what has become of this island?" said Rémy. "Should a man have to choose between his life and his career? Can anything be done to put some sanity in the situation?"

Fournier got up and walked toward the window. He looked outside at the ash-covered rooftops, the people wandering aimlessly over the muddy streets, the dead cattle floating in the harbor. His eyes clouded over as he stared out over the gray, pumice-covered water.

"Don't think for a minute I don't sympathize with the people of Saint-Pierre," he said at last. "I know they are starving and in need of adequate shelter, but my hands are tied. Under the circumstances, my best advice to you is to offer them food and drink supplied by the sisters of Saint-Paul de Chartres. There are tents erected on the grounds of the church on rue des Ursulines where they can find shelter. That should help calm their nerves until this thing blows over. Beyond that, it's out of my control."

"If you'll forgive me, mon colonel, that seems a bit inadequate," said Rémy.

"I'm afraid there's nothing more I can do," said Fournier. "I've been recalled, and I'm leaving the island today."

"What?" said Rémy, uncomprehendingly.

Fournier held up a telegram from Mouttet. Rémy snatched it out of his hand and read it, his face a mask of bewilderment.

"It seems I'm being transferred to Guadeloupe, which means my services here are no longer required," said Fournier in a voice tinged with irony. "Captain Renoult will be in charge for the time being. I trust you'll be in good hands."

Rémy felt nauseous and light-headed. He was overcome with disgust. Fournier was the most experienced, levelheaded commandant on the island. This was the last nail in the coffin as far as Rémy was concerned.

"But, sir, how can he just ship you off like that?" said Rémy.

Fournier placed his helmet on his head. "I've learned not to question orders from the Colonial Office. I think the governor asked for my transfer. It came as a shock to me as well. Now if you'll excuse me, I have to send this telegram to Paris immediately, while we still have some working undersea cables. It's been an honor serving with you, Rémy. You're a good man."

Rémy watched as the colonel buttoned his tunic and marched out the door. Standing alone in Fournier's office, Rémy realized all at once how truly dire their predicament was.

Left with no recourse, Rémy rejoined his men at the roadblock on the outskirts of Saint-Pierre. Fatigue and hunger showed on the soldiers' faces, but even worse were the faces of the refugees, which were beyond hope. They were tired, hungry, and desperate to leave. Children were barefoot and crying; the women were disheveled and pitiful, their clothes covered in ash and soot. There was so little food and drink to go around that soon the sisters of Saint-Paul de Chartres had to start turning people away. Slowly Rémy felt his resolve slipping. When a family of peasants with a meager donkey cart and a flock of chickens begged for the chance to pass through the checkpoint, he had no choice but to turn them away. Standing firm with his hands on his sides, he told them it was forbidden to leave the city, by order of the governor. He ordered them back to town, but inside he was crushed with guilt. He knew the orders were politically motivated and were not based on public safety or common sense, but he could not countermand a direct order. He remembered the grim warning of his commandant back in Senegal that any further misconduct on his part would get him shipped off to the penal colony in French Guiana, a veritable death sentence.

When news began to spread that the avalanche had smashed through the Guérin sugar factory, burying people alive, turmoil broke out in the city. Debris from the avalanche swept out to sea, driving back the tide more than three hundred feet before it rushed back in a tidal wave that crashed into place Bertin, sweeping several people out to sea. That set off a wave of alarm. People ran through the streets, shouting and screaming, seeking shelter or trying to reach higher ground. The Mouillage Quarter was evacuated to points higher up, but the once-peaceful town was now a disaster zone.

Fearing a stampede out of the city, Rémy ordered his soldiers to hold firm, even to the point of using force, although he knew his orders were dangerous, possibly illegal given the circumstances. But he had no recourse. Everywhere he looked, frightened citizens closed their shops and homes and fled with everything they could carry in their haste to escape the doomed town. Those who lacked anywhere to go resigned themselves to their fate and camped outside the cathedral or the army barracks. Others watched the commotion from their balconies with anxious, distraught faces, waiting for the end to come.

Sergeant Aubert, looking uncharacteristically grim, strode up to Rémy. He saluted and said, "Mon lieutenant, before the situation gets out of control, I believe we should allow small groups of civilians to evacuate, perhaps a dozen at a time. If we keep them here, civil disorder will break out, and more lives will be lost."

Rémy shook his head. "Colonel Fournier made it clear that no one is allowed to leave the city save for military personnel, gendarmes, and clergymen. Everyone else must remain in their homes until the volcano calms down."

"That doesn't appear to be likely anytime soon," said Aubert. He shielded his eyes and scanned the mountain. "I believe our keeping the people here is downright cruel."

"While I sympathize with their plight, I cannot countermand a direct order from my commanding officer," said Rémy. "Between you and me, Colonel Fournier shares our view, but his hands are tied. He told me to forget the idea of allowing citizens to evacuate. Instead, he urged me to offer them food and drink supplied by the sisters of Saint-Paul de Chartres."

Aubert scowled. "The old man's gone mad. Too much malaria, rum, and dengue fever. What about Captain Renoult?"

"No chance," said Rémy. "He won't allow it. If he finds out we're letting people through, he'll relieve me of duty and put me in jail. I can't risk running afoul of the brass again."

"I don't suppose there are any volcanoes in French Guiana, am I right?" said Aubert wryly.

"No, just alligators, piranhas, and rats the size of dogs . . . not to mention the dry guillotine."

"That puts things into perspective," said Aubert. "I guess I'll be heading back to my post now."

"Before you leave," said Rémy, "do not, I repeat, do not turn your gun on anyone. If the people attack out of desperation, shoot in the air or use the butt of your rifle to turn them back. There is to be no shooting at civilians under any circumstances. Is that clear?"

"Oui, mon lieutenant," said Aubert, saluting.

"Carry on," said Rémy, returning the salute. "Let's hope this whole thing blows over shortly." As he watched Aubert return to his post, Rémy felt a wave of nausea, a sinking feeling that the situation would not improve but would soon spiral out of control.

Chapter 36

Tuesday, May 6

In the early morning hours, Rémy was shaken by a startling sight. The summit of Mount Pelée exploded with loud detonations. The blast sent a ball of flame and a mushroom cloud of black smoke over a thousand feet into the air, sending shock waves through the city. Lightning flashes lit up the purple-gray sky, and the explosions shook the town to its foundations. A bank of electric generators at the power station on rivière Roxelane failed when they clogged with ash, plunging half the town into darkness. Streetlamps ceased functioning, and a rash of burglaries broke out, adding to the alarm. And now rivière Blanche turned into a raging torrent, cutting off traffic to and from the northern half of the island, adding further alarm. Fear and despair were starting to show in the people's faces. Frantic residents wandered through the streets with parcels on their heads, their paths lit by kerosene lamps as they yelled, "Get out now! Save yourselves! The river has burst its banks!"

The volcano sounded like the discharges of artillery, while the windows rattled from aerial vibrations. It set off a wave of panic. Homeless people thronged the Mouillage district, and the churches were packed with people desperate for absolution. Mudslides continued rumbling on the mountainside, tumbling down toward rivière Blanche, throwing up clouds of dust, adding a terrifying show to the onlookers. To the residents of Saint-Pierre, it looked as if the world had come to an end. And for the vast majority, there was no escape.

While Rémy was out making his rounds, he was shocked by the sheer number of posters hanging all over town depicting Mayor Fouché assuring the public they were in no danger. The mayor urged them not to yield to groundless panic and to resume their normal business to whatever extent possible. But by the looks of things, no one was taking him seriously. The normally bustling marketplace was like a graveyard. The schools were empty, and food was running out. Even place Bertin looked like a ghost town. And there were only a few stalwarts huddled outside the Chamber of Commerce waiting for supplies to come in by ship, desperate for any sign that la Mère Patrie had not forgotten them.

At noon Governor Mouttet and his entourage left on the *Topaz* for Prêcheur to drop off food supplies and to aid in the evacuation of the sick and elderly, but they returned an hour later reporting that a panic onshore had caused several people to fall in the water and almost drown. Since there was not enough room on the *Topaz* to take everyone, fighting and scuffling broke out, resulting in several injuries. It did not help matters that Prêcheur was coated in five inches of ash and rivière Blanche had become a roaring torrent, cutting the villagers off from the relative safety of Saint-Pierre. By the time Governor Mouttet returned to Saint-Pierre, he appeared shaken and distressed. When he alighted ashore, he looked like he had aged ten years. He mirrored the hopelessness of the people of Prêcheur, who had to face another night of torment in the shadow of Mount Pelée.

A large group of travelers hoping to flee Saint-Pierre had assembled on the wharf. They were loaded down by packages and trunks and were clamoring to board one of the steamers of the Compagnie Gerard to Fonds-Saint-Denis, Morne d'Orange, or Le Carbet. But there was not enough space for everyone. Rémy estimated over three hundred panicked travelers were trying to cram aboard a single steamer. It was an impossible situation that was reaching a boiling point. Wending his way through the crowd, Rémy approached the governor. "Excellency, I'd like to have a word with you if possible."

"Yes, yes, what is it?" said Mouttet, ashen-faced.

"I was wondering if you would reconsider your decision to keep the people in Saint-Pierre. I believe we would have a better chance of maintaining order if we permitted small groups of people to leave. I fear the situation will deteriorate due to the shortage of food and accommodations." Mouttet's eyes were unfocused and glazed. He seemed to be staring off at some uncertain point in the distance. After Rémy made his request, he only shook his head.

"There is to be no change to my policy as of the present," he said. "I'm still awaiting orders from the Colonial Office. In the meantime, I've put in a request for more supplies, but so far there's been no word. I'll let the garrison commander know as soon as I hear something."

"But, sir . . ."

"Lieutenant, as I stated previously, the safety of Saint-Pierre is completely assured. I have sent troops to patrol the road to Fort-de-France, with orders to turn back refugees who are trying to leave. That should go a long way to restoring order."

They were enveloped by the crowd. People were pushing and shoving in an attempt to board the ships. To alleviate the situation, gendarmes pushed them farther back, but Rémy felt as if his body were being crushed by the onslaught.

"But, sir, as you can see, the situation is growing desperate," said Rémy. "Look around you. I fear a breakdown of law and order. We can't hold out much longer."

"I'm sorry, Lieutenant, there's nothing more I can do now," said Mouttet, pushing past Rémy. "I'm heading down to Fort-de-France to check on the situation there, but I'll be back later this afternoon. As far as I'm concerned, there's nothing in the activity of Pelée that warrants a departure from Saint-Pierre. There will be no evacuation."

Stunned, Rémy stared at the governor and then walked away.

The governor's words fell like a sharp sword on his neck. So that was it. There was to be no evacuation. No assistance from the Métropole. No hope of rescue. They were on their own, cut off from the rest of the world in their hour of need. He watched the governor wend his way through the crowd, feeling a gnawing ache in his gut. The governor was handling the matter like a career bureaucrat when the situation demanded a more aggressive approach. A large-scale evacuation was warranted, even by sea if necessary. There were just a scant five miles between Saint-Pierre and the rumbling volcano. Tremors and ashfall had become a daily occurrence. Mudslides were an ever-present danger. Already the people were showing signs of fatigue and despondency. If the situation deteriorated, there could be a stampede, riots. Hundreds could die. Shaken by this realization, Rémy returned to his makeshift post guarding the southern route, but the plight of the refugees was getting worse. He feared the soldiers would soon be forced to use their weapons, if only to save their own lives.

An hour later, Governor Mouttet stepped off the *Topaz* in Fort-de-France and hurried to the telegraph office. He glanced at his pocket watch. He had only an hour to collect his messages and tend to his errands before the next sailing back to Saint-Pierre. Time was precious; the people in Prêcheur were desperate for supplies and relief, and the fumes from the volcano were becoming intolerable. Most of the refugees were camped along the shore, waiting for ships to take them farther south, away from the volcano. His last attempt to evacuate the sick and elderly on the *Topaz* had resulted in a debacle, with several people falling into the water and nearly drowning. He couldn't risk another catastrophe like that. If word got back to Decrais at the Colonial Office that he had botched the rescue attempt, there's no telling how it would end. He looked up and saw the naval cruiser *Suchet* bobbing in the harbor, and an ingenious plan formed in his head. Salvation was close at hand. When he pushed open the door to the telegraph office, the clerks jumped to their feet.

"Good afternoon, Governor," said Jules Coppet, doffing his cap.

Mouttet looked at their expectant faces. "Good afternoon, gentlemen. Has anything arrived for me from Paris?"

"Not yet, sir," said Coppet. "But I received this message from our office in Saint-Pierre."

He sorted through a pile of messages and handed a telegraph to the governor.

CABLE LINK WITH ST. LUCIA BROKEN. BELIEVED SEISMIC ACTIVITY PELEE RESPONSIBLE. ROUTING ALL EXTERNAL TRAFFIC VIA YOU.

"What do you make of this?" said Mouttet.

"Exactly what it says, sir," said Coppet. "It means we'll be responsible for sending all the messages from Saint-Pierre and Fort-de-France, which means double the work. We could be backed up for several days. They say the cable lines to Saint Lucia and Saint Vincent were damaged in the avalanche that destroyed the Guérin sugar factory. Now we have only one working cable, the one to Dominica."

Mouttet furrowed his brow. "Only one cable?"

"Yes, sir," said Coppet.

"That sounds serious."

"It's very serious, sir," said Coppet. "It means it could take hours or even days for us to get through to Paris. All messages will have to be routed through Dominica and from there to Saint Thomas and New York. It's a disaster."

"Some of the messages have already gotten lost in the shuffle," added another operator. "Dominica is complaining of backlogs. It could take weeks to sort through all this mess. We need help."

Mouttet felt a tightening in his chest. The situation was starting to escalate. How did things manage to deteriorate so quickly?

"I noticed the cruiser in port," said Mouttet. "Please send an urgent cable to the Colonial Office. Do you have some paper?" Coppet handed him paper and a fountain pen. The governor scratched out a message and handed it back. "I need that cruiser at my disposal as soon as possible. Give this message top priority."

"Yes, sir," said Coppet.

He put on his headphones and began tapping out a message in Morse code:

Fort-de-France 6 May.

To Decrais, Minister of Colonies: Request you put Suchet *at my immediate disposal. Heading up to Saint-Pierre to coordinate the evacuation of Prêcheur. Please advise soonest possible. Imperative you send me five thousand francs for immediate relief.*
L. Mouttet

"Here's your copy, sir," said Coppet.

"Good work," said Mouttet, pocketing the message. "I'll be heading back to Saint-Pierre in an hour. You know where to reach me with any messages. I'll be at my suite in the Hôtel Intendance. Please forward any messages to me straightaway."

"Yes, sir," said Coppet, doffing his cap once more. "Consider it done."

After the governor had left, Jules Coppet turned to his companion and said, "What do you suppose he plans to do with the *Suchet*—shell the volcano?"

"He's only been here a few months, and I think he's already lost his mind," said the other telegrapher.

The two men burst into laughter.

Chapter 37

Wednesday, May 7

Just before dawn, a violent scene erupted on Mount Pelée. Clouds of ash and bolts of lightning with reddish flames lit up the early-morning sky. Huge projectiles shot out of the crater with terrifying booms, rocking the town with explosions like cannon fire. Black smoke billowed out of the crater, creating a sense of impending doom. Glasses fell off tables, windows shattered, and barometers plummeted. The explosions knocked Rémy out of bed. Stumbling to his feet, he made his way to his desk, feeling the floor shaking beneath his feet. He grabbed his binoculars and made his way to the window to study the scene up close.

"Good Lord, it looks like the end of the world," he said, feeling a profound sense of doom. The summit of Mount Pelée was alight with orange-red flames. Ash was spurting everywhere. The harbor looked like a scene from the last days of Pompeii. The once-sparkling blue water was dull and gray, littered with the corpses of farm animals, tree trunks, and deposits of ash and pumice stones that seemed to stretch on for miles.

He threw on his uniform and boots, refilled his cartridge with bullets, and went to receive his orders. Then he headed down to the courtyard, where his men were already assembled. Dividing them up into two groups, he sent the first group to patrol the town and keep order, and he sent the second group to guard the southern road to make sure people stayed safely in their homes.

More refugees flooded into Saint-Pierre. Some of them were survivors of the Guérin sugar factory disaster or had lost family members in the tragedy and were in a state of shock. Sisters from the convent brought them inside and gave them food and drink; the rest just wandered aimlessly through the throng or crowded into the marketplace, but food was scarce and money even scarcer. A shipment of food brought in by steamer went quickly. Bags of rice and beans and loaves of bread were handed out to famished residents, who grabbed them and fled back to their homes. Some people were too mesmerized by the pyrotechnic display on Mount

Pelée to do anything but gape and stare. As the morning dragged on, more people flooded into Saint-Pierre since, by everybody's estimation, it was the safest place for the displaced residents from the northern half of the island. Placards all over town announced that the volcano was on the wane and the people should sit tight and wait out the end of the eruption, but by the looks on their faces, few believed it anymore.

Rémy was exhausted from pursuing looters and squatters, yet more people arrived by steamers and small ferries or in simple donkey carts and horse wagons. The stream of refugees continued unabated. He reckoned the population had swelled by several thousand. But the volcano seemed no closer to quieting down. A thick layer of ash now covered every surface. Everyone's clothes were covered in soot and ash. Children sat on the ground and played with the volcanic dust as if it were sand. The women were noticeably distressed. Their normally vibrant faces reflected fear and distress. For Rémy, the work was endless. He broke up countless fights, arrested dozens of disorderly civilians, and emptied houses of illegal squatters, but there was nowhere for them to go. They had taken up every inch of available space in the barracks, the inns, and the guesthouses. Some refugees were reduced to sleeping in the alleyways. Others crowded into the cathedral to hear mass or to baptize their children. Later, news began to spread like wildfire that the Soufrière volcano on Saint Vincent had erupted. This caused a wave of panic to spread throughout the crowd. They now began to collect outside the mayor's office, demanding answers. As Rémy watched the faces of the angry citizens, he sensed a rising tension in the air, a sense of impending doom.

The latest issue of *Les Colonies* did little to calm everyone's nerves. At his post guarding the southern road, Rémy scanned the headlines, disturbed by Marius Hurard's carefully crafted front-page interview with Gaston Landes that looked to be no more than political showmanship:

> *According to observations made by M. Landes, in the early morning hours of yesterday, the central crater of the volcano vomited out a yellow and black powdery substance at various intervals. The bottom of the neighboring valleys should be evacuated and those remaining should keep to a*

certain height to avoid being overwhelmed by the muddy lava, as were Herculaneum and Pompeii. Vesuvius, added M. Landes, claimed only a few victims. Pompeii was evacuated in time and few corpses were found in the buried cities. In conclusion, Mount Pelée presents no more danger to Saint-Pierre than Vesuvius poses to Naples.

The article ended with the coup de grâce—a statement by Governor Mouttet himself:

The security of Saint-Pierre remains uncompromised.

Incensed, Rémy threw the newspaper on the ground, where it was trampled by the feet of the crowd.

He looked up suddenly and saw a cloud of black ash billowing out of Mount Pelée like a giant cauliflower, filling the skies with swirling black ash and volcanic dust that blocked out the sun and cast a gloomy shadow over the town. There was an audible hush among the crowd. Everyone stared at it in horror. The ominous nature of the cloud told Rémy one thing: the end was near.

As he stood with his soldiers guarding the highway, the crowd grew agitated. They began yelling and shouting, demanding to be let out. Men shook their fists and women screamed and cursed at him, but Rémy and his soldiers were forced to turn them back at the point of their rifles. For several hours they guarded the road, not permitting anyone to pass except occasional gendarmes and clergymen, no matter how much the people screamed and shouted.

By late afternoon, a new group approached. They claimed to be survivors from the Guérin sugar factory. They begged and pleaded to be allowed to leave. Rémy was at once distressed by their plight. There were two dozen of them, men and women with soot-covered clothes, haunted eyes, and panicked faces. Their voices were both pleading and demanding. Something in the tone of their voices bothered Rémy. The men carried machetes, and the women were armed with knives. They didn't look like normal refugees with mattresses, pots, and pans. There was something sinister about them, almost as if they were in a voodoo trance.

Standing firm, Rémy ordered the soldiers to turn them back, but upon refusal, the refugees lunged at the troops, attacking them with their weapons, slashing at the soldiers' throats with cutlasses. A scuffle ensued, during which one of the refugees lunged at Aubert's throat with his machete, slashing him across the neck. Blood spurted everywhere. Aubert fell to the ground. Rémy stared in horror. A jolt of electricity shot through his veins. Grabbing his revolver, he jerked the hammer back, aimed at the attacker, and squeezed the trigger.

A blast rang out. The man collapsed on the ground, writhing in agony. The blood-soaked machete landed only inches from Aubert's body. The refugees turned and fled, screaming. Trembling and in a state of shock, Rémy knelt down beside Aubert and cradled his friend's head in his arms. Aubert's eyelids fluttered, and he had a pulse, albeit weak. But the sergeant was quickly losing blood from the gash on his neck. Blood soaked his shirt and the ground where he lay.

"Hang in there," said Rémy. "You're going to make it. You're a fighter. You're the best soldier I've ever known . . ."

"Forget about me . . ." said Aubert, struggling to speak. "Go . . .find the girl . . .before it's too late . . ." His eyelids fluttered and closed.

"Stay with me," Rémy screamed, clutching his friend tighter. "Don't leave me!"

He grabbed a shawl from a woman and wound it around Aubert's neck several times like a tourniquet. It turned bright red almost immediately. Rémy tried to hide the horror he felt, but Aubert was losing massive amounts of blood. He didn't have much longer to live. Rémy cursed the stupid politicians and the inept bureaucracy that created this disastrous situation.

"Don't worry, you're going to be all right," he said, hugging his friend.

Aubert clutched his arm. "G–get the girl, or you'll regret it the rest . . ."

Rémy could see the life slipping out of his eyes. They were starting to roll back. He held his friend and begged him not to leave, but Aubert was too weak to answer. His muscles stiffened and his eyes rolled back, then he went completely still. Rémy stared in shock at the lifeless body of his friend: Sgt. Jean-Alfred Aubert was dead.

Rémy yelled for two gendarmes. They came running when they saw the commotion and asked what happened. They laid Aubert's body on a stretcher and carried him away. Sickened by the unnecessary bloodshed, Rémy staggered to his feet and ordered his men to fix their bayonets.

He ordered two soldiers to chase after the machete-wielding refugees, but they were already dispersed in the crowd. The situation was now out of control. He did not know how much longer they could hold out under these conditions. His hands and clothes were soaked with Aubert's blood, an unnecessary casualty of the volcano. It was exactly as he'd feared. Aubert was brutally murdered, and the onlookers were shaken by the ordeal. The people of Saint-Pierre and the refugees were desperate to survive. It was only a matter of time before a riot ensued, and more innocent lives would be lost.

He felt his limbs shaking. His heart beat like a kettledrum, and he was gasping for breath. Something inside of him snapped. He knew he was in shock, that he was losing control. He felt his nerves shattering. He raised his hands and stared at Aubert's blood. Sapped of energy and sickened beyond belief, he decided he could no longer wait to find Emilie. He had to find her before it was too late. He knew her life hung in the balance. He was through waiting for the right time, through taking orders, through having no control over his life. He decided once and for all that he would rescue her no matter what happened, even if it cost him his life.

Leaving a corporal in charge, Rémy marched back to the fort and headed straight to the office of Captain Renoult. He made no attempt to hide the blood on his hands or clothes. The only thing he tried to hide was the disgust he felt at the unnecessary bloodshed, the terrible loss of his best friend.

Renoult was drinking a cup of coffee and dictating a telegram to an orderly. When he saw Rémy, he raised an eyebrow and dismissed the clerk. He motioned for the lieutenant to enter.

Rémy marched in and saluted.

"Yes, Rémy, what is it?" said Renoult, with obvious impatience.

"Mon capitaine, there is something I have to report."

"Yes, what is it?"

"One casualty: Sgt. Jean-Alfred Aubert. He was hit with a machete by refugees desperate to flee the city. He died of his wounds."

"I will inform his family by telegram while we still have one open line to Dominica," said Renoult. "It may take a day or two to reach France. Is there anything else?"

"Yes, mon capitaine, there's an urgent matter I must take care of," said Rémy.

"What is it?"

"I have to go to the hospital to see about a patient."

"Who is it?" said Renoult.

"A young woman who—"

"That's impossible," said Renoult. "Return to your station at once. Dismissed."

"But, sir, it's very important," said Rémy, struggling to control his breathing.

"The answer is still no," said Renoult. "You are responsible for guarding the southern road. I have put an entire contingent of men under your command. Have you lost your senses? Do you wish me to relieve you of your command?"

"No, sir, but a woman's life may be at stake," said Rémy.

"Lieutenant, we have an entire city at stake. I cannot relieve you of your duty to take care of one woman who is obviously being taken care of. Now return to your post at once. Our orders are to keep the people contained. No one is allowed to leave the city without express permission from the governor."

"But, sir . . ."

Renoult's face clouded over. "Lieutenant, we are in a state of emergency. Return to your post at once, or I will arrest you for dereliction of duty."

Rémy trembled inside. His mind raced, and he felt dizzy. Sweat and soot poured down his temples, and his limbs were shaking. He had a sinking feeling that if he didn't rescue Emilie, she would be dead by morning. In his mind's eye, all he could see was carnage and death: a beautiful woman reduced to ashes. Perhaps he was going mad. Perhaps he had lost his sense of reason. Perhaps he was a disgrace to his uniform like his commanding officer had told him back in Senegal. Perhaps he deserved to be sent to the penal colony in French Guiana. None of that mattered now. The only thing that mattered was finding Emilie. He had to rescue her, even if it meant he was court-martialed and sent to prison. Even if it meant his name was ruined. So be it. He had nothing else to live for.

Red-faced and gasping, Rémy shook his head. Then he took two steps backward and fled the fort, Renoult's shouts ringing in his ears.

It was dusk by the time Rémy arrived at the Colonial Health Institute. He realized he was now a fugitive and could be arrested on the spot. This knowledge kept his heart racing and his senses on high alert. Luckily the hospital workers were oblivious to this fact. They were sweeping the accumulated ash into piles, closing the shutters, and getting ready to lock up the hospital for the night. The rivière Roxelane was gushing loudly in the background and the wind rustled the trees overhead. He had arrived just in time. Another minute more, and it would have been too late. He assessed the property. The hospital consisted of a main two-story building built of stone, with a red-tiled roof, and several smaller buildings. Surrounding the entire complex was a stone wall with an iron gate, which had not yet been locked. This was his first piece of luck.

Pushing open the gate, Rémy headed up the path to the entrance, and after several insistent knocks, an elderly nun opened the door.

"Yes, sir, can I help you?" she said, studying his face inquisitively.

"I'm here to see a patient."

The nun shook her head. "I'm sorry, but visiting hours are over. Come back tomorrow." She tried to shut the door, but when Rémy prevented her, she added, "Please remove your boot, sir. I must close the door. It's almost vespers . . ."

"I must get in," said Rémy. "I can't come back tomorrow. It's an emergency. I must see her now."

He fixed his stare on the elderly nun. When she saw his insistence, she pouted and reluctantly let him in.

"You do realize I'm breaking hospital policy by letting you in," she said. "The doctors are very strict around here. It's for the patients' safety."

"Bless you, Sister. It's extremely important."

"What is the name of this patient?" she said as she led him to an office where keys were dangling from hooks on the wall.

"Emilie Dujon."

She eyed him sharply. "There's no one here by that name."

Rémy was stunned. "I'm certain she was brought here. Perhaps she was admitted under a different name. A gentleman by the name of Lucien Monplaisir brought her here several days ago."

"Did you say Monplaisir? We have a young lady here by that name. No one has been to see her. Come with me."

She snatched the key off the wall and led Rémy down a darkened corridor lit by gas lamps. When she reached the correct room, she inserted the key in the lock and flung open the door.

But the room was empty.

Rémy was shocked when he saw the empty bed, the half-used jar of morphia, the pillow streaked with blood, evidence of a struggle, and Emilie's shawl lying forlorn on the floor. He picked it up and smelled it. It still had traces of orange flower, hyacinth, jasmine, musk, and sandalwood. It was her scent.

"As you can see, she's not here," said the sister. "Which seems very odd. We keep strict records of our patients, and no one has been discharged for days."

"Could she have gotten out by herself?" asked Rémy.

"That's impossible," said the sister. "The doors are locked from the outside. Somebody must have let her out. I shall have to investigate what happened. Dr. Bertrand will be very upset when he hears about this tomorrow morning. This is very troubling."

The sister began questioning the other nurses, who had begun to congregate outside the room out of curiosity. No one had any knowledge of Emilie's disappearance until a wide-eyed young novice revealed that a mysterious doctor had appeared late one night claiming to have authorization from the young woman's family to fetch her. He had pushed his way inside and arrogantly demanded to be taken to the young woman's room and given the keys to unlock her restraints. Since the young nun was the only one on duty that night, she had no choice but to comply. Rémy shuddered at the news. It was clear Emilie had been coerced or threatened into leaving against her will, and possibly by someone she didn't know or trust. But something still didn't add up. Who was this mysterious doctor, and why did he come in the middle of the night? Was this unknown doctor, in fact, Lucien Monplaisir? And if not, who was he? And where did he take her? Rémy asked the young nun for a description of the doctor, and when she described a suave older gentleman with tufts of white hair, a commanding presence, and piercing eyes, he knew it was Gaston Faustin Jacquet, the notorious quimboiseur. Thanking the sister, Rémy doffed his pith helmet and rushed out of the hospital.

Chapter 38

Rémy hurried through the streets of Saint-Pierre, aware that Renoult probably had soldiers out looking for him, ready to arrest him and haul him off to jail. He figured he had only minutes to find Emilie. By now there was a constant rain of ash and cinders all over the city. Visibility was limited. People scurried through the ash-covered streets in desperation, searching for any means of escape, but all exits were blocked. Their faces were frantic, streaked with ashes and soot, their clothes a disheveled mess. Some pulled small children by their arms, crying and miserable. Other people resigned themselves to their fate, peeking out through wooden shutters, doorways, or from balconies, casting wary eyes toward the mountain. Occasionally a carriage would pass through the streets, its wheels muffled by the ash on the cobblestones. The streetlamps were dark due to the loss of electricity, which lent a gloomy aspect to the town. The only light came from the kerosene lamps that glowed in the windows, like tiny beacons of light in a snowstorm. Saint-Pierre by all appearances was a ghost town and her people, the walking dead.

Sporadically, explosions like cannon fire reverberated from the mountain, causing people to cry out in fear. They would stare at the summit of Mount Pelée with eyes widened in terror as orange-red flashes of lightning lit up the evening sky. In their eyes, Rémy saw raw fear. Tremors added to the surreal atmosphere. To make matters worse, the air was growing increasingly noxious from sulfur and ash. People coughed and wheezed; horses snorted and collapsed on the street. Dogs and cats cowered in the alleyways, frail and near death from hunger. Rémy wondered how much longer the people would hold out under these conditions. The only thing that was keeping him sane was the hope he would find Emilie and save her. If he lost this chance, there was no point in going on. No more point in living.

He was breathless by the time he reached the voodoo shop on rue Longchamps. He looked up at the sign: "GASTON FAUSTIN JACQUET, HERBALIST AND HEALER." Yes, this was the place. He was sure it was the same store he had seen Emilie coming out of the other day. The front door was locked and the shutters were drawn, but he thought he heard faint footsteps coming from inside. He peeked in through the shutters and saw only a tiny candle glowing in the back. A figure hovered near it and then disappeared behind a wooden screen. Other than that, it appeared empty. He cursed the fact that he couldn't see more clearly. Somehow, he had to get inside. He banged on the door, but no one responded. He called out, "Open up!" but still no one came to the door. A few passersby stopped and stared as if he had lost his mind. A gendarme let out a derisive howl and muttered an insult under his breath, but Rémy ignored him and continued banging with all his might. Soon a pair of heavy footsteps thudded toward the door.

"What do you want?" said a deep voice behind the door.

"I wish to speak to M. Jacquet," said Rémy.

"The shop is closed now. Come back tomorrow."

Rémy clenched his fists, his face reddening and his temples sweating.

"Open up. I have to talk to you," he said.

"I said go away and come back tomorrow," said the voice. "We are closed now."

By now his heart was pounding in his temples. His muscles were clenched, and all his senses were on high alert. Strangely, for all the ash and cinders, his mind was alert. He was in full control of his faculties. He didn't know how much longer the city would last. He didn't even know if he would still be alive by morning, but he was not about to back down now. He was not going to leave without Emilie.

He pounded on the door. "Damn you! Open the door!" But there was no sound from inside the shop.

Rémy took a step backward and, in one swift motion, slipped his revolver from his holster, cocked the hammer, and blew his way into the shop. The door flew open in a burst of gunpowder.

The first thing that struck him was the acrid odor of burning incense, combined with the smell of rum, cigar smoke, and burnt chicken feathers. In a corner he spied a garish altar with a skull that grinned menacingly. The ghoulish display was surrounded by statues of Catholic saints and African deities and a hideous mural depicting various forms of death. Behind a mahogany desk sat the quimboiseur, dressed in an expensive sack suit and waistcoat. He was poised and cunning in his chair, his chin resting in his upright hands and his eyes following Rémy's every move. There was nothing friendly about his eyes.

Rémy charged at him, his revolver aimed at his chest. "Where is she?"

The Grand Zamy lifted an imperious eyebrow. "The spirits are not satisfied with you barging in here uninvited. Leave at once."

"Where is Emilie Dujon?"

"Get out," said the Grand Zamy, his eyes blazing.

"I am not leaving without her. I know you have her."

The Grand Zamy's face hardened. He placed his hands on the desk and glared at Rémy through smoldering eyes. "Who are you, and what is your business with her?"

"That's none of your business. I know who you are and what you do for a living. I know you drug people and extort them. I can arrest you for suspicion of kidnapping and assault."

The Grand Zamy sneered maliciously. "Put your gun away, Lieutenant. What evidence do you have?"

"I have witnesses who say you kidnapped her out of the asylum."

"That's a lie. Get out now."

Rémy circled the desk and pressed the revolver to the older man's temple. The quimboiseur's body twitched and sweated profusely, but he remained impassive. The veins in his forehead pulsed, and his muscles clenched. Rémy realized this would not be like interrogating a common criminal.

"Tell me where she is," said Rémy. "Or I will shoot you."

"By the Holy Virgin, Saint Michael, and Saint Benoît, I will tell you nothing."

Rémy pressed the cold steel into the Grand Zamy's forehead. "Start talking."

The quimboiseur eyed him. "I will only speak if you put the gun away. We must be reasonable. You look upon me as some malicious character, but that is unfair, and it insults the spirits. My work is vitally important. You must look upon quimbois as a sort of spiritual valve. It fulfills the supernatural needs of the people. It makes life and misfortune more bearable, since through voodoo lies a door that is always open to luck, love, and beauty. It makes the impossible possible."

"But you lie to them and extort money out of them."

"That is too harsh. You look at me as a charlatan, but that is not the case at all. I am a master of suggestion. I use it like a powerful lever. I've even heard they use it in America to sell laundry detergent. But for healers such as myself, I use it to sell dreams. If a customer believes—or even wants to believe—anything can happen, I show him the way. Now put the gun away so we can speak like proper gentlemen."

Rémy hesitated for a moment. Then he uncocked the hammer and holstered the gun.

"Sit down over there," said the Grand Zamy, motioning to the seat across from him. "I assure you I mean you no harm. Would you perhaps like a glass of rum?"

"Is it poisoned?"

The Grand Zamy roared with laughter. "You're a funny man, Lieutenant. I like your sense of humor. What did you say your name was?"

"I didn't. Now tell me, where's the girl?"

"She is my guest for the time being. She's very ill and needs proper care. I operate an informal *clinic* here. At the moment, she is not receiving any visitors."

"I want to hear it from her lips."

The Grand Zamy eyed him. "Do you doubt me?"

"I've heard you're the man they call the Grand Zamy, the notorious quimboiseur."

The Grand Zamy tented his hands and eyed him. "My name is M. Gaston Faustin Jacquet, a respected herbalist. I practice an ancient art the slaves brought over from Africa. My job is to heal the sick. I also relieve people of their suffering. But it is not really me who does the healing; it is the saints. I close my eyes and listen. The saint searches for the cure, and I listen to what he says, then I apply the correct remedy. Sometimes the patient is so ill, he needs closer examination and a much stronger medicine to uproot the sickness. I'm afraid Mam'selle Emilie falls into the latter category. She is in need of a great cure. Her body needs purification, and only *I* have the remedy."

Rémy's eyes widened. He had no doubt the quimboiseur was delusional. Insane. He was like the old witch doctor Aubert had told him about at place du Fort selling amulets, fetishes, and magical ointments made from the grease of serpents. Aubert had seen the old man serving a strange brew of tafia mingled with gunpowder and crushed wasps, while the dockworkers gathered around, clamoring for the potion as if it were a life-giving elixir until they had drunk themselves into a state of madness. It sickened Rémy that people could be so gullible, yet at the same time so desperate to believe that a potion could solve all their problems. This quimboiseur was even more dangerous.

"In addition," continued the quimboiseur, "the young lady owes me a great deal of money. So great, in fact, that she could never pay it back in one lifetime. So I have arranged for her to become a gagé, so that she will have several lifetimes to pay off her debt." The quimboiseur gave him a cold stare that made him shudder. "As you can see, our relationship is mutually beneficial."

"You madman," said Rémy, his hand hovering over his holster. "You're nothing but a common thief."

The Grand Zamy's face clouded over. "You speak from ignorance. You know nothing about the spirit world. There are misguided fools who invoke the spirits and are tormented by them, for once you call down a spirit, it is difficult to get rid of it. The young lady is a victim of her own ignorance. She called down the spirits, and now they torment her day and night. She has created her own misfortune. For her there is only one solution, and that is the work of the herbalist. But my healing goes beyond the body. I heal men's souls and give them higher purpose. It is only through me that her soul will find its purpose."

Good Lord, the man is a megalomaniac, thought Rémy, *a cruel and powerful manipulator of men. A danger to the public.*

"I believe you're holding her against her will," said Rémy. "That makes you a common criminal."

"What do you know?" said the Grand Zamy, bolting to his feet. "If you rebel against my will, I will bring upon you all the curses and excommunications in my power. I will condemn you on behalf of the Most Holy Trinity and cast you into the Lake of Fire and Brimstone. I will call upon Beelzebub and all the demons to make you disappear forever."

Rémy didn't flinch. "How many people have you killed or turned into zombies?"

"You are displaying a dangerous level of ignorance," said the Grand Zamy with malice. "I'm a patient man, but even I have my limits. Unlike you, I solve people's problems. I help them. I cure my customers of whatever is keeping them from reaching a state of pure holiness. Can you say the same thing?" The Grand Zamy's face softened for a moment. "You have no idea of the amount of good I do for people. I bring love, fortune, success, happiness. . . I fulfill their worldly needs."

"Did you tell Mlle Dujon you could solve her problems?"

"Who better than me?" said the Grand Zamy. "She came here in a troubled state. She needed someone to intercede on her behalf with the spirits. I make miracles happen. My customer list contains the most important politicians and society figures from all over the Lesser Antilles and as far south as Port of Spain. I'm discreet and professional. I get results."

Rémy extracted his revolver and pointed it at the Grand Zamy. "Not anymore. I've heard enough. I'm going to get her out of here. Hand her over to me now before I shoot you."

Suddenly he felt the muzzle of a gun in his back.

"Drop the gun, Lieutenant," said a woman's voice behind him.

Left with no choice, Rémy dropped the revolver on the floor.

Chapter 39

Rémy turned to face his adversary.

It was a beautiful mulâtresse with exotic eyes, fiery lips, and a long and graceful neck. She wore a muslin dress lined with expensive lace and a yellow turban that accentuated her high cheekbones and bronze skin. Around her neck she wore a necklace of gold beads that glinted in the candlelight. She regarded him with smoldering eyes, and in her hand she held a Browning semiautomatic pistol. She chambered a round with expert precision, flipped the safety catch, and pointed the pistol at Rémy's chest.

"Don't move, Lieutenant," said the Grand Zamy. "She's trained to shoot robbers and looters and is an expert marksman. Unlike me, Alphonsine is not interested in healing people." His mouth twisted in a cunning smile.

"That's a fancy pistol for a lady," said Rémy.

"Quite necessary when you engage in a dangerous business such as ours," said the Grand Zamy. "Jealous boyfriends, enraged husbands, swindled business partners, vengeful neighbors. We get all kinds."

"Yes, I'm starting to get the picture," said Rémy, keeping his eyes on the pistol. Beads of sweat rolled down his forehead, and his heart pounded. Somehow he had to get the pistol from her. He had to disarm her. "Still, I'm not used to seeing a beautiful lady brandishing a weapon such as this. For a soldier, a woman with a gun is quite alluring."

He inched closer to the woman and, in an instant, grabbed her hand and pointed the pistol up. She pulled the trigger and a blast rang out, sending plaster showering from the ceiling. The woman screamed, and Rémy twisted her arm, forcing her to drop the weapon. Then he gave her a forceful knock that sent her hurtling to the floor. Before Rémy could retrieve his own weapon, the Grand Zamy brandished a cutlass and lunged at him.

Quick as a flash, Rémy dodged the blade as it slashed past his throat. All at once he kicked the Grand Zamy in the groin and punched him in the face. The quimboiseur screamed with fury. Heaving the cutlass over his head, he swung it at Rémy, but the latter lifted a chair and swung it into the Grand Zamy's body, knocking the blade out of his hand and sending him flying backward. The quimboiseur groaned and crumpled to the floor. Enraged, he grabbed the cutlass and sprang at Rémy once more, but the officer ducked and tripped the quimboiseur, sending the blade flying out of his hand. In an instant, the quimboiseur pounced on Rémy, and the two tumbled to the ground, rolling and pummeling each other with forceful kicks and punches. For his age, the Grand Zamy was surprisingly agile. He wrapped his powerful hands around Rémy's neck and squeezed the life out of him until Rémy saw his world turning black.

Mustering every last ounce of strength, Rémy smashed his fist into the quimboiseur's face, sending him reeling backward, blood spurting everywhere. He followed with well-placed punches that left the Grand Zamy writhing in pain until he was motionless. Gasping for breath, Rémy retrieved his revolver and the woman's pistol, which he stuffed in his holster, and then went to search the back rooms. He was certain Emilie was hidden somewhere on the premises.

His mind raced, and his heart beat furiously as he went from room to room searching for her, fueled by rage that he may have come too late. At last he came to a nondescript room sealed by a locked door. He took a step back, lifted his knee, and kicked it open.

He saw her immediately. Emilie was lying on a bed looking deathly pale. She was semiconscious, possibly drugged. Her legs were tied to the bed. He tried to shake her awake, but she only partially came to. She mumbled something incoherent and tried to lift her head, but she was too weak; upon inspection, he saw her pupils were dilated. On the bedside table Rémy spied a bottle labeled *passiflora guadrangularis*. He had no idea what it was, but he was certain Emilie had been drugged. He slipped the bottle into his trouser pocket and said, "My dear lady, what have you got yourself into?" He tapped on her cheeks and tried to rouse her, but all she could do was groan in response. "Emilie, try to stay awake. You've been drugged. Can you hear me?" She nodded in response. "Good," he said. "I'm going to get you out of here. I'm going to get you help." The girl mumbled something, and her eyelids fluttered.

Picking her up gently, Rémy carried Emilie out of the voodoo shop, out into swirling torrents of ash and cinders, leaving the quimboiseur and his beautiful accomplice to their own fate. All around, the town looked like a wintry scene. The mounds of ash reminded him of his home back in France during the cold of winter. He thought it odd that during this time of crisis and death, he was reminded of his childhood home.

Having no other choice, he took Emilie to the same inn on rue Petit Versailles where he had put her previously during their impromptu rendezvous. Remembering the young couple, the innkeeper gave her the only room he still had available now that the city was flooded with refugees. When he saw Emilie's condition, he asked what had happened, and Rémy explained that she was ill. He asked the kindly innkeeper to send a doctor as quickly as possible to their room.

Rémy laid Emilie on the bed and tried to keep her from falling asleep again. He gave her fragrant tea that the innkeeper had sent up and put a cool cloth over her burning forehead. She mumbled a few incoherent words, but Rémy told her to save her strength. She smiled and touched his hand, which he took as a good sign. After the longest half hour of his life, there was a knock on the door, and a doctor entered with a look of concern on his face. He sat down beside Emilie and immediately went to work checking her vital signs. He checked her pulse and temperature, and then he opened her eyelids and peered at her pupils.

"Who is this patient?" said the doctor, eyeing him suspiciously.

"Her name is Emilie Dujon," said Rémy.

"Are you the woman's husband?"

Rémy shook his head. "No, sir, I'm just trying to help her. I think she's been drugged."

"Is there any chance that she's pregnant?" said the doctor, pressing on her abdomen.

"Not likely, but I believe she's been dabbling in voodoo. I found her in a drugged state in the back of an herbalist's shop. I found this on the table beside her."

He handed the doctor the suspicious bottle. The doctor examined it and immediately assumed a grim countenance. "This is a powerful narcotic. The root of the *passiflora guadrangularis* is so toxic it's considered poisonous. Its symptoms are passivity and lethargy. Too much of it can result in death. Do you know how much of this she has ingested?"

Rémy was stunned. "I have no idea. Can you help her?"

"Probably," said the doctor. "If it's caught early, we prescribe the crushed leaves of the *passiflora*, also known as the giant granadilla. It's quite common in these parts. It also helps heal snakebites by reducing hemorrhaging and is quite effective at treating whooping cough and bronchitis. My wife makes a jelly out of it." He wrote out a prescription and handed it to Rémy. "Get this filled right away and give her a double dose to start. She should feel better within a few hours. It's good you came to see me when you did. With all the ash and sulfur fumes, I have a huge caseload ahead of me. I have to get down to the hospital right away. Several women went into early labor because of fear and anxiety over the volcano. I suspect the young lady will be in good hands with you, though, Lieutenant. I think she owes you her life."

Rémy thanked the doctor and offered to pay him, but the doctor shook his head.

"Good luck to you both," he said, doffing his hat. "Check back with me in a day or two. I'm just down the street over the chemist's shop. Dr. Leon Roseta."

"If we should live that long," said Rémy, showing him the door.

The doctor nodded grimly, then left.

Chapter 40

Thursday, May 8

For the next several hours, Rémy stayed by Emilie's side, feeding her the antidote the innkeeper was kind enough to procure from the local chemist. She slept intermittently, during which time he kept vigil over her, and gradually the color returned to her cheeks. The initial dose did wonders for reducing her stupor and bringing her back to a state of wakefulness. A few hours later, she was sitting up and drinking tea. She asked all sorts of questions about what had happened to her, but Rémy was reluctant to fill her in on all the details. He worried the shock would be too much for her. He hoped that with time, the memory of that horrible experience would fade for good. When she expressed sorrow and guilt over what she had done, he brushed the hair away from her face and kissed her gently.

"You're not to blame," he said. "You were under tremendous strain. I know what kind of man Lucien is. I did some checking up on him. He has a bad reputation all over the island. He's known for using women and abandoning them, just like the planters of old did with their slave women. He's a ruthless cad. When I asked people about him, they warned me to keep away from him. The look of fear was palpable on their faces. God only knows how many lives he's ruined."

"I fear as long as he's alive, he'll never leave me alone," she said with a weak voice. "He'll harass me to no end. He loves to hurt people. It gives him a perverse form of pleasure."

"Don't worry about that now," said Rémy. "We'll cross that bridge when we get to it. I'll make sure Lucien keeps his distance."

"I feel terrible for all the trouble I've caused," she said with innocent, childlike eyes.

Rémy reached out and caressed her cheek. "I think the person you hurt most was yourself," he said. "Your cousin, the priest, will recover, and I see you're recovering nicely. Lucien is the one who should pay for all the grief he's caused. But there'll be plenty of time for that later. Right now just get better."

"I'm already feeling better," she said. "But something is troubling me. How did you get me away from the Grand Zamy?"

"We sparred a little, but he got straight to the point," said Rémy. "You're lucky I came when I did. M. Jacquet is a ruthless criminal. I also had a little tête-à-tête with his charming lady companion." He pulled out the lady's pistol from his jacket pocket.

"Clever," said Emilie, smiling. "Somehow you figured it all out. You're very clever. I wish I knew more about you."

"There'll be time for that later," he said.

"Tell me something. . . how did you find me?" she said.

"It wasn't too hard. I went looking for you at the Colonial Health Institute, but by then you were already gone. A nurse gave me a description of the man she claimed took you away, and I put two and two together."

Emilie's face turned white. "I think you saved my life."

"I had a little help from the spirits," he said. "My main concern now is getting you safely out of here and up to Morne-Rouge. Here, take some more medicine."

He measured out a teaspoonful of the antidote and mixed it into a glass of tea.

"Drink up," he said.

She took the glass and drank it. As the liquid entered her system, it seemed to cleanse her from within. Her skin glowed, and her eyes looked clearer. She looked healthy again. She gazed at him with love-filled eyes that spoke of innocence and trust. He would do anything in his power to make sure she didn't end up with that ruthless sugar planter. Now that he had her he would never let her go.

"Tell me something," he said. "Why did you agree to marry Lucien?"

Her eyes turned downcast. "I thought he loved me. In the beginning he put me on a pedestal and treated me like a queen. He bought me flowers and chocolates and made me feel special. I had my doubts about him, but I blocked them out. I see now how foolish I was. I should have listened to my instincts. I knew he had a dark side to him, but I prayed he would never turn that side against me."

"And I'll make sure the despicable cad never gets another chance," said Rémy. "Please try to get some sleep now." He pulled the sheet up and left her to go sit by the window. As the night wore on, he kept vigil over her as he checked the pistol and revolver to make sure they were loaded. From time to time, he would glance out the window and see groups of soldiers marching through the murky streets, no doubt looking for him. It would take a miracle to keep from getting spotted. He poured himself a glass of rum. It was going to be a long night.

At four a.m. he was shaken by a great roaring from Pelée. A loud rumble like thunder shook the town, and lightning flashed through the clouds that cloaked the mountain's heights. Smoke poured out of the crater and filled the atmosphere with ominous gray swirls that lit up with orange-red flashes. Eeriness pervaded the town. Rémy stared at the pyrotechnics with a growing trepidation. His senses were on high alert. Something was going to happen. He could feel it in his bones.

The church bells rang early in honor of Ascension Day, yet Rémy was filled with a dire sense of foreboding. All of his instincts were telling him to flee, yet he was trapped by his uniform and his circumstances. To leave the inn meant capture, yet to remain meant certain death. He was sure of that. The minute he reached a roadblock, he would be discovered and detained. If he even made it that far. For now, he and Emilie were trapped like the tens of thousands of others who were awaiting rescue—or death.

Emilie's eyes fluttered open. She cried out and sat up in bed. Ash blew in through the shutters, invading their quiet. He told her they should evacuate the city as soon as possible and that he had a bad feeling about the volcano no matter what the mayor and governor had said. She rubbed the sleep from her eyes and asked him what time it was.

"Five o'clock," he said, flipping his pocket watch open. "If we hurry, we can make it out before the streets fill up with people. I can take you up to your cousin's house in Morne-Rouge. You'll be safe there."

"What about you?" she asked.

Rémy took a deep breath. "Everything will be just fine. I'm sure of it."

She looked at him skeptically.

Rémy turned his back. "You'd better get dressed now. We have to leave soon."

Emilie was crestfallen. "But I can't leave without saying goodbye to Abbé Morel. He must be worried sick about me. As far as he knows, I'm still locked up in the hospital. Please, I must go and see him."

Rémy pondered her request. They were only a few blocks from the prison. He supposed it wouldn't be too difficult to find Abbé Morel. The streets looked fairly safe; most of the people would be heading to mass, and Emilie seemed to have a filial bond with the priest. Under the circumstances, he felt it was the least he could do.

"All right," he said. "But if anything happens, I want you to be able to protect yourself." He pulled out the pistol from his jacket pocket. "Don't be frightened. I'll show you how to use it." He sat down next to Emilie. "There are only two rounds left, which means only shoot if absolutely necessary, if you feel your life is being threatened. But first you'll have to flip the safety latch out of the safe position." He showed her how to do it. "Understand?" She nodded with utmost seriousness. "Good girl. Remember, only use it as a last resort to save your life."

Emilie took the pistol and hid it in her pocket.

After paying the innkeeper, they left the inn and headed down the muddy sidewalk. Ash was raining down like snow, coating them and making breathing difficult. They hurried down rue Petit Versailles as shops were beginning to open. At the corner, he spied two soldiers talking to some merchants. As they spoke, they brushed ash off their shoulders. Dodging them, Rémy pulled Emilie into a nearby alleyway and waited until the soldiers moved on. Sweat snaked down his temples. That was a close call; the soldiers had almost seen him. Slowly the town was starting to come alive. Soldiers would be out looking for him. It would be almost impossible to get through the roadblocks, but no matter, they had to try. They had to trust in fate to see them to safety. Taking Emilie by the hand, they left the safety of the alleyway and headed toward the prison. His mind raced. Somehow he had to find a way out of there. Survival, he felt, was close at hand.

Chapter 41

They hurried down rue Petit Versailles and made their way over to rue de la Prison. Emilie's heart was racing. Freedom seemed so close. Luckily the streets were quiet aside from a few faithful heading to church. It was Ascension Day, and mass was starting at precisely five a.m. It was already a few minutes after five. They had to hurry. Emilie was filled with anxiety. There was always the possibility of discovery: by Lucien, by the Grand Zamy, by anyone who might recognize her. They waited outside until most of the guards had left for mass and the prison was quiet. Rémy looked especially wary. She uttered a silent prayer that Abbé Morel would be there and he would bless their journey. It was her last hope.

As soon as the way was clear, they hurried up to the prison gate and begged the guard on duty to see Abbé Morel. When he permitted them to enter, they hurried down the hallway until they reached his office. To Emilie it was like a refuge from the uncertainty and fears of life. She could feel his presence everywhere. When at last Abbé Morel appeared, she threw herself into his arms. Her beloved cousin's embrace was so comforting. It felt just like the old days. Abbé Morel shook Rémy's hand and immediately recognized him as the same lieutenant who had come to Domaine Solitude in search of Emilie. Abbé Morel's relief at seeing Emilie was palpable. He told her how he had been worried sick about her ever since Lucien put her in the psychiatric hospital. He praised Rémy for rescuing her so quickly.

Emilie brought Abbé Morel up to date with everything that had happened, and Rémy wasted no time in informing the priest that he intended to spirit Emilie out of Saint-Pierre as quickly as possible. He told the priest he feared the volcano would erupt at any moment, sending the town into a frenzy. A look of gravity came over Abbé Morel's face. He agreed with the lieutenant that something terrible was bound to happen soon, and he offered to give them a horse and a donkey to carry them safely to Morne-Rouge.

"There's just one complication," said Rémy. "I have no permission to leave the city. They will spot me at the first roadblock because of my uniform and detain me. They will probably arrest me for desertion. I left my post to rescue Emilie."

Abbé Morel thought about it for a minute. "Then I shall give you a cassock and wide-brimmed hat. As a priest, you will be allowed to leave the city. Tell them you are taking the young lady to her family in Morne-Rouge for safety. I give you my blessing for a safe journey."

"What about you, Tonton Abbé?" said Emilie. "Can't you come with us?"

Abbé Morel shook his head. "I'm afraid not. I can't leave the convicts alone at a time like this. The whole world has forgotten about them. They need me now more than ever. I promised to say mass for them and give them communion. I'll join you in a day or two, God willing."

Emilie clutched his arm. "I can't leave you behind, Tonton Abbé. Please come with us. It may be your only chance."

Abbé Morel shook his head. "Please go, my child. It is for the best." The gravity in Abbé Morel's face sent a chill through Emilie. She had never seen him with such a somber face. It left her so disheartened, she was at a loss for words. Rémy thanked the priest profusely, and Emilie hugged Abbé Morel.

"Thank you for everything, Tonton Abbé," she said. "I love you and shall await your return."

"I love you too, my child," he said. "There's no need for thanks. Perhaps this is the reason why I had to come back to Martinique. My only wish is for your happiness. I know you will be in good hands with Lieutenant Rémy. He risked everything for you."

Abbé Morel gave Rémy a cassock, which he threw on over his tunic and trousers. Then Abbé Morel took them to the stable and gave them a donkey and a horse. Rémy saddled them and helped Emilie mount the donkey. Abbé Morel accompanied them to the road, and they took their leave of him.

"Goodbye, Tonton Abbé," said Emilie.

"Go and may the saints protect you," said the priest.

Heading down the cobblestoned street, Emilie suppressed a tear. She watched as Abbé Morel grew smaller and smaller by the side of the road. He looked so tired and forlorn. So frail. He bore a great burden of responsibility on his shoulders. For the prisoners, he represented their only link to God, their only link to absolution and heaven. He could not leave them now. She understood this. Now her beloved Tonton Abbé was truly alone in the world. That realization broke her heart.

The clattering of hooves alerted them that a posse of mounted soldiers was trotting up the road. Thinking quickly, Rémy turned down an alleyway, but no sooner did they think they were free than a carriage overtook them, blocking their path. Rémy had no choice but to halt his horse. In a flash, Lucien jumped out and advanced toward him with furious eyes.

"Just where do you think you're going with my fiancée?" he said.

"I'm getting her out of here," said Rémy. "She's not safe here."

"She's coming with me," said Lucien. "I've been watching the prison, waiting for the rats to flee the sinking ship, and now I've caught you. You're a coward and a disgrace, and I'll be damned if I'll let her go with you."

"No, Lucien," said Emilie. "Let us pass. I don't belong to you anymore."

Enraged, Lucien tried to pull her off the donkey, but Rémy slid down from his horse and shoved him away. "Leave her alone. She doesn't want to go with you."

"She doesn't know what she wants," said Lucien, panting. Red-faced and huffing, he pointed at Emilie. "This girl, who I considered beneath my stature, I was prepared to marry until I discovered her treachery. I can only describe her actions as a form of temporary insanity brought on by the sulfurous fumes of the volcano and her primitive instinct for survival. Naturally she was mistaken. She thought her best chances for survival were you, a warrior and a soldier. How tragically wrong she was! I bought two tickets on the *Roddam*, which sails tomorrow at noon. I paid ten thousand francs for them. Sadly, she won't be on the steamer."

"And do you think you'll be on that steamer?" said Rémy. "If you do, you're a fool."

"No, you're the fool," said Lucien, his eyes blazing. "And now my dear Emilie is one as well. The both of you have made a foolish choice, and the two of you will die here together."

Then, with hate-filled eyes, Lucien pulled out a pistol and pointed it at Rémy.

Rémy locked eyes with Lucien. "You must be going mad, because if you kill us, you'll never board that ship. Right now there's a whole contingent of soldiers searching for me. You'll never get away with it." Rémy inched closer to Lucien, his eyes on the pistol. Sweat poured down his temples. His breathing was heavy, and Emilie could see his muscles tightening.

"I've been waiting hours, days, weeks for this moment," said Lucien in a voice dripping with contempt. "Finally I will have my satisfaction."

"Put the gun down," said Rémy, panting, sweat pouring down his face. "You're not a murderer. You're not a criminal."

"Did you think I was going to let you run away with my fiancée?" said Lucien, cocking the hammer. "Now I know why I bought this pistol. You're nothing but a lying, thieving scoundrel. Prepare to die, you bastard!"

Emilie uttered a terrifying scream.

Lucien turned to look at her, and in a flash Rémy lunged at Lucien, grabbed his arm, and pointed the pistol away. Rémy struggled against his adversary to control the weapon, while Lucien fought like a demon. Emilie watched in horror as the men were locked in a life-and-death struggle, each one attempting to seize control of the weapon. Lucien's face contorted with rage as he strove to wrestle the pistol away from Rémy, while the latter twisted Lucien's arm in an unnatural position. Using every ounce of strength, Lucien turned the pistol until it was barely pointing at Rémy's neck. Rémy's jaw set and his muscles bulged as he tugged and pulled with all his might, but it seemed hopeless. He could feel the cold metal pressing against his neck.

Suddenly a blast rang out. Lucien's eyes bulged. Blood poured from a gaping wound in his chest. He stared at Emilie, dropped the pistol, and collapsed face-first on the ground. He twitched for a moment and lay still.

Stunned, Rémy turned to see Emilie holding a smoking pistol in her hand.

"Did I . . . ?" she said, her face drained of color.

"You handled that elegantly," said Rémy. "You shot him in pure self-defense."

"Is he dead?" she asked, watching a pool of blood collecting near his body.

"As dead as Robespierre," said Rémy with admiration. "Come on; let's get out of here."

"What about the body?" she said. "We can't just leave him here."

Rémy picked up Lucien by the shoulders and dragged him toward the carriage. Before he threw him in headfirst, he managed to seize the two steamship tickets out of his pocket, and then he smacked the horse's rear. The animal took off down the street, carrying the lifeless body of its owner away forever. "Good riddance," said Rémy. "I suppose that's the last we'll see of Lucien."

He mounted his horse and pulled up Emilie behind him. "Let's ride together. I think we'll make better time if we leave the donkey here." He kicked the horse's side, and together they cantered toward the city of Morne-Rouge, leaving Lucien and Saint-Pierre far behind them.

Chapter 42

Emilie clutched Rémy around his middle and held on tight as they cantered past the Savane du Fort, skirted the rivière Roxelane, and continued past the Jardin des Plantes, where the palm trees were coated in a thick layer of ash, giving them a skeletal look. They rode through the village of Trois Ponts and began to climb the steep mountain road toward Morne-Rouge. It would be a long, arduous climb with no water anywhere to drink. The horse panted but continued trotting with every muscle and sinew in its body, carrying them closer to safety with each herculean stride. The road zigzagged through great forests that looked more like a wintry scene under the volcanic dust. Soon they reached a plateau bordered with fields of sugarcane that had turned gray. Rémy urged the horse on. Deliverance seemed close at hand.

After about an hour, a strong wind began to blow, and the ground trembled. And then the sky darkened. It was an eerie sort of darkness, like a sudden storm. The passersby they encountered by the side of the road cried out and clutched each other in fear. Some knelt by roadside shrines to pray. Most of them looked spent, ready to collapse with exhaustion. Emilie calculated they had ridden about two miles. With each stride of the horse, Saint-Pierre grew smaller and smaller until it slowly disappeared from view. Still, the change in atmosphere filled her with terror. The air smelled ominous. She could see the sweat pouring down Rémy's temples and soaking his shirt, but he kept urging the animal forward.

They continued climbing up the steep mountain road for another half mile, then suddenly the wind picked up. All at once they were assaulted by a downpour of ash, cinders, and muddy rain. The pellets beat down on their faces, hands, and bodies, lacerating them, burning them. Now they were surrounded by swirling clouds of ash. The horse reared, almost throwing them off. Rémy did his best to calm the animal, but they were at the mercy of the onslaught. The volcanic rocks were raining down like hailstones, pelting them with fury. The horse was near collapse, unable to breathe. Emilie and Rémy choked on the fumes that swirled around like the inside of a furnace. She thought that at any minute they would be asphyxiated. In the distance they heard wailing voices. There were a dozen people clinging together by the side of the road, their voices barely audible above the noise of the bombardment. That was the only way they knew they weren't alone. But it was impossible to see them through the ash clouds.

Every now and then they detected flashes of lightning emanating from on high, adding to the ghostly atmosphere. They covered their noses and mouths with handkerchiefs, but it did little to filter the noxious fumes. Everything was coated with gray ash, including their hair and skin. It soaked into their clothes and streaked down their faces. The downpour was so overpowering, Emilie felt as if they were drowning under a waterfall of ash and cinders. Still, Rémy urged the horse with all his might, even beating the poor animal to keep moving. Emilie prayed silently, but it seemed as if they had entered the gates of hell itself. The ground was covered in a thick layer of ash, pumice, and cinders, giving it the appearance of a moonscape. Suddenly Emilie screamed. Several feet away lay the body of a woman buried beneath a layer of volcanic debris. Beside her was a basket with all her worldly belongings and a tiny infant, his body gray and still, frozen in time.

Rémy told her to avert her eyes. There was nothing they could do for the baby, he said. Tears streaked down Emilie's face. Death was close at hand now. How much longer could they take the ferocious pounding of volcanic debris? The cinders pummeled them with a fury, like the daggers of an invading army. As they coursed their way up the mountain road, they began to see more bodies strewn about under the debris. Emilie recoiled in horror. The dead looked like the pictures she had seen of the victims of Pompeii— gray, still, and lifeless.

"Hold on tight," said Rémy. "We have to stay together."

Emilie clutched him tighter. She buried her face in his back, hoping to shield herself from the assault, but the pain from the falling rocks was becoming unbearable. The fumes were entering her lungs with each breath, causing her to choke. She could hear the horse snorting. The poor animal was nearing collapse. Rémy kicked its side, urging it to continue, but Emilie was sure the animal would soon give up and sink into the mud. Then they would all asphyxiate and succumb to the mercy of the volcano.

"Are we almost there?" yelled Emilie. "How much longer?"

"I can't see anything," he said. "The volcano is . . . in full eruption now. God only knows how it will all end. Probably hundreds . . . thousands may die. I think we left at the last possible moment. Are you all right?" He turned to look at her. Emilie forced herself to smile, but she was literally gasping for breath. She was able to hide her face in his back, but Rémy was taking the attack head-on, shielding her with his body. She tried to calculate the distance from Morne-Rouge, but it was impossible. Minutes ticked by, and still they had not arrived. Rémy coughed into his handkerchief. Emilie could see spots of blood staining the cloth. He was getting sick too! *Dear Lord, please save us from this calamity!* Emilie was seized with terror. She couldn't bear the thought of losing Rémy so soon after they were reunited. Her heart was overflowing with love for him. The thought of Rémy dying now was like a dagger to her heart. The pain was too great.

Suddenly there was a terrifying explosion. The roar was deafening. The ground rumbled and shook, causing the horse to stumble and lose its footing. Emilie cried out in fright. She half expected to see the ground open up beneath them and swallow them up. Looking up through the swirling clouds, she could see an enormous column of ash shooting up in the sky thousands of feet like an enormous cyclone,—gray, black, and menacing. It had a power all its own, a force that came from inside the volcano. It was like nothing she had ever seen before. It filled the sky and was accompanied by huge projectiles that shot out of the crater and rained down in the direction of Saint-Pierre and the harbor. The noise was earsplitting, and the bombardment continued for several minutes, sending a heavy shower of red-hot cinders and boulders blasting out of the volcano, swirling through the air like massive cannonballs. The eruption rained down on the city of Saint-Pierre like an enemy attack, blasting everything in its path.

Emilie clung to Rémy. She was certain they would die together, buried alive under layers of ash, hot cinders, and rocks. Certainly the odds were against them. But at least they were together. Rémy squeezed her hands. She could feel his love in his grip. It soothed her through all the pain and torment. They spoke not a word as ash and cinders rained down all around, pelting them with fury. Emilie closed her eyes and tried to block out the pain. She was sure the end had come. She mouthed a silent prayer and waited for death to take them.

Chapter 43

Thursday, May 8
Morne-Rouge

At the first explosion, Da Rosette sank to her knees before the statue of the Virgin Mary and prayed with all her might. The house shook, dishes rattled in the cupboard, and glasses smashed to the floor. The servants screeched and ran outside for safety. A loud rumbling noise drowned out all sound, but Da Rosette was sure the Virgin could hear her prayers. It seemed as if the volcano was out for revenge. With her own eyes she had seen a column of smoke pouring out that was bigger and more terrifying than anything she had ever seen. Her only weapon now was repentance; her only shield was faith. She poured her heart out to God and prayed for salvation. She prayed for Emilie's safety. She prayed that Mme Dujon would be comforted in her widowhood, and she prayed that Maurice would be cured of his consumption. And lastly she prayed for her beloved island, Madinina, *l'île aux fleurs, l'île des revenants* . . . the island of flowers, the island of ghosts. She could feel the spirits all around her. It seemed as if the Bon Dieu and the spirits were out for revenge. She prayed for forgiveness. She prayed for grace.

The house of Luc Aubéry was thrown into turmoil. Servants ran around picking up broken plates and dishes, while M. Aubéry ran outside to check on the volcano. It was he who came back and reported seeing an immense column of black smoke that rolled upward, forming a gigantic mushroom cloud that darkened the sky while sending forth intermittent bursts of lightning that crackled and danced on the summit like gigantic firecrackers. He described a rush of wind, a mass of smoke, and gases that blew out of the summit and tore through the countryside, wiping out everything in their path. He stared out the window, ashen-faced, and said, "I have witnessed the gates of hell."

The women listened in horror. Mme Dujon sat huddled on the couch with Mme Aubéry and Da Rosette, while the servants prayed and cried. Mme Dujon looked most shaken up. She wept into a handkerchief. She wailed and cried, wondering what had become of

Maurice, who had left the house an hour before and still hadn't returned. She also cried for Emilie, certain she would never see her beloved daughter again.

Suddenly Maurice burst through the door, seized with terror.

"There's been a major eruption," he said. "I think the whole town of Saint-Pierre has been destroyed. Huge ash clouds burst out of the crater. There were at least seven of them, large black columns of twirling ash and smoke hell-bent on destruction. And then, right before my eyes, a massive cluster of rocks shot out of the crater at an enormous speed and hurled toward Saint-Pierre. It was like a thousand cannons blasting at once. I fear everyone in Saint-Pierre may be dead."

"Mon Dieu," said Mme Dujon, frantic. "How did you manage to see everything?"

"As soon as I heard the blast, I ran like the devil and took shelter between two houses. Then I saw an enormous reddish-gray cloud shoot out of the crater and rush down the slopes toward the city. It was smoldering and looked alive with lightning flashes. The roar was deafening. Fire, smoke, ash, and gases exploded all at once, burning and scorching everything in their path. My heart was pounding, and I was frantic. Several minutes later, I got a good look at the crater. It was smoking hot and looked like a big black gaping hole in the mountain. There was not a living thing for miles."

Mme Dujon turned white from shock. Mme Aubéry stared at Maurice with horror-filled eyes. The two women shuddered. Both had family members who were in the path of the volcano and who surely must now be dead. There were probably hundreds if not thousands of people who died from the eruption.

Da Rosette clutched her chest and cried out, fearing for Emilie's safety. She did not know how much longer her heart would hold out. She tried to be strong for Madame's sake, but with this news, she had lost all hope. She was sure her heart had broken the day M. Monplaisir had taken Emilie away to the lunatic asylum. That day she had cried an ocean of tears. And the gruesome death of her patron, M. Georges Dujon, was also a great shock to her system. Tall, strong, kind, and gallant, his death was horrid and unnatural. Surely it was the work of the devil! She was sure the Bon Dieu wept on his throne the day M. Dujon was buried alive, but the news that

Emilie was caught in the burning clouds from Mount Pelée, this news was too much to bear!

She loved that child as if she were her own flesh. As if they were mother and daughter. For as long as she lived, she would never forget the moment they put the squalling baby in her arms, with her amber eyes and soft auburn curls. Emilie was the most beautiful baby she had ever seen. She thanked the Bon Dieu for giving her this beautiful child to care for as if she were her own. Mme Dujon had no patience for children. She was melancholic and brooding, spending most of her days locked in her room, unable to bond with her own children. Emilie needed Da Rosette's constant care and attention, and she rewarded her with her undying love and affection. How Da Rosette had loved that child! How she had sacrificed for that child! Surely the Bon Dieu would not take her away now . . .

She wailed and cried. Where was her beloved Emilie?

Da Rosette got up from the couch and began to pace about the room. She fretted and wrung her hands, praying to the Bon Dieu for one last chance to see her beloved Emilie again before she was called up to heaven. She couldn't bear the thought of leaving this world without seeing her baby girl one last time. The thought caused an ache in her heart that would not go away.

Sainte Vierge, I would give anything to see my Emilie again, she prayed. I would give a mountain of gold. I would give my very soul. Take me instead!

Tears ran down Da Rosette's cheeks, creating glistening rivulets that moistened her silk foulard. She glanced at Mme Dujon. She was being comforted by Mme Aubéry, while Maurice and M. Luc Aubéry stood by the window with a pair of binoculars, surveying the devastation wrought by the volcano. There was the terrible whiff of death in the air. Surely thousands of souls were now ascending to heaven. The smell was oppressive, almost choking her. Grasping her cane, she shuffled off to the kitchen for a soothing cup of coffee. Luckily M. Aubéry had opened his home to Mme Dujon and her entourage during this trying time. He had paid the doctor's bills for Maurice and bought sedatives for Madame so she could sleep through the night. He had even given Da Rosette her own guest cottage on his large estate.

The coffee was soothing. It revived her along with a few bites of cassava bread. She had no appetite, but she knew she had to keep her strength up for appearances' sake. It wouldn't do for her to get weak and sick, leaving Madame all alone in her time of need. But without her doudou Emilie, Da Rosette had no reason to go on living. For the sake of Maurice and Madame, she would will herself to live a little longer. Now was not the time for goodbye with Madame so out of sorts. But oh, she was so tired! Her limbs ached, and her knees weren't getting any younger. The thought of dying before seeing Emilie's beautiful face again was almost too much to bear. She felt her heart shattering into a thousand pieces.

She put down the coffee mug and shuffled outside to see what had become of her beloved island. "Bon Dieu," she prayed. "I have served you faithfully all these years. Please don't take away my beloved Emilie. She's all I have left in the world. Take pity on your humble servant! Bring her back home to me!"

Outside the street was in chaos. People were running from their houses in search of loved ones. Most had gathered near the cathedral as soon as the rumbling started. They held on to each other as the volcano disgorged its fiery contents, spewing forth black clouds and cinders in the direction of Saint-Pierre. Through the rumbling and ash clouds, all eyes were focused on the summit of Mount Pelée, which looked like the smoking barrel of an enormous cannon.

Down the street she caught sight of two straggling figures making their way toward the cathedral. They were covered in soot and ash, their clothes in tatters. There was a young woman astride a horse and a man covered in ashes, blood trickling down his soot-covered face. He was staggering, as if returning from the battlefield. The young woman's hair lay in clumps about her face, her eyes hollow and her hands clutching a sooty shawl around her shoulders. They looked like they had wandered from far away and were on their last legs. They looked near to collapse. When they reached the church, the man helped the young woman off the horse, and she crumpled to the ground, panting and gasping. The man stood beside her on trembling legs, as if keeping vigil over her. Their faces looked battle-scarred and haunted; their eyes looked half-dead. Yet something about the young lady looked familiar.

Da Rosette let out a cry of shock, raced toward them, and then flung herself on the young woman. She hugged her with all her might, tears streaming down her face. Bon Dieu, it was a miracle! Her beloved doudou was alive! People began crowding around; they pointed at the young couple, who looked like they had escaped the gates of hell. For the longest time, Da Rosette clutched Emilie in an embrace of thanksgiving, while Lieutenant Rémy stood by watching them as if in a state of shock. Of the three figures in the town square of Morne-Rouge, the officer looked the most overcome with emotion. While the women cried and hugged each other and thanked God for the miracle, he stared at the smoldering volcano in bewilderment and raised his fist in defiance. He had fought his greatest battle and won.

Chapter 44

Over the next few days, news began to trickle up to Morne-Rouge that the entire town of Saint-Pierre was obliterated by the volcano. All that remained of the glittering city of rum, music, and culture was a smoldering ruin. Empty shells of buildings and thousands of corpses. Around thirty thousand people were asphyxiated from the clouds of hot gases that raced down from the mountain at enormous speeds. The buildings and almost all the ships in the harbor were demolished by fiery hot gases and incandescent volcanic bombs, some of which weighed several tons. The destruction was massive. Even the fort was reduced to a smoldering ruin. There was not a trace of the theater, and the churches were reduced to rubble. Word spread quickly that one soul was discovered alive among the wreckage: August Cyparis, a convict who was being held in the dungeon. When the volcano began its final eruption, he grew desperate and begged for last rites from the prison chaplain. From the stories that were passed down, Abbé Morel stayed by his side throughout the eruption, which filled the desperate prisoner with an enormous sense of peace and calm. As he sat in his dark cell praying for salvation, he knew the priest was nearby, praying alongside him. Several days later, when rescuers dug through the ruins, they found Cyparis near death. He was burnt, starving, and delirious. Sprawled nearby was the corpse of Abbé Morel, his hand gripping his rosary. Like all the others, he had been incinerated. The mourning for the dead went on for days and days.

A week later, Rémy lathered his face and brought the razor to his cheek. He winced at the pain. It still stung under his bandages where the hot cinders had lacerated his flesh. But every day he was improving. M. Aubéry was kind enough to have given him use of one of his guest cottages. It was comfortable and quiet, the perfect place to recuperate from the most trying ordeal of his life. A doctor and a nurse came every day to check on their progress and change the bandages. As he shaved, it dawned on him that to the entire world, Lt. Denis Rémy was dead. As far as anyone knew, he had died alongside his comrades in Saint-Pierre during the catastrophic eruption of May 8. He realized he had been given an extraordinary opportunity to start his life over. Under the circumstances, a new start was just what he needed.

But what he most needed was redemption.

In many ways he felt he had redeemed himself when he saved the life of Emilie Dujon. Through an extraordinary set of circumstances, he had rescued her from the jaws of death. She was young and innocent, a victim of incredibly cruel circumstances. She deserved a new life, a second chance as well. And he had given it to her by spiriting her out of Saint-Pierre. In that regard he felt as if he had restored his sacred honor. He took a deep breath and stared at his image in the mirror. The lines looked deeper and the scars were still painful, but he was a survivor. Yes, he had survived two attempts on his life and a volcanic eruption the likes of which the world had never seen before. What were the odds of that? His brow furrowed. He knew they were infinitesimal, but he was living proof that one human could beat the odds.

He dried his face with a towel and put on the civilian clothes that M. Aubéry was kind enough to lend him. Inside, he had the nagging feeling there was still some unfinished business to attend to. There was the matter of Emilie. He had saved her from her abusive fiancé, but she was all alone in the world. Her father was dead and her plantation in ruins. Their money was all gone: obliterated in the ruined banks. She was probably penniless. And now homeless. He knew the only honorable thing to do was to marry her. That is, if she would have him. Yes, he would marry that beautiful béké girl, and they would start over together. They would rebuild Domaine Solitude on the wreckage of the plantation and build a future together. He would cast aside his identity of a soldier and take on the new identity of planter, and together they would build a family and a future. The past would stay buried forever. That thought filled him with hope.

Over in the Aubéry villa, Emilie was recuperating in the salon. While Da Rosette patiently dressed her wounds, she sipped herbal tea and listened to Cousin Rose play the harp. The music soothed her. It helped her to forget the ordeal they had overcome. With each passing day, she was feeling stronger and more resilient. She knew the city of Saint-Pierre had been destroyed, but she was lucky to be alive, to have escaped a veritable inferno by a hair's breadth. She would never forget the horrifying explosion and the sight of the gigantic black mass that had rolled down toward Saint-Pierre, as if the mountain itself were bearing down upon the city. After the volcano had vomited out a dark cloud, a shower of hot mud and glowing rocks rained down on the countryside, obliterating everything in its reach. She had felt as if they had entered the gates of hell. At that point, the horse was near collapse. The poor wretch was bleeding profusely, laboring for each breath. She did not know how much longer it would last, but the brave beast would not give up. And then, to their horror, the blast caused a terrifying displacement of air that sent the branches of the trees spinning out of control, like a tornado. The force seemed to almost pull them up into the air. That is when Emilie had screamed and nearly passed out. All the vegetation around them was burning out of control. The heat was unbearable. They were in mortal danger of asphyxiation. They did their best to protect their noses and eyes from the ashes and volcanic mud that assaulted them, but it soon became unbearable. Just then, a sudden gust of wind blew the glowing cloud from over their heads, sending it rushing toward Saint-Pierre. That's when she knew salvation was at hand. She had hugged Rémy with all her might and then fainted from exhaustion.

And now, a week later, it was all like a bad dream. She closed her eyes and listened to the soothing music, trying to push aside the memory. Over and over she saw the terrifying black cloud wreaking havoc on the land. She knew the beautiful city of Saint-Pierre was gone forever. From now on, it would exist only in their memories. She set aside the teacup and brushed a tear from her eye. *Thank God we made it. Thank God we escaped that terrible ordeal! Poor Tonton Abbé. How I will miss him! He was brave right up until the end. Cher Tonton Abbé, que Dieu t'accueille dans son paradis avec ses saints anges. Dear Tonton Abbot, may God welcome you to his paradise with his holy angels.* Searing pain gripped her heart.

Just then Rémy entered the salon, and their eyes met. In an instant he was by her side, and her heart was at peace. He caressed her cheek, and she kissed his hand. No words passed between them. Everything they felt was in their eyes. Together they strolled outside arm in arm, still haunted by the catastrophe they had witnessed and narrowly escaped. They held on to each other and looked down at the smoldering ruins of Saint-Pierre. The buildings were hollowed-out shells; the entire town had been reduced to rubble. The ships in the harbor were bobbing bits of driftwood or completely sunk. There was no movement at all, no life anywhere. The entire town was dead. The only sound they heard was the wind blowing over the blackened massif of Mount Pelée.

But they were alive and free. Their hearts were beating, and their eyes were aglow. Yes, they had suffered a terrible trauma, but they were free. *Free.* The word sounded beautiful to Emilie. Rémy took her in his arms and kissed her. She felt his warmth envelop her, like a soothing glass of rum. She gazed into his eyes and knew his unspoken thoughts. Her heart swelled with love. They had come through so much together in so short a time. Now all she wanted to do was forget the past and forge a new destiny. The island of Martinique would recover from this catastrophe, and one day, if they were lucky, the beautiful city of Saint-Pierre would recover as well. She laid her head against Rémy's chest and felt the beating of his heart. And if she was even luckier, this beautiful man would join her in the task of rebuilding. Side by side they would start over. She could think of no greater happiness in the world.

Author's Note

At the turn of the twentieth century, Saint-Pierre, Martinique, was known as the Paris of the West Indies. It was an important political, commercial, religious, and cultural city, the capital of the French West Indies. Music, theater, and art thrived there. Thousands of hogsheads of sugar and rum were exported annually from this important seaport. Great fortunes were made here, and political dynasties were born here. But on May 8, 1902, Mount Pelée erupted violently, killing thirty thousand citizens and obliterating the city within a matter of minutes, a shock from which the city is still recovering. It was the eruption of Mount Pelée that gave the world the term *pyroclastic surge* (*nuée ardente*) to describe the incandescent cloud of gas, ash, and lava fragments that swept down from the mountain, scorching, burning, and incinerating everything in its path. The term *nuée ardente* was coined by Alfred Lacroix (1863–1948), a French mineralogist and geologist who published an exhaustive volume about the eruptions in Martinique. Before this time, the concept of pyroclastic surges was unknown in the world, although scientists began to suspect their existence in 1883 after the eruption of Mount Krakatoa.

The novel is based on the events recorded between April 21 and May 8, 1902. For the most part, the scenes follow the established timeline in most history books, including each volcanic eruption, the mudslide that destroyed the Guerin Sugar Factory, the telegraph messages, newspaper headlines, and the movements of Governor Mouttet. The only times the narrative differs is when historians disagreed, when the historical record lacked sufficient information, or for dramatic purposes, as in the mudslide that destroyed Domaine Solitude. While Governor Mouttet did create a scientific commission to study the problem, they never left Saint-Pierre. However, I did discover that a group of climbers led by Eugène Berté did reach the summit of Mount Pelée on April 27. They discovered that the Étang des Palmistes, the crater lake of cool spring water, had become a pit of bubbling black lava. I substituted their experience for the experience of my fictional scientific committee for purposes of dramatic tension. The real Scientific Commission met with the governor in the dining room of the Hotel Intendance on the evening of May 7, mostly as a means to quell the public's anxiety. When word got out that the governor was holding a meeting, a crowd gathered outside in hopes of hearing some news. When the meeting was over, the governor addressed the people from the front steps of the hotel, assuring them that they had already seen the worst of the volcano. He told them that the "relative positions of the craters and valleys opening toward the sea assure the complete safety of Saint-Pierre." Tragically, in less than twenty-four hours, they would all be dead.

I blended fact with fiction to create my story. The characters of Prof. Gaston Landes, Fernand Clerc, Governor Mouttet, Mayor Rodolphe Fouché, Amédée Knight, Paul Mirville, and Marius Hurard were real people. They are important figures in the history of Martinique. The rest were either composites of other characters or completely fictional.

To this day there is a dispute among historians whether or not Governor Mouttet exacerbated the situation by preventing the people of Saint-Pierre from leaving. The fact is, quite a few citizens were able to leave on steamers and schooners or by carriage. But the death count stands at approximately thirty thousand. The controversy began when a French journalist named Jean Hess arrived in Saint-Pierre in the aftermath of the tragedy to investigate what happened. Piecing together the bits of information including telegraphs, newspaper articles, and eyewitness testimony, he came to the conclusion that the main culprit was Albert Decrais, the Minister of Colonies back in Paris. He claimed in his book *The Catastrophe of Martinique, Notes of a Reporter* that Decrais had pressured Mouttet into keeping the citizens calm and contained to not disrupt the election. One of the survivors, Fernand Clerc, alleged that the governor, under orders from Decrais, deliberately ignored the many danger signals and even threatened his civil servants with dismissal if they left their posts so that the election could take place as planned. There is a general dispute also regarding whether or not Governor Mouttet used his soldiers to prevent an exodus of the citizens. There is no doubt he believed they were safe given that both he and his wife stayed overnight in Saint-Pierre. That is how they came to perish alongside the other unfortunate victims.

Today the volcano is currently in a quiescent state, which means it is not active but is registering seismic activity. Mount Pelée remains a popular excursion for visitors and locals alike. People regularly climb the mountain to view its summit. The city of Saint-Pierre was never fully rebuilt. Some people can even be found living among the ruins. I found a couple who had set up house inside the ruined fort! Tourists can freely explore the ruins of Saint-Pierre and visit the city's volcanic museum. The tourist office on rue Victor Hugo offers free walking guides, which are most helpful for navigating the old cobblestoned streets. Visitors can visit the dungeon of Ludger Sylbaris (1875–1929), the city's most famous survivor.

Bibliography

Alibert, Pierre Barthélémy. *Martinique 1902: L'Apocalypse.* Paris: Éditions Orphie, 2016.

Cœur Créole (pseudonym). *Saint-Pierre-Martinique: Annales des Antilles Françaises—Journal et Album de la Martinique Naissance, Vie et Mort de la Cité Créole.* Paris: Berger-Levrault & Cie. Éditeurs, 1905.

Dujon-Jourdain, Elodie, and Renée Dormoy-Léger. *Mémoires de Békées.* Paris: L'Harmattan, 2002.

Forster, Elborg, and Robert Forster. *Sugar and Slavery, Family and Race: The Letters and Diary of Pierre Dessalles, Planter in Martinique, 1808–1856.* Baltimore: Johns Hopkins University Press, 1996.

Garaud, Louis. *Trois Ans à La Martinique.* Paris: Librairie D'Éducation Nationale, 1909.

Garesche, William A. *Complete Story of the Martinique and St. Vincent Horrors.* Chicago: L. G. Stahl, 1902.

Georgel, Thérèse. *Contes et Légendes des Antilles.* Paris: editions Pocket Jeunesse, 1994.

Hearn, Lafcadio. *Two Years in the French West Indies.* New York: Harper & Brothers, 1890.

Heilprin, Angelo. *Mont Pelée and the Tragedy of Martinique.* Philadelphia: J. B. Lippincott Company, 1905.

Hess, Jean. *La Catastrophe de la Martinique: Notes d'un Reporter.* Paris: Librairie Charpentier et Fasquelle, 1902.

Loomis, Justin R. *The Elements of Geology; Adapted to the Use of Schools and Colleges.* Boston: Gould and Lincoln, 1852.

Morgan, Peter. *Fire Mountain: How One Man Survived the World's Worst Volcanic Disaster.* New York: Bloomsbury, 2003.

Scarth, Alwyn. *La Catastrophe: The Eruption of Mount Pelée, the Worst Volcanic Disaster of the 20th Century.* Oxford: Oxford University Press, 2002.

Sérafini, Dominique, Jacques-Yves Imbert, and Patrick Sardi. *Saint-Pierre: L'Escale Infernale.* St. Pierre: S. Quemere Imbert, 2015.

Thomas, Gordan, and Max Morgan Witts. *The Day the World Ended*. New York: Stein and Day Publishers, 1969.

Whitney, John Randolph. *True Story of the Martinique and St. Vincent Calamities*. National Publishing Company, 1902.

Zebrowski Jr., Ernest. *The Last Days of St. Pierre*. New Brunswick: Rutgers University Press, 2002.